Yan Lianke was born in 1958 in Henan Province, China. He is the author of numerous novels and short-story collections, including *Serve the People!* And *Dream of Ding Village*, which in 2012 was shortlisted for the Man Asian Literary Prize and the *Independent* Foreign Fiction Prize and adapted into a film (retitled *Til Death Do Us Part*). He is the winner of two of China's most prestigious literary awards, the Lao She, for *Lenin's Kisses*, and the Lu Xun.

Carlos Rojas is Associate Professor in Chinese Cultural Studies and Women's Studies in the department of Asian and Middle Eastern Studies at Duke University. He is the translator, with Eileen Cheng-yin Chow, of *Brothers* by Yu Hua and the author of several books about Chinese culture and history. Of his translation of *Lenin's Kisses*, Ha Jin said, 'Carlos Rojas's translation captures the vigour of the original, funny, poised, peculiar but always rational.'

YAN LIANKE

Lenin's Kisses

TRANSLATED FROM THE CHINESE BY
Carlos Rojas

VINTAGE BOOKS
London

Published by Vintage 2013

First published in Chinese as *Shuohuo* in 2004

2 4 6 8 10 9 7 5 3 1

Copyright © Yan Lianke 2004
English translation copyright © Carlos Rojas 2012

Yan Lianke has asserted his right under the Copyright, Designs
and Patents Act 1988 to be identified as the author of this work

First published in Great Britain in 2012 by
Chatto & Windus

Vintage
Random House, 20 Vauxhall Bridge Road,
London SW1V 2SA

www.vintage-books.co.uk

Addresses for companies within The Random House Group Limited
can be found at: www.randomhouse.co.uk/offices.htm

The Random House Group Limited Reg. No. 954009

A CIP catalogue record for this book
is available from the British Library

ISBN 9780099569480

The Random House Group Limited supports the Forest Stewardship
Council® (FSC®), the leading international forest-certification
organisation. Our books carrying the FSC label are printed on FSC®-
certified paper. FSC is the only forest-certification scheme supported
by the leading environmental organisations, including Greenpeace.
Our paper procurement policy can be found at:
www.randomhouse.co.uk/environment

Printed and bound by Clays Ltd, St Ives plc

Translator's Note

"The time is out of ioynt: Oh cursed spight,
That ever I was borne to set it right."
                              William Shakespeare, Hamlet

While still alive, Chairman Mao had insisted that he wished to be cremated after his death, but instead his corpse was embalmed and placed on display in a crystal coffin in Beijing's Tiananmen Square. Despite persistent speculation that the corpse currently on display is actually a replica (reinforced by reports by his personal physician that the initial embalming process had been badly botched), the mausoleum remains enormously popular, frequently drawing lines of tourists that extend half a mile or more. Commemorating a man who is credited with founding modern China but is also tacitly blamed for many of its attendant disasters, the Mao Zedong Mausoleum is a curious hybrid—part historical relic, part religious shrine, and part tourist attraction. Emblematic of a broader proliferation of Maoist artifacts that are alternately treated as fetish, kitsch, and good luck charm—a contemporary phenomenon that Geremie Barmé calls "shades of Mao"—Mao's embalmed corpse literally embodies some of the contradictions that mark the peculiar historical juncture at which China currently finds itself, as it shifts abruptly from communist austerity to what is euphemistically described as "socialism with Chinese characteristics."

Taking its inspiration from this fascination with Mao's corpse, Yan Lianke's *Lenin's Kisses* revolves around the corporeal remains of another communist forefather: Vladimir Lenin. After learning that Russia may no longer be able to afford to maintain Lenin's corpse on display in Moscow's Red Square, a local Chinese official by the name of Liu Yingque proposes to purchase it and install it in a special Memorial Hall that he will construct in his home county. By developing an extensive tourism industry around this communist relic, Liu hopes to bring his county unimaginable wealth. But first he must find a way to raise the vast sum of money needed to purchase the corpse from the Russians, and for this he turns to an isolated village located at the outer margins of his county. One of the distinctive aspects of this village is that most of its residents are disabled and have developed a variety of special skills to compensate for their physical limitations, and Liu therefore comes up with the idea of having the villagers perform their disabilities, reinventing themselves as spectacular commodities.

The village is said to date back to the Ming dynasty, when a couple of disabled peasants (and an old woman) unable to keep up during an obligatory large-scale relocation from one province to another were permitted to drop out of the procession and establish a home in the mountains. Word soon spread of this unique community in the mountains, and before long disabled peasants from all around came to join them. Throughout much of the village's history, its residents enjoyed a bountiful existence in which all their basic needs were easily met. Until the 1950s, the villagers were so isolated that they—like the inhabitants in the remote utopian community in Tao Yuanming's famous fifth-century fable "Peach Blossom Spring"—remained blithely unaware of the political changes unfolding in the rest of the country.

As a result of this isolation, the villagers speak a dialect of Chinese with many terms and phrases that would be unfamiliar to most outsiders. Some of these terms reflect actual usage in the region (Yan Lianke is from Henan), while others are the author's own invention. In the novel, these terms are explained in a series of notes labeled "further reading." For instance, the first note explains the verb *shouhuo,* translated here as "to liven": this binome—which is borrowed for both the name of the village and for the original Chinese title of Yan's novel itself—is composed of two Chinese characters that literally mean "to receive life," but in the novel's regional dialect are used to refer to enjoyment, pleasure, or even sexual intercourse.

At the same time, however, these notes do much more than simply explain obscure terminology. Like Nabokov, who once observed that "human life is but a series of footnotes to a vast obscure unfinished masterpiece" —and whose famous work *Pale Fire* is essentially a volume of footnotes—Yan Lianke uses the extensive notes in *Lenin's Kisses* as crucial structural and conceptual elements of the work itself. These notes not only provide a convenient pretext for a series of flashbacks that help flesh out the histories of the protagonists and of the village itself, they also exemplify the peculiar temporal disjointedness that is a central concern of the novel as a whole.

As the text jumps back and forth between the narrative present and events from years, decades, and even centuries earlier, it generally uses the traditional Chinese calendar's sixty-year "stem-and-branch" cycle, complemented at times with the corresponding animal from the twelve-year zodiac cycle. For readers who may be unfamiliar with the Chinese calendar, Gregorian dates have been added to the English translation (though it should be noted that few contemporary Chinese readers would know without consulting a chart that, for instance, the *wuyin* Year of the Tiger corresponds to 1998 and the first several weeks of 1999 in the Western calendar). Similarly, the novel also alternates between the modern metric system and traditional Chinese units for length, weight, area, and so forth. To preserve this distinction, we have retained the metric units while translating most traditional Chinese units into their English equivalents. For instance, a Chinese *chi* is approximately the same length as an English foot, so we simply call it a foot. For a few Chinese units that don't have a close equivalent in the English system (for instance, a *li* is equivalent to about a third of a mile, and a *mu* is equivalent to 0.165 of an acre), we have retained the original Chinese terms.

Just as *Lenin's Kisses* alternates between disparate chronological periods and measuring systems, it also delicately negotiates a compromise between social critique of political permissibility—like many of Yan's other works. For instance, his novel *Serve the People,* in which the Maoist injunction to "serve the people" is twisted around to justify the pursuit of erotic bliss, was never officially released in Mainland China, while *Dream of Ding Village,* which focuses on China's rural AIDS epidemic, was technically banned after its publication (though it remained widely available). *Lenin's Kisses,* meanwhile, was not banned—and, in fact, it was awarded China's prestigious Lao She Literary Award—though its unflattering portrayal of contemporary China did lead the People's Liberation Army, which had employed Yan as an author since the 1980s, to ask him to step down. Yan Lianke is forthright about the restrictions that many contemporary Chinese authors continue to face, and notes that he himself often engages in a process of self-censorship, attempting to anticipate what the State censors will find objectionable in his own work. In a recent blog post, he compares these processes of censorship and self-censorship to an act of castration, asking rhetorically, "Is not a literature that can only dance within a tightly constrained space also a castrated literature? Can a castrated literature still be considered literature? And, if it is not literature, then what *would* it be?"

Despite his trenchant criticism of the "castrating" effects of the Chinese state's censoring apparatus, Yan Lianke appears to delight in his ability to dance at the very margins of what is politically permissible. Just as the villagers of Liven learn a variety of "special skills" to compensate for their physical disabilities, Yan Lianke has developed an uncanny ability to use allusion and innuendo to dramatize the stark inequities of modern China. In *Lenin's Kisses,* this careful dance with the specter of censorship is reflected in the volume's unusual numbering scheme, in which only odd numbers are used for the notes, chapters, and so forth. While Yan explains that the work's discontinuous numbering expresses the tragic sentiment of the novel as a whole (since in China odd numbers are considered inauspicious), we might also view the "missing" even-numbered chapters and notes as a tacit reminder of everything the novel necessarily leaves *unsaid* as a result of Yan's delicate courtship with China's censorship system. In particular, the work's fantastical descriptions of the hardships and sorrows endured by the residents of Liven speak evocatively to the fate of the countless ordinary citizens who risk falling through the proverbial cracks produced by contemporary China's tectonic shift from high communism to hypercapitalism—citizens inadvertently sacrificed by a logic of economic progress that purports to be advancing the interests of the nation as a whole. In this way, the structure of the novel mirrors the historical juncture against which it is set—a juncture in which, to borrow the work's opening description of a freak mid-summer snowfall, time itself might appear to have fallen "out of joint."

—Carlos Rojas

LENIN'S KISSES

Book 1: Rootlets

Chapter 1: Heat, snow, and temporal infirmity

Look, in the middle of a sweltering summer, when people couldn't liven,[1] it suddenly started snowing. This was hot snow.[3]

Winter returned overnight. Or perhaps it was more that summer disappeared in the blink of an eye—and since autumn had not yet arrived, winter instead came hurrying back. During that year's sweltering summer, time fell out of joint. It became insane, even downright mad. Overnight, everything degenerated into disorder and lawlessness. And then it began to snow.

Indeed, time itself fell ill. It went mad.

The wheat had already ripened, but the succulent wheat fragrance that had blanketed the land was dulled by this snowstorm. When the people of Liven[5] had gone to sleep that evening they hadn't bothered to pull up their sheets, and had lain naked in bed idly cooling themselves with fans made from paper and cattail leaves. After midnight, however, a fierce wind began blowing and everyone frantically reached for their covers. Even wrapped in their sheets, the villagers felt as though the bitterly cold air was cutting straight to their bones, and immediately started rummaging for their winter quilts.

When the villagers opened their front door the next morning, the women exclaimed, "Oh, it's snowing! It's hot summer snow."

The men paused and sighed. "Damn, it's a hot blizzard. It's going to be another famine year."

The children cried out brightly as though it were New Year's Day: "It's snowing! . . . It's snowing! . . ."

The elms, poplars, mangroves, and pagoda trees were all blindingly white. In winter, it is merely the trees' trunks and branches that get covered in snow, but in summer their canopies are transformed into enormous white umbrellas. When the leaves are no longer able to support the weight of the snow, it cascades to the ground.

This hot snow came just after the wheat had ripened, and many sites[7] throughout the Balou mountains were transformed into winter wonderlands. In one field after another, the wheat stalks were pinned cruelly to the ground by the snow, and while an occasional ear of wheat might be visible, the vast majority of the stalks were splayed out as though they had been blown over by a tempest. If you were to stand on the ridge above the fields, however, you would still be able to smell the scent of wheat, like incense that lingers long after a coffin has been carted away.

Look, the hot snow that fell in the middle of this sweltering summer transformed the entire land into a winter wonderland, leaving everything pristinely white.

Needless to say, for the village of Liven—nestled in a valley deep in the Balou mountains—this snowfall in the fifth month of the *wuyin* Year of the Tiger, 1998, constituted a veritable natural disaster.

Further Reading:

1) **To Liven**. DIALECT (*used mostly in western Henan and eastern Henan's Balou mountains*). *The term means to experience "enjoyment, happiness, and passion," and also carries connotations of finding pleasure in discomfort, or making pleasure out of discomfort.*

3) **Hot snow**. DIAL. *Refers to summer snow. People from this region usually call summer the "hot season," and refer to summer snow as "hot snow." They sometimes also speak of "hot flurries" and "hot blizzards." It is unusual for*

snow to fall in the summer, but upon consulting local gazetteers I discovered that there is generally at least one such snowfall every decade or so, and there have even been periods in which there was hot snow for several summers in a row.

5) **Liven**. Legend has it that the origins of the village can be traced back to the Great Shanxi Relocation near the beginning of the Ming dynasty, between the reigns of the Hongwu and Yongle emperors. Imperial regulations specified that in each household with four members, one person would be exempt from the relocation order; in households with six members, two would be exempt; and in those with nine members, three would be exempt. The elderly and disabled in each household stayed behind while the young and healthy were relocated, and during the resulting exodus wails of partings resounded across the land. The first wave of relocations was followed by vigorous protests, which led the Ming court to announce that those unwilling to cooperate should gather beneath a large pagoda tree in Shanxi's Hongdong county, while everyone else should return home and wait to be summoned. News of this announcement spread like wildfire through the region, and soon virtually the entire county was headed toward the tree. It is reported that there was one family in which the father was blind and the eldest son was a paraplegic, and in order to demonstrate his filial piety the family's youngest son used a cart to haul his father and elder brother to the pagoda tree, whereupon he himself returned home to await relocation. Three days later, however, Ming troops forcibly relocated the hundred thousand people who had gathered beneath the tree, while allowing those waiting at home to stay behind.

For the purposes of the migration, no distinction was made between the blind, the crippled, and the elderly, or even between women and children. Consequently, the old blind man with a crippled son had no choice but to trudge along with everyone else, his son strapped to his back. The sight of a crippled boy guiding his blind father, who was carrying his son with his own elderly legs, was absolutely heartrending. Each day, the procession would start at dawn and march until nightfall, gradually making its way from Shanxi's Hongdong county to the Balou mountain region in Henan province. The old man's legs became swollen and his feet bloody, while his son cried and repeatedly tried to kill himself. The others watched them in despair, and petitioned the officials to allow them to drop out of the procession and return home. Each official relayed this petition to his superior until it finally reached the minister of migration, Hu Dahai. Hu's response, however, was vicious: Whoever dares to release even a single person will be executed, and furthermore his entire family will be exiled to a distant province.

Everyone from Shandong to Shanxi to Henan knew about Hu Dahai. He was originally from Shandong, but near the end of the Yuan dynasty he fled famine and ended up in Shanxi. He was reputed to be ugly, but robust; straitlaced, but evil; unkempt, but heroic; outspoken, but narrow-minded; powerful, but lazy. The people held him in deep contempt, and when he went begging for alms everyone avoided him like the plague. Even if he showed up at people's homes while they were in a middle of a meal, they would refuse to let him in. He arrived in Hongdong one day hungry and thirsty, and saw an expensive tile and brick house. He extended his hand to ask for alms, but not only did the owner of the house refuse to give him any food, he taunted Hu by taking a freshly baked scallion pancake and using it to wipe his grandson's butt before feeding it to his dog.

As a result, Hu developed a deep and abiding hatred for the people of Hongdong. He subsequently made his way to the Balou mountain region in eastern Henan, and by the time he arrived he was famished, parched, and on the verge of collapse. He saw a thatched hut in a valley, and inside an old lady was preparing a simple meal of grain husks and bread made from wild weeds. Hu hesitated, but eventually decided not to ask her for anything. As he was about to leave, however, the old woman suddenly gestured for him to come in. She offered him a seat, gave him some water to wash his face, then cooked him a delicious meal. Afterward, Hu showered her with appreciation, but the old woman didn't utter a single word in return. It turned out that, in addition to being as thin as a rail, she was also deaf and mute. Hu decided that Balou's generosity was the precise inverse of Hongdong's depravity, and became determined to express his gratitude to the former while seeking vengeance against the latter.

Hu eventually stopped begging for alms and joined troops under the direction of the future Ming emperor Zhu Yuanzhang. He bravely risked his life on the battlefield, cutting down his enemies like blades of grass, and in this way this former vagrant helped contribute to the establishment of the Ming dynasty. In the first year of the new dynasty, the new emperor surveyed the war-ravaged landscape, and cried out in anguish. The Central Plains region lay barren, its population decimated, with corpses piled high in mass graves.

One of the emperor's first projects, therefore, was to organize a series of mass relocations to help repopulate these barren regions, and he appointed Hu Dahai to serve as his minister of migration. Using Shanxi's densely populated Hongdong county as his base of operations, Hu proceeded to organize a mass migration from Shanxi to Henan. His primary target, however, was the family of the rich Hongdong man who had used a scallion pancake to wipe his grandson's butt and then fed it to his dog, and Hu insisted that everyone in the man's village—including even the blind and crippled—be forcibly relocated.

When Hu Dahai heard that the migration procession included an old blind man with his crippled son, not only was he unsympathetic; he was filled with vengeful rage. He refused to even consider allowing the two of them to drop out—leaving them with no choice but to continue trudging forward. When the procession was passing through Henan's Balou mountains several months later, the blind man and his son collapsed, and sympathizers again petitioned Hu Dahai to permit them to remain behind. Just as Hu was about to grab a knife to kill the petitioners, he happened to notice the same deaf-mute woman who had cooked him a meal when he had wandered into the Balou region. He immediately threw down his blade and knelt before her.

Under the woman's imploring gaze, Hu Dahai agreed to let the blind man and his crippled son stay behind. He left them with many taels of silver, and ordered a hundred soldiers to build them a house and help them cultivate several dozen mu of farmland, to be irrigated with water from the river. As Hu was about to leave, he told the deaf-mute woman, the blind father, and his crippled son:

> The soil in this valley is rich, and the water abundant. I am
> leaving you with plenty of silver and grain, so that you may
> settle down to farm and to liven.

From that point on, this gorge came to be known as Liven Gorge. When word got out that a deaf-mute woman, a blind man, and a cripple had set up a household here and were enjoying a heavenly existence, disabled people from throughout the region began pouring in. The deaf-mute woman supplied them with land and silver, thereby permitting them to live comfortably, raise families, and establish a village. Although many of these villagers' descendants inherited similar physical handicaps, the deaf-mute woman continued to provide them with everything they needed. The village came to be known as Liven, and the old woman was recognized as the ancestral mother.

This is merely a legend, but it is a legend that has become common knowledge.

On the other hand, a Shuanghuai county gazetteer reports that although Liven has existed since the Ming dynasty, its recorded history dates back only to the previous century. It claims that Liven was not merely a location where disabled residents established a community, but a sacred revolutionary site where a soldier by the name of Mao Zhi from the Red Army's Fourth Regiment settled down to live.

In the fall of the bingzi year, 1936, General Zhang Guotao's Fourth Regiment separated from the rest of the Red Army, and consequently at the end of the Long March they didn't stop at Shaanxi with the rest of the army, but rather continued westward. Zhang was initially concerned that his injured troops would fall behind, but he subsequently began to fear that they would return to Yan'an and disclose his separation from the Red Army. He therefore ordered all of the injured troops to disband and return home. However, shortly after the soldiers tearfully bade farewell to the comrades with whom they had fought day and night, they were attacked by Nationalist forces and more than half of them were slaughtered, leaving the remainder with no choice but to remove their uniforms and continue toward their respective hometowns disguised as peasants.

This gazetteer reports that Mao Zhi was the youngest female soldier in the Red Army—noting that she was only eleven when she joined and fifteen when she left the Fourth Regiment. In the guihai year, 1923, when she was a year old, her father had been imprisoned and killed during Zhengzhou's Great Railroad Strike, at which time her mother took her to join the revolutionary forces. After her mother was killed during the Fifth

Encirclement Campaign, Mao Zhi became a revolutionary orphan who knew that her hometown was somewhere in Henan province, but wasn't sure of the town or district. She subsequently joined the Fourth Regiment with her mother's comrades, and together they embarked on the Long March. As the troops were crossing the snow-covered mountains, Mao Zhi lost three toes to frostbite and broke her leg falling into a ravine, leaving her unable to walk without the aid of a crutch.

Most of Zhang Guotao's injured troops either died or simply disappeared after he ordered them to return home, but Mao Zhi managed to survive by hiding in an open grave. She subsequently lost contact with the army and had to resort to begging for alms. When she arrived at the Balou mountains and saw the disabled people living in Liven, she decided to stay with them. The gazetteer reports that while there was no record of Mao Zhi's having officially joined the Red Army, everyone in Liven—and throughout the entire county—regarded her as a bona fide revolutionary leader. Thanks to her, therefore, Balou came to have glory, Liven came to have direction, and the villagers, despite being physically disabled, were able to live happy and fulfilled lives in the new society.

When this local gazetteer was revised and published in the gengshen Year of the Monkey, 1980, the section on Mao Zhi reported that she and the other villagers were content. In this way, the village of Liven truly lived up to its name.

7) **Site**. DIAL. Place, location. **That site:** That place, that location.

CHAPTER 3: THE VILLAGERS OF LIVEN BECOME BUSY AGAIN

Heavens! The snow fell continuously for seven days—seven long days that virtually killed off the sun.

These seven days of hot snow transformed summer into winter.

Once the snow finally began to taper off, some villagers tried to begin harvesting the wheat. Rather than using sickles, they lifted the wheat stalks out of the snow with their bare hands and snipped off the ears with scissors. They placed the wheat in a bag or basket, which they carried to the front of the field.

The first person to head into the fields that day was Jumei, leading three of her surtwin[1] daughters—her three little nins.[3] They spread out with their crates, bags, and wicker baskets like flowers in a field of grass—each reaching one hand into the deep snow to pull out the ears of wheat, and then snipping them off with a pair of scissors in the other hand.

All of the villagers, including those who were blind or crippled, followed Jumei's lead and went to harvest their own snow-covered wheat.

Everyone was very busy on this snow day.

The people gathering wheat were scattered like a herd of sheep through the white hills, and the clicking of their scissors echoed crisply across the snow-covered landscape.

Jumei's family plot was positioned against the wall of the gorge, abutting two adjacent plots and opening onto a path that led up to Balou's Spirit Mountain. Her several-*mu*-large plot was oddly shaped, but was basically a large square. Jumei's eldest daughter, Tonghua, was blind. She never went to work in the fields, and instead would sit in a corner of the courtyard for a while after each meal before eventually going back inside. She had never ventured beyond the entrance to the village, where the path up to the ridge began, and regardless of where she went, all she could see was an indistinct haze. At high noon, she could see a light pink sheet. She didn't actually know that what she was seeing was the color pink, and instead described it as being like running her hand through muddy water. In the end, however, what she saw was basically pink.

Tonghua didn't know that snow is white, or that water is clear. She didn't know that tree leaves turn green in the spring, turn yellow in autumn, then fall off and turn white in winter. Accordingly, she was expected only to dress and feed herself, and paid scant attention to this hot blizzard in the middle of the sweltering summer. Meanwhile, Jumei's second and third daughters, Huaihua and Yuhua, together with her youngest, Mothlet, all followed their mother like a flock of chicks to harvest the snow-covered wheat.

The landscape was completely transformed. A pristine white sheet covered the mountains and valleys, broken only by a river that, from above, appeared as black as oil. Jumei and her daughters were harvesting wheat in those snow-covered fields, their hands red from the cold even as their foreheads were covered with a sheen of perspiration.

It was, after all, still summer.

Jumei led her daughters through the rows. They resembled a three-pronged wheat drill, and left the snow-covered field looking as though it had been the site of a cock- or dogfight. Some neighbors came over the ridge, and one, upon seeing the piles of wheat along the path, called out to Jumei:

"Old Ju, I want to come over to your place this year to borrow some grain. . . ."

She responded, "If there is any left, you are certainly welcome to have some."

Another added, "If you don't have any to spare, you could always simply marry out one of your daughters."

Jumei smiled happily, but didn't reply.

The neighbors returned to harvest the wheat in their own fields.

The entire snow-covered ridge became a swarm of activity. If a blind man's family found itself shorthanded, even the blind man would need to go to the fields and help out. A sighted person would lead him there, pull a wheat stalk out of the snow, and place it in his hand; and in this way the blind man would make his way down the row until there were no more stalks, and then would turn around and head back. Cripples and paraplegics also had to work in the fields just like wholers.[5] They would sit on a slick wooden board, and each time they cut a handful of wheat they would nudge their body forward, sliding the board along with them. In this way, they were able to move through the snow even faster than wholers. Those who didn't have a board would instead use a wicker dustpan, pulling themselves over the snow along the ridges on the underside of the pan. The deaf-mutes were not impeded from working, and given that they could neither speak nor hear they therefore had less to distract them, and consequently were able to work even faster and more diligently than everyone else.

By noon, the entire ridge was suffused with the scent of freshly cut wheat.

When Jumei and her daughters reached the other end of the field, they saw three men waiting there for them. These men were wholers from the city, and they whispered to each other as they gazed out over the snow-covered fields. The snowy wilderness muffled the sound of their voices, the way a well might swallow an errant snowflake. Jumei said, "Go see what they are doing." Before these words had even left her mouth—and before Huaihua had a chance to respond—Mothlet had risen up out of the white snow and glided over to the ridge.

Huaihua said, "Mothlet, you're like a spirit."

Mothlet looked back and said, "Sis, are you hoping that I die and return as a ghost?"

Mothlet appeared to float like an insect or sparrow. Her tiny figure startled the men, one of whom stepped forward and knelt down before her.

"How old are you?"

"Seventeen."

"How tall are you?"

She became bashful. "Mind your own business."

He laughed. "You look like you're only about three feet tall."

She retorted angrily, "*You're* the one who is only three feet tall."

He chuckled as he patted her head, and told her that he was the township chief. He gestured to the other two men, explaining that one was the county chief and the other was his secretary. He asked her to go find whoever was in charge of the village and have that person come over—telling her to say that the township chief had personally come to investigate the hardships the village had suffered.

Mothlet laughed and replied, "Grandma Mao Zhi is my grandmother, and my mother is right over there gathering wheat."

The township chief gazed at her with an odd expression, then laughed. "Really?"

She replied, "Really."

The township chief turned to look at the county chief, who had gone pale. The corners of his mouth were twitching, as though something was either tugging at his heart or pulling at his face. He slowly shifted his gaze from the top of Mothlet's head over to the vast snow-covered region next to the mountain, whereupon his face gradually reverted back to its normal hue.

The county chief's baby-faced secretary was tall and slender, and he kept staring at Yuhua and, particularly, Huaihua—whose svelte physique was accentuated by a bright red sweater that made her look like a flame blazing in the snow. As a result, he never managed to shift his gaze over to Mothlet, who intuited what he was thinking and glared at him angrily. She eventually called out over her shoulder,

"Ma, someone's asking after you—he's looking for Grandma!"

Mothlet fluttered mothlike back to the field.

The other girls all turned toward their mother, as though it were unprecedented and somehow inappropriate for someone to come looking for her. Jumei's front pockets were stuffed full of wheat, making her look as though she were pregnant. She lumbered forward, removed the bag of grain from her shoulders, and laid it down in the snow. She then wiped the sweat from her brow with her ice-cold hands and stared at Mothlet.

"Who is that over on the ridge?"

"It is the township chief, the county chief, and his secretary."

Jumei briefly felt faint, but immediately recovered her composure. Even though she had already wiped her brow, sweat began to pour out like vapor erupting from a steamer. She stood up and used her hand to support the bag of wheat hanging from her chest. Gazing at her daughters, she said coldly,

"They are cadres—cadres looking for your grandmother."

When Huaihua heard that it was the county and township chiefs, her face initially froze in disbelief, then erupted in joy. It goes without saying that these little nins all resembled one another, but if you looked carefully you would notice that Huaihua was fairer and more distinctive-looking than her sisters. She, too, recognized this, and therefore always tried to take the lead. She stared back at the men on the ridge for a long time, then turned to her mother and said, "Ma, Grandma is crazy. If it really is the county chief, wouldn't it be better for you to go see him instead? Why don't you. I'll go with you."

Mothlet said to Huaihua, "If the visitors say we should get Grandma, then she must not be crazy after all."

Jumei sent Mothlet back to the village to look for the girls' grandmother.

Huaihua continued to gaze at the ridge, but appeared disappointed. She kicked the snow several times, blushing anxiously.

The girls' grandmother was the heroic Grandma Mao Zhi described in the county gazetteer, and she was now hobbling with Mothlet across the field. By this point Grandma Mao Zhi was already in her seventies and had gone through several dozen crutches—though she, unlike the other villagers, used hospital-style crutches consisting of two white aluminum tubes screwed together to yield a pair of perfectly proportioned tubes, with a rubber stopper fastened to one end to keep them from slipping, and several layers of cloth wrapped around the other end, which rested comfortably in her armpit. No one else in the village had such nice crutches, and at best they used canes fashioned from willow or pagoda tree branches, from which a carpenter had sawed off the tip, chiseled a hole in the side, and then nailed it together with a wooden or iron nail.

Grandma Mao Zhi's crutches not only were attractive and durable but also granted her a sense of dignity and authority. Whenever there was a crisis, all she had to do was tap the ground with her crutch and everything would immediately be resolved. For instance, when the township government had sent several imposing wholers to the village of Liven to demand that everyone pay a hundred-yuan transportation tax, hadn't those men immediately turned back the instant Grandma Mao Zhi brandished her crutch at them? And the winter that the government tried to make everyone in Liven pay two pounds of cotton in taxes, wasn't it Grandma Mao Zhi who'd removed her cotton jacket and thrown it in their faces and then, standing before them with her sagging breasts, demanded indignantly, "Is this enough? If not, I'll also take off my pants," and before they could react had begun to unfasten her belt?

The officials had exclaimed, "Grandma Mao Zhi, what on earth are you doing?"

She'd waved her crutch at them. "If you want to collect cotton, I'll take off my cotton pants right here and now, and hand them to you."

The officials had dodged her crutch and departed.

Grandma Mao Zhi's crutch was her weapon, and now she was alternately leaning on it and pulling it out of the snow. She hobbled along behind Mothlet, followed by two crippled dogs she had adopted. By this point, everyone in the village knew that the county and township chiefs had come to investigate the crisis. Given that the Balou region had endured a hot snow that had fallen for seven straight days and left more than a foot of accumulation that completely buried the wheat crop, it was only natural that the government would come investigate the villagers' hardships, comfort them, and offer them money, grain, eggs, sugar, and cloth.

Administratively, the village of Liven belonged to the county of Shuanghuai, and the township of Boshuzi.

The villagers noticed that the county chief waiting on the ridge was getting impatient.

They also saw Grandma Mao Zhi striding up to meet him.

She passed a pair of blind men leading each other down from the ridge. They were each carrying a basket of wheat, and one called out in greeting: "It's Granny Mao. I can tell it's you from the sound of your crutch. Other people's crutches make a hard thump in the snow, but yours sounds like a soft puff of air."

Grandma Mao Zhi asked them, "Are you returning from harvesting wheat?"

The blind man replied with a request. "Please ask the county chief for more money. Ask him to give every family in the village ten thousand yuan."

Grandma Mao Zhi asked skeptically, "Would they even be able to spend that much money?"

He replied, "If they can't spend it all, they can always stuff it under their mattresses for their grandchildren."

A deaf man came over and called out, "Granny Mao, please tell the county chief that all he needs to do is provide everyone in Liven with a pair of those headphones that are all the rage back in the city."

A mute approached and used his notepad to communicate the fact that his family had endured considerable suffering, and that their wheat was buried so far down beneath the snow they couldn't dig it out. He worried that this year he once again wouldn't be able to find himself a wife, and asked Mao Zhi to request that the county chief help him find one.

Mao Zhi asked him, "What kind of wife do you want?"

He gesticulated to indicate a tall figure, a short one, a fat one, and a slender one, and then waved his hands in the air.

A one-armed carpenter walked over and instantly understood what was going on, explaining, "He means that any kind of wife is fine, as long as she is a woman."

Mao Zhi turned to the mute and asked, "Is that correct?"

The mute nodded.

In this way, Mao Zhi took the hopes and wishes of the entire village with her when she went up the ridge.

The two chiefs were waiting anxiously, their impatience written all over their faces. When the township chief saw Mao Zhi hobbling, he quickly stepped forward to help her. To his surprise, however, before she reached him she stopped in front of the county chief and brought her icy gaze crashing down on him, whereupon he immediately looked away and stared off in the direction of a mountain on the far side of the ridge. The township chief said, "Mama Mao Zhi, this is the county chief and his secretary." Mao Zhi turned pale and placed her crutch behind her for support. Whenever she was about to use her crutch to hit something, she always began by positioning it behind her for support.

The township chief said, "This is the recently appointed county chief, Chief Liu. . . ."

Mao Zhi looked intently at the county chief, then dropped her gaze and cried out, "*This* is the county chief? My god, how could *he* be the chief? He is but a pig, a goat, a maggot crawling in a putrid piece of pork! He is a flea on the corpse of a cold dead[7] dog!" And then . . . and then, she puckered her toothless mouth and spit in his face. The sound was surprisingly loud, reverberating through the air and blowing away the clouds on top of the ridge.

As things began to calm down, Mao Zhi abruptly turned and began hobbling back to the village, leaving the township chief, the county chief, and his secretary—together with Jumei and her surtwin daughters—all staring after her in shock.

After a long pause, Chief Liu kicked at a stone and cursed, "Blast your grandma. What's her problem? *I'm* the only real revolutionary here!"

CHAPTER 5: FURTHER READING— COLD DEAD DOG

1) **Surtwin**. In Balou, multiple births of three or more siblings are called surtwins. In the middle of the twelfth month of the gengshen year, nothing particularly noteworthy was taking place in Balou—or in the rest of the country, for that matter. Apart from a Party Assembly being held in Beijing, everything was the same as before. On television and in newspapers, however, that assembly was subsequently compared to Mao Zedong's founding of the People's Republic of China thirty-one years earlier. The event lasted for five days, and on the last day Jumei went into labor. Her belly was swollen tight as a drum, and she cried in agony as she delivered three daughters—this being the triple phoenix birth that everyone in Balou had heard about but never before witnessed. Although the babies were no larger than kittens, each was nevertheless a tiny person, able to wail and nurse. As Jumei lay there, her blood flowing down the legs of the bed and her forehead bathed in sweat, Mao Zhi elatedly brought the midwife one bucket of boiling water after another. The midwife washed her hands and placed a hot towel on Jumei's forehead, asking, Is your belly livening yet? Jumei replied, It hurts, and feels like I'm still having contractions. The midwife was eating a bowl of bean noodles that Mao Zhi had prepared for her, and asked in surprise, You're still having contractions? I've been delivering babies my entire life, but this is the first triple phoenix birth I've ever seen. How could there possibly still be a fourth or fifth child in there?

After finishing her noodles, the midwife got ready to leave. Before she left, however, she again felt inside Jumei, then cried out in astonishment: Heavens, there really is another baby in her belly!

Jumei proceeded to give birth to a fourth child.

This was Balou's legendary surtwin birth. All four of the infants were girls. The eldest was called Tonghua, or "Tung-Oil Tree Blossom"; the second was called Huaihua, or "Pagoda Tree Blossom"; the third was called Yuhua, or "Elm Blossom"; and because there happened to be a moth flying around the room when the fourth was born, she was called Si'e, or "Fourth Moth," and was nicknamed Mothlet.

3) **Little nin**. *A girl whose growth is stunted. Because Jumei gave birth to quadruplets, each of them was born small, and therefore everyone called them little nins.*

5) **Wholer**. *A term of respect used in Liven to refer to healthy people. The term is used to designate those of us who are normal and are neither blind, deaf, mute, nor missing any limbs.*

7) **Cold dead**. DIAL. *This was originally used to refer to cold weather, but here it is used to suggest that someone's heart is as cold and hard as that of a dead man.*

There was a reason why Mao Zhi cursed the new county chief like this. The chief's name was Liu Yingque, and he was once just an ordinary person like us. Prior to the dingji year, he had been a soc-school babe[1] in the county seat, and it was from there that he ended up as a temporary worker in the township of Boshuzi. Every day he would sweep the courtyard of the town hall and fill the boilers in the canteen, for which work he was paid twenty-four and a half yuan a month.

During that era, people throughout the land were deeply engrossed in the dance of Revolution, though in remote Balou they were concerned primarily with trying to fill their bellies. The people of Balou eventually came to realize that they needed knowledge and enlightenment, just as the nation needed to develop a socialist education movement, promote soc-ed,[3] and emphasize rationality and pedagogy. Personnel were needed to promote soc-ed, so Liu Yingque was summoned. Given that he was young and fit, and was regarded as the soc-school babe, he was sent to Liven a hundred li away to help promote soc-ed and lead the people.

In Liven, Liu asked the villagers if they had ever heard of Wang, Zhang, Jiang, and Yao.

The villagers stared at him blankly.

Liu explained that Wang, Zhang, Jiang, and Yao were the infamous Gang of Four, and asked how it was possible that the villagers didn't know about them.

The villagers continued staring at him blankly.

Liu then convened a meeting, during which he read from some official documents. He explained that the Gang of Four was comprised of Deputy Party Chair Wang Hongwen, the conspirator Zhang Chuqiao, Chairman Mao's wife Jiang Qing, and the hooligan Yao Wenyuan. At this point, the villagers nodded and Liu, his work complete, prepared to return to the commune. As he was leaving, however, he happened to notice a wholer walking over from the other side of town. She appeared to be about sixteen or seventeen, and as she walked her braids waved back and forth like a pair of black crows perched on her shoulders.

You can just imagine what it must have been like to hold a meeting in Liven and gaze down from the stage at the crowd of blind, crippled, deaf, and mute people below. In this sea of disabled people, Liu's eyes would have felt to himself like a pair of lanterns, his legs like flagpoles, and his ears like satellite dishes. Here, he would have felt like a commander in chief, even an emperor—but even so, he wouldn't have wanted to stay too long; he would have been afraid that if he did his eyesight might begin to fade, his legs might grow weak, and his hearing might deteriorate.

This was the third lunar month. The vegetation was green, flowers were in bloom, and a refreshing fragrance hung in the air. In Liven there was a pair of century-old honey locust trees, whose canopies shrouded the entire village in shade. The village was located in a gorge at the base of a cliff, and consisted of a scattering of houses connected by a road. The region facing the ridge to the west was comparatively flat and populous; most of the inhabitants were blind, but when they went out they didn't need their canes as long as they stayed close to home. The central region was hillier and less populated; most of the residents were cripples but, since their eyesight was good, if they needed to get around they could hobble along by leaning on their crutches and against a wall. In the easternmost region, meanwhile, *the terrain became extraordinarily steep and the road was exceedingly poor. Most of the residents there were deaf-mutes, but since they had good eyes and strong legs they were not particularly concerned over the condition of the road.*

Liven's main street was two li long, and extended from the river to the mountain. The region to the west with the concentration of blind inhabitants was called the blind zone, the region to the east with a preponderance of deaf-mutes was called the deaf zone, and the region in the middle where cripples predominated was naturally called the cripple zone.

The wholer was walking over from the cripple zone, though she herself was not crippled and instead seemed to flutter along like a leaf blowing in the wind. Liu Yingque had set out from the commune early the previous morning, and after spending the night on the road had arrived in the village around noon. He had originally planned to convene a meeting under one of the honey locust trees, read his official documents, and then leave this world of the crippled and the blind and the deaf and dumb as soon as possible—spending the night on the road and returning to the commune the next day. Upon seeing this young wholer appear before him, however, he resolved instead to stay in Liven another night. He stood in the middle of the road, his white shirt tucked into his pants, waiting for the woman to approach so that he could examine her delicate figure, flushed cheeks, florid shirt, and embroidered shoes. Back in town, those shoes were as ubiquitous as the zongzi bamboo leaf wrappings that always end up scattered everywhere after the annual Duanwu Festival, but here in Liven she was the only person who wore them, her shoes resembling a couple of blossoms in the middle of a winter landscape. Liu stood in the middle of the road as though trying to block her path, and asked, Hey, what's your name? Why didn't you come to the meeting today?

She blushed and looked around, as if trying to escape, explaining, My mother is sick, and I needed to get her some medicine.

He introduced himself as Cadre Liu from the commune, and asked if she knew who Wang, Zhang, Jiang, and Yao were. When she didn't respond, he proceeded to educate her, explaining that an event had taken place in China that was so momentous that it was celebrated throughout the land as a second Revolution. He asked her how it was possible that she didn't know

21

who Wang Hongwen and Zhang Chuqiao were, or even that Jiang Qing was Chairman Mao's wife. Afterward, he still didn't leave, but stayed in Liven another night. He was determined to teach this girl and her isolated village many things about the outside world—about the commune, the provincial capital, and indeed the entire nation.

It wasn't until many days later—after he had gotten to know the girl well—that Liu finally returned to the commune.

And at the end of that year Jumei miraculously gave birth to four daughters.

After the birth, Jumei's mother, Mao Zhi, went to the commune to look for Cadre Liu. Given Liu's willingness to promote soc-ed in remote mountainous villages like Liven, he had become recognized as the most outstanding soc-ed cadre in the commune—or perhaps the entire county—and consequently was no longer charged with such lowly tasks as sweeping the courtyard or boiling water, and instead had become a prominent national cadre. Therefore, shortly after Mao Zhi arrived at this commune that functioned as the township office to look for him, she promptly turned around and returned home. When she arrived at her daughter's bedside after having spent two days on the road, she said only one thing—that Liu Yingque had died, having been crushed like a pancake after falling into a ravine while promoting soc-ed in the countryside.

Further, Further Reading:

1) **Soc-school babe.** This was a designation that dated from when Chief Liu was a child, and was the product of several unforgettable pages from the history of the nation. Soon after the founding of new China, there began to appear many socialist academies and cadre training centers, which developed into Party institutes or Marxist-Leninist academies. People called these institutions socialist schools, or soc-schools, and within a decade they could be found in every city and county, with some provinces and districts having as many as three or four of them. Some continued to be called socialist education institutes, but most were referred to simply as soc-schools.

The Shuanghuai County Institute was known as a soc-school. It was located in a field to the north of the city and consisted of several red-tiled buildings arranged around a white-brick courtyard. This school was founded in the early years of the People's Republic, and the county's Party secretary doubled as the school president, while the county chief served as the school's vice president. Cadres from throughout the county regularly came to study, and anyone who wanted to be promoted had to study for three to six months. There were also periods, however, when attendance was very light. The school had only one full-time teacher, whose name was Liu, and all of the other classes were taught by the secretary, the county chief, and various visiting experts. During the farming season, the government wouldn't initiate many new policies and movements, and therefore the school would send all of its employees home to tend their crops, leaving only Teacher Liu to oversee the premises.

Liu Yingque had grown up in this school, and had been adopted by Teacher Liu.

That was the gengzi year, 1960, or the first of what people subsequently referred to as the Three Years of Natural Disasters, when the entire country endured a series of nightmarish famines. The county stopped sending cadres and Party members to the Shuanghuai soc-school, and the cadres and teachers who were already there were told to return home, leaving only Teacher Liu and his young wife. One day after the forty-year-old Teacher Liu and his wife had gone out to forage for wild plants, they returned to the freezing-cold school and discovered a bundle next to the door, inside which there was a several-month-old infant so emaciated that its legs were as thin as its arms. Teacher Liu and his wife turned back toward the fields and began cursing:

Damned father! Damned mother! Did you leave your child on our doorstep to die?

If you have any conscience at all, you'll take your child. We'll even give you a quart of sorghum if you do.

Are you really dead? If so, you didn't deserve to die a good death, and may your corpse be dug up by hungry dogs and wolves.

By the time Teacher Liu and his wife finished cursing, the sun had already set behind the mountains and the fields were once again shrouded in darkness. Teacher Liu's wife wanted to toss the baby into the field, but he wouldn't hear of it. Years earlier, when the Eighth Route Army had passed through Shuanghuai, they needed to hold an urgent training course for Party members, and since Teacher Liu had good handwriting they appointed him—despite his "rich peasant" background—to be their transcriber. Liu was subsequently admitted into the Party, and following the defeat of the Nationalists in the jichou year and the founding of a new China, Teacher Liu's boat was lifted by this rising tide and he was promoted to the position of secretary of the county chief. When the Shuanghuai soc-school was established a few years later, Liu became the school's only full-time teacher. So, therefore, as a Party member, cadre, and intellectual, how could Teacher Liu permit his wife to throw out a living child? Accordingly, he took the baby from her and proceeded to raise it as his own.

The boy survived, and was given the surname Liu. Since there were sparrow hawks circling around overhead when Teacher Liu found the bundle, he decided to name the child Yingque, or "sparrow hawk."

The famine eventually subsided, and the Shuanghuai county soc-school once again became a flurry of activity. Party members and cadres from throughout the county—and sometimes even from neighboring counties—began returning to the school. Each day that the school's brick chimney was spitting out red flames and billows of black smoke, Liu Yingque could go down to the school canteen to eat. Everyone knew Yingque was the abandoned child Teacher Liu had found outside his door, and since those studying at the school were all cadres and Party members—which is to say, enlightened and kindhearted people who had devoted their lives to struggling on behalf of the Party—they felt it was perfectly appropriate for the child to come eat in the canteen as he wished.

As a result, Liu Yingque did not merely survive, he thrived.

He would carry his bowl to the canteen when it was time to eat, and when the cadres were finished he would follow them to the classroom, sitting on a little stool in the back of the room. At night, he would retire to a small room in the school's storage area and go to sleep.

When Liu Yingque was six, Teacher Liu's wife gave birth to a girl. It was said that she had married Teacher Liu—who was more than ten years her senior—precisely because she could no longer bear children. Who would have thought, therefore, that Teacher Liu would manage—at the age of forty-seven—to get her pregnant? Once she had her own daughter, her attitude toward Yingque became increasingly cold, until eventually he was forced to eat at the school canteen every day. All of the cadres and Party officials regarded him as a son of the school, to the point that many of them stopped calling him by his name and instead referred to him as "soc-school child" or "soc-school babe." When Yingque was twelve, Teacher Liu's wife left their daughter behind and ran away with a man from another county who had come to study at the school, and it was only then that Teacher Liu truly accepted Yingque as his own son and proceeded to raise him as the elder brother of his daughter.

3) **Soc-ed.** A technical term referring to the socialist education movement. **Soc-ed cadres.** those who were charged with implementing the socialist education movement.

Book 3: Roots

Chapter 1: Looking at this person, this official, this Chief Liu

The snow finally stopped falling. Like a visitor who had dropped by Balou and decided to cool his heels for a week, the snow eventually got up and departed.

No one knew where it went.

Summer returned to the mountains and the village.

Having endured this blizzard, summer did not have a trace of happiness on its full face[1] when it returned. The sun refused to come out, and a heavy mist hovered over the village and the ridge—a mist so thick that it flowed through your fingers as if you were holding them under running water. In fact, the fog was so dense that if you got up in the morning and reached out your hands, they would get damp enough that you could then use them to wash the sleep right out of your eyes. The only problem is that your hands would be left slightly muddy from the dirty fog.

The snow melted.

The wheat that had not been harvested during the snowfall began to grow mold. Without sun, the air became stuffy and the wheat began to turn black. The wheat grain turned black, as did the wheat germ, and people who ate them would develop a bad case of the runs.

The wheat stalks in the fields mildewed, and the following winter the cattle didn't have any hay to eat.

That autumn, there weren't any wheat seeds to plant.

That's when the county chief, the township chief, and the township chief's secretary came to investigate the hardships the village had endured. The three of them were staying together in a courtyard inside[3] the village. Before Liberation, this courtyard had been a Buddhist temple adorned with statues of bodhisattvas; Lord Guan, the god of war; and Lady Livening, the town's sacred ancestor. It is said that the village owed its existence to the deaf-mute Lady Livening, in that it was precisely because she had prepared a nice meal for Hu Dahai—who had been humiliated while begging for alms in Shanxi's Hongdong county—that Hu subsequently agreed to allow the blind Hongdong man and his crippled son to drop out of the migration procession and settle down here, even going so far as to provide them with silver, land, and water. They were therefore able to enjoy a heavenly existence, leading disabled people from throughout the land to flock over to join them. The result was the village of Liven.

All of this was thanks to that deaf-mute woman.

Eventually, however, the statues of the bodhisattvas disappeared, as did those of Lord Guan and of Lady Livening. The courtyard was swept clean, beds were built, and the three-room tile building was transformed into a guest house. Seventeen or eighteen years earlier, when Liu Yingque had been teaching at the soc-school, he had stayed in this very temple when he visited Liven, and now he was staying there again. The location was the same, but the people had changed. In the blink of an eye, the nearly forty-year-old county chief had reached middle age. As Liu looked back on his life—from his humble beginnings as a grounds-sweeper and water-boiler for the township's soc-school; to being a teacher in Liven's own school; to being appointed a township cadre; to being promoted to deputy township chief, township chief, and deputy county chief, and finally to his current position as county chief—he felt a distinct twinge of nostalgia.

Shuanghuai had long been dirt-poor. While much of the rest of the nation was enjoying an unprecedented wave of economic expansion, even the street directly in front of the Shuanghuai county government building remained unpaved. When it rained, the puddles in the street were deep enough to swallow an ox, and once a child fell into one and drowned. The county didn't have any factories or mines, merely mountains and gorges, and until only a few years earlier, its county offices didn't even have enough money to pay for electricity or phone service. At one point, representatives from the county committee and the county government got into a heated argument over who should be responsible for fixing a blown bicycle tire, whereupon the county chief at the time smashed the glass of pickled vegetables he was holding and the county committee secretary snapped in half a dust mop for cleaning the windows. The district Party committee secretary, Secretary Niu, had come over to try to work things out, and spoke to each of the county's cadres in turn.

He first approached the county chief and demanded,

"What are you going to do to help this county get rich?"

The county chief replied, "That's easy. I would need you to cut off my head."

Secretary Niu then spoke to the county committee secretary, saying,

"If you can't help the county shed its poverty, you shouldn't be here."

The county committee secretary bowed abjectly and replied,

"If you can transfer me somewhere else, I will kowtow to you right here and now."

Secretary Niu replied,

"Then I'll have you fired!"

The county committee secretary said,

"As long as you can get me out of here, I'd be happy to be fired."

Furious, Secretary Niu smashed his teacup afoot.[5]

He continued making the rounds to each of the other county cadres.

He told Deputy County Chief Liu, "Your fields look like they are nicely maintained."

Deputy Chief Liu replied, "No matter how well we farm, we will still remain this poor."

Secretary Niu asked, "Do you have any suggestions on how to help the county become rich?"

Deputy Chief Liu replied, "That's easy."

Secretary Niu stared at him intently, and said, "Then tell me."

Deputy Chief Liu explained, "Given that we have neither factories nor mines, we must therefore use our scenery to manufacture pleasure."

Secretary Niu asked, "What kind of pleasure can you manufacture with this kind of yellow earth and muddy water?"

Deputy Chief Liu replied, "Secretary Niu, does Beijing have many pleasure-loving residents?"

The secretary replied, "Beijing is the nation's capital, and was the historic capital of many previous dynasties."

The deputy chief responded with a question: "Do many people go visit the Chairman Mao Memorial Hall?"

The secretary said, "Sure, lots. So what?"

Deputy Chief Liu said, "We should allocate a large sum of money to fund a trip to Russia to purchase Lenin's embalmed corpse and bring it back here. We could then display it at Shuanghuai's Spirit Mountain." He added, "Secretary Niu, have you been to Spirit Mountain? It is located two hundred *li* from here, and has a forest of cypresses and pine trees, with deer, monkeys, wild boars, and kiwi trees. It is a veritable forest park. If we were to display Lenin's corpse there, the site would become peak[7] important, and people from around the country—and even the entire world—would come to appreciate it. If we were to charge five yuan per ticket, ten thousand visitors would net us fifty thousand yuan; and if we charged ten yuan per ticket, ten thousand visitors would bring in a hundred thousand yuan. If instead we charged fifty-something yuan per ticket, then ten thousand visitors would bring in more than five hundred thousand yuan. Aren't admission tickets directly translatable into banknotes? How many banknotes would ten thousand visitors bring in? Could the entire county succeed in raising even a hundred thousand bank-notes from merely farming the land? Shit! Dogshitpigshitcowshit-horseshit! If waves of visitors were to come to Spirit Mountain from all over, we could easily have more than ten thousand visitors a day. We could have visitors from Jiudu, Henan, Hubei, Shandong, Hunan, Guangdong, and Shanghai. We could have visitors from around the country, even from around the world. We could consistently have ten thousand, thirty thousand, fifty thousand, seventy thousand, even ninety thousand visitors a day. And, furthermore, about a tenth of those ninety thousand visitors would be foreigners, who naturally wouldn't use our own Chinese money to buy tickets, but rather U.S. dollars. Would five, fifteen, or even twenty-five dollars be too much to charge per ticket? To view Lenin's remains, twenty-five dollars wouldn't seem expensive at all. If we were to charge twenty-five dollars per person, then eleven people would bring in two hundred and seventy-five dollars, and ten thousand visitors would bring in two hundred and fifty thousand dollars."

Deputy Chief Liu continued, "There would also be food and housing expenses, as well as tourist items and local specialties. I'd even be concerned that the streets would be too narrow, leading to traffic jams, and that there might be too few hotels and guest houses, leaving visitors with not enough sites to visit and spend their money."

Deputy Chief Liu discussed this plan with Secretary Niu in the county guest house, and as Secretary Niu listened he idly picked at a cigarette hole in the arm of the sofa where he was sitting, until the pea-sized hole gradually grew to the size of a date, a walnut, and finally a persimmon. Secretary Niu was nearing sixty, dressed in plain clothes, and had a tall and slender build. What little hair he had left had all gone gray. He had toiled on behalf of the Revolution his entire life, and had met countless officials and cadres. In fact, Liu Yingque was himself someone Secretary Niu had promoted from the ranks of township cadres.

When Secretary Niu had first arrived in the county several years earlier, he had heard that there was a township with a paved road, where every house had electricity and running water, and each kitchen had a faucet that, if left open, could flood the entire house. Secretary Niu asked where the money for the running water came from, and was told that someone had paid for it. He asked who this was, and was told that before Liberation someone from the township had moved to Southeast Asia and opened a bank. One day, the banker decided to return to his hometown for a visit, and when he did Liu Yingque, who at the time was the township chief, forbade the peasants from working in the fields that day, despite the fact that this was harvest season, and gave all the local children the day off from school.

As a result, everyone, young and old alike, lined up along the road to greet the visitor. There was a fifty-seven-*li*-long dirt road from the township center to the visitor's village, and most of the road was so muddy that cars and trucks couldn't use it. When the visitor left the township center, he found that both sides of the entire length of the road were lined with peasants. The road was covered in red, though this was not a conventional red carpet but rather a patchwork of red cloth, red paper, and the red silk that the villagers ordinarily used only for weddings. Each village had been assigned a different stretch of road, and the villagers who didn't have any red silk or cloth instead used women's red shirts and jackets. It was raining that day, and when the visitor got out of the car that had brought him to that point, he was immediately met by a red silk wedding sedan-chair. Upon seeing this endless stretch of red road, the visitor initially refused to climb into the sedan, whereupon the sedan carriers knelt down before him, leaving him no choice but to climb in.

After the visitor finally mounted the sedan, the carriers began making their way along the fifty-seven-*li*-long red-carpeted road to Liven.

The peasants lining the road were beating their drums, blowing their horns, and rhythmically clapping their hands.

The visitor would periodically try to get down from the sedan to walk on his own, but each time he did so the carriers would immediately kneel down before him. Even if he still tried to proceed astep,[9] he didn't dare tread on the red cloth, red silk, and red brocade. The peasants lining the road immediately stopped clapping their hands, beating their drums, and blowing their horns, and everyone—young or old—also knelt down before him. They said he brought glory to his homeland, and that if he refused to ride in the sedan-chair along the red-carpeted path, it would suggest he didn't appreciate the welcome they had prepared for him. He therefore had no choice but to return to the sedan. When he finally arrived at the village, he tearfully knelt down before the village elders and promised he would pay whatever it took to pave that fifty-seven-*li*-long road, and would supply the entire township with water and electricity.

Afterward, Secretary Niu had gone down to the township to take a look, and met with the township chief, Liu Yingque.

Secretary Niu asked him, "Would you be able to provide all of the villages in the county with electricity and running water?"

Liu replied, "I am the township chief, and am only responsible for this single township. How could I be responsible for an entire county?"

Shortly afterward, Liu Yingque was promoted to deputy county chief, whereupon he did indeed become responsible for all of the villages in the county. Secretary Niu knew that Liu had fixed up the road to the village quite nicely, permitting cars to drive along it as smoothly as ships on the sea.

Now, looking at this person, this official, this Chief Liu, Secretary Niu recognized that he was a wise official, and that he was full of astonishing wisdom. Nevertheless, when Liu raised the idea of buying Lenin's corpse and displaying it on Spirit Mountain, Secretary Niu jumped in alarm as if he had just seen someone shatter a stone with a touch of his bare foot or the mere sound of his voice. At first he looked scornfully at this short and burly deputy county chief, as though he were fashioning a statue out of mud softened with his own piss. When he heard Liu calculate the projected revenue from selling admission tickets, however, his look of disdain was gradually replaced by a slight smile. When Liu paused, Secretary Niu stopped picking at the cigarette hole in the sofa's armrest and looked sternly at Liu Yingque, the way a father might regard a son wearing tattered clothes and covered in piss-mud, uncertain whether to hug or hit him.

Secretary Niu pondered for a while, then lowered his voice and asked, "Do you know what Lenin's original name was?"

Deputy Chief Liu looked down at his feet, then laughed. "Yes, of course. How could I not know his name? While looking over my documents, I repeated his name several times to memorize it. It is thirteen Chinese characters long: *Fuo-la-sai-mi-er Yi-li-qi Wu-li-yang-nuo-fu*: Vladimir Ilyich Ulyanov." He added, "Lenin was born in the fourth lunar month of the *gengwu* Year of the Horse from two sixty-year *jiazi* cycles ago, and he died in the twelfth month of the thirteenth year of the Chinese Republic." Liu specified, "Lenin died three months short of his fifty-fourth birthday, meaning that he fell more than ten years short of our current life expectancy."

"Do you know what books he wrote?"

"His most famous works are *What Is to be Done?; Materialism and Emperio-Criticism; Imperialism, the Highest Stage of Capitalism;* and *The State and Revolution.* Lenin was the progenitor of our country's socialist system, and the father of our socialist state. What child wouldn't be aware of his father's circumstances?"

"But why would the Russians be willing to sell us his corpse?"

At this point, Deputy Chief Liu took a document pouch out his bag, from which he removed a copy of *Reference News,* together with a pair of internal documents available only to county-level cadres and above. It was an old issue of *Reference News,* from the *gengwu* Year of the Horse, 1990, and in the lower right corner of the second page there was a three-hundred-and-one-character-long article entitled "Russia Wishes to Cremate Lenin's Remains," describing how a critical question confronting all of Russia's political parties following the breakup of the Soviet Union was whether to preserve or to cremate Lenin's embalmed corpse, currently on display in Moscow's Red Square, and concluding that those opting for cremation seemed to be gaining the upper hand.

One of the two internal documents was written three years and the other six and a half years after the *Reference News* article, with the latter of the two documents having been published just three months prior to the present meeting between Niu and Liu. Both of the documents focused on instances in which peasants committed suicide or disrupted county government to protest excessive taxation, or banded together to destroy county government gates, furniture, and vehicles in order to protest perceived injustices. They also described a case in which officials from one southern township went to a village to collect taxes, whereupon a woman who couldn't pay climbed into bed with one of the tax collectors in order to receive an exemption. From that point on, all of the village women unable to pay their taxes attempted to sleep with government officials, and deeply resented those who declined their advances.

Secretary Niu needed to read these internal documents immediately, before going to bed—just as children all over the world need to drink a glass of milk before going to sleep. He didn't notice any of the other astonishing international news stories that appeared during this same six-and-a-half-year period, and instead focused only on a couple of short reports—each only about a hundred characters long—detailing Russia's current economic difficulties. These reports described how there were insufficient resources for maintaining Lenin's preserved corpse, how parts of the corpse had deteriorated owing to financing shortfalls, and how the officials looking after the corpse often had to run down to the government office to seek additional funds. The reports noted that some high-ranking Russian officials had recommended the corpse be entrusted to a company or political party—but given that the political parties willing to accept the corpse didn't have the funds to pay for it, while the private corporations that had the funds had no interest in it, nothing ultimately came of this proposal.

Secretary Niu carefully examined the two reports, and then read back over the earlier *Reference News* article. He read the article again, then turned once more to the reports. He placed both the documents and the yellowed newspaper on a table and gazed intently at Deputy Chief Liu for what seemed to be an eternity. Finally, he said,

"Liu Yingque, pour me a glass of water."

Deputy Chief Liu went to fetch him a glass of water, and asked,

"Secretary Niu, why do you think we should worry about the county's economic state? There is actually treasure everywhere, and the question is really whether or not one is willing to go look for it."

"Deputy Chief Liu, how old are you?"

"I was born in the year of the great famine."

"This water is not hot enough. Go get me another glass."

Deputy Chief Liu went to fetch another glass and Secretary Niu, left alone in the room, again glanced at the *Reference News* article and the two internal document reports. He picked them up and was about to read them again, but instead placed them down on the table.

About a month later, there was an upheaval in the county government, as a result of which the county chief was transferred to an office in the district seat of Jiudu and the district Party committee secretary was sent elsewhere to study. As a result, Deputy County Chief Liu was promoted to the position of county chief.

Under the expert direction of the county's standing committee, County Chief Liu selected a date for purchasing Lenin's corpse, and then went to an area outside the city to spend the night and reflect on his decision. The prospect of purchasing Lenin's remains struck him as cold and tragic—though he wasn't sure if this feeling was due to his sentiments about Lenin or to his misgivings about the idea itself. This was late autumn—the crescent moon hovered over the harvested wheat field ends,[11] and the fragrant scent of crops and soil was everywhere. Chief Liu sat there deep into the night, pinching his leg and slapping his face to stay awake, then awkwardly knelt down and bowed three times in the direction of Lenin's hometown in Russia, silently offering his apologies. The next day, he composed a document entitled "Shuanghuai County's Directives Concerning Fund-raising and Attracting Investment in Order to Purchase Lenin's Remains," and distributed it to every council, office, township, and village throughout the county.

Several months passed in the blink of an eye, and the county's tourism industry began to show signs of life. A road was opened running from the county seat to the Spirit Mountain forest, and although it was initially paved with cement, the visitor from Southeast Asia who had supplied the county with roads, electricity, and running water agreed to subsidize the entire cost of repaving it with black oil.[13] On Spirit Mountain, various stones and other landmarks throughout the canyon were given distinctive names. One stone was called

Horse-Whinny Stone, and another was Deer Looking-Back Stone. A cypress with a chinaberry tree growing out of a hole in its trunk was called the Husband and Wife Embracing Stone; and there was also a Guillotine Cliff, a Black Dragon Pool, and the Cave of the Green and White Serpent.

For each landmark, people were invited to come up with explanatory stories. For instance, the name "Horse-Whinny Stone" was inspired by the rebel Li Zicheng, who helped bring down the Ming dynasty. (It was said that after Li Zicheng's defeat at Mount Funiu, he passed through here with a dozen or so followers, not realizing that more than ten thousand Qing imperial troops were waiting in ambush behind the next mountain, intent on finishing him off right then and there. When Li and his entourage arrived at this particular stone on Spirit Mountain, however, his horse suddenly came to a full stop and began whinnying incessantly. Eventually, Li had no choice but to turn around and head west, foiling the Qing ambush.)

The Deer Looking-Back Stone was said to have been inspired by a hunter who shot a deer and then pursued it for three days and three nights until he finally succeeded in trapping the animal at the edge of a cliff. As the deer was about to fall over the precipice, however, it suddenly turned to look back at the hunter, and at that moment it was transformed into a beautiful girl. The hunter married the girl, and proceeded to give up hunting and become a farmer, after which he and the girl lived happily ever after. The Husband and Wife Embracing Stone had a very moving story, and the Guillotine Cliff a tragic one. The Black Dragon Pool was once the home of an evil spirit, and the Green and White Serpent Cave was named after Xiao Qing and Bai Suzhen, the protagonists of the popular opera *Legend of the White Snake*.

In addition, a waterfall was being constructed that would be called Nine Dragon Cataract, and each county board and committee was expected to fund the construction of a new hotel or guest house on the mountain, which would be built in a classical Ming-Qing style. The heads of these local boards and committees began going to the bank to apply for credit, and some county boards—such as the wealthy postal-electric and transportation boards—even made direct investments of their own.

Construction had already started on a Lenin Memorial Hall, which from the outside would resemble the Chairman Mao Memorial Hall in Beijing, and inside there would be a crystal coffin containing Lenin's preserved corpse. In the front of the hall there would be a room with Lenin's corpse, a gallery of his images, and a collection of his writings, while in the back there would be a small theater showing films about his life and work. On both sides of the hall there would be temperature and humidity machines, to help preserve the remains. There would also be a break room for the workers, as well as a tea and a meeting room for distinguished guests. In front of the memorial hall there would be a garden, beyond which there would be a field flanked by parking lots, ticket booths, and gift shops. In the immediate vicinity of the memorial hall there would of course be plenty of restaurants and restrooms. The food in the restaurants wouldn't be too expensive, and while there was some dispute within the county's standing committee over whether or not the restrooms should be free or available for a fee, everyone agreed that they definitely needed to be clean. The stone path up the mountain would have a specified number of turns, and each of the hundred-year-old trees in the forest would be labeled with plates claiming that they were three hundred or even five hundred years old, while the five-hundred-year-old trees would be fenced off and labeled with plates claiming they were eleven hundred, nineteen hundred, or even two thousand years old. These sorts of arrangements were already well under way.

At present, the most important consideration was how to raise enough money to fund the trip to Russia to purchase Lenin's remains. The district informed Chief Liu that it would help provide half of whatever was needed, but that Chief Liu would have to find the remaining half himself. Over the preceding several months, Liu had raised as much as he could, yet had managed to secure only a small fraction of the total amount. He worried himself sick about how to go about obtaining the remaining funds to be able to take someone to Russia to negotiate a price and sign a contract for the corpse.

Further Reading:

1) **Full.** DIAL. **Full** means "entire," and **full face** means one's "entire face."

3) **Inside.** DIAL. Means "in the middle of," "in the center of."

5) **Afoot.** DIAL. Means "under his foot."

7) **Peak.** DIAL. Means "highest" or "most."

9) **Astep.** DIAL. Means "walking."

11) **Field ends.** The front or sides of a field.

13) **Black oil.** Asphalt. Because it is black, locals call asphalt "black oil."

Chapter 3: Guns go off, clouds disperse, and the sun emerges

Chief Liu, together with his secretary and the township chief, had been on his way to Spirit Mountain, where construction on Lenin's Mausoleum had already been under way for three months. The ground in front of the mausoleum had been broken, and the bricks and stones for building the structure had been brought up from the plateau below. But the work group had taken the pair of Hanbai jade tablets erected at either end of the plateau and placed them on the walls of the provisional latrines that had been erected for the construction site, and as a result they had become splattered with urine and excrement. Spirit Mountain was under the jurisdiction of Boshuzi township, and consequently Chief Liu had asked the township chief to take care of the situation.

The township chief had ordered, "Take the Hanbai jades down from the latrine walls."

The head contractor replied, "This is just temporary, and besides, what are you worried about? We'll rinse them off afterward, leave them as good as new."

The township chief said, "I'll fuck your mother, that's what I'll do. This is some of the Han jade that we'll be using for the mausoleum."

The head contractor said, "There's no need to insult my mother. When we were building a bank in Jiudu, we almost used gold bricks to build the bathroom."

The township chief said, "I *will* fuck your mother. Are you or are you not going to take them down?"

The contractor said, "You really don't need to talk about my mother. The county chief has overseen all the plans, and any changes would have to be approved by him."

The township chief then spent the entire day driving down to the county seat to negotiate with the county chief. When he arrived, Chief Liu was animatedly cursing the mother of a man from Singapore. The man's mother had died. She was from Shiliu Village in the western part of the county, and many years earlier her son had joined the army and been sent somewhere in Taiwan. For a while it was unclear whether or not he was even alive. Years later, it turned out that the son not only had survived but had gone on to become a successful businessman in Singapore. It was said that he became so rich that he could construct a building out of bricks made from actual cash.

Despite all of his money, however, he couldn't transfer his mother's remains to the coast from the village where she was buried. His sister went to take a look, as did his brother, together with many other relatives who owed him favors. But given that the mother had already died, it was determined that her remains had to remain in the village. The people in the county told her son that she had passed away two months earlier. By this point the son was sixty years old, and although he was a man, he often wore the sort of floral outfits that resembled a jujube tree covered with tropical bananas and mangoes. As soon as the son returned to Shuanghuai, Chief Liu himself had gone to the Jiudu train station to join the visitor's honorary escort, and the entire ride back he enthusiastically regaled the visitor with descriptions of the fabulous plans the county had made. When he finished, he announced, "We plan to buy Lenin's corpse from Russia."

The Singapore visitor was astounded. "Is that even possible?"

Chief Liu laughed. "With money, anything is possible."

The visitor reflected for a moment, and then observed sadly that his mother had passed away. While she was alive, she had not been able to enjoy even half a day of happiness with him, but now that she was deceased, he wanted to give her a magnificent *sheng* burial.

He had heard that a *sheng* burial wasn't necessarily very expensive, and all that was needed was some bricks and stones with which to construct the tomb. The problem, however, was that theirs was only a single family in the village; it would seem just too desolate if there weren't other relatives to help carry the coffin. He said, "Chief Liu, if you can find me another filial son, I will donate ten thousand yuan to the county, and if you can find me eleven filial sons, I will donate a hundred and ten thousand yuan. This should help you make up some of the funding you need to buy Lenin's corpse."

Chief Liu asked, "And what if I find you a hundred and one filial sons?"

"Then I'll give you a million and ten thousand yuan."

"And if I find you a thousand and one filial sons?"

The visitor replied, "Then I'll give you ten million and ten thousand yuan." He then added that regardless of how many filial sons the county managed to provide, the most he would be able to donate would be fifty million yuan, because if he were to give more, it would cut into the financial backbone of his business. Fortunately, with that fifty million yuan, the county would have a total of about a hundred million yuan, and if it could raise a hundred million, the higher-ups would contribute another hundred to bring the total to two hundred million—with which the county would surely have enough to negotiate an agreement to purchase Lenin's remains.

Chief Liu placed all of his hopes on this visitor from Singapore, and on the day of the mother's burial not only did he come up with more than seven hundred residents of Shiliu Village—including both men and women, young and old—all wearing filial caps and gowns, but he recruited more than a thousand additional filial sons from neighboring villages and townships. In this way, he organized a filial procession consisting of more than two thousand people. The caps and gowns were all prepared at the township level, for which every store throughout the township and indeed the entire county sold all the white cloth it had in stock, and garment factories worked around the clock for seven straight days. Even then, there were some people in the procession who were not able to obtain clothing for the occasion. It was agreed that those who did receive funeral garb would be allowed to keep it, and after washing it they could use it as regular clothing.

The resulting assemblage didn't resemble a funeral procession as much as an endless sea of white-clad mourners descending the mountainside like a cloud of mist. They trampled the wheat sprouts on either side of the road, and walked all over the hill on which the grave was located. Their wailing scared off all of the crows and sparrows on the mountain; the birds dispersed like clouds in the distant sky. After the funeral, the visitor returned to Singapore, and the money he had promised disappeared without a trace. As a result, all the owners of the fabric stores and heads of garment factories went to Chief Liu demanding payment.

Chief Liu had swallowed the Singapore visitor's bait—hook, line, and sinker—and subsequently grew so anxious his mouth became filled with painful sores that wouldn't go away unless he sucked on some bitter melon. He decided there was no need to reimburse the stores for the cost of the fabric used to make the mourning outfits, since he would consider it their collective contribution to the Lenin Fund.[1] He added that the garment factories didn't need to be reimbursed either, and that if the factory heads were to ask for payment, Chief Liu could simply replace them. The factory heads were so terrified when they heard this that they didn't dare ask again. Meanwhile, everyone else who participated in the funeral procession was compensated—in the sense that they not only received a brand-new set of white clothes, but for the next several days also had something new to talk about whenever they got bored. In the end, however, the Lenin Fund did not reach its target.

If it had been only a question of the visitor from Singapore that would have been one thing, but as it turns out there was something else that had infuriated Chief Liu even more, leaving him utterly speechless. The previous night, Chief Liu and his wife had had a falling-out—one that was as unexpected as the summertime blizzard that would suddenly befall Liven. While Chief Liu was out hosting a fund-raiser to help purchase Lenin's remains, his wife was home watching television.

45

Around midnight, he returned to their house and he and his wife went to bed. Since it was the weekend, they theoretically should have had their customary conjugal enlivening. This was their agreement, which they had written down, signed, and sealed with their finger-prints. They had agreed that they needed to carry out their connubial enlivening every weekend, in order to keep the chief from getting too big for his britches and forgetting his own wife. She was almost seven years younger than he, and after they slept together the first evening following his appointment as township chief, she took advantage of his good spirits and made him write down this vow. Therefore, every weekend they would make sure to have an enlivening.

But after Chief Liu began planning to purchase Lenin's corpse and realized he would need to raise a large sum of money in order to bring it back and install it on Spirit Mountain, he forgot all about his weekly conjugal enlivenings. His head[3] was filled with plans to build a mausoleum to house the corpse, but now the Singapore visitor was nowhere to be found and the Lenin Fund, which was supposed to have become bigger than a mountain and higher than the sky, had similarly failed to materialize. Chief Liu was exhausted and furious at the Singapore visitor, and when he got out of his fund-raiser that weekend and returned home after midnight, he fell asleep as soon as his head hit the pillow, his snores reverberating through the house. Just before dawn, his wife woke him up and said something astounding:

"Liu Yingque, I want a divorce."

He rubbed his eyes and stared back at her. "What?"

She said, "I've been thinking about this all night, and decided that it would be best if we got divorced."

Chief Liu finally understood what she was saying. He sat up in bed, and his shoulders began to feel a little chilly, as the night breeze washed over him like a bucket of cold water. He wrapped his shoulders with a big red quilt cover, looking as though he were holding up a large, fluttering flag. His wife was sitting in a chair in the center of the room, in the same moon-colored underwear she had been wearing the previous day, together with the kind of pink cotton tank top that had recently become fashionable among women in the

Shuanghuai county seat. Underneath this white and pink outfit, her skin was as bright and supple as pristine white jade, while her hair looked as though it had been painted black. Though she was only seven years younger than Chief Liu, she looked as though she was not even thirteen, pretty and refined. As she sat in the chair in front of Chief Liu, she looked like a coquette girl[5] sitting in front of her much older brother.

He asked, "Fuck, is this because I haven't been enlivening you recently?"

She replied, "It's not because of that. Besides, the enlivening is not just for me."

He said, "Nowhere else would you find a preschool teacher willing to divorce a county chief."

She said, "I want to get divorced. I really do."

It was at this point that the township chief had arrived at the government building where Chief Liu and his wife lived. He stood in the doorway listening for a while, then walked in, smiling. Standing next to Chief Liu, he said, "Girl, have you forgotten? Have you forgotten that the county chief is the head of the county, and that you are his wife? After he is promoted to district commissioner or district Party committee secretary, you would then become the wife of the district commissioner or Party secretary, and if he is promoted to provincial governor or provincial Party committee secretary, you would then become the wife of the governor or Party committee secretary."

She stared at the township chief with a disdainful smile lurking in the corners of her lips and her eyes.

Chief Liu added, "I'm telling you, by marrying me you have fallen into a nest of riches, and your family will burn incense for three generations."

She replied softly yet firmly, "I don't want to enjoy riches, and I don't want to be your wife."

He said, "After I become as famous as Lenin, then even if you die, there will still be someone around to make you a memorial tablet and build you a memorial hall. Do you realize that?"

47

She shouted back, "I'm only interested in what happens when I'm still alive. I couldn't care less what happens after I die."

He paused, then retorted, "How could your parents have given birth to someone like you?"

The township chief interjected, "Chief Liu, let it go. Don't argue with her. Besides, she's just a woman. You should go up to Spirit Mountain to take a look, and see if the contractors have put the Hanbai jade back on the latrine wall again."

Chief Liu said, "Fuck his grandmother. Make them come down."

The township chief said, "Fuck them back for eight generations. They say that they aren't willing to listen to anyone other than the county chief."

Chief Liu called out to his secretary, "Let's go. Secretary Shi, have the driver bring my car around."

His wife said, "Go, go! If you can, then stay away for ten days or two weeks."

Chief Liu laughed coldly. "In fact, I won't come back to this house for another month."

His wife retorted, "You shouldn't come back for another two months."

He said, "I won't come back for another three months."

She said, "If you return, you won't even deserve to be called human."

Chief Liu said, "If I cross this threshold within the next three months, you can consider me a bastard and tear down that memorial hall I just built, so that after we bring back Lenin's remains, we won't be able to sell even half of an admission ticket. You can leave me to wander the streets, burning up when the sun shines in the winter and freezing to death when it snows in the summer."

And, in fact, that summer it did snow.

Once he left the house and was on the road, the driver complained, "Fuck. This bedeviled day is getting colder and colder, and the car windows are covered with snowflakes."

Chief Liu and the township chief stuck their hands out the window to try to catch a snowflake.

The township chief said, "That's what the weather's like here in Balou. Every year it snows a bit during the third lunar month, and there is a major blizzard once every few years."

Secretary Shi said, "That's crazy. I can't believe it."

The township chief replied, "Secretary Shi, everything I said is the absolute truth, and if there is even the slightest falsehood, may this summer snow freeze me to death, and the winter sun burn me up."

Secretary Shi asked, "Really?"

The township chief said, "Really. Have you ever seen red dates growing on a peach tree? Or a one-legged man outrun a two-legged one? Or a blind person who can use his hearing to find where everything is? Do you believe any of this? Or a deaf person who, by feeling your ears with his fingertips, can hear everything you are saying? Or someone who has been dead for seven days and buried for four, but is still able to come back to life? Have you ever seen anything like that? Or a black crow that bears and raises chicks that look just like doves? If you don't believe these things, then when we arrive in Liven I will show you, thereby expanding your horizons. Okay?"

He added, "Secretary Shi, these things are all common occurrences in the Balou mountains. Fortunately, you are still a college student, because I'd really love to take a crap on your college textbooks and wash your blackboard with my piss. After studying for so many years, you earn more each month than I do, and sleep with more women, but you don't even know that here in Balou the temperature can drop to four or five degrees below zero in the summer, and can rise to thirty-four or thirty-five degrees in the winter. Don't you agree that I should take a crap on your textbooks, and wash your blackboard with my piss?"

Secretary Shi said, "Chief, your mouth is like a toilet."

The township chief replied, "Ask the county chief whether I was telling the truth."

Both of them turned to Chief Liu, and noticed that his face had turned a deep shade of purple and he was trembling from head to toe. Back in the county seat, he typically wore only a T-shirt, but now his entire body was covered in goose bumps. He was hugging his shoulders, and his teeth were chattering madly. In front of the car, snow was falling heavily and the windshield wipers kept trying to clear it from the windows.

The entire mountain was covered with a layer of pristinely white snow.

The township chief asked, "Chief Liu, are you cold?"

He shivered, but didn't respond.

In order to reach Spirit Mountain, they had to traverse the Balou mountains and take the road up to Liven. The base of Spirit Mountain was located about seventeen *li* or so beyond Liven. They were driving an old car with all the windows open, but even then they'd each had sweat pouring down their bodies. When they'd started out on their drive, warm wheat fragrance had wafted over the car, and the peasants beside the road had disappeared into the wheat fields. It was more than a hundred *li* from the county seat to the Balou mountains, and it took them more than half a day to cover the distance, since the driver was afraid that if he went too fast they might get a flat. When they had arrived in the Balou mountains, they drove through a forest of pagoda trees, where they were able to enjoy a breeze. As the temperature dropped, however, the fragrance of ripe wheat began to fade. The smell of summer gradually changed to that of fall, and as the car scurried over the mountain the weather became increasingly cool, even downright chilly. If the car's occupants hadn't kept the doors and windows tightly shut, they would have felt as though they were out in a field in the dead of winter.

The driver said, "It's getting colder and colder. What's going on?"

The township chief replied, "Fuck your family for eight generations. That's just how the weather is here. In the third lunar month they sometimes have peach blossom flurries, while in the middle of winter it can be scorching hot."

The driver said, "Fuck, if it really is snowing, we should use the windshield wipers to clean the snow off."

Secretary Shi asked, "Chief Liu, are you cold?"

The township chief said, "Why worry whether he's cold or not? Let the heat bake him to death, and the cold freeze him to death."

Chief Liu said, "I didn't bring any other clothes. If it's this cold in Shuanghuai, where will I get warm clothes?"

The township chief said, "If you wear heavy clothes you will burn up, but if you take them off you will freeze to death."

The township chief added, "It's snowing. Let's go—we need to get the county chief a padded jacket."

Secretary Shi said, "Let's pull into the village up ahead."

Chief Liu said, "Fuck, I simply can't believe it could possibly get too cold for me."

As he was saying this, the car pulled into a village halfway up the mountain and stopped at a wheat factory, where they borrowed a jacket and an army coat. After the driver stored the new clothing, they continued making their way up the mountain. It was on that snowy day that they encountered Jumei and her three nin daughters, and succeeded in finding Grandma Mao Zhi.

They arrived at Liven's guest house, where they stayed for the night.

The snow finally stopped falling.

The temperature, however, remained bitterly cold. When they woke up the next morning, the sky was still overcast and snow was blowing everywhere. Chief Liu hadn't slept well. The statues of the bodhisattvas, Lord Guan, and Lady Livening that had been in his room in the former Buddhist temple were no longer there. The three-room tile-roofed house was split into three sections by two partition walls. Chief Liu slept in the northernmost section, with a bed all to himself. The bed had two mattresses and two quilts, and therefore was certainly warm enough, but he couldn't sleep. Instead, he kept thinking about some of the things that had taken place eighteen years earlier when he was a soc-school teacher in Liven, and particularly about a woman who had given birth to quadruplets.

He thought that once he was able to bring back Lenin's remains and install them on Spirit Mount,[7] he could help promote tourism throughout the county and bring wealth to the district. He would surely be promoted then from county chief to deputy district commissioner or deputy district Party committee secretary. By that point, he would become a major figure, even an international personality, and not even the district Party secretary would be his equal. Four-fifths of the dozen or so counties in the district were poor, but he had already decided that once he was appointed deputy district commissioner or deputy district Party secretary, he would order that a memorial hall be erected in each of those poor counties, and then would have Lenin's remains circulate from one county to the next, thereby bringing each of them additional tourism revenue and greater wealth. He would also institute a global Lenin Day for the district. On this day, he would place Lenin's corpse on display in the city square in Jiudu, the district seat, so that everyone could revere and better understand him. Anyone wanting to read Lenin's works—together with those of Marx and Engels, and of course Mao Zedong—could gather together. As for whether or not those who revered Stalin and read his works would be permitted to visit, Chief Liu had not yet fully made up his mind, since he had heard that Chinese and foreigners had differing opinions about Stalin.

He had thought about many things that night, as he listened to the township chief and Secretary Shi snoring away in the next room like an old *erhu* melody, to the point where he almost couldn't resist going over and stuffing their mouths with dirty socks, and covering their noses with cotton and old shoes.

But given that now he was the county chief, he had no choice but to simply tolerate the noise.

So, he woke early and got out of bed.

The temple courtyard was half a *mu* in size, and had several old cypresses, a young elm, and a couple of middle-aged tung-oil trees. The branches and leaves of the tung-oil trees were pushed down to the ground by the weight of the snow. The old bird's nests in the cypresses had been pulled down by the weight of the snow, and a branch was lying at the base of the courtyard wall. There were also a couple of chicks that had hatched in the middle of the summer, but had fallen to their death and frozen into little balls of ice—only their tiny beaks poking out of a ball of snow, as though they were trying to peck their way out of an eggshell. The courtyard wall was made from adobe, and was covered by a thatched roof made from cornstalks. The cornstalks had dried up, and one by one had fallen to the ground. Under the influence of the elements, various sections of the wall itself inevitably began to collapse.

Chief Liu draped his coat over his shoulder, and stood in the doorway gazing at the courtyard.

Out in the street there was a cripple who had just gotten out of bed and was drawing water from a well. He hobbled over on his crutches, and as he walked through the snow his feet didn't make a conventional *zhizha zhizha* sound; rather, the sound of his lame leg gently coming down was followed by that of his other leg forcefully lifting up and back down again into the snow. This alternation of light and heavy thumps had a melodious quality, and to Chief Liu this sounded as if off in the distance there was a pair of wooden mallets, one large and the other smaller, taking turns pounding in the snow. As Chief Liu walked away and everything began to grow quiet, he looked up and saw that behind the clouds over the eastern mountain there was a sheet of whiteness that looked as though it would have oozed out if it hadn't been held in place by the mountains. But there were tiny cracks between the clouds that allowed several silvery white strands to pour through as though they were liquid.

Chief Liu stared intently at the white liquid.

It oozed out and accumulated like a pool of mercury, but was gradually covered up by dark clouds.

As Chief Liu stared at the rapidly disappearing white liquid, he glanced once again at the courtyard, and noticed that next to the southern wall there was a rusty shovel. He went over and pulled it from the snow, and then placed it in a notch in the wall. With the shovel's blade pressed close to his collar, he aimed it toward the silvery clouds to the east, and as he was aiming, his right index finger kept tugging at his chest as though he were pulling a trigger. Each time he pulled the trigger, he shouted *bang,* imitating the sound of a gun.

Ready, aim, *bang*!
Ready, aim, *bang*!
Ready, aim, *bang*!

Ready, aim, *bang*!

As he shouted *bang,* the black clouds in front of the white liquid began to part, allowing it to further ooze out into a small pool.

When Chief Liu heard the sound of the white liquid pouring through the clouds, his face immediately turned scarlet. He proceeded to fire even faster while continuing to make a thorough[9] *bang*ing sound. Eventually, the sun reappeared, and the silvery white liquid turned golden yellow, creating a golden yellow world.

"Chief Liu, the sky has cleared up," Secretary Shi remarked as he approached from behind, rubbing his sleepy eyes. "As you were firing toward the east, the sky cleared up and the sun came out."

"How would the sun dare *not* to come out?" Chief Liu turned around and, grinning happily like a general who had just won a battle, said, "Come here, Secretary Shi. Why don't you give it a try."

Secretary Shi picked up the shovel and, resting it on the courtyard wall, aimed it toward the eastern sky and pulled an imaginary trigger with his right index finger while shouting *bang, bang, bang*. But even as he was firing and shouting, the clouds moved back toward the center of the sky, once again covering up most of the golden yellow and silvery white pool.

Secretary Shi said, "I can't do this."

Chief Liu suggested, "Let the township chief give it a try."

The township chief walked out of the latrine and quickly tied his pants back up, then he too used the shovel as a gun and aimed it at the eastern mountains. He fired more than ten times, but as he did the clouds reconverged and the silvery white liquid was once again fully covered up.

The sky was filled with dark clouds.

Even in the temple courtyard, the air turned humid and steamy.

Chief Liu patted the township chief on the shoulder and said, "With your skills, I'll appoint you secretary of tourism after we bring Lenin's corpse back." As he took back the shovel, he shifted his position and aimed, then fired it three times. Sure enough, another fissure appeared in the clouds.

As the gun sounded, the clouds dispersed, and the sun came out again.

He fired ten or so more shots, and along the ridge of the eastern mountain there appeared a silver mat.

He fired another ten or so shots, and several gold mats appeared.

He fired another ten or so shots, and the gold and silver areas grew as large as a wheat field.

In the blink of an eye, a bright blue sky emerged behind the eastern mountain, and the black clouds that had not yet dispersed became covered by the gold and silver mats. The snow shone brightly in the sunlight. The tree branches poked out in all directions, silver-coated. Throughout the snow-covered fields along the mountain range, there were occasional clumps of wheat sticking out, like thorns piercing through the snow-white bed covering the ground. The air was unusually fresh, and if you took a few breaths and savored them, a distinctive aftertaste would linger in your mouth—and this aftertaste, while initially pleasant, would subsequently become nauseating.

The entire village was filled with the sound of retching.

After they finished coughing, these people who had just gotten out of bed all slapped their foreheads.

The men said, "Ah, the sky has cleared. At least now we can harvest some of the grain and recover somewhat from this natural disaster."

The women said, "Ah, the sky has cleared. The mildewed sheets can be hung out to dry. Even during a natural disaster, you shouldn't let your sheets get moldy."

The children said, "Ah, the sky has cleared. The next few days will be great fun. Each day that it snows is another day we can stay in bed and not go to school. Having to go to school is worse than starving to death."

There were also some people staring at the temple guest house, who said, "Ah, the county chief arrives and the sky immediately clears up. Even the weather recognizes that he just isn't like the rest of us."

Chief Liu heard these remarks from the other side of the courtyard wall, whereupon he took down the shovel and stuck a fistful of snow into his mouth, which was parched from all of his *bang-bang-bang*ing. He reflected for a moment, then turned to the township chief and asked, "Is it normal for it to snow here in the middle of the summer?

The township chief replied, "There was one such snowstorm just before the three years of natural disaster, and another during the lost decade, but neither was as big as this one. Those were mere dustings that immediately melted as soon as the sun came out."

Secretary Shi said, "So, in other words, this summer snowstorm is really a once-in-a-century occurrence?"

The township chief replied, "Fuck, if this miraculous incident isn't newsworthy, then I don't know what is."

Chief Liu said to the township chief, "I want to contribute to the disaster relief. Why don't you go to Spirit Mountain and have someone take the Hanbai jade down from the latrine wall. They should clean it thoroughly, and use the cleaning water to cook some food." Then he suggested to his secretary, "Why don't you go back to the township and urge each board member to donate ten yuan to Liven, even if it means that they have to go hungry to do so. Then, write about how the entire township dedicated its efforts to disaster relief and send the report to the district and provincial seat. After the disaster relief has concluded, I'll have Liven convene a several-day-long livening festival[11] to express their gratitude to the government for its efforts on their behalf."

After finishing his breakfast, the township chief headed off to Spirit Mountain to clear snow.

Secretary Shi returned to the county seat.

Chief Liu stayed behind in Liven.

Further Reading:

1) **Lenin Fund.** *A fund specifically reserved for purchasing Lenin's corpse. This became the most frequently used term after Shuanghuai resolved to purchase Lenin's remains.*

3) **Head.** Skull.

5) **Coquette.** Coquettish.

7) **Spirit Mount.** An abbreviation for Spirit Mountain.

9) **Thorough.** Continuous.

11) **Livening festival.** A major festival held every year after the wheat harvest, this being a tradition unique to Liven.

CHAPTER 5: THE LIVENING FESTIVAL OF THE INTERCALARY FIFTH MONTH OF THE *WUYIN* YEAR OF THE TIGER

The harvest season was almost over.

The period of hurried walking was almost over.

In the end, it was still summer. When the sun briefly came out, the snow quickly melted, leaving the ground soaking wet—to the point that if you were to pick up a fistful of soil, you would find it half full of water. Just when the sun was needed most, they got day after day of fog. The fog was so thick, in fact, that it was not much brighter during the day than at night, and although Chief Liu continued waving his shovel at the sky every day, the fog continued to envelop everything in sight. Every day, Chief Liu would pick up the shovel when no one was around, and wave it at the sky. Squatting down in the excrement-covered ground of the latrine, he would aim his imaginary handgun toward the area of the sky where the sun should have been and fire several shots, but the fog continued flowing inexorably forward. By the fifth day, he was so anxious that his mouth was filled with cold sores, to the point that he took a real rifle and fired it three times into the fog. All three bullets hit squarely in the middle of the clouds and fog.

As a result, the fog finally dispersed.

The water-laden soil dried up to the point that you could walk on it.

The grains in the ears of wheat were all mildewed. The sediment was greenish, and when people ate it they would vomit and get the runs. The wheat stalk also became mildewed, turning green and black and emitting a foul odor. The cattle refused to eat it, even though they were half-starving. That winter, there would be no wheat stalks to feed the cattle, and no family would have any grain, or even a bowl of snow-white noodles every three to five days. There wasn't even enough flour to prepare the flatbread[1] that they traditionally ate on New Year's. Nor were there enough wheat seeds to plant in the fall.

Throughout the land, this was truly a year of disaster. On the villagers' faces there was no trace of the happiness they would normally feel after the wheat harvest. In the past, Grandma Mao Zhi would always organize a three-day festival after the harvest. Every household would extinguish the fire in the hearth and go to whoever had the biggest field, where the villagers would gather together to eat and drink for three straight days. During that period, one-legged cripples would compete with two-legged people to see who could run the fastest. Deaf people would demonstrate their ability to tell what someone was saying simply by touching the speaker's earlobe, using their hands to feel the sound of the words. Blind people would compete to see whose hearing was the sharpest by having someone drop a needle onto a stone, wood, or dirt surface and trying to determine where it had fallen. And then there were the one-armed people, who held their own competitions.

That three-day festival was like New Year's, and young men and women would come from miles around to participate. Amid the festivities, young men and women would meet one another, and young men from out of town would often marry the disabled women from the village, while the village's disabled young men would marry young women from outside. But sometimes, a tragedy would unfold. Once, for instance, an attractive and able-bodied young man from another village came to watch the festivities, and noticed a crippled, not terribly attractive young woman who, although she was lame, could embroider seventy to ninety flower blossoms in the blink of an eye. The young man felt that if he didn't marry her, he simply wouldn't be able to continue living, and therefore tried to kill himself after his parents refused to approve the match. In the end, however, he went to live with her. She subsequently got pregnant and gave birth to a child, leaving the young man's parents with no alternative but to acknowledge their new family member. There was also a beautiful young woman who came to Liven to enjoy the festivities, at which she met a deaf man who not only had not lost his ability to speak, but could tell what you were saying from your expression and the movement of your lips.

The young woman said, "I feel sorry for whoever has to marry you."

The deaf man replied, "Why would you feel sorry for her? I would wash my wife's feet, bring her water, cook her meals, and let her relax at home rather than having to work in the fields. Why in the world would you feel sorry for her?"

The young woman laughed. "Your words are prettier than a song."

The deaf man said, "That's not true. Just listen to me sing."

He then lowered his voice and sang her a Balou tune.[3] The lyrics went as follows:

When the sun comes out in winter, the ground warms up.
Two people are lying on the ground sunning themselves.
The young man clips his wife's nails,
While the wife picks her husband's ears.

There is a rich landlord in the eastern village,
With piles of silver and gold, he lives in a tile-roofed house.
But one day the landlord struck his wife eight times.
I ask you, whose life is bitter, and whose is sweet?

The young woman didn't laugh when she heard these lyrics. Instead, she thought for a while, then gently placed her hand in his and asked if he could hear her. He held her hand and replied, "As long as I'm touching you, I'm not deaf at all, since I can feel what you are saying." She then removed her hand and announced that she had to return home to consult with her parents—and even though no one in her family agreed to the marriage, she still returned to Liven to marry him.

There was also a blind man whose eyes were pools of darkness, but whose heart was deep, and who could steal a woman's heart with just a few words. He was going out to the fields to listen to the livening festival, but on the way he tripped over a stone and almost fell. Fortunately, a young woman from outside the village was there to grab him.

He asked, "Why did you grab me? Why not just let me fall to my death?"

She said, "Brother, you mustn't be like that. It's always better to live than to die."

He said, "That's easy for you to say. You not only can see, you are also very pretty. Of course it is good for *you* to live."

She stared at him, "How can you tell I'm pretty?"

He said, "Precisely because I'm unable to see, I can see everything beautiful in the world, including everything beautiful about you."

She said, "I'm short and fat."

He said, "I see that your waist is like a willow."

She said, "You can't see. I'm dark and swarthy."

He said, "Because I can't see, I therefore can see you as light and tender, just like my own sister. You are like a fairy maiden."

She said, "You can't see, and therefore your eyes are clean and untainted."

He said, "You can see, and therefore you see the entire world as dirty. I can't see, and therefore I see the entire world as pristine and pure." He added, "I can't see, and am always saying that I should be allowed to fall to my death. But actually, I never really want to die. You can see, and although you've never said that you wanted to die, I'm sure that you think about death many times every day." It's unclear whether or not the young woman really did always think about death, but when the young man said this, her eyes immediately started to tear up. She said, "Brother, I'll lead you out to the field to watch the livening festival." The blind man started to hand her one of his

61

canes, but was worried that it would get her hands dirty. Therefore, he decided to keep this cane that had just fallen to the ground for his own use, and instead handed her the one he himself just had been using. She could feel the warmth of his hand on the cane, and where he had worn it smooth.

Together, they went to watch the livening festival.

Afterward, they proceeded to spend the entire rest of their lives together. They had a son and daughter, as one generation begat another.

However, this year's livening festival was not hosted by Grandma Mao Zhi, nor was it held in celebration of the harvest; rather, it was hosted by Chief Liu in celebration of something he himself was organizing. Chief Liu had gone to see Grandma Mao Zhi, who was in her courtyard feeding her dogs as though they were her children. The dogs were also disabled—some of them were blind, some were crippled, and others had lost all their fur and their backs were full of scabies, like the uneven surface of a mud wall. There was also a dog that for some reason didn't have a tail and was missing an ear. This courtyard abutted an earthen cliff, and on either side of the courtyard there was a small building. On the south side, there was a thatched hut that served as Grandma Mao Zhi's kitchen, and on the north side there were two earthen dugouts that Mao Zhi used as doghouses. In front of the dugouts were a pig trough, an old washbasin, a handleless wok, and a new earthen pot, all of which Mao Zhi used to feed the dogs. Dogs don't fight for food the way pigs do, and they ate the corn-paste gruel that Grandma Mao Zhi put in their basins, pots, and woks. The courtyard was full of the sweet scent of ripe corn, and the sound of the dogs lapping it up. There was a mutt that was already more than twenty years old, which in dog years was equivalent to about ninety human years. The dog was so old it could no longer move, and therefore Grandma Mao Zhi placed half a bowl of corn gruel in front of it, and it just lay there and slowly extended its tongue into the bowl to lick up the food.

By that point, the sun was already high in the sky, and the courtyard was completely still. You could hear the sound of villagers working in the fields, calling out to their oxen as they plowed the fields—their

voices rising and falling like the music to the Balou tune "Birds Flying."
As Grandma Mao Zhi fed her dogs, she heard the door behind her
open, and when she turned she saw Chief Liu standing in the doorway.

She looked over at him, then turned and continued feeding her
dogs.

Chief Liu remained in the doorway, as though he had expected
this and was not at all embarrassed. He gazed at the two buildings
on either side, and then at the row of dogs eating their food, as they
all silently stared back at him. He wanted to come inside, but seeing
the dogs standing there as though they were ready to rush at him as
soon as Grandma Mao Zhi gave the word, he decided instead to wait
in the doorway.

Standing with her back to him, Grandma Mao Zhi asked, "What
do you want?"

Chief Liu tried to walk forward as he replied, "That's a lot of
dogs you are feeding."

"Did you come to see my dogs?"

"I've come for disaster relief."

"Then relieve it."

"Our disaster relief funds and grain reserves are almost exhausted.
When it hailed in Lianshu township the year before last, I didn't go,
and didn't send them any money or grain. Last year when there was a
drought in Zaoshu township and their entire harvest was lost, I didn't
go, and just sent them a hundred pounds of wheat seeds for each *mu*
of their land. But this year, when it snowed in Liven in the middle of
the summer and many households had to pull their grain out of the
snow, I came to assess the situation and personally distribute money
and grain. It's entirely possible that, this way, you may end up receiving more grain than you normally would have gotten from simply
harvesting it."

Grandma Mao Zhi poured the remainder of the food into the
dogs' bowls, and said,

"In that case, I should thank you on behalf of the entire village."

Chief Liu shifted his gaze to some date trees growing on top of
the dugouts. The trees had lost all their leaves in the blizzard, but

under the sunlight of the past several days several green buds had begun to emerge, as if spring had just arrived.

"No need to thank me," said Chief Liu. "You should thank the government. You should host a livening festival, as you have in the past."

Grandma Mao Zhi said, "I'm old, and don't have the energy to organize one."

Chief Liu said, "In that case, I'll do it myself."

Grandma Mao Zhi said, "As long as you are able to."

Still standing behind Grandma Mao Zhi, Chief Liu began to laugh. "You've forgotten that I'm the county chief."

Grandma Mao Zhi also laughed and, without turning around, replied, "How could I forget? I still remember when the higher-ups[5] asked me to be township chief and I declined. You weren't even born then, much less a soc-school teacher in the Boshuzi commune." Chief Liu didn't reply. He stood for a while longer behind Grandma Mao Zhi, snorted, then walked out of the house.

Actually, Liven didn't have any village cadres. In fact, it hadn't had a village cadre since Liberation, and instead it was loosely structured like a large family. Nearly forty years earlier, in the *renchen* year, 1952, the members of the commune wanted to join a larger brigade, but discovered that no brigade was willing to accept a village consisting of more than two hundred disabled residents. They therefore suggested that they form their own large brigade, but there were not enough villagers for that, and they had only enough to form a small production brigade. In the end, they weren't considered either a large or a small brigade, but rather were merely a village in Boshuzi. Since they had all been brought to this township and county by Grandma Mao Zhi after Liberation, it was therefore only natural that she should take charge of village affairs. For instance, she was responsible for holding meetings, distributing grain, selling cotton, and helping relay urgent political announcements from the higher-ups. When two neighbors quarreled or a mother- and daughter-in-law got into a spat, Grandma Mao Zhi would need to resolve the rifts. Had Grandma Mao Zhi not agreed to settle down in Liven, by this point she probably would have already become a township or county chief. But given that she merely wanted to pass her days in Liven, she naturally became the village's director.[7]

If Liven was going to hold a livening festival in a wheat field, it was expected that she would be responsible for organizing it. Aside from famine years, she had been organizing the annual livening festival for several decades, and more generally was responsible for handling all of the village's activities, big or small. Grandma Mao Zhi wasn't exactly what people nowadays would call a village or town cadre—like the village head, Party branch secretary, production brigade leader, or village leader—since the people of Liven, unlike those in other towns, had not selected a village cadre, and neither the previous township or commune, nor the current township government, had come to Liven to announce who the village cadre should be. Whenever there was anything that needed to be done, however, the higher-ups would invariably come looking for Grandma Mao Zhi. She would consider their request, and some things she would manage herself while others she would decline on behalf of her fellow villagers, making the higher-ups go home empty-handed. Without her, there was no one who could take the lead.

For instance, if people wanted to open a road, build a bridge over the creek running through the bottom of the gorge, build a reservoir, or clean out the village well after leaves, branches, or a child's hat or shoe had fallen in—or after someone jumped into the well himself in a moment of despair, thereby contaminating the water and making it necessary to dredge the well and scrub its inner walls—Grandma Mao Zhi would take responsibility for handling these things, since there was no one else in the village who could.

And, of course, there was also the annual livening festival.

But this famine year the festival ended up being organized by Chief Liu himself. Even without Grandma Mao Zhi, Liven was still a bustling community. When Chief Liu left Grandma Mao Zhi's house, he had been in Liven for nine days. On four of those days there had been good weather, and many people had already begun planting corn in the pockmarked fields, but because both the slope and the flat fields had absorbed so much water, it was advisable to let them dry out for several more days before planting. As for the grain funds that had been brought in from the county seat, Secretary Shi would have to return with the survey and some cash before nightfall. Of course, it was necessary to hold the livening festival now, in order to distribute the grain funds to the people. The government looks after its people, and the people should remember the government's kindness; this is the way things had been for thousands of years.

In the end, Grandma Mao Zhi did not show up to organize the livening festival. But actually, Chief Liu had not even really asked her to host it, since he was afraid that if she did show up, she might say and do things that would confuse everyone. For better or worse, however, she was seventy-one years old, and a survivor of the events around the *bingzi* year, 1936, and the only villager who had been to Yan'an. The higher-ups regarded her as a member of the older generation who had participated in the Revolution, and therefore someone who must be respected. Chief Liu consequently had no choice but to go and speak to her. Though how could she imagine that he wouldn't be able to host a tiny livening festival without her help?

What a joke!

After visiting Grandma Mao Zhi's house, Chief Liu went straight to the old honey locust tree in the center of the village to ring the bell. The sun was directly overhead, and a group of cripples had gathered in the clearing near the tree to have lunch. Among them were an old carpenter and several younger men. Apart from one man who was missing a leg, the others had never used crutches. Holding their rice bowls, they stood up to greet Chief Liu. They lifted bowls and asked with a smile, "County Chief, have you eaten yet?"

Chief Liu replied, "I have. And you?"

The cripples said, "We just finished. Why don't you come to our house to have a few bites."

Chief Liu replied, "No, thank you," then asked, "Would you like to take part in a livening festival?"

The young cripples' faces started glowing, and they said, "Yes, of course. Who wouldn't? We've all been waiting for Grandma Mao Zhi to host one."

Chief Liu stared at them. "So, if she doesn't host it, you won't participate?"

A young cripple asked, "If she doesn't host it, then who will?"

Chief Liu said, "I will."

The young cripple said, "The county chief certainly has a sense of humor!"

Chief Liu said, "I'm serious. I'll host it."

The cripples stared at him in astonishment. After studying him carefully and seeing that he wasn't joking, they all turned away. The older cripple looked off into the distance while eating his lunch, and said,

"Chief Liu, there are one hundred and ninety-seven of us here in Liven, of which there are thirty-five blind people, forty-seven deaf people, and thirty-three cripples, together with several dozen more who are missing an arm or a finger, have an extra finger, stunted growth, or some other handicap. Does the county chief want to see us make a spectacle of ourselves?"

Chief Liu turned slightly pale. He replied to the older cripple, "I know you are a carpenter, and can carve with lightning speed. I certainly don't want to see you make a spectacle of yourself. I am your parental official, and therefore am in effect your parent. All eight hundred and ten thousand inhabitants of the county are my virtual children, and I need to look after what they eat and wear. After your midsummer blizzard, I was here the next day with rescue funds and grain. Therefore, tomorrow I want to organize a livening festival, at which I will personally give each of you a ration of funds and grain. If you attend the festival, you will receive grain and money, quite possibly more than you would normally receive in a normal year. If you don't attend, however, you won't receive anything."

Everyone stared at him.

Chief Liu walked away.

He left before they were able to see anything in his face. In this village, there was only this one road, which was also a street. The sun shone down furiously, and even the chickens and pigs tried to hide in the shadow of the wall. The county chief was muscular but rather short and fat, and his shadow was only half as long as he was tall. This black shadow followed behind him like a silent ball. He was wearing a pair of leather sandals that slapped loudly on the ground, and he walked very briskly without looking back, as if he were angry.

In front of him, the village's oxcart wheel bell was hanging from the honey locust tree. The tree was as thick as a man's waist, and at the height of a person's head there was a branch as wide as a plate, from which the bell was hanging. Because the villagers were afraid the wire holding up the bell might cut into the tree branch, they had padded it with rubber shoe soles. Chief Liu saw not only the bell, but also the rubber padding. The old honey locust tree gave off a scent of fresh sprouts, while the rubber padding emitted a mildewed smell. The bell, rubber tire, and metal wire all emitted a sharp oxidized odor. Needless to say, the bell had not been used for several years, the last time anyone rang it having perhaps been before the land redistribution campaign of the *wuwu* Year of the Horse, 1978. When other villages wanted to hold an occasional meeting, they would ring a bell to call the meeting to order if they didn't have a horn to blow. In Liven and the surrounding county and township, however, everyone remembers the meeting times, and it is very unusual for anyone to sound the bell.

But it was evident that Chief Liu intended to ring the bell himself, thereby once again using it to summon everyone together. He had walked over to where the bell was hanging, and was about to look for the brick used to strike it, when One-Legged Monkey, who had been eating with the older cripple, suddenly grabbed his crutches and hobbled up behind him.

"Chief Liu," he shouted, his face turning scarlet.

Chief Liu turned around.

"You don't need to strike the bell. I'll go door-to-door notifying everyone for you. In the past, whenever there was an event of some sort, this is what Grandma Mao Zhi would always have me do." Having said this, he grabbed his crutches and headed off in the direction of the blind area of the village. He walked very briskly, his right crutch lightly touching the ground as his left foot left the ground, and as he was waiting for his left foot to come back down again, he would lean into his right leg. He wasn't walking as much as he was hopping, but in this way was able to proceed as fast as a wholer could. In no time, he arrived at a blind man's house, and entered through the main gate.

Chief Liu was right behind him, staring in astonishment at his hop-running, as if he were watching a deer or a small horse galloping along a mountain pass.

In this way, One-Legged Monkey notified each household.

He called out, "Hey, Lead Blind Man, tomorrow morning there'll be a livening festival. The county chief wants to distribute grain and funds. Whoever doesn't attend runs the risk of starvation!"

He called out, "Hey, Fourth Blind Man, tomorrow there will be a livening festival, though of course if you plan to starve to death next spring there is no need for you to attend!"

He called out, "Hey, Crippled Auntie, didn't you say you wanted to see the county chief? Then you should turn out for the livening festival tomorrow."

He said, "Little Piglet, why don't you run home and tell your parents that tomorrow at the break of dawn a three-day livening festival will begin."

And in this way, everyone was notified.

When the sun came up the next day and the eastern sky was enveloped in a rosy glow, everyone finished breakfast and proceeded to the main field in the village. The weather was warm and pleasant, and there was a slight breeze. The men were all wearing loose-fitting gowns, while the women wore comfortable blouses. The field was a large clearing that was as flat as the surface of a lake. Originally, this was used as the communal threshing ground, but after the land was redistributed it came to be used as the blind men's threshing ground, and therefore whenever the villagers held an event, they would always attempt to include the blind men. The blind men in Liven were well looked after, like babies who are always given a few extra gulps of breast milk. Although this was now the blind men's field, the village would use it whenever there was a public event for which everyone needed to gather together. The field therefore came to be used as the village's meeting space and performance stage. It was one *mu* in size, with one side abutting the road, two sides abutting a set of fields, and along the fourth side a three-foot-high earthen dam, on top of which there was a pockmarked slope.

The owner of this slope was fifty-three years old. He had only one arm; the other was merely a stub. But even with only one arm, he could still plow the fields, turn the soil, and use a hoe to smooth the earth. When people came to observe the festivities during the livening festival each year, if there wasn't enough room for them in the main field, they would go over and sit on that pockmarked slope. The slope had been plowed and hoed, but after being trampled for three straight days, it was left as flat as a pancake. After the livening festival, the owner once again needed to hoe and turn the soil, and as he was using his ox to plow the field a second time, he complained vehemently that people had destroyed his field. But even as he was complaining vociferously, he continued smiling broadly.

Once, someone noticed that after the harvest every year, the one-armed landlord would invariably go and plow his field beforehand. The person said, "Uncle, the livening festival has not even taken place yet. What's the point of plowing the field now, if it will only be trampled flat again?" After looking around to make sure no one else was listening, he laughed softly and said, "Nephew, don't you know, when I plow this field and then allow it to be trampled, all of the dust from everyone's shoes and the filth from their bodies will go directly back into the soil, making it unnecessary to add any additional fertilizer for the rest of the year."

This year, the one-armed man once again plowed the slope. He originally assumed that, on account of the summer blizzard, there wouldn't be a livening festival this year, but now it turned out that there would be one after all and that the county chief would host it himself. The one-armed man, therefore, was the first to arrive at the field, and the other villagers soon followed. They brought chairs, benches, and mats, and some of them notified their relatives in neighboring villages, urging them to come take part in the excitement. They also brought seats for their relatives, in order to reserve a spot for them. By the time the sun had risen three pole-lengths in the sky, when everyone would normally be working, the field was already full. There were bundles of beams bound together with wire resting on some piles of wood, on top of which there were some door planks covered with reed mats, which functioned as a makeshift stage. This stage had been erected by the one-legged Lame Carpenter, with the assistance of several young men. They brought saws, hammers, axes, and other tools, and in no time at all they completed their work.

The benches in front of the stage were arranged in neat rows.

Men and women from neighboring villages were invited to come sing Balou tunes.

In the past, the musical troupes would come to Liven several days prior to the festival to discuss their proposed compensation, but since this year the festival was being hosted by Chief Liu, the percussion and musical troupes didn't know how to organize, or whom to approach. The news that the county chief would personally host the livening festival spread quickly through the villages, like the aroma of food at mealtimes. When the sun came up that morning, the entire mountain pass was filled with visitors from neighboring villages who had come to observe the excitement. By the time the sun reached the head of the village, a huge crowd had gathered in the field, and the slope along the dam was completely full of people. The fifty-three-year-old one-armed man walked around shouting, "You're all trampling my field! . . . You're all trampling my field! I just plowed this field, but if I had known you were going to trample it like this, I wouldn't have bothered." Even as he was complaining, he continued smiling broadly. When he saw relatives and acquaintances from other villages who didn't have anywhere to stand, he said to them, "Why don't you go sit over there in my field. I can always plow it over again later."

As a result, there were more and more people sitting in his field.

The crippled woman who worked as the village pharmacist took a portable coal burner to the field, and used it to prepare a pot of dark tea-eggs, the fragrance of which quickly spread everwhere.

A deaf man was roasting peanuts by the side of the field.

Someone selling sunflower seeds set up a stand right next to his.

71

A woman from the neighboring village cooked tofu strips on the slope. The tofu strips were dipped in hot oil, then strung up on a skewer and dunked in a pot of boiling water. Although the pot contained only water and no oil, and was seasoned with only salt, pepper, anise, and MSG, those tofu strips were so fragrant they could be smelled from miles away. A balloon seller arrived, as did a whistle peddler. People selling candied apples and poached pears also arrived. Someone selling clay Buddha and fat boy figurines set up a water basin on a tall bench, and after the figurines were dunked in water, they turned bright red. Because the water was hot, when the peddler pulled out the fat boy figurine, its little pecker stuck straight out and a thin stream of liquid flowed from it, as if it were a real boy peeing into the air. Everyone laughed at this, and someone even forked over money to buy it and the Buddha figurine that was still sitting in the water. The field was raucous, with more and more people arriving at every moment. It was like a temple ceremony in the mountains. Even incense and paper money sellers arrived.

The livening ceremonies that Grandma Mao Zhi typically hosted were also intended to celebrate the year's harvest. After working hard all year, the villagers were permitted to relax, to gather together for three days to eat and drink. But this year the ceremony was hosted by the county chief, and for this reason people came surging in like the tide. They not only filled the one-armed man's field on the slope but also lined the sides of the field.

The sun rose another pole-length in the sky.

The percussion troupe and musicians were all set up on the eastern side of the stage.

Jumei and Mao Zhi didn't come to watch this livening festival, but Jumei's daughters were dispersed throughout the field. The sun was searingly hot. A man standing in one of the sunlit areas had taken off his shirt and gown, and his sweat-covered head and back shone in the sunlight. Someone demanded impatiently, "Why haven't things started yet?" Someone else replied, "The county chief and his secretary have not arrived yet. How could we start without them?" Half-crazed under the blazing heat of the sun, even the goats grazing on the distant mountains were startled by the tumult, as they stared down in surprise at the crowd.

In the cobalt blue sky, there were a few traces of white clouds. The clouds were as white as cotton, while the sky was as blue as a deep pool of water. The entire world was a boundless reservoir of calm, and only the field at the entrance of the village was bustling. It was very hectic, but at the same time very solitary. It was like a pot of boiling water in the middle of a field of calm. The children who had climbed the trees along the side of the road were waiting, and began shaking the tree branches, causing the twigs and leaves that had been damaged by the hot snow to fall to the ground. Someone shouted out sharply,

"The county chief and his secretary have arrived! .... The county chief and his secretary have arrived!"

The crowd spontaneously parted to open a path for them. The cripples and the people who were missing an arm or leg all crowded up at the very front of the stage. The deaf and mute people sat down behind the cripples. The blind people, meanwhile, could hear but couldn't see, and therefore they didn't compete with anyone for space and instead just tried to find a secluded spot from which they could listen to the Balou tunes. Of course, the ones who really crowded up to the stage were the half-deaf old-timers. Given that they were only partially deaf and could hear loud voices quite clearly, the villagers pushed them right up to the edge of the stage. In Liven, there was always a strict set of rules dictating who at any meeting, performance, or livening festival should be in front, and who should be in back.

A blind man crowded forward, and some people said, "Given that you can't see, why do you need to crowd your way forward?" The blind man laughed and walked instead to the back of the field.

Most of the mutes were also deaf. A deaf-mute crowded up to the edge of the stage, but someone asked, "Given that you can't hear, why do you need such a good seat?" The deaf-mute therefore yielded his seat to someone else.

For the deaf-mutes who could still hear a little, some people would shout out, "Third Uncle, if you sit here you'll be able to hear"; "Fourth Auntie, if you sit here you will be near the musicians."

73

In this way, the seats were distributed. Of course, the wholers all sat up in front, and if they arrived early they would claim a good seat, or they would send one of their children to save them a seat. Once the seat was secured there would be nothing anyone could say. Among those from the same village, everyone treated everyone else's relatives as their own, and so naturally no one was going to complain. But when people came from other villages, they understood that this was Liven's festival and not theirs, and therefore they naturally should sit or stand along the outermost rings.

Actually, you could also see and hear from there, but the problem was that those spectators were closer to the peddlers, and therefore everything was very smoky. Children would run around amid the peddlers' stands and between their legs, making it difficult for the spectators to concentrate on the villagers' special-skills performances.[9] If people were watching from the ninth ring or beyond, the performers' heads looked like black beans in an autumn wheat field. On the other hand, everyone had come for the excitement, so they were generally content to stand back.

Chief Liu and his secretary arrived. By this point the sun had already risen to who knows how many pole-lengths in the sky. When Chief Liu and Secretary Shi arrived, they were smiling broadly, and they entered the field accompanied by One-Legged Monkey. The crowd parted to open a path for them. The musicians put down their reed pipes, bamboo flutes, drums, and three-stringed fiddles. The county chief and his secretary were given the best seats in the house: two red chairs that were only a few inches tall. They were woven from bamboo and painted red, but the yellow matrimonial "double happiness" character underneath remained visible. Needless to say, these chairs had been part of the dowry that some young woman's parents had given her when she married a man from Liven, but were now gloriously being used by the county chief and his secretary as their special stools.

Chief Liu had removed his army coat several days earlier, and underneath was wearing a round-collared white sweatshirt, which was tucked into his underwear. He had a red face, a flattop, and a slightly protruding belly, and his hair was speckled with gray, such that when he got older he would look just like a bona fide county chief, and not at all like the other peasants from the Balou mountain region. At the same time, however, he also didn't resemble those important personages from Jiudu or the provincial seat who frequented fancy restaurants. Instead, he appeared a bit rustic, though compared with the other Balou peasants he actually seemed rather Westernized. But even his Westernized appearance, if compared with that of other outsiders, was rather rustic.

Of course, the important thing was not how provincial or cosmopolitan he was, but rather the fact that his secretary was tall, thin, and fair-skinned, with a snow-white shirt tucked into his pants and shiny black hair that was carefully parted, as though he were an important personage. To be accompanied by a secretary who could pass for a celebrity added immeasurably to the county chief's own prestige. Therefore, Chief Liu walked empty-handed in front, while his secretary followed behind with his water glass. The glass was originally a jar filled with pickled vegetables, but Chief Liu was one of the only people at the livening festival who had his own glass, and therefore he walked with his head raised high while his secretary looked around at eye level. The people of Liven and visitors who had come to attend the festival had no choice but to gaze up to the county chief and his secretary. Everyone watched as they walked past, and the shouts of the peddlers selling tea-eggs, tofu strips, and candied fruit all suddenly grew silent, and even the children stopped running around. The field grew so still that the only sound that could be heard was the musicians resting their mallets on the ground.

The livening festival was about to begin.

First, someone had to speak. In the past, it had always been Grandma Mao Zhi who would say a few words. For instance, she might say, "Last night a blind dog came to our house. Both of its eyes had been gouged out, the poor thing, and pus was oozing from its eye sockets. I have to go back and take care of it, but meanwhile you can all sing and watch the performances. No one is permitted to work for the next three days. No one is permitted to cook, either, and if relatives come to visit, they can eat at the livening festival as well."

75

Or she might say, "I won't speak today. What do you think, do you want to sing Balou or Xiangfu tune?"[11] Someone might shout that they should sing a Balou tune, and they would proceed to do just that. If, instead, someone stood up and cried out, "I want to hear some Xiangfu tunes," then they would first sing some of those.

Or, alternatively, she might not get up on stage at all, but rather would stand in front and simply say, "Let's begin!" With this, the musicians would start playing their fiddles and the performers would start singing. As for Liven's trademark performances, those would come after the main event.

This time, however, Grandma Mao Zhi didn't show up. Instead, One-Legged Monkey walked up to the front, following the path that had already been opened up for Chief Liu. When he arrived at the front of the field, he went to the edge of the meter-high stage, threw his crutches to the ground, and hopped up onto the stage, shouting, "Please welcome the county chief to say a few words!" Then he hopped down again.

Once One-Legged Monkey was back on the ground, he patted the shoulder of a deaf man watching the stage, then pulled away the stool that the man was sitting on in order to use it as a stage-step.[13]

Chief Liu used this stage-step to climb onto the stage and then, standing on a raised area at the center of the platform, he gazed out at the crowd of Balou peasants who had come to watch the festival. The bright yellow sun shone on people's heads, making them look as though they were glowing. The people standing on the slope all leaned forward as they peered at the stage. Chief Liu was about to start speaking, but after opening his mouth he immediately closed it again, having suddenly realized that the hundred-odd people in the audience had not yet applauded him. So, instead of speaking, he simply waited.

Perhaps it was because the people of Liven don't attend meetings as often as people elsewhere, or perhaps it was because this was the first time they had seen the county chief host a livening festival, but whatever the reason, they didn't realize that no matter where the county chief was, before he started speaking they were always expected to break out into applause, just as you must bring food to the table before starting to eat. Perhaps they hesitated because they couldn't understand why Grandma Mao Zhi hadn't accompanied Chief Liu and his slender secretary to say a few words. All of this, after all, was something she typically would be responsible for, but this time for some reason it seemed to be the completely insignificant One-Legged Monkey who was taking responsibility for things. As a result, Chief Liu and the villagers found themselves at a stalemate, as Chief Liu waited for the villagers to applaud, while the villagers waited for him to begin speaking. As for Secretary Shi, he was paralyzed with confusion as he watched the county chief up on stage and the crowd below.

A sparrow fluttered over the field, and the sound of its wings echoed over the crowd.

Chief Liu became increasingly anxious, and cleared his throat to remind the crowd of what was expected of them.

The crowd heard him clear his throat and assumed that he was about to speak, and therefore they became even quieter than before. They became so quiet, in fact, that from one side of the field you could hear the tea-egg water boiling all the way over on the other side. As Chief Liu waited up on stage and the crowds remained frozen down below, it seemed as if time itself had come to a standstill. Secretary Shi wasn't sure what the problem was, so he made his way to the front of the stage, where he raised his glass and whispered, "Chief Liu, do you want some water?" Chief Liu didn't answer, but his face turned slightly green. At that point, One-Legged Monkey suddenly hopped onto the stage and, without saying a word, started to applaud. With this, Secretary Shi suddenly realized what was wrong, and therefore he too jumped onto the stage and frantically started clapping, saying, "Everyone, please give the county chief a hand!"

Just as rain follows lightning, the crowd immediately came to their senses and began applauding enthusiastically. From soft to loud, and from sparse to dense, the applause quickly became a solid mass of sound. As long as Secretary Shi didn't stop applauding, the crowd naturally wouldn't stop either. Secretary Shi kept clapping until his palms were red, as did One-Legged Monkey, and the crowd also clapped until their hands were in agony. The sparrows in the trees next to the field were startled and flew away, and the village pigs and chickens were so frightened that they all scurried home. It was only then that Chief Liu's face began to regain its normal color. He raised both hands and gestured for everyone to stop applauding, whereupon Secretary Shi stopped.

The sound of applause abruptly ceased.

Chief Liu advanced to the edge of the stage, and although his face still had some traces of green, his original reddish tint had mostly returned. He coughed again to clear his throat, and then said slowly,

"Fellow villagers and village elders, I am County Chief Liu. Most of you haven't seen me before, and therefore I don't blame you." As he continued, his voice became even louder. "You had a hot blizzard here in Liven, a natural disaster. Although each family was able to preserve some of their harvest, of the one hundred and ninety-seven people in the village, there are thirty-five who are blind, forty-seven who are deaf, and fifty-something who are missing an arm or a leg, not to mention the dozen or so who are retarded or insane. No more than a seventh of the population of the village are wholers, and consequently this hot blizzard is truly an enormous disaster for you."

Chief Liu paused, and gazed down at the crowd.

"Fellow villagers and village elders. We have eight hundred and ten thousand people in our county, and I am their parental official. Out of those eight hundred and ten thousand people, everyone—regardless of whether their surname is Zhao or Li, Sun or Wang—as long as they were born in this county, they are all my children. I am the parental official of those eight hundred and ten thousand people. I can't bear to see a single child go hungry, regardless of where they are from, and certainly can't permit any of my children to starve to death."

Chief Liu gazed down at the crowd below.

Secretary Shi also gazed at them and, as he did, he and One-Legged Monkey began applauding. The crowd once again erupted in applause.

Chief Liu gestured for them to stop, and said,

"I have decided, given that this hot blizzard has brought great hardship to Liven and that your wheat harvest has been devastated, to compensate each family for its losses."

He gazed again at the crowd of blind and deaf people, cripples, and other disabled villagers, and this time Secretary Shi didn't need to start clapping for the crowd to break out into raucous applause. The applause went on and on, like a storm raining down on the rooftops, enveloping the entire village. It continued for so long that eventually the leaves on the trees were shaken to the ground. The county chief looked out at the ruddy glow on the faces of the crowd, and the gloomy expression that had haunted his face disappeared, leaving behind a satisfied smile. He said,

"Please, don't applaud. If you clap for too long, you will hurt your hands. To tell the truth, there is no parent in the world who would allow his or her children to starve to death. I am the parent of the entire county, and as long as I have a single steamed bun, then everyone in Liven will be able to have a bite, and as long as I have even half a bowl of soup, then everyone in Liven will be able to take a sip. Not only will I distribute grain, I also want everyone in the county who earns a salary to take out their wallets. In a few days, I will have someone bring over the grain and distribute some to every family, and as for the money, my secretary has already brought it over and divided it up. After this festival has concluded, everyone in Liven will receive more than fifty yuan. If your family has two people, they will get more than a hundred yuan; if you have three people, you will get more than a hundred and fifty yuan; if you have four people, you will get more than two hundred yuan; and if you have seven or eight people—"

Chief Liu wanted to continue calculating, but the crowd once again erupted in wild applause. It turned out that he didn't merely want to host a livening festival; he was also going to distribute money and grain. One-Legged Monkey stood on the left-hand side of the stage with both hands lifted over his head, as if he were reaching for something. He was not tall enough to be seen, and normally when he stood up he would lean into the willow crutch wedged in his armpit, with the majority of his weight supported by the crutch. But now that he tried to straighten his body, the crutch slipped from under his arm and fell to the stage, leaving him no choice but to continue standing there on one foot. No one had any idea he could stand on one leg for so long. It seemed that he would stand there as long as the applause continued, while the crowd looked as though it was prepared to continue applauding enthusiastically as long as he didn't fall over.

By this point, the sun was almost at its zenith. The people's faces were flushed and their bodies were covered in sweat, and they were clapping so hard that it seemed as though their hands were getting swollen. Chief Liu was profoundly moved by the applause, and repeatedly gestured for the crowd to stop. But the more he gestured, the louder the applause grew, until it seemed to fill the entire world, alternating between rhythmic clapping and utter cacophony. The sound echoed from the mountaintops to the sides of the gorges, reverberating as it spread farther and farther. It was as if the livening festival had been held not for the sake of the shows and performances, but rather merely for the sake of applauding. A feeling of happiness coursed through Chief Liu's heart like a stream of fresh water through a drought-plagued region. He turned and pulled a stool out from under one of the musicians, then placed it at the front of the stage and hopped onto it. Shouting into the wall of applause, he said,

"I have taken note of who isn't applauding. Those leading the applause were all from Liven, while those who didn't applaud were all outsiders."

As he shouted this, the applause gradually died out, and the people from Liven looked around for the outsiders from other villages. The field immediately grew quiet and there was a chill in the air. The outsiders gazed up at Chief Liu, as some of them tried to hide behind other people or behind a tree, but Chief Liu continued smiling brightly.

He stepped off the stool and took several more sips from the glass of water Secretary Shi was holding, then shouted at the top of his lungs,

"Friends from other towns and villages, you shouldn't feel I am playing favorites simply because I am giving the inhabitants of Liven grain and money. I realize that when Liven had its summer blizzard, each of your towns and villages also experienced hot snow, and even in places where it didn't snow there were strong winds that affected your crops. I want to give you all some good news. You have all heard that I will travel to the Russian Federation to purchase Lenin's remains? You all know that at Spirit Mountain we have created a national forest park, and have already begun construction on what will be Lenin's Mausoleum? I am happy to report that we have already raised some of the money that we will need to make the purchase, and the district government has already agreed to match all of the funds that we raise. If we raise ten million yuan, the government will donate another ten million, for a total of twenty million; if we raise fifty million, the government will donate another fifty million, for a total of a hundred million. Given that Lenin was a world leader, Russia certainly won't give us a discount on his corpse. The price will be in the hundreds of millions, and consequently I have asked everyone in the county to donate more money. I heard that one peasant sold his pigs and chickens, and even hauled his parents' coffins to the market in order to raise money. Some people sold the grain they were planning to plant next year, while others married off their young daughters. I would like to offer my apologies to all of you from the Balou mountain region, and to everyone in the entire county. I, Chief Liu, have let you down, and have also let down the eight hundred and ten thousand residents of the county."

As he was speaking, he solemnly bowed down, and the crowd grew even more solemn. He continued, "What good news do I have to report to you at this time? I'm happy to say that I've already raised a sizable Lenin Fund. I just need to raise another large sum to bring the total to fifty million yuan, which, combined with the government's matching funds, would leave us with a hundred million."

"One hundred million yuan—that's more money than you could carry on a shoulder pole, or even in an oxcart or a horse carriage. For that much cash, you would need a Dongfeng truck, and I intend to drive this truckful of cash to that country called Russia and sign a contract to purchase Lenin's corpse. If I don't have enough money, I can pay an advance deposit and sign an IOU for the rest, whereupon I would bring Lenin's remains and deposit them here in the Lenin Mausoleum in our Spirit Mountain. Fellow villagers and elders, when that time comes, you will have more tourists here than ants. For those of you selling tea-eggs by the side of the road, if you originally sold them for twenty cents, you will find that now you are able to sell them for thirty or fifty cents, or even a yuan or more. If you open a small roadside restaurant, you will find that you'll never be able to shut your door, that customers will flock in like students just released from school. If you wanted to open a hotel, you would find that even if the bed is dirty and the ceiling leaks, or the comforter is stuffed with straw rather than cotton, or the bedding is full of lice and fleas, you wouldn't be able to keep customers away even if you were to break their legs with a stick.

"I tell you, after having endured this year's calamities, next year's heavenly days are almost upon us. The sun rises in the east, but it will shine only on your houses and courtyards. People in other counties might have mountains and trees and water, but they won't have Lenin's corpse. Neither the sun nor the moon will shine down upon them.

"It's okay if you didn't applaud for me today, but after I bring Lenin's corpse, it will be too late to bow before me.

"Today everyone can watch the livening festival. I won't say another word, and instead will listen to the performance of Balou tunes with everyone else. These will serve as my opening remarks for this year's livening festival."

As soon as he said this, the stage became completely silent.

It was not quiet for very long, however—just long enough for a leaf to fall to the ground, whereupon the crowd once again erupted in wild applause, and the musicians on stage began playing their drums and gongs. The musicians playing gourd pipes and percussion looked upward as they played, while those playing fiddles and drums had to look down at the crowd below, and occasionally glanced upward at the sky as though there was an extraordinary scene up there. They performed *Birds Flying Toward the Phoenix*. The music sounded like millions of birds flying and singing in a forest.

The sun was shining, bathing the field in a deep warmth, covering everyone's face in sweat. Chief Liu and his secretary sat in their red bamboo seats below the stage, and periodically took out their handkerchiefs to wipe their faces. One-Legged Monkey didn't have a seat, so he stood in a corner of the stage leaning on his crutch. He glanced around for a fan for Chief Liu and, as he was doing so, Jumei's daughter Huaihua suddenly showed up in a pink shirt, with a smile that made her face look like a flower. She was carrying two large cattail leaf fans, and handed one to Chief Liu and the other to his secretary. One-Legged Monkey noticed that when Secretary Shi accepted the fan he smiled as he nodded to Huaihua, and she also smiled as she nodded back to him, as though they had known each other for more than a hundred years.

One-Legged Monkey felt a bit at a loss, as if something that had been his responsibility had been taken over by someone else. As Huaihua walked past him, he hissed, "Huaihua, you're like a ghost." Huaihua stared at him in shock, then ground her teeth and retorted, "You think that, just because my grandmother is not here, that makes you the village official?" Then they parted. The performance of *Birds Flying Toward the Phoenix* was almost over. Next, there was an upbeat musical interlude, which brought everyone together. This was followed by the main event, which featured a singer named Cao'er who specialized in Balou tunes and had been invited to Liven specifically for this purpose. Cao'er was not her original name, but rather a stage name she had adopted as a teenager after performing the part of a character named Cao'er in *Seven Head Turns*. Cao'er the singer was now forty-seven years old, and after performing *Seven Head Turns* for the past thirty-three years she had become more famous in Balou than all of the previous county chiefs combined. But regardless of how famous she was, she still had to report to the county chief, and when Secretary Shi said that Chief Liu wanted her to perform at Liven in the Balou mountains, she had no choice but to agree.

The excitement of this year's livening festival was thanks in large part to her.

The performance costumes were the same ones that were typically used for auspicious occasions, while the accompaniment was performed by Cao'er's own personal troupe, which she had brought with her. When she arrived, the crowd immediately stopped applauding as everyone looked up, and even the peddlers hawking their goods gazed at the stage. At that moment, the children who had been waiting for this opportunity snatched some tea-eggs from the pot and grabbed several skewers of tofu slices and candied apple sticks. The peddler shouted at them,

"You're stealing my candied apples! . . . You're stealing my candied apples!"

In the end, however, the peddler merely shouted at the children and didn't dare try to chase them as they ran away laughing. Because the performance had already begun, no one really cared if something was stolen, and the peddler was afraid that if he left his stand to chase after the kids he might return to find everything else had been taken as well. Consequently, he couldn't focus on the performance as he cautiously guarded his stand.

On stage, they were performing *Seven Head Turns*, also known as *The Middle Shadows Path*.[15] The play featured a disabled woman named Cao'er, who was paraplegic, blind, deaf, and mute, and although she suffered unimaginable torment while alive, after her death she had the opportunity to become a wholer blessed with a beautiful singing voice. That is to say, she had the opportunity to go to heaven. It took seven days to traverse the flower- and grass-filled path from the mortal world to heaven, and as long as she followed her guide along this path for seven days without glancing back, she would be able to leave behind this sea of bitterness. But during those seven days, she discovered that she couldn't bear to abandon her blind husband, her deaf-mute son, or her paraplegic daughter, and that she couldn't bear to give up her family's pigs, chickens, cats, dogs, cattle, and horses. She therefore glanced back at every step. When, on the seventh day, she finally reached the gates to heaven, she ended up going through the wrong door and missed her chance to be reincarnated, and as a result she returned to earth once again as a severely disabled woman.

Cao'er performed the role of this disabled woman named Cao'er, and a man who frequently performed with her played the part of the high monk who was leading Cao'er to heaven. One of them was in the mortal world, kneeling at the funeral altar and chanting Buddhist sutras, while the other was in the spectral world, singing as she advanced toward heaven. As they walked, they conversed and sang:

THE HIGH MONK SINGS:

The bodhisattvas and other spirits have mercy
And protect everyone who attempts to cross the sea of
bitterness.
Cao'er has been disabled her entire life
So she should be able to escape this bitter world and enter
paradise.

You walk along the flowery path.
As you continue forward you are not allowed to look back.
This was the first of the seven days
But seven days later you will cross the shady path.

CAO'ER SINGS:

The fragrance along the sunlit path assails the nostrils,
A blue aroma.
I comfortably walk forward
But my husband is weeping in front of the coffin.
What I smell are flowers and grass,
While what he smells is incense.
I'm heading to heaven to enjoy happiness,
How could I leave him, blind, to take care of our
children?
(She looks back)—Oh, my husband!

THE HIGH MONK SINGS:

Cao'er, you can hear clearly while walking along the
shady path.
Today is already the second day of the first week.
The flowers and grass are still as fragrant as before,
But you still can't resist looking back.

CAO'ER SINGS:

The sun is rising on the second day of the first week.
The sun looks like gold and the moon like silver.
The left side of the road is lined with red peach
     blossoms,
The right is lined with new pear blossoms.
This is the red and white road to heaven,
But my deaf-mute son won't have a mother to look
     after him.
As his mother, how can I proceed?
Seeing my motherless son,
I can't help worrying who will interpret for him when
     he can't hear,
And who will speak for him when he can't talk?
When they are still young, who will make them
     clothes?
And when they grow up, who will serve as their
     matchmaker?
(Pauses, looks back)—My son!

THE HIGH MONK SINGS:

Today is your third day on this shadowy path.
Cao'er, you must be sure to listen carefully along the
     road,
The flowery and grassy path to heaven.
After seven days you will enter heaven.
In the meantime, if you are thirsty there are sweet
     pomegranates
And if you are hungry there is fried wheat grain.
For the past three days you have enjoyed yourself as if
     it were New Year's.
But if you look back you will not able to cross
     heaven's gates.
Remember this, remember this:
You hold your fate in your own hands.

CAO'ER SINGS:

Every day I spend on the shady path,
Is like the first day of the new year.
White clouds, blue skies, and a golden sun,
But my daughter struggles to walk with her crippled
* legs.*
If she rips her clothes, who will mend them?
When it is time to eat, who will bring her chopsticks?
I cry out to my daughter:
You are weeping in front of your mother's coffin.
(Looks back, says)—Oh, my dear daughter!

THE HIGH MONK SINGS URGENTLY:

Cao'er, Cao'er, you heard clearly,
Of the seven days, you have already used up three,
And the fourth is already more than half over.
When you turn back there is no shore and no
* brightness,*
When you were alive you had no legs with which to
* walk,*
But now in the shadows you can walk like the wind.
When you were alive, all you could see was a sheet of
* darkness*
But in the shadows you can see a sheet of light.
When you were alive you couldn't hear the thunder,
But in the shadows you can hear a pin drop.
When you were alive you would open your mouth but
* no words came out.*
Now in the shadows you open your mouth and a
* beautiful song pours forth.*
Remember, remember, remember,
If you turn back, you will face a sea of endless
* bitterness and eternal regret*
Like grass without roots,
Like a tree without a trunk,

Like rice sprouts without water,
Like a river without a shore, without movement, and
    without moisture.
If you look back, you will see endless bitterness and
    eternal regret.
If you continue forward you will encounter a deep sea
    of good fortune.
Think carefully before you act,
And don't let this opportunity become lost in the shadows.

CAO'ER SINGS:

Alternating between wandering and continuing forward,
Alternating between cloudy rain and clear skies,
Alternating between floral fragrance
And bitter tears of exhaustion.
When I reach heaven will I be as blessed as the eastern sea?
If I return to the mortal world will I experience a sea
    of eternal bitterness, and will my sleeves be wet
    with tears?
I wander and wander and wander some more.
I walk forward, then double back, my heart not at rest.
If my husband's clothes get dirty, who will wash them?
If my children get hungry, who will cook them noodle
    soup?
When the pigs enter the pigpen, who will shut the gate?
Who will give the chickens their feed?
Who will give the ducks their slop?
Who will cut some grass for the ox?
Who will give the horse some grain?
Who will give the cat some water?
Who will cut the dog's dirty fur? Who will sweep the
    courtyard in the fall?
Who will stay home to watch the house during the
    busy summer months?

Oh, my home, my home, my home,
How can I bear to enjoy my fortune alone, and
    abandon my home?
(Looks back, says)—My home, my sweet home!

THE HIGH MONK SINGS:
You will walk along the shadowy path for seven days.
On this fifth day it is drizzling.
You mustn't miss this opportunity.
If you look back again, you will miss this opportunity.
The heavenly gates in front of you will then be shut.

CAO'ER SINGS:
The flowers are not as fragrant as they used to be,
The grass is no longer as green.
If I look back and waver, I will miss this opportunity.
After reflecting, I can't bring myself to look back.

THE HIGH MONK SINGS:
Five days have already passed, and now it is the sixth.
Yesterday you did not look back, and today the rain
    and wind will cease and the sun will come out.
The grass is still as green as before,
And the flowers are still as fragrant.
The bodhisattva and other spirits are already at the
    gates waiting to welcome you.
The gates to heaven are shining a light in your
    direction.

CAO'ER SINGS:
Six days have already passed.
When the sun sets it will leave a rosy glow.
I hesitatingly proceed forward.
I anguish over whether or not to look back.

THE HIGH MONK SINGS:

The seventh day is already upon us.
The purple cloud and rose-colored dawn.
The gates to heaven are wide open.
Cao'er, you should go forward.
If you step forward you will be as fortunate as the
      eternally flowing eastern sea
But if you step back you will endure a sea of endless
      bitterness.

CAO'ER SINGS:

The sun of the seventh day is already upon us.
Purple clouds and rose-colored dawn.
The gates to heaven are open.
And I have no dark thoughts.
If I step forward I will be as fortunate as the eternally
      flowing eastern sea
But if I step back I will endure a sea of endless
      bitterness.
I have already seen the smiling bodhisattvas standing
      at the gate.
    The gate to heaven is brightly illuminated,
    The gold-paved road is broad,
    And the silver-plated walls are bright.
I can already see various spirits standing next to the
      bodhisattva
With their long sleeves, broad belts, and benevolent
      expressions.
Young boys happily welcome me with dimpled
      cheeks,
and jade-like girls with long braids laugh.
If I advance, there is the road to heaven,
But if I retreat, there is the road to hell.
If I advance, there is the gate to heaven,
But if I retreat, there are the depths of hell.

If I advance, there is eternal happiness,
But if . . . But if . . .
But how can I bear to see my blind husband enter the
*   kitchen*
Handling the spring planting and autumn harvest all
*   alone?*
Harvesting the grain alone,
Tears stream down his face as he cuts the beans.
Who could help him sharpen his sickle?
Who would help him wash his clothes?
How can I endure this, how can I endure?
How can I bear watching my deaf-mute son walking
*   alone along the street,*
Wanting to ask for directions, but having no voice?
When other people speak to him, he merely stares in
*   confusion.*
How can I endure this? How can I endure?
How can I bear to watch my daughter lying paralyzed
*   in bed?*
Struggling to crawl forward,
When she tries to close the chicken cage, she is unable
*   to walk over to it,*
When she tries to feed the pigs, she is unable to lift
*   even half a pail of scraps,*
When she tries to feed the horse, she is unable to cut
*   the hay,*
When she tries to lead the horse, she cannot untie the
*   bridle,*
When the dog is hungry all she can do is stay in the
*   doorway,*
And when the cat can't find its way home she simply
*   cries her eyes out.*
My home, my sweet home!
Although this thatched hut may be dilapidated and
*   run-down,*

It is still my home.
The chicken coop and pigpen are also my home.
How could I forget? I don't dare forget.
The blind, crippled, deaf, and mute are still my family.
I am my husband's wife and my children's mother.
Whatever fortunes heaven might hold, I wouldn't be
     able to enjoy them.
The roads are paved with gold and silver but I cannot
     see their brilliance.
Difficulties and travails I would willingly enliven.
The endless sea of bitterness is my fate.
(She suddenly turns, and shouts loudly)
—Oh, my husband, my children, my ox, horse, pigs,
     goats, and chickens!

Further Reading:

1) **Flatbread.** Dumplings, but because they are flat, they are called "flatbread."

3) **Balou tunes.** A kind of local theater popular in the Balou mountains. It is a hybrid of Henan opera and drama, but with more emphasis placed on singing than on acting, and therefore does not lend itself to being performed by large groups.

5) **Higher-ups.** This refers to upper-level agencies and organizations. These upper-level agencies and organizations are called higher-ups by the people of Liven, of the Balou mountain region, and even of the entire province, and they elicit a feeling of awe among the common people.

7) **Directors.** This is what the residents of Liven call village cadres or people who would use a cadre's authority to resolve problems.

9) **Special skills.** Special technique. The residents of Liven and of the Balou mountain region all refer to technique as a kind of skill. Mixed technique,

therefore, becomes mixed skills, and artistic technique becomes artistic skills. Special skills, accordingly, are really a kind of special activity practiced by those who happen to possess an unusual ability.

11) *Xiangfu tunes.* An antecedent of Henan opera. Originally, these tunes developed in the Xiangfu township of Henan province, and therefore they are called "Xiangfu tunes."

13) *Stage-step.* Stage stairs.

15) *Middle Shadows.* This refers to the legendary region between light and shadows. After passing through the Middle Shadows, one reaches the Shadowy Region.

CHAPTER 7: CAO'ER DEPARTS, AND PEOPLE'S AFFECTIONS TURN TO CHIEF LIU

Chief Liu felt strangely furious.

By the time Cao'er finished singing *Seven Head Turns*, her voice was completely hoarse. The real Cao'er sobbed as she sang, soaking two handkerchiefs with her tears, but the fictional Cao'er had spent her entire life blind and crippled, deaf and mute. It would have been very easy for her to have simply died and gone to heaven, but in the end she couldn't bear to relinquish her mortal life, and therefore when she arrived at the silver and golden gates of heaven, she looked back at the mortal world, resolving to resume her former life of bitter toil. How could this performance not bring the disabled inhabitants of Liven to tears? When Cao'er finished singing, the crowd was a teary mess, and everyone—the blind, the deaf, the crippled, and the otherwise disabled—was sobbing inconsolably. After everybody finished crying, the audience thunderously applauded as Cao'er stood at the front of the stage for her curtain call.

The applause was far louder than what had followed the county chief's opening remarks, and it lasted for longer than a shovel handle. Cao'er came down from the stage and walked over to greet Chief Liu. She had changed out of her performance costume and put on her street clothes, but even then she was still surrounded by applauding people. This made Chief Liu feel somewhat nonlivened.[1] He was quite certain that the applause for him had not been nearly as long or as loud. However, he was not a wimpy chick-bellied, duck-gutted loser, so he stood in front of the stage and shouted, "Fellow townspeople, my fellow townspeople! You have endured a natural disaster. Everyone should now get in line, and I will issue each of you fifty-one yuan. Everyone come take your money!"

It was true that fifty-one yuan was, in fact, more than fifty. Chief Liu personally distributed to each of the townspeople these allotments of "more than fifty" yuan: one fifty-yuan bill and a one-yuan bill. He sat at a table, and as the head of each household approached one after another, he gave the families their money. If the family had two members, he would give them one hundred-yuan bill and two one-yuan bills; and if the family had five members, he would issue them two hundred-yuan, one fifty-yuan, and five one-yuan bills. In all, there was just enough to give everyone exactly fifty-one yuan.

The field was in turmoil, as outsiders with family in the village accompanied their relatives to eat boiled vegetables from the communal pot, as those who didn't have relatives in the village bought food from local peddlers, and as those finishing their lunch prepared to go watch the people of Liven perform their specialties. These performances had a different ending from that of the Balou tune *Seven Head Turns*, and rather than making people cry they made them burst out laughing as their jaws dropped in astonishment. For instance, in the back of the village there was someone who had lost an eye, and therefore had to view the world through just one eye. But if you put five needles in a row, he could thread them all in a single try. Of course, everyone who couldn't thread a needle would simply laugh, while the women and girls in the audience would stare in astonishment. There was also One-Legged Monkey—also known as One-Leg—who was always following Chief Liu around like a shadow. He dared to race against the fastest two-legged men in the village, and as long as he had a good crutch, he could always beat them. And there was also Paraplegic Woman, who could embroider both sides of a piece of cloth with identical images of a cat, a dog, and a sparrow. This was known as double-faced embroidery, and she could even embroider on a tree leaf—as long as it was a large one, such as that of a poplar or tung-oil tree.

These Liven special-skills performances were renowned throughout the Balou region.

As Chief Liu was distributing the money to the residents of Liven, he gave the money to the wholers without any questions, but if the recipient was disabled he would ask, "What kind of special skill can you perform?"

The recipient would smile, and rather than specifying his special skill, he would say,

"Chief Liu, please have Cao'er sing another tearjerker as an encore."

Chief Liu's face would harden with displeasure.

A middle-aged blind man walked over. He carefully felt the money Chief Liu gave him, then lifted it into the air, blindly holding it under the sunlight.

Chief Liu said, "You can rest easy. How could I, the county chief, give you counterfeit money?"

The blind man laughed and took the money, then begged him,

"Cao'er sings so refreshingly well, could you please have her sing an encore?"

Chief Liu asked, "Which is more important, money or listening to the opera?"

The blind man replied, "If you can convince her to sing again, I'd be perfectly happy not to take this money." It was almost as if what Chief Liu had given him was not money to help him survive the spring famine, but rather merely a handful of new bills.

The embroidering Paraplegic Woman came to the center of the village to receive the disaster relief funds for her family. She sat on a wheeled plank, and each time she nudged herself forward the wheels would squeak. Chief Liu said, "You should oil those wheels." She replied, "I have already cried my eyes out. Please have Cao'er sing a new song." Chief Liu suggested, "For the encore, why don't you simply perform your embroidering-leaf specialty." She responded, "After hearing Cao'er sing, who could bear to watch someone embroider?" She accepted two hundred and fifty-five yuan in disaster relief funds for her five-person family. As she was accepting the money, she didn't say a word—not thanking the government, or even nodding to Chief Liu—but rather continued staring reverently in the direction in which the costumed Cao'er had departed.

Chief Liu was furious.

He called Cao'er up to him and said, "You performed quite well, but now you are competing with me for the spotlight." Therefore, he handed her a hundred-yuan bill, and said, "Leave now, and you should be able to be out of the Balou mountain region before nightfall."

Cao'er stared at him in confusion, and said, "Chief Liu, did I not sing passionately enough?"

He repeated firmly, "Go now."

Cao'er pushed away the money he was offering her, and said, "If I didn't sing well enough, then for my encore I'll perform *The Injustice Done to Dou E*."

Chief Liu said evenly, "Are you going to leave or not? If you don't, then I will. You can stay here and help with disaster relief, and next year if the villagers don't have enough grain, I'll come looking for you."

Cao'er glanced at Secretary Shi, standing next to Chief Liu, and noticed that he was discreetly nodding to her, so she packed up her performance wardrobe and walked away, her musicians following close behind. At that point, the sun was directly overhead, leaving the mountain covered in a yellow aura. In the center of the stage, countless specks of dust were flying around like tiny stars. Once Cao'er had departed, everyone shifted their attention to Chief Liu, who again began distributing the money. Each time a head of household approached, One-Legged Monkey would record his name in a little booklet, and if the person reported that there were three people in the household, Secretary Shi would hand Chief Liu one hundred and fifty-three yuan. Chief Liu said,

"I know this isn't very much money. Please accept it as a gesture of goodwill from the county. Together with the grain, your family will be able to make it through the winter and spring famine."

After taking the money, the person would either gaze gratefully at Chief Liu or say a few words of gratitude, whereupon the county chief would blush in response. Some of the older villagers in their sixties and seventies would accept the money and bow at the waist, whereupon Chief Liu would blush like a flower about to bloom, as colorful as persimmon leaves in autumn. But there were only forty-something households in Liven, and before Cao'er left, Chief Liu had already distributed money to about half of them, and consequently the persimmon-colored flush on his face did not last for very long.

At this point, some people began finishing their lunch and returned to the field. The tall and short stools that had originally been arranged in the field were restored to their original positions, and the bricks and stones that had been used as seats were returned to their original locations. The first people to return to the field, however, surreptitiously rearranged the seats, shifting the low ones up to higher ground and the outer ones to the middle of the field. As for the visitors who didn't have relatives in town, after buying some snacks at the food stalls on the edge of the field they now returned to their seats.

They were all waiting to watch the encore performance of the livening festival.

Chief Liu had not yet had his lunch. After he gave all of the households their money, the people of Liven naturally cooked several dishes for him, including stewed chicken, scrambled eggs, and stir-fried chives, together with some wild fowl and fresh hare from who knows where. All of the dishes were laid out on a table in one of the rooms at the temple guest house. Originally, these dishes were also intended for Cao'er and her musicians, but now the entire table was just for Chief Liu and his secretary. Chief Liu washed his face and hands, whereupon Secretary Shi said, "Chief Liu, please eat."

Chief Liu just sat at the table without moving.

Secretary Shi asked, "Shall I have them cook you some other delicious dishes?"

Chief Liu replied, "This is fine."

Even after saying this, however, Chief Liu still didn't move his chopsticks. He sat at the table on a stool, his back to the door and staring straight ahead, both hands behind his head as if he were afraid it might fall off. It was as if his hands and his head were fighting one another, each pushing in opposite directions, even as his eyes continued staring at the newspapers plastered all over the white temple wall.

Secretary Shi said, "Cao'er has already left. So be it. You shouldn't keep thinking about her."

Chief Liu remained silent.

Secretary Shi said, "The encore is a special-skills performance, and after eating you will need to say a few more words."

Chief Liu stared at a couple of flies buzzing around in front of him. He watched as one landed on a dish and nibbled, then flew to another dish and nibbled some more.

Secretary Shi shooed away the flies and said,

"Chief Liu, if you have finished eating, why don't we go to Spirit Mountain to look at the future site of Lenin's Mausoleum. Once you are there, you won't have any reason to be unhappy."

Chief Liu rested his gaze on Secretary Shi's face, and asked,

"Is it not true that I gave each of them fifty-one yuan?"

"It's not a small amount," Secretary Shi answered. "With fifty yuan, you can buy one hundred pounds of grain."

"I had thought they would all kowtow to me in gratitude. But in the end they didn't do anything."

Secretary Shi suddenly realized what was wrong, and therefore promptly started for the door.

Chief Liu asked, "Where are you going?"

The secretary said, "I'm going to ask the cook to prepare another soup."

And, with that, he left.

Soon, he returned.

When Secretary Shi reappeared, he was carrying a delicious bowl of hot-and-sour soup with chives and coriander floating on the surface, which was emitting a pungent pepper smell. He was followed by more than a dozen villagers, men and women, all of whom were over forty. When they entered, they promptly knelt down in front of Chief Liu and that tableful of food, and some of them even knelt down in the courtyard outside the temple. They had been brought over by One-Legged Monkey and Lame Carpenter, who naturally knelt down in front and, like standard-bearers, announced,

"County Chief Liu, this morning you distributed famine relief money to all of us here in Liven. There was no way for us to bow down to you in gratitude while down in the performance field, and therefore we are all here now to express our thanks."

The crowd proceeded to kowtow to Chief Liu three times in unison.

Chief Liu became somewhat anxious, and immediately dropped his chopsticks. His face flushed bright red, and he asked urgently, "What is this? What is this?" As he was speaking, he quickly pulled the carpenter to his feet, and then did the same to several of the other villagers, while angrily rebuking them. In the end, he invited them all to sit down and eat with him. The villagers naturally didn't dare eat and drink with the county chief, and therefore he accompanied them out to the temple courtyard. When he returned, his face was bright as he reprimanded his secretary, ordering him to never again bring people in to bow down before him. After this, the two of them finally began eating their stewed chicken, fresh hare, and chicken wings with mushrooms and vegetables.

Chief Liu wolfed down his food, and in no time at all he had eaten his fill.

Secretary Shi said, "Chief Liu, you ate very quickly."

Chief Liu replied, "Everyone is waiting in the field for the encore performance. How can we make them wait for us?"

With that, he threw down his bowl and chopsticks and proceeded to the field. When he arrived, he discovered that it was, in fact, already packed with villagers eager to watch the performance, while those waiting to perform their special skills were assembled below the stage.

It was during this encore that many things finally came to light, as though the performance had succeeded in pulling back an enormous curtain. Chief Liu suddenly had an epiphany, and realized that he had not rescued the villagers from six months of famine following the summer blizzard, but rather that it was he himself who had been rescued by this summer blizzard. More specifically, the blizzard had rescued his grandiose plan to purchase Lenin's corpse.

Further Reading:

1) **Nonlivening.** DIAL. Means "unable to put up with." This is an antonym of livening.

CHAPTER 9: CHICKEN FEATHERS GROW INTO A SKYSCRAPING TREE

The encore performance included a variety of different specialty acts. The race between cripples and able-bodied people was an old favorite. One-Legged Monkey and a young man by the name of Niuzi lined up on the edge of the field, and when someone shouted "Go!" they both shot out like a pair of arrows. Needless to say, the young man ran like the breeze, while One-Legged Monkey—who had just turned twenty-three—borrowed a red sandalwood crutch that was smooth on the outside but had a flexible core inside, and each time it struck the ground it flexed slightly. When One-Legged Monkey leaned into the crutch, it bent so much that it looked as though it were about to break. Everyone thought it was going to snap in two and One-Legged Monkey would fall to the ground, so who could have imagined that instead it would flex as he stepped forward, sending him flying through the air. In this way, he was able to leap forward, and while he lagged behind the other young man throughout most of the race, by the time they reached the finish line Monkey—inspired by the crowd's cheers of encouragement—had somehow managed to pull ahead.

In front of everyone, Chief Liu gave One-Legged Monkey a hundred-yuan bill, and also agreed to give his family an extra two hundred pounds of disaster relief grain. In addition, One-Eye, who the previous year had been able to thread five needles at once, was now able to thread eight to ten of them. Paraplegic Woman not only could embroider a pig, dog, and cat on thick paper and rags, but could even embroider two identical cats and dogs on each side of a leaf. Deafman Ma, living in the rear of the village, was able to light firecrackers next to his ears, with only a thin board to protect his face. And then, there was Jumei's eldest daughter, Tonghua, who, as everyone knew, was blind.

Tonghua was already seventeen, but didn't know that leaves are green, clouds are white, and the rust on iron shovels and hoes is brown. She didn't know that the sun's rays are golden in the morning, or that they are blood red at dusk. Her sister Mothlet explained, "Red is the color of blood." Tonghua asked, "Then, what color is blood?" Mothlet replied, "Blood is the color of hanging couplets that have been left up after the new year." So Tonghua asked, "What color is a pair of couplets?" Mothlet responded, "Couplets are the color of autumn persimmon leaves." Tonghua asked, "Then what color are autumn persimmon leaves?" Mothlet responded, "You blind person, you! Persimmon leaves are the color of persimmon leaves."

Mothlet walked away, not wanting to discuss the matter further.

Tonghua stood in complete darkness, even as the sun was shining down brightly around her. From the day she was born, she had never seen anything other than pure blackness. Daytime was black, and nighttime was also black. The sun was black, and the moon was also black. For the past seventeen years, everything had been pitch black. Beginning from when she was five, she'd walked around using a cane made from a date tree, tapping this way and that. With her cane, she made her way from inside her home to outside, from her doorway to the center of the village. During previous livening festivals, she would come with her mother and her cane and find a spot on the side of the field, listening intently to the Balou and Xiangfu tunes, together with the plays, song and dance routines, and so forth, but then would leave when they got to the grand finale, asking her mother to stay and watch in her stead. All Tonghua could see, after all, was utter darkness.

But this year, Jumei said that she was too busy to leave the house. Tonghua told her mother that everyone claimed the county chief would give whoever went to watch the performance a hundred-yuan bill. Her mother was silent for a long time, as though recalling the festivals they had attended, but in the end still insisted she couldn't leave the house. Tonghua waited for her sisters—Huaihua, Yuhua, and Mothlet—to leave, then stood in the doorway, listening to the sound of footsteps in the street and the hubbub in the field. Then, *tap tap tap,* she made her way to the side of the field, where she stood next to the crowd and listened to the entire special-skills performance. She heard people's searingly black shouts, their reddish black laughter, their whitish black applause flying back and forth through the air. She heard Chief Liu applauding One-Legged Monkey, shouting, "Go! Go! If you win, I'll give you a hundred yuan!" She heard Chief Liu's shouts flying back and forth in front of her eyes and next to her ears, and heard him give One-Legged Monkey his hundred-yuan bill and the latter kowtow in appreciation, knocking his head on the ground with a bright black sound. (Chief Liu was so moved by this that he gave him another fifty yuan.)

Tonghua also heard Paraplegic Woman embroider a two-sided sparrow on a tung-oil leaf. When Chief Liu handed her the money, he looked at the leaf and asked, "Are you also able to embroider on a poplar leaf?" She replied, "A poplar leaf is too small, so all I would be able to embroider would be a grasshopper or butterfly." He then asked, "Are you also able to embroider on a pagoda tree leaf?" She replied, "A pagoda leaf is even smaller, so I could only embroider a few baby faces." Chief Liu grabbed her hand and stuffed who knows how much money into her fist, saying, "Such skill, such exquisite skill! Before I leave, I will definitely make you a plaque with an inscription saying, *The most skilled in the world.*"

During the encore performance, it seemed as if the entire mountain was full of people, and their jostling and clapping sounded as though the entire world was filled with the sound of black rain. When Chief Liu awarded the performers their money, that sound of black rain suddenly stopped and the crowd went silent, becoming so quiet that you could hear a pin drop. After Chief Liu had awarded the money, however, the person accepting it would kowtow to him, and that intensely black sound of applause would once again ring out like black rain, enveloping the mountain range, the village, the trees, and the houses, as though mosquitoes had flown into the darkness.

This was the first time that blind Tonghua had clearly heard the village's livening festival, including the villagers' special-skills routines: the one-legged race, the deaf-person-lighting-fireworks, the one-eyed needle-threading, the paralyzed woman's embroidery, the one-armed arm-wrestling. There was also the nephew of the village carpenter who lived in the back of the village. He was only about ten years old and small like a bug. He had contracted polio as an infant, and it had left one of his legs as thin as a twig and his foot as tiny as a bird's head. He was, however, able to insert his tiny foot into a bottle and use it as a shoe to walk around.

Chief Liu's eyes were opened by Liven's special-skills performances, and blind Tonghua heard him clap so hard that his hands turned black-and-blue. She heard him distribute money, and speak and laugh until his voice became black-hoarse, such that his every word became as black and shiny as the black blade of the carpenter's saw. In the end, as the sun was about to set and the temperature turned from hot to cool, many of the outsiders chatted and joked as they prepared to return together to their own villages. Chief Liu stood on the stage and shouted with his pitch-black words, "Who else has a special skill to perform? If you don't speak now, you won't get another opportunity. Tomorrow my secretary and I will leave, and afterward there won't be anyone left to hand out awards!"

At this point, Tonghua climbed up onto the stage and used her date-wood cane to make her way to the center. When she reached the spot where only the special-skills performers were permitted to stand, she stopped, delighting her sisters, who all started shouting, "Tonghua! Tonghua!" as they rushed to the front of the stage. The sun by this point was black red and searingly hot, shining down from the western mountain ridge. Tonghua was wearing a pink shirt, blue pants, and square shoes, and stood there like a sapling, her shirt and pants rustling in the black-cool breeze that blew over from the back of the stage. Her pretty blind eyes were as bright and black as a pair of grapes covered in mist. Her figure was pristine and unblemished by dust, and while she was not as blindingly beautiful as her sister Huaihua, she was nevertheless blessed with a delicate figure. The raucous crowd abruptly grew still. Tonghua's sisters also stopped shouting out to her. They were all waiting for Chief Liu to offer her something, and for her to offer something in return. It seemed as if the entire world had been plunged into silence. Chief Liu gazed at her as if the scorching sun had suddenly disappeared and been replaced by the moon.

Tonghua waited there in the darkness, and heard Chief Liu standing slightly to the south of the center of the stage—which is to say, to her left. She heard Secretary Shi standing behind him, and One-Legged Monkey standing to his right. When she heard their gazes she was somewhat surprised, feeling as though late autumn leaves were about to fall onto her body. She heard her sisters watching her, as their gazes flew up onto the stage like a breeze blowing on her face through a crack in a window.

Chief Liu asked, "What's your name?"

She said, "I'm Tonghua."

"How old are you?"

"I've seventeen."

"Whose daughter are you?

"My mother's name is Jumei, and my grandmother is Mao Zhi."

Chief Liu turned pale, but quickly recovered his composure.

He asked her, "What is your special skill?"

She said, "I can't see anything, yet I can hear everything."

"What can you hear?"

"I can hear a leaf or feather fall to the ground."

Chief Liu therefore asked someone to go fetch a gray sparrow feather with a white stem. He held the feather tightly and extended his fist toward her, waving it back and forth. He said, "I'm holding a feather from a Plymouth Rock rooster. What color is it?"

She said, "Black."

Chief Liu then took a white fountain pen and waved it in front of her, asking, "What is this?"

"There's nothing there."

"This is a pen. What color is it?"

"Black."

Chief Liu passed the feather from one hand to another, then held it behind his head. He said, "Listen to where this feather lands." Tonghua opened her eyes wide, and the fog that had hung over her black eyes disappeared as they became so bright they looked fake—appearing unspeakably moving and enticing. The field became deathly silent, and the people who had been preparing to leave immediately returned to their places. The people sitting in chairs or on bricks all stood up to get a better view, and the children who had climbed down from their trees all climbed back up again to watch. The paralyzed, crippled, and blind spectators couldn't see the performance, so they just sat there without moving, waiting for the people around them to tell them what had happened. The entire world became still, to the point that the sun could be heard setting on the other side of the mountains. Everyone's eyes were riveted on the feather Chief Liu was holding.

He released the feather and it slowly fluttered to the ground, flipping over a few times before landing next to Tonghua's right foot.

Chief Liu asked, "Where did it land?"

Tonghua didn't answer, and instead simply bent down with her head raised, and reached out to grab the feather.

Everyone on and below the stage was astounded. Yuhua blushed brightly, as did Mothlet. But Huaihua, looking surprised, was blushing with envy. Her blush was not merely red; it also had a tint of yellowish green. As for Chief Liu, he stared carefully into Tonghua's eyes. He took the feather from her and once again waved it in front of her face, and saw that her black eyes were still beautifully vacant. So, he handed the feather to Secretary Shi and signaled for him to drop it.

Secretary Shi gently dropped the feather to the floor.

Chief Liu asked, "Where did it fall?"

Tonghua said, "It fell into an indentation in the ground in front of me."

After having someone pick up the feather for him, Chief Liu held it in the air without dropping it, and asked her again, "Where did it fall this time?"

Tonghua pondered for a long time, then sadly shook her head, "This time I didn't hear a thing." Chief Liu walked over and stood in front of her for a long time, and then stuffed three hundred-yuan bills into her hand, saying, "You answered correctly three times, so I'm giving you three hundred yuan as a reward." He watched Tonghua accept the money, and her face light up as she stroked these brand-new hundred-yuan bills. Chief Liu, looking intently at her face, asked, "Is there anything else you can hear?" Tonghua put the money in her pocket, and asked, "Will you offer another reward?"

He said, "If it is a performance that doesn't involve listening, I'll give you another reward."

She laughed and said, "I can tap a tree with my cane and tell whether it is a willow, pagoda, elm, mahogany, or tung-oil tree." He therefore led her to an elm, a chinaberry, and two old pagoda trees on the edge of the field, and she indeed was able to identify each of them correctly, so he gave her another hundred-yuan bill. He told someone to bring over a stone and a brick, together with a piece of quartzite, and then asked her to tap them with her cane—and, sure enough, she was able to tell which was which. He gave her another hundred-yuan bill. By this point, everyone on and off stage was in a hubbub. Seeing Tonghua earn five hundred yuan in the blink of an eye, they all marveled and discussed it excitedly. Tonghua's sister Huaihua was the first to climb onto the stage and grab her hands, saying, "Sister, Sister, tomorrow I'll lead you down to the market, where I'll buy you anything you want."

The sun slipped behind the western mountains, bathing Liven in a red glow. Those people who still wanted to perform no longer could, as darkness had fallen. The visitors from other villages gradually recovered from their surprise and excitement, and returned home. The person who had cooked a big pot of food in the middle of the village for all of the residents of Liven called out for everyone to come over and eat some cabbage and boiled meat. At this point, Chief Liu's initial feeling of confusion was suddenly lifted, replaced by an enormous tree of clarity.

He decided to establish a special-skills troupe in Liven and give performances throughout the country. The admission fees for their acts would provide him with just enough money to purchase Lenin's corpse.

Book 5: Stem

CHAPTER 1: A TUMULT BREAKS OUT, AS THOUGH SOMEONE HAS JUST WALKED OUT A DOOR AND INTO A TREE

In the blink of an eye, Liven was thrown into a tumult, as though, in the middle of the night, instead of the moon, the sun were to suddenly rise—replacing the moonlight that had shone every night with the blindingly bright light of the sun. It was decided that Liven would establish a performance troupe, which would tour outside the Balou region. They would wear costumes and perform on stage in city theaters. Each of Liven's special-skills performers was given a title by Chief Liu, as Secretary Shi wrote down their stage names and the names of their respective routines:

> *One-Legged Monkey: One-Legged Flying Leap*
> *Deafman Ma: Firecracker-on-the-Ear*
> *One-Eye: One-Eyed Needle-Threading*
> *Paraplegic Woman: Leaf-Embroidery*
> *Blind Tonghua: Acute-Listening*
> *Little Polio Boy: Foot-in-a-Bottle*

There was also the sixty-three-year-old Blind Fourth Grandpa, who lived in the front of the village, and because he was blind from birth, his eyes were merely a fallow field, and he was able to drip molten wax onto his eyeballs. Third Auntie, who also lived in the front of the village, had broken her hand at an early age, but was able to slice turnip and cabbage thinner and more evenly with one hand than most people could with two. In the back of the village there was Six Fingers, who had an extra digit on his left hand—a second thumb growing out of his first one. In Liven he almost couldn't be counted as being disabled, since he was virtually a wholer. But ever since he was a little boy he had despised that extra thumb, and every day he would bite it until, gradually, it became reduced to merely a piece of flesh with a fingernail as hard as a chrysalis. He wasn't afraid of biting it off, and would even have dared to barbecue it over a fire, as though it were a piece of old wood, or a hammer or something. Everyone in the village, both young and old, had a special skill[1] on account of their disability, and they were all recorded in Secretary Shi's notebook, and were told they would all go on to become actors in the special-skills performance troupe.

They would immediately stop farming and leave Liven, and instead would earn a salary every month. This salary would be astonishingly high. Chief Liu announced that he would give a hundred yuan per performance to anyone whose special-skills routine could be included in the show. Therefore, if they had a performance every day, in twenty-nine days they would have twenty-nine performances, and in thirty-one days they would have thirty-one performances. If they received a large payment for each performance, then each month they would receive a sizable pile of cash. If a family with two wholers stayed behind in Liven to farm the land, then even if they had perfect weather all year long and planted all of their land into heavenly fields,[3] enjoying overturned days,[5] they probably still wouldn't be able to earn a comparable amount of money.

Who wouldn't want to perform with that sort of special-skills troupe?

One-Legged Monkey had already asked the carpenter to make him one of those special crutches. Paraplegic Woman had already returned to her mother's house to borrow some money in order to pay for some traveling clothes. Deafman Ma went to find some hard cedar in order to make a partition box for his firecrackers. The parents of the thirteen-year-old little Polio Boy had already prepared his travel bag.

The village's special-skills performance troupe was established overnight, and would leave the village the following day. The troupe consisted of sixty-seven performers, including eleven blind people, three deaf people, seventeen cripples, three people with broken legs, and seven with deformed hands or arms. There was also one member with six fingers, three who had only one eye, and one with a burn scar on his face. The remainder were wholers and virtual wholers. Disabled people were the stars, and wholers played only a supporting role, such as moving boxes and setting up props. They could help the disabled wash their costumes and cook food. They could help them fix or replace their props when they broke, and after the disabled villagers finished performing in one location and were preparing to go to another, the wholers could help them with the strenuous task of moving everything.

Tonghua, needless to say, was one of the troupe's star performers. When Huaihua heard that the village was going to establish a special-skills troupe to perform throughout the land, she immediately went to look for Secretary Shi. Secretary Shi asked her what kind of special skills she could perform, and she replied that she didn't have any, but she could comb hair and therefore could make sure that the performers were all impeccably groomed. Secretary Shi wrote her name in his notebook as well, and smiled as he caressed her face, treating her as tenderly as he might his own child.

After this smile and caress, Huaihua couldn't sleep at all that night after returning home, and the following morning she had a huge smile on her face. She was beautifully pink, like a butterfly, and spent the entire day sauntering through the streets of the village, telling everyone she met that she was the troupe's hairdresser. She hadn't slept at all the previous night, either, being a knot of nervous energy, and when the sun came up the morning after her meeting with Secretary Shi, she finally drifted to sleep, and dreamed she was leaping off a cliff.

She asked, "Uncle, do you think I've grown taller?"

She explained, "I've heard that if you dream of leaping off a cliff, that means you are growing taller. Auntie, do you think perhaps I'm a little taller?"

Her uncles and aunties did indeed feel that she had grown a little taller, and was prettier than Tonghua, Yuhua, and Mothlet. Huaihua's three sisters were like three early spring flowers on a pockmarked field that had not yet bloomed, while Huaihua herself was a fully bloomed peony blossom, a beautiful red rose. She felt she was no longer a nin, but rather a petite wholer, an attractive little hummingbird. When Huaihua returned home and compared her height with that of Tonghua and Yuhua, she confirmed that she was in fact a bit taller than they. They felt that her growth spurt was a direct result of Secretary Shi's caress, so she hoped that he would caress her again, maybe kiss her, thereby helping her grow from a petite nin into a wholer. She felt she was not only the troupe's hairdresser, but also suited to be the troupe's announcer.

Needless to say, the person playing the role of the announcer needed to be a pretty wholer.

Yuhua, meanwhile, was not quite as tall of Huaihua, but was nevertheless determined to become the troupe's ticket seller. Only Mothlet obeyed her mother and grandmother, saying that she had no intention of leaving with the troupe and instead would remain in Liven. About half of the village's nearly two hundred residents left with the troupe, and those who stayed behind were only children and the elderly, together with the mentally disabled, who'd never developed a special skill and consequently had no choice but to stay behind and farm the land.

On that day, the village was in a complete tumult, as though someone had raided the granary. Everyone was in the streets borrowing things. One-Eye, who was preparing to perform his needle-threading act, collected several sets of unused needles and went from house to house to exchange them for used ones, both large and small; because those needles were dull from having been used to sew clothing and repair shoes, their openings were very slick and therefore easier to thread. Polio Boy's mother sat in the doorway of their house making her son a shoe for his left foot, since from that point on he would always wear a bottle on his right foot, and therefore the sole of his left shoe had to be particularly firm. There were also many people who, as they prepared to leave, suddenly discovered that several generations of their family had never really left home, apart from traveling into town to go to the market, and that consequently they didn't own a handbag or knapsack, or even a pocket in which to stuff their clothing and other things. As a result, they all needed to borrow a bag of some sort from one of the other families.

The village seamstress once again became busy, sewing clothing for one person after another.

The carpenters also became busy making crutches and canes for the seventeen cripples and the three people with broken legs, together with the eleven blind men—all together, thirty-one people who needed crutches and canes, of whom there were eighteen who couldn't do without their crutches, including thirteen who wanted to exchange theirs for new ones. As a result, the sound of the carpenters' pounding echoed nonstop throughout the village. The sound of people trying to collect or borrow things for the trip was like an incessant river. One family had a half-blind son who, because he didn't have any special skills, was removed by Chief Liu and his secretary from the performance troupe. The child therefore sat sobbing in the middle of the road, adding to the tumult, and as he cried he stomped with both feet, kicking up a cloud of dust.

This, then, was the state in which the village found itself.

The next morning, these sixty-seven residents of Liven, all of whom had been given special stage names, were getting ready to depart. Jumei had not left the house for ten days—not since Chief Liu and Secretary Shi moved into the village temple.

But now, her daughters Tonghua, Huaihua, and Yuhua were all running through the house, preparing their clothing and luggage in order to follow the performance troupe out of the village.

Jumei sat on a stone in the middle of her courtyard as the noon sun transformed it into a steam bath. There was no breeze, and sweat dripped from her face. The shade from the trees had shifted away from the spot where she was sitting, leaving her under the searingly hot sun, feeling like a handful of greens tossed into a hot wok. The courtyard consisted of two halls with four rooms each, between which there was a two-room main quarters. Jumei and Tonghua slept in the main quarters, while Huaihua and Yuhua lived together in the halls on either side. Everyone kept her clothes at the head of her bed. There was no chest of drawers, because there wouldn't have been enough room to even turn around. They had lived in that small room for more than ten years, like birds in a crowded nest, and now they were finally ready to leave. One of the girls asked their mother, "Where did my pink shirt go? I distinctly remember that yesterday it was folded at the head of the bed, so how could it have suddenly disappeared?" Her sister asked, "Where did my velveteen shoes go? A couple of days ago I took them off and put them under my bed."

Without saying a word, Jumei sat there watching her daughters come and go. Her thoughts were in turmoil; she felt like an immense field that had been cultivated—planted in the spring and harvested in the autumn—but was now on the brink of abandonment by those responsible for working it. The field would be left barren, just like her heart. She knew that in the past few days enormous changes had come over the village. She knew that the performance troupe would change the village's destiny, just as her own destiny had been changed by the same person. But this time the entire village was at stake. It was like a sudden rain in the middle of a drought, and if it were to become a flood no one would be able to prevent the villagers from surging out. It seemed to Jumei that if her daughters wanted to leave, they would, just as water will always find a way to flow downhill, just as even a crow must eventually leave the nest. As they prepared to depart, however, Jumei sighed desolately, and finally stood up from the stone where she was sitting.

She walked out the door.

She felt she had no choice but to go see that man.

So, she went to the temple guest house.

This happened to be naptime, though that particular afternoon people were rushing around as though they were preparing for a major performance. It was as if they were all going to become somebody else, and live someone else's life. The residents of Liven, regardless of whether they were blind, crippled, or able-bodied, were blushing with excitement.

Jumei ran into someone, who said, "Jumei, how are you doing? Three of your four daughters have joined the performance troupe."

She smiled weakly, but didn't respond.

The person said, "Jumei, soon your family will have more money than they will be able to spend. When I come to borrow some, I hope you'll be forthcoming!"

She smiled weakly, but didn't respond.

Then she proceeded to the temple guest house, where a couple were kneeling on the ground—a wholer and his wife were appealing to Chief Liu on behalf of their son. Chief Liu was sitting in a chair in the center of the room. It was the middle of the day, and he was feeling somewhat drowsy, as a tide of laziness flowed over his face and body like yellow mud. Secretary Shi had gone somewhere, leaving Chief Liu alone with the visitors. Because he was feeling drowsy, he seemed to glare angrily at the couple in front of him, and said, "If you have something to say, go ahead and say it."

The kneeling couple knelt more resolutely, and said,

"County Chief, if you don't agree to our request, we will kneel here until we die."

He said more patiently, "So, what can your son do?"

"Although our son is rather ugly, he can smell the scent of wheat from miles away."

Chief Liu replied, "Even I can smell the scent of wheat from several miles away."

The couple said anxiously, "He can tell which family in the village is steaming buns, and can even tell whether the buns are stuffed with sesame or with scallion and chives."

Chief Liu pondered for a moment, then asked, "Really?"

The kneeling couple said, "We'll bring him over, and you can see for yourself; he can tell where in this room it is damp, where there is coal smoke, and where there are old rat droppings."

But even though they'd described their son very accurately, Chief Liu waved them away, saying, "Please leave and let me rest; bring the child over later, and then we'll see." The couple once again kowtowed to him, then got up and left. The old cypresses in the temple courtyard covered it in shade, but even standing in the shade of the trees, Jumei immediately became bathed in sweat. She watched the couple leave, and saw that it was the village's bricklayer and his wife. The couple looked at each other, and seemed as though they wanted to say something, but in the end they didn't. Jumei saw that the couple looked unhappy, and realized that it was because three of her own daughters had managed to join the performance troupe while their child had not. They therefore felt resentful toward her, and stared at her coldly. Their footsteps echoed brightly on the brick floor of the courtyard, like the soft wood of a tung-oil tree striking a stone slab.

Jumei paused at the door of the temple as she peered inside. Chief Liu had already closed his eyes and begun to nap. He was leaning back in his chair, his hands clasped together behind his head. He gently rocked the chair, but his body and soul were both in the process of falling into a deep slumber. Having established the performance troupe, he felt as though he had stepped outside and stumbled onto a money tree, from which the funds he needed to purchase Lenin's remains had suddenly dropped to the ground. He hadn't even needed to exert any significant effort to obtain it. How could this not make him feel relaxed and enlivened?

The room in the temple remained as it had been before, and the three rooms were separated by two partition walls. Along the beams at the top of the partition walls were drawings of dragons, phoenixes, and spirits, while the walls themselves were covered with old newspapers. There were four portraits hanging on the center wall, and the first three featured Marx, Lenin, and Chairman Mao. The ones with beards had dust on their beards, while the clean-shaven one had dust on his lips and nose. The paper had already turned yellow with age, and looked as though it would rip at the lightest touch. The last portrait, however, was brand-new. It depicted a middle-aged man with straight hair and a bright smile.

As Jumei stood in the doorway staring at this row of portraits, she felt shocked. It occurred to her that before leaving home she should have remembered to comb her hair and put on some new clothes. She regretted not having changed before coming, and now that she was really there and gazing at those four portraits, a knot of anxiety started pressing against the side of her heart, then suddenly became a ball of terror. The fourth image was a formal portrait of Chief Liu himself, and Jumei was startled to see it positioned alongside the first three. She stared in astonishment, as the knot of anxiety in her heart solidified. Still standing motionless in front of Chief Liu, just outside his front door, she looked as though she had just run into an old acquaintance. She finally began to understand why that knot of anxiety had become wedged in her heart. First, it was because Chief Liu had put on weight; his face looked fat, and his former slenderness was nowhere to be found. Second, it was because he had hung his own portrait on the wall beside those other three; this immediately made her feel that there was a vast gulf between him and her.

As she stood at the door, she found that her feet were frozen in place, unable to propel her over the threshold. She looked at Chief Liu, then around at the walls of the center room. After what seemed like an eternity, she softly cleared her throat.

It turned out he was already awake. He heard her cough, but because he was trying to sleep he didn't open his eyes. Instead, he impatiently shifted in his chair and asked, "Whatever you want, can't you wait until I've finished my nap?"

She replied, "I am Jumei."

He immediately brought the four legs of the chair to rest on the floor, opened his eyes, and looked around the room. He stared at her for a while, then gazed coldly at the gate to the temple guest house.

He said, "Given that I didn't ask you to come, what are you doing here?"

She said, "I came to see you."

He said, "I admitted your daughters into the performance troupe. They will each earn a salary, and you will live comfortably from now on." He looked at her as he said this, then continued, "You should try to save some money, and after I've bought Lenin's corpse and installed it on Spirit Mountain, there will be a constant stream of tourists coming up along Liven's mountain ridge road. If you establish a restaurant, hotel, or something along that road, you will be able to enjoy a heavenly existence. Even better than mine."

Jumei wanted to say a few more things, but after hearing this, she didn't know what else to say. She looked up again at the three portraits hanging on the wall, glanced at him, then turned and slowly walked out of the guest house.

He hesitated for a moment, then got up from his chair and also looked up at the portraits on his wall. He called out after her, explaining, "These were all hung by my secretary, who was trying to flatter me."

She slowed down as she walked through the courtyard.

He, however, said, "You can find your way out on your own. I won't escort you any farther."

She left the temple courtyard. The sun was shining brightly, generating wave after wave of heat, while a chill emanated from that shady courtyard. Jumei suddenly began to feel somewhat light-headed, as though she were being boiled alive. She didn't regret having gone to see Chief Liu, and neither was she pleased to have failed to get anywhere with him. But when she turned into the alley leading back to her house, and saw that no one was around, she suddenly began sobbing inconsolably. She stood there a while, bitterly slapping her face and cursing,

"How humiliating! How could I have debased myself in this way?"

After she finished slapping and beating herself, she stopped crying. She stood there for a while longer, then returned home.

Further Reading:

1) **Special skill.** DIAL. *An extraordinary skill. Because many of the inhabitants of Liven are disabled, they need some area in which they can compensate for their shortcomings, simply to survive. Blind people, for instance, use their acute hearing, and deaf people use their exquisite sense of touch.*

3) **Heavenly fields.** A heavenly field is not a field that is literally in heaven, but rather a field that is as attractive as heaven. Many years earlier, the valley in which Liven was located had fertile soil and abundant water. There were flat fields that could be easily irrigated in times of drought, and hilly ones that could be drained in periods of flood. Regardless of what disability people had, as long as they worked on their family's land, they would always have something to harvest. All year round, the people of Liven had more grain than they could eat, so they sowed and harvested broadly, and didn't fear natural disasters. The villagers could always be found in the fields, either busily sowing or leisurely harvesting, and in this way one year followed another. Everything changed, however, in the gengyin Year of the Tiger, 1950, when the land was collectivized and this leisurely pattern of existence finally came to an end. As a result, a family's land was no longer managed in such a leisurely and abundant manner, and the residents of Liven lost a way of life, a dream, and a fantasy. It became one of Grandma Mao Zhi's goals to continue farming these heavenly fields, and this became a source of direction and sustenance for the entire village.

5) **Overturned days.** Refers to a kind of nostalgia that is closely related to heaven. This is a special mode of existence that only the residents of Liven have experienced or can understand. Its uniqueness lies in its freedom, relaxation, substance, lack of competition, and leisure. The residents of Liven call this sort of halcyon age "overturned days," "lost days," or "fallen days."

CHAPTER 3: GRANDMA MAO ZHI
TUMBLES OVER LIKE
A BUNDLE OF STRAW

Grandma Mao Zhi emerged from her house, the greenish tint in the deep wrinkles on her face resembling frozen mud on the side of the river in the dead of winter. The hospital crutch that she was carrying made a bright and resonant sound each time it struck the ground. She walked briskly and without saying a word, as though she were flowing down a river like a piece of dry and sturdy bamboo. The sun had already begun to move toward the west, and the streets were much calmer than they had been over the previous few days. It seemed as though all of the villagers with special skills who had been anxiously rushing about preparing to leave were now finally ready. Many had borrowed travel bags, and those who hadn't simply ripped a bed-sheet in half and used each half to wrap up their clothing and other belongings. The women who had been rushing around to make new clothes and shoes were once again leisurely doing their regular sewing. The carpenters who had been frantically making new crutches had dropped their axes and saws and begun stretching out their sore backs. Everything became much calmer, as even the dogs and chickens began sauntering aimlessly up and down the street as they used to.

It was only after Grandma Mao Zhi had finally gotten ready to leave the house that she learned that Chief Liu had decided to establish a traveling performance troupe, for which he had recruited sixty-seven of the villagers. Apart from a handful of wholers, the rest of the recruits were all deaf, blind, paralyzed, or crippled. Ten days earlier, Mao Zhi had spit in Chief Liu's face, but when he, Secretary Shi, and the township chief wanted to stay in the village, she had asked One-Legged Monkey to send someone to straighten up the temple guest house, and to arrange for each household in the village to take turns sending them food. She explained that if a home was clean, the family should cook them the meal and invite them over to eat it; if the house was messy, the family should instead bring soup, steamed buns, stir-fried vegetables, and rice to the guest house.

It occurred to Grandma Mao Zhi that she, too, should cook the guests something, given that Chief Liu was the county chief and was visiting Liven—despite the fact that she bore lifelong hatred toward him. Therefore, she sent One-Legged Monkey to make arrangements. One-Legged Monkey lived just east of Grandma Mao Zhi. He was very quick, and whenever Grandma Mao Zhi had something to announce, she would dispatch him to go door-to-door relaying the information. Alternatively, he would go ring the village bell, stand on a stone, and shout out the news. Grandma Mao Zhi was not a village cadre, but it often seemed as though she must be one. By the same token, One-Legged Monkey was not a particularly significant person within the village, but given that Grandma Mao Zhi was always dispatching him to do things on her behalf, he became an important personage in his own right.

Grandma Mao Zhi had said, "You'll see to it that Chief Liu and the other visitors get what they need while they're staying at the temple guest house?"

One-Legged Monkey agreed to look after them.

Ten days later, however, when they were a third of the way into the month, Grandma Mao Zhi suddenly realized that during the ten days One-Legged Monkey had been looking after the guests, she had never once asked how they were doing, and neither had Monkey come over to give her an update. It was as if this were all his responsibility, and there was no need for her to ask about it. It was as if he really were a village or town cadre. Even though her house was separated from his by only a single wall, he nevertheless had not bothered to utter a word to her that the village had decided to establish a traveling performance troupe, or that the following day half of the villagers would go on tour, leaving behind the elderly, the children, and the mentally retarded to farm the land.

Instead, Grandma Mao Zhi learned all of this from Mothlet. Mao Zhi was at home sewing her burial clothing, on her straw mat under a tree in the middle of the courtyard. Using light and heavy silk, black and green fabric, coarse and fine imported fabric, she cut and sewed, making herself one piece of clothing after another. Each time she finished an outfit, she would fold it and place it in the red box at the head of her bed. No one knew how many sets of clothing she had sewn, or how many more she planned to make. Ten years earlier, when she turned fifty-nine, she had prepared a set of burial clothing for herself. Since then, she had sewn herself twelve years' worth of burial clothing, and whenever she had any spare time she would take the opportunity to sew some more. Given that she didn't want to see Chief Liu while he stayed in the village, she locked herself at home every day and worked on her burial clothing. This is how she had spent the preceding ten days. As she was about to sew the edge of a black silk burial gown, Mothlet came rushing into the courtyard.

"Grandma, Grandma, come quickly. Mother isn't letting my sisters join the performance troupe. They are determined to go, but Mother just cried and had a huge fight with them."

Grandma Mao Zhi paused her sewing, and asked what had happened in the village over the past few days. After she listened to Mothlet, the wrinkles in her face began to resemble frozen mud.

She then walked out of her house.

The pack of dogs saw her angry expression. They were originally going to follow her, but instead they all simply looked at her, stood up, then lay back down again. Grandma Mao Zhi slammed

126

her door shut with such force that even Mothlet—who was accompanying her—was startled. Grandma Mao Zhi walked in front, as little Mothlet fluttered after her. Mothlet initially thought that her grandmother was going to their home, but instead she went to One-Legged Monkey's house.

"One-Leg, come out. Come and explain to me what's going on."

This was one of those houses consisting of a three-room thatched hut, a square adobe courtyard, and a front gate that looked as if it were about to collapse but somehow managed to remain upright. One-Legged Monkey was sitting in the doorway of the main room, using a soft cotton cloth to polish the new crutch the carpenter had made him. When he heard Grandma Mao Zhi calling out to him, he leaned on the crutch and hopped toward the outer gate.

"Grandma Mao Zhi, what on earth are you so angry about?"

"Is it true that Chief Liu recruited sixty-seven villagers to leave Balou and spend all their time performing?"

One-Legged Monkey replied, "It is true. He hired sixty-seven villagers, and the troupe is called the Shuanghuai County Special-Skills Performance Troupe."

Granny Mao Zhi stared at him as though she didn't recognize him, and asked, "How is it that you didn't inform me of such a major undertaking?"

One-Legged Monkey stared back at her as if he didn't recognize her, and said, "Chief Liu told me not to bother informing you, given that you are not a village cadre."

Grandma Mao Zhi was momentarily flummoxed, then replied,

"It is true that I'm not a village cadre, but if I don't give the word, how will that Liu character manage to lead those sixty-seven villagers out of Liven?"

One-Legged Monkey laughed. "How would he *not* lead them out of the village?"

"Are you going?'"

"Of course. I'm the troupe's cadre and deputy director. How could I not go?"

"If I don't let you leave the village, would you be able to leave?"

127

"Grandma Mao Zhi, Chief Liu says that you are old and can no longer manage the village's affairs. He says that from now on, I should be responsible for everything that goes on in the village. He says that in a few days he will announce that Liven is an administrative village, and will install me as Village Head, meaning that I would be the one giving the order that no one be allowed to leave the village."

Grandma Mao Zhi stood in shock at the gate of One-Legged Monkey's house. The searing afternoon heat seemed as though it was leaving a plating of gold on her gray head. She looked as though she had been cast out of gold—both her face and her body seemed somewhat stiff. One-Legged Monkey gazed at her, and suddenly began laughing like a child. He said, "Grandma Mao Zhi, you are already old and sewing yourself a burial outfit. Why don't you just let me try out the position of village cadre for a few days." He added, "Once I become a village cadre, everyone's lives will be vastly improved, becoming even better than those heavenly fields that were planted by our eight hundred forebears." After saying this, he turned and went back inside, closing the outer gate behind him and slamming the door in Grandma Mao Zhi's face as though she were just a beggar.

The mountain range and the village suddenly became deathly quiet.

The sound of One-Legged Monkey slamming the door echoed through the village streets like the sound of an awl.

Mothlet stood behind Grandma Mao Zhi, her face pale with shock. She cried out *"Grandma!"* and then ran over to support her, as though afraid her grandmother might collapse like a piece of decayed wood.

But Grandma Mao Zhi stood firm, as stable as a tree. She stared intently at the willow gate outside One-Legged Monkey's house, fiercely lifting up her crutch and striking it against the willow several times, creating a crack in the tightly sealed gate. She then shouted through the crack, "One-Leg, you're dreaming! Your fantasy is to die and become a cadre!"

With this, she spun around and, leaning on her crutch, hobbled out into the middle of the street. Her footsteps were slightly louder than they had been when she left home, and her limp was significantly more pronounced. Her crutch resonated each time it struck the ground, and it almost seemed as though she were faking her limp in order to attract attention—using her limp and her crutch to demonstrate to the villagers the urgency of the situation. She was determined to halt the villagers' attempts to leave the village, and began at Deafman Ma's house in the center. Deafman Ma's Firecracker-on-the-Ear routine was one of the troupe's prize attractions, so if he didn't go, the troupe would lose one of its key assets. Deafman Ma was in the process of stuffing his shoes, socks, pants, and shirts into a bag. His firecracker board was about as large as a shovel blade, and was leaning against a table leg. Grandma Mao Zhi walked into his house, stood behind him, then cleared her throat and called out, "Deafman Ma!"

He immediately stopped what he was doing.

Grandma Mao Zhi shouted, "Turn around."

Deafman Man turned so that his left ear, which could hear a little, was facing her.

Grandma Mao Zhi demanded, "So, you too are going to join the performance troupe?"

He seemed afraid that Grandma Mao Zhi wouldn't be able to hear him, so he cleared his throat and shouted, "For several thousand yuan a month, how could I not join?"

Grandma Mao Zhi said, "You'll regret this."

"I won't regret it. This will be better than farming heavenly fields or living overturned days. I'll never regret it."

"Listen to me. You must not go."

Deafman Ma shouted back, "My entire life, I've listened to you, and have never had an opportunity to enjoy myself. This time, I'll leave the village even if it kills me."

Grandma Mao Zhi went to One-Eye's house. One-Eye's bags were already packed, and he was sitting in his room changing into the shoes his mother had made him. Grandma Mao Zhi said, "It is a profound humiliation for both you and your eye to thread needles for an audience. It is a loss of face, and basically reduces you to the status of a performing monkey."

One-Eye said, "Being in Liven is not a humiliation, but what *is* humiliating is the fact that I am now twenty-nine years old and still haven't managed to find a wife. How could I not go?"

Grandma Mao Zhi then went to Paraplegic Woman's house, and said, "So, you also feel that you have no choice but to go?"

Paraplegic Woman said, "If I were to stay here in Liven, I would die of poverty."

Grandma Mao Zhi said, "Don't forget how you came to be paralyzed. Don't forget how you came to Liven."

"I do remember. And precisely because I remember, I therefore have no choice but to leave with everyone else."

Grandma Mao Zhi then went to see the thirteen-year-old Polio Boy. She said to his parents, "This child is only thirteen years old."

His parents replied, "In a few years his foot will no longer fit in the bottle. He is not too young, so we should give him the opportunity to leave home."

"You can't put your son's disability on display for others to see."

"If we don't let them see this, what will they see?"

Grandma Mao Zhi left Polio Boy's house. The village was increasingly tranquil. The afternoon sun was shining down on the summer leaves throughout the village, making them look as though they were shining. The temple guest house was sitting empty, like a silent old man who, as time passes, no longer feels the need to say anything. The old cypress cast its shade over the village street, leaving it in semidarkness. Grandma Mao Zhi was not walking as quickly as before, and her limp became increasingly pronounced. The hard, yellow sheen that had congealed on her face disappeared, and was replaced by a gray pallor. She slowly hobbled forward, several strands of gray hair falling onto her forehead. When she arrived at the guest house door, she paused and peered inside, then entered.

Chief Liu was drinking his tea, and Secretary Shi was folding and packing the underwear and undershirt he had just washed. Chief Liu said, "Let me put my own underclothes away." Secretary Shi replied, "There's no need. They aren't dirty. Even if they had been used to cover a steamerful of buns they wouldn't be dirty." So, Chief

Liu let him pack the underwear—watching with a look of delight and pleasure, as though he were a father watching a son who had grown up and was able to help him do things, thereby permitting him to leisurely sit back. As Chief Liu sipped his tea, he suddenly remembered something. He turned and gazed at the portrait of himself hanging on the wall, then said to Secretary Shi,

"Take that down; it's not appropriate."

Secretary Shi replied, "Let's keep it up. There's nothing inappropriate about it."

"If we are going to keep it up, we should at least move it down a little. How can I be on the same level as the others?"

Secretary Shi therefore climbed onto a table and shifted Chief Liu's portrait down two chopstick lengths, so that his head was now level with Chairman Mao's shoulder. Secretary Shi asked, "Is this okay?" Chief Liu considered, then said, "You could move it up a little." Secretary Shi moved the portrait back up a little, such that it was now only half a head below that of Chairman Mao, and then refastened the corners of the portrait to the wall. At that point, Grandma Mao Zhi walked through the doorway and stood there without speaking, gazing at Chief Liu. She no longer had that look of disdain with which she'd regarded him ten days earlier when she saw him on the snow-covered mountain ridge, and no longer had that majestic look of a mother standing in front of a child. Instead, now she looked as though she had something to ask of the child, and furthermore was afraid the child would not heed a pitiful old woman, and might even strike her. She looked timid and weak, as though she would have toppled over if she hadn't been grasping her crutch. Chief Liu regarded her the same way she had regarded him ten days earlier, with a look of impatience and disdain. He continued sitting at the table holding his teacup, without speaking or moving. He continued looking straight ahead, as though he hadn't seen her.

"Are you really going to establish that disabled performance troupe?"

"It's a special-skills troupe. We are leaving tomorrow. First we will go perform in the county seat, and we have already sent people to put up posters."

"You will destroy Liven."

Chief Liu laughed. "What is there to destroy? I'll make it possible for every family in Liven to have a white-tiled house, and will give every disabled villager more money than they can possibly spend. They will all enjoy heavenly days."

Grandma Mao Zhi said, "If you agree not to lead them away, I will kowtow to you in gratitude."

Chief Liu smiled, "I don't need your kowtows. After I bring back Lenin's remains, *everyone* will kowtow to me."

Grandma Mao Zhi said, "If you let the residents of Liven stay in the village, I'll hang your portrait in the main hall of my home. I won't hang anyone else's portrait there, just yours, and will burn incense in front of it all day long."

Chief Liu smiled again, and said softly, "I know that from the moment you let the residents of Liven enter society,[1] you always hoped that they would burn incense for you every day. But you have let Liven down, and haven't let them enjoy a good life. Unlike you, I am not trying to get them to burn incense for me. I am not seeking fame; I just hope that they will think fondly of me. I know that, with your crippled leg, you are able to predict the weather. Actually, you could also join the performance troupe and perform a weather-forecasting act. If you come with us, I'll pay you a salary that will be at least fifty percent—and perhaps even a hundred percent—higher than that of anyone else in the troupe."

Upon saying this, Chief Liu gazed at Grandma Mao Zhi as though she were a girl he was exhorting, as if he imagined that what he had said had entered her heart and was able to transport her across a river. A look of immense happiness appeared on his face. Grandma Mao Zhi, however, glared at Chief Liu without saying a word. She looked as though he had just slapped her, and all of a sudden her face turned purple, as though she wanted to brandish her crutch at him, the way she had done ten days earlier. But as she was on the verge of doing so, she discovered that her body was no longer steady, and even before she lifted her crutch she suddenly tumbled over like a bundle of straw. As she was falling, her face twitched and she started foaming at the mouth. She cried out to the sky in words that only she—or someone else from Liven—could truly understand: "I have let Liven down. I helped Liven enter society, and in the process have let down the village and its people. . . ." It seemed as though she was having an epileptic attack. When Mothlet, who was standing in the entrance to the temple guest house, saw Grandma Mao Zhi collapse, she rushed inside, but at the same moment she immediately withdrew. She ran home, shouting, "Ma! Ma! Come quick. Grandma is not well.

"Quick, quick! Grandma is not well."

The villagers immediately rushed to the guest house. Jumei and her daughters all rushed to the guest house. The entire village was a cacophony of running feet.

Chapter 5: Further Reading— Entering society

1) **Enter society.** *This is a historical term that only the people of Liven would recognize, as it relates to a story that pertains only to Liven. Several decades ago, in the* jichou *Year of the Ox, 1949, there was a monumental occurrence. At that point Grandma Mao Zhi was only twenty-seven or twenty-eight years old. Even so, she had been the wife of the stonemason for several years. But she had not yet had children. Her leg was somewhat lame, but not excessively so, and if she walked slowly no one could tell she was disabled. The stonemason had picked her up when he came to the Balou mountains to work as a stone polisher. No one knew where she had come from, or where she was going. She was rail-thin from hunger, more dead that alive. The stonemason had carried her more than twenty li, from deep in the mountains back to the village, where he fed her water and soup. After a few years, she became his wife.*

At the time, it was quite common for people from Balou to bring back a woman when they returned from a trip, and therefore there was nothing remarkable about this. The extraordinary thing about Mao Zhi, however, is that even though she was an outsider, she wore the traditional clothing of the village. Despite already being seventeen, she still couldn't farm or sew, though she could recognize quite a few Chinese characters. She had been rescued by the stonemason, who at the time was a thirty-one-year-old bachelor—almost fifteen years older than she—and therefore was anxious to get married as soon as possible. Because she was young and he was comparatively old, they didn't marry immediately, and instead she stayed in his house, though they slept apart. Even after they settled down, they were attracted by the possibility of leaving Liven and the heart of Balou. While Mao Zhi was physically living in Liven, her heart was floating in the world beyond the Balou region. She never did make up her mind to leave Liven, and everyone assumed this was because the stonemason was so good to her.

In reality, this was not entirely the case. When Mao Zhi was little, she had marched tens of thousands of li with her mother and the Red Army, and one night during the Battle of the Fifth Encirclement Campaign, when she and her mother were sleeping in a cave, her mother was seized by a group of male Red Army soldiers. When the sun rose the next morning, her mother was executed along with another two Red Army soldiers, and her corpse was left on the riverbank.

It wasn't until three days later that Mao Zhi learned her mother had been executed by a colonel whom Mao Zhi had called "Uncle," and that her mother and those other two soldiers—whom Mao Zhi had also known as uncles—had been labeled traitors. For several months the regiment had been unable to shake the enemy's pursuit, and it was said that it was all due to the fact that Mao Zhi's mother and the other two soldiers were secretly revealing the regiment's position to the enemy. Because Mao Zhi was now the daughter of a traitor, none of the other soldiers dared bring her any food, and consequently she spent three days alone in the cave without eating.

Finally, on the fourth day, a battalion commander went into the cave and carried her out. He gave her a bowl of soup and three hard-boiled eggs, and told her that it wasn't her mother who was the traitor, but rather several other soldiers who had already been executed. Their army contingent could now safely eliminate its enemies and realign itself with the main army. The soldier told Mao Zhi that her mother had been officially recognized as a revolutionary martyr, thereby making Mao Zhi the descendant of a martyr, and of the Revolution. In this way, Mao Zhi became the youngest female soldier in the Red Army.

Mao Zhi had followed the army contingent from Sichuan back to the Northwest. One year followed another, and she gradually grew up and learned to fight and carry a gun. When the army contingent finally reached the Northwest, they were scattered by a surprise attack, and all of Mao Zhi's sister soldiers fled to other areas. During her time with the army contingent, Mao Zhi had grown up in fear, with gunshots of the enemy and of her mother's execution reverberating through her dreams. Under this unimaginable terror, she said that she wanted to leave, but in the end she stayed in Liven.

She remained in Liven, but never forgot her desire to leave. Whenever she had any free time, she would go up to the mountain ridge road, and when she encountered travelers from beyond the mountains she would ask them many questions, such as, What is the outside world like? Is the war still going on? Have the Japanese made it to Shandong or Henan province? But most of the people she encountered couldn't tell her anything, and in this way she finally came to understand just how remote the Balou mountains were from the rest of the world—like a fragment of a rock that had been left behind in a long ravine, or a clump of grass in a vast forest. When Mao Zhi encountered other people along the mountain ridge path, they were almost invariably also from Balou, and knew very little about the outside world. News about the Japanese came and went, but it was impossible to determine what was reliable and what wasn't. The people of Liven gradually realized that she had walked over with the regiment, and in the process her heart had been wounded, her body scarred, and her leg crippled. After she began to put down roots in Liven, she couldn't stray far even if she had wanted to. The village was so isolated that there wasn't even reliable news about the Revolution, and this became the best reason for her to remain there. It was as if she was trying to let time swallow up the past.

Liven had abundant fields and inexhaustible grain, and Mao Zhi gradually got used to living there. She learned to farm and to sew, and in the process became a villager. The stonemason's mother was a seventy-three-year-old paraplegic. She was the oldest resident of Liven, and knew the ins and outs of the village better than anyone else. Everything regarding the village's origins and its legends came from her mouth. Mao Zhi was with her every day, and always called her "Grandmother." One of the villagers remarked, You should have Mao Zhi call you "Mother." The mother replied, Don't worry about things that don't concern you; I know perfectly well what I want Mao Zhi to call me. The villager said, You should tell your son to sleep *with her. Mao Zhi glared at him and replied, If you have nothing better to do, then why don't you give your mouth a rest and mind your own business.*

As a result, the villagers came to respect Mao Zhi even more than before.

But even as the villagers came to believe that Mao Zhi would never marry the stonemason, one winter the two of them finally tied the knot. It was only later that the villagers realized that they married the same winter the stonemason's mother fell ill. Just before she passed away she hugged Mao Zhi and began to weep. As she wept, she told Mao Zhi many things, and Mao Zhi also cried, and told her many things in return. For decades no one knew what they discussed, though, in the end, Mao Zhi agreed to marry the stonemason.

After Mao Zhi agreed, the stonemason's mother peacefully passed away.

That night, she and the stonemason finally slept together.

That year, Mao Zhi was nineteen years old, while the stonemason was almost thirty-five.

The next day they buried the stonemason's mother, and he never again went out to polish stones. Instead, he stayed home, watching over Mao Zhi and farming the land. As for Mao Zhi herself, she would sometimes hear news from outside the village—including reports that the Japanese had advanced to the ninetieth parallel—and she would turn slightly pale. When she heard reports that the Japanese were going from the city to the countryside to collect grain, and that when they encountered children they would give them some foreign candy, Mao Zhi looked very suspicious. She would listen carefully to news about the weather and the war, but never again mentioned wanting to leave Liven.

Mao Zhi truly became a resident of Liven. When the stonemason went out to plow the fields, she would lead the ox; and when he went to harvest the grain, she would follow behind to collect the grain into bundles. When the stonemason came down with a fever, she would go into town to buy garlic and scallions to cook him some soup. They were just like all the other families in the village, who—although they might have members who were blind or deaf—would diligently sow and harvest the grain, staying busy throughout the summer and autumn, such that each household would have so much grain and vegetables that the family wouldn't be able to eat it all. The events of the outside world remained distant from the lives of the residents of Liven, as though the village were located a hundred and eighty thousand li from anywhere else. Aside from a handful of villagers who would travel to nearby towns to buy oil and salt, and in the process bring back news of the war—which could have been either true or false—the residents of Liven remained completely cut off.

In this way, one day followed another.

And one month followed another.

Spring, summer, fall, and winter all came and went.

Directly on the heels of the jichou Year of the Ox came the gengyin Year of the Tiger, which is to say, the thirty-ninth year of the Republic. It was that year—and, specifically, the fall of that year—that Mao Zhi went to a market several dozen li from Liven. Previously it had always been men—and, specifically, wholers—who would go to the market, taking with them the various items that each family wanted to sell, and bringing back the various items that each family needed to buy.

This particular fall, by the time autumn leaves were covering the ground, as Mao Zhi was picking persimmons from her fields, she glimpsed in the distance someone in a Mao suit coming from the mountain. From the persimmon tree, she called out,

"Hey! Do you know what is going on outside?"

The person looked up at her.

"What do you want to know?"

"Up to where have the Japanese advanced?"

The person replied with surprise that the Japanese had returned home long ago. Five years had already passed since their surrender in the Year of the Cock—in the eighth month of the thirty-something year of the Republic—and now it was clear that not only did the Republic no longer exist, but many of the towns around Liven had already entered into cooperative societies.

The person at the base of the tree couldn't imagine what kind of surprise and turmoil his simple remark would elicit in the person up in the tree. He walked away, while Mao Zhi stared out at the land beyond the Balou mountains. The white autumn clouds were drifting across the sky, and the sun was as bright as if it had just been washed, and everything illuminated *by this sun underwent a remarkable transformation. Mao Zhi cast a final glance toward the parting shadow of the man in the Mao suit, then climbed down from the tree and went home.*

The next day, she woke up early to head into town to go to the market. A round-trip from Liven to Boshuzi Street and back was well over a hundred li, and therefore she got up at the first cock crow and was on the road by the second. By the third cock crow, she had already traveled more than ten li into the mountains, and by the fourth she had left the mountains entirely.

By the time it was light enough to see several li into the distance, Mao Zhi witnessed a remarkable scene. She saw a village with a wheat field on the top of a hill. The field was several mu in size, and there were a few dozen men and women hoeing the soil together, systematically working their way from one end of the field and back. Mao Zhi couldn't understand who could possibly own such a large plot of land, or whose family could have so many people. The largest plot of land in Liven was Deafman Ma's, which was only eight-point-five mu. But this plot was so large that it covered the entire hill. No matter how big a family might be, it couldn't possibly have more than twenty youthful members able to work the fields. Such a family would need to have more than fifty members in all, if children and the elderly were included as well.

How would a family of fifty-something members not divide the family land between them?

How would a family of fifty-something members manage to cook enough food for everyone?

How would a family of fifty-something members ever make enough clothes for everyone to wear?

How could a family of fifty-something members ever find a large enough house for everyone to live and sleep?

Mao Zhi stood in front of that plot of land, bathed in sunlight. The soil of the recently plowed field was red and moist, as though there were an invisible river flowing through the air. It was precisely in the midst of this dark red color that Mao Zhi noticed that at the head of the field there was a wooden sign that read: Songshu Village Second Mutual Aid Team. The sign had been blown by the wind and drenched by the rain, and consequently the words were somewhat blurred. It looked as though the sign had been there for at least two years, if not longer. Mao Zhi didn't understand what a mutual aid team was, and she just stared at the sign in astonishment. At that point, a young man walked over from the gully at the head of the field and called out, Hey, what are you looking at?

She asked, What is a mutual aid team?

The young man stared at her in amazement, and asked, So, you can read?

She looked at him disdainfully and said, Why wouldn't I know how to read?

He replied, If you can read, then why don't you know what a mutual aid team is?

She blushed.

He asked, Is it possible that your village has never organized a mutual aid team or a cooperative society?

The mutual aid teams brought together households which didn't have an ox with those that did, he told her. They paired strong laborers with weaker ones, and households with plows with those that had only hoes. They brought together households that had a lot of land with those that had less. The teams brought everyone together, so that some would sow, some would harvest, and others would apportion grain for consumption. As a result, there were no longer any landlords and hired hands, or poor people who needed to sell off their own children, and instead every day there would be a new harmonious society. As the young person was speaking, he tied his belt, picked up a hoe that was stuck in the ground, and went to rejoin the crowd of people working in the field.

Mao Zhi continued standing there, stupefied. It was as if the young man's remarks had opened up a window into a room that had long been shrouded in darkness, letting in a ray of light that illuminated her innermost thoughts. She watched the young man and the group of people hoeing the field, and suddenly realized that profound changes had taken place in the world. The people of Liven knew absolutely nothing of these changes. It was as if the rest of the world had a sun and a moon, while generation after generation of Liven residents had lived in pitch blackness. It was as if the Liven villagers were so cut off from the rest of the world that not even a hint of a breeze could get through. She didn't know why she hadn't heard news of this collective farming from the village's own wholers, who went to market at Boshuzi Street. She didn't know whether it was that the wholers simply didn't see anything when they went to market, or that they saw things but didn't mention them after they returned to Liven. Or, perhaps it was just that the one day they discussed these things in the village canteen, she happened not to be around.

The world had changed enormously over the preceding few years.

Throughout the land, the people had been liberated.

After Beiping was named the nation's new capital, peasants from all over had been called together to the center of the city, and after their land had been redistributed they were sent to continue farming collaboratively. All of the land now belonged to the government, and was not assigned to specific families or individuals. It was allocated to those who were actually farming and using it, but did not belong to them in the same way that families' bedding belonged to them. After the world was thrown into disorder, the people were also thrown into disorder. Households were divided into finely calibrated categories of landlords, rich peasants, poor peasants, middle peasants, and lower-middle peasants, but the people of Liven had no knowledge of any of this. They had not even heard the faintest whisper of these developments. So many enormous developments had taken place in the world, but Liven remained ignorant of them all.

Mao Zhi proceeded forward, her heart heavy, as if she didn't belong to this world. By the time she passed a town and arrived at a village, the sun had already come up and the air was filled with warmth. She saw some more people walking back to the village from the hill behind the town, carrying hoes and wicker baskets. One group followed another, and if they weren't carrying hoes and shovels, they were carrying wicker baskets. Needless to say, this was a mutual aid team, and whenever one team went to work in the fields, another returned home. They were like soldiers returning to their barracks after having just won a battle, singing as they carried their war trophies. There were singing Henan tunes, and while Mao Zhi couldn't hear the lyrics clearly, she could see the joyous melodies shimmering like moisture in the morning sky. She stood at an elevated point along the mountain ridge path, gazing down at the peasants as they entered the town, and her eyes filled with envy.

However, envy is merely envy, and gradually that feeling was transformed into a form of pain. She saw slogans painted on the town walls with white lime, all of which either praised the mutual aid teams and cooperative society or had been written many years earlier. She had seen these slogans when she was a teenager, and she herself had helped people write some about overthrowing landlords or local tyrants and dividing up the land. Those slogans were now old and faded, but they still sparkled in the sunlight. When Mao Zhi saw these big-character slogans, her heart started racing, like a dammed-up underground stream that had suddenly been opened. This stream had originally flowed as a small trickle, through gunfire and rain, from north to south, from snowy mountains to grassy plains, and was ultimately transported on shoulders and horseback.

Back then, because Mao Zhi was still young, she became exhausted easily and yearned to stop and rest, and as she made her way alone, village by village, from the yellow-earth hills of Shaanxi toward western Henan, whenever she encountered another regiment she would follow it, and if she encountered an appropriate family she was prepared to settle down with it. In this way she made her way from village to village, day after day, until she finally reached the Balou mountains, where she encountered the stonemason and the village of Liven. It was as if Liven had been waiting for her there for several centuries—or even millennia—and as soon as the village saw her it forced her to stay behind. As for Mao Zhi, it was as if she had been searching for Liven as she made her way from Shaanxi to western Henan, and it was precisely when she couldn't take another step that she spotted the village.

After living in Liven for several years, Mao Zhi found that her wounds gradually healed, and even after the stonemason's mother passed away and Mao Zhi wept and lay sobbing on her mother-in-law's corpse, she made no mention of the wounds, which she had already started to forget. Other than herself, there wasn't a soul in the world who had any knowledge of those events. No one knew that when she was part of the army, she had known a Red Army platoon leader from Hubei. After that secret order disbanded the army contingent, she and the wounded platoon leader left together. Later, when they ran into enemy troops, they hid in a tomb. It was raining heavily, and she started running a fever. She lost consciousness, and didn't know how much time had passed before the rain stopped and the sun came out and she finally woke up.

However, the platoon leader, who had regarded her as his sister, was nowhere to be seen. More important, she discovered that her lower body was sticky and smelled of menstrual blood. It was only later that she realized he had taken advantage of her while she was unconscious. She had been deflowered by that platoon leader who had somewhat loved her. She squatted inside the tomb and wept inconsolably. The platoon leader never returned, and no one else passed by. After night fell, she finally dragged her body, defiled by the platoon leader, out of the tomb.

She staggered in the direction of her hometown.

It was then that she encountered her future husband, the stonemason. It was also then that she encountered the village of Liven, which had been waiting for her for centuries or even millennia, and decided to settle down there. Her tearless wounds gradually healed, her body matured, and she recovered her strength. The world had changed dramatically. She had to take care of things—take care of some things in Liven.

Of course, she couldn't forget that she had been to Yan'an, or that she had contributed to the Revolution. Even though now, after so many years, she was the wife of a stonemason and a resident of Liven through and through, she was nevertheless still a Red Fourth[1] revolutionary. She still kept a folded Red Army uniform from the Red Fourth Regiment in a chest at home, and was still young and full of energy, so how could she not do something?

She thought, I want to help advance the Revolution. I want to lead the people of Liven into society.

CHAPTER 7: FURTHER, FURTHER READING—RED FOURTH

1) **Red Fourth.** *As with "entering society," the term "Red Fourth" derives from a period of Mao Zhi's personal history. She was a famous female soldier in the Red Army's Fourth Regiment when she was a teenager, but in autumn of the bingzi year, 1936, she was like a stone rolling down a hill, unable to return to the elevated position from which it began, and therefore with no choice but to quietly wait at the bottom of the hill. Over the following decade, Mao Zhi matured into a woman and became a member of this village of disabled people. Even though it had been many years since she was a female Red Army soldier, the Red Fourth was like a seed planted in her heart that was only now beginning to sprout.*

She wanted a revolution. She wanted to lead the people of Liven into a mutual aid team and a cooperative society.

It was sixty-nine li from Liven to Boshuzi Street, meaning that a round-trip was one hundred and thirty-nine li. Traditionally, when the people of Liven needed to go to the market, they would leave home one day and return the next, and if they couldn't find a place on the road to sleep overnight, they would at least stop somewhere to rest. But the one time Mao Zhi went to the market, she left and returned the same day. Her husband waited for her in the moonlight, and when he saw her bounding down the mountain path like a deer, he called out to her, Where did you go? I woke up early and didn't see you. I spent all day looking everywhere for you, and have been waiting here all night! She gazed at that man fifteen years older than she, and said excitedly, Hey, Stonemason, did you know what all of the other villages and towns have become? Everyone has combined their land into five-household teams or eight-household groups. They even share their oxen and their plows. Each household has renounced every last sliver of private land that they once owned, and when the bell rings after each meal the entire village happily goes out to farm the land together. If the field is far away, someone returns to the village to fetch water for everyone. After drinking the water, some of the villagers sing Xiangfu tunes or clapper opera arias. Mao Zhi asked her husband whether he had seen or heard of any of this when he had been at the market.

She didn't wait for his answer, and instead grabbed his hand and plopped down on a stone beside him. She exclaimed, I'm exhausted! I've walked more than a hundred li today, and my feet are covered in blisters. If you don't carry me, there's no way I'll be able to make it home. It turned out that although the two of them had been living together, that night was the first time he had seen her express anger toward him. He sat on the stone next to her and tried to pull her up, but as soon as he grabbed her hands she immediately collapsed into his lap as though paralyzed. He then carried her home under the moonlight.

After they arrived, he gave her some warm water and washed her feet—massaging her toes and the soles of her feet, and popping her blisters. He asked, So, you went to the market just to observe people's farming partnerships? She said, The world has changed. Do you know who is now in control of everything? He replied, I don't know. She said, It's the Communist Party. She then asked, Do you know what the farming partnerships are called? He said, No. She looked disappointed, but precisely because of her disappointment she appeared happy and excited, and said, It's not just you who doesn't know! I suspect that no one in Liven knows about this! She added, Now that we've been liberated, our leaders are the Communist Party and Chairman Mao, and each family and household must unite into mutual aid teams to work the land together. These mutual aid teams unite together into cooperative societies. Stonemason, I want to coordinate Liven's entry into society, and organize each family and household into teams to farm together, harvest together, and distribute the grain together. She continued,

145

There is a bell hanging from the tree at the front of the village, and when it tolls, everyone immediately drops their bowls and goes out to the fields. This afternoon, I'm going to go and tell all of the villagers to return home and eat. In the city they have running water, and with a flick of the wrist they can have water come pouring into their pots, buckets, and washing basins. We still have to haul water every day from the gorge back up to the village. People report that in Jiudu they even have electrical lights instead of gas lamps; and that behind their front door there is a cord, and when you pull it the entire house fills with light, as if it were full of sunlight.

She said, Stonemason, carry me to bed, and tonight you can do with me as you please. I am your woman, and you are my man. You can do with me as you please. She said, I want to lead the people of Liven into society, and allow them to enjoy a heavenly existence. I want to give you a son and daughter; I want to give you a whole passel of children and grandchildren. I want them to have more grain than they can eat, and more clothes than they can wear. I want them to enjoy a good life in which they have lights that don't need oil, flour that doesn't need to be ground, and when they go out they don't need to ride in an ox-drawn carriage. The stonemason had never ejaculated the way he did that night while lying on top of her. Previously, she had not been well, and he didn't dare touch her. But that night, he rubbed his body against hers as though he were polishing a stone, while she was like soft clay beneath him. By the time they finished and were panting, she asked, Did you enliven?

He replied, I did.

She said, After we enter society, I'll enliven you every night.

He asked, When will we enter society?

She said, Tomorrow we will hold a meeting, so tomorrow we will enter society.

He said, But if you say that we have entered society, does that mean we necessarily will? Liven doesn't have a town above us. If we did, we could have them send someone down to hold a meeting, and if they told us to enter society, the villagers would have no option but to do so. But we have no higher-ups, and there is no one to send down. Therefore, if you say we should enter society but there is someone in the village who pays you no heed, what will you do?

Mao Zhi didn't say another word.

In the end, Liven was a village that had been forgotten by the world. Located in the Balou mountains at the junction of three separate counties, it was more than ten li from the nearest village. From its Ming dynasty origins, the entire village had been made up of blind people, deaf people, and cripples. Able-bodied men would marry out of the village once they grew up, as would able-bodied women. Disabled people from outside would come in, and the village's wholers would leave. This is how things had stood for centuries. However, there was no canton or county that was willing to accept Liven as its own.

One year followed another, and the Kangxi reign was replaced by the Yongzheng and Qianlong reigns, right up to the reign of Empress Dowager Cixi, the Xinhai Revolution, and the Chinese Republic. For several centuries, Liven never paid grain taxes to any dynasty, province, canton, district, county, or township, and no one from the other districts, towns, or villages in the adjacent counties of Dayu, Gaoliu, or Shuanghuai ever came to Liven to collect grain taxes.

Liven was a village outside the world.

That night, Mao Zhi sat in bed, in a daze. Suddenly, she got up and threw on her clothes.

The stonemason asked, What are you doing?

She replied, I'm going to Gaoliu. Do you want to go with me?

What are you going to do there?

I'm going to see the higher-ups.

Her husband lit a fire, kneaded some dough, and then placed the griddle in the fire and baked her five oil buns. They left Liven before dawn, setting off for Gaoliu.

Gaoliu was three hundred and nine li from Liven, and they asked for directions as they proceeded. Each day, they would resume their journey at dawn, and stop to rest at dusk. They would eat when they were hungry, and drink when they were thirsty. Whenever they needed something, the stonemason would offer to polish people's stones.

Twenty-five days later, they finally arrived in Gaoliu. The county seat had two streets, at the intersection of which was the government office. The building was a triple courtyard-style structure, with three separate entrances.

In the late Qing, this courtyard had been used as the county yamen, and during the Republican period it was the county seat, but in the new era it was called the county government. The stonemason sat down in the garden in front of the government office and waited, while Mao Zhi entered the second courtyard of the county government building. The county chief was pushing a slightly used foreign cart,[1] and Mao Zhi ran into him as he was about to leave for the countryside. The county chief asked, What do you want from me? She said, I am from Liven, in the Balou mountains. I see that the entire land has been liberated, and there are cooperative societies everywhere, so how is it that in Liven we are all still operating as individual households? Why has no one been sent to organize us and help us enter society?

The county chief stared at Mao Zhi in astonishment, then called her into his office and asked her many questions. He went to a map hanging on the wall, and searched it for a long time. On the outer edge of the map, he found several of the villages that Mao Zhi had mentioned, but for the life of him he couldn't find Liven. Eventually, he stepped out of the room and went to speak to someone in an adjacent office for a while. When he returned, he told Mao Zhi very solemnly, You should not have come to Gaoliu for this. According to the geographic plan, you belong to Dayu county. It is Dayu that has forgotten you. Dayu's county chief is truly a piece of work.

Therefore, Mao Zhi and her husband proceeded on to Dayu, and after another month of walking all day and resting at night, they finally arrived. Dayu's government was located in a mansion that formerly belonged to a rich landlord, and the county chief was a few years older than Gaoliu's. He was a local, and knew the surrounding towns and villages like the palm of his hand. When Mao Zhi saw him, he knew why she had come before she even had a chance to finish speaking. He exclaimed, Fuck, the Shuanghuai county chief really has balls! How dare he treat one of his own villages like this, having everyone divide into cooperative societies while leaving a single village to continue operating as individual households? Where does he get off, letting one of his villages fall through the cracks, to the point that they don't even know which district they belong to? As the county chief was cursing, he took out a map of Dayu and spread it out on a table, then asked Mao Zhi to examine it carefully. He used a ruler to measure out the distances on the map, and then drew a dot on the paper outside the margins of the actual

148

map. He said, Look. The Balou mountain range is here and Liven should be about here, but it is about five-point-three inches from your village to our county's Honglianshu township, while you are only about three-point-three inches from Shuanghuai's Boshuzi township. Don't you agree that your village must belong to Shuanghuai?

After another half month, Mao Zhi and her husband finally arrived in Shuanghuai. County Chief Yang had gone to the district center for a multiday meeting concerning the establishment of mutual help teams and cooperative societies, so Mao Zhi and her husband stayed in a mill near the front gate of the county government building for several days. When Chief Yang finally returned from the county seat, riding on a mule, it was already summer and sweltering hot. Chief Yang was from a military background, and was wearing a full uniform. Once he reached his office, his secretary, little Liu, gave him some water and reported on a number of things that had occurred during his absence, including the fact that a woman named Mao Zhi, who was staying in a mill house outside the government office, claimed that her village still didn't know what county or district it belonged to. She claimed that, even now, each household in the village worked independently, and none of their ancestors had ever paid any imperial grain taxes. No one in the village knew what a landlord, rich peasant, poor peasant, or farm laborer was. Secretary Liu solemnly reported all of this to Chief Yang, who maintained a placid and expressionless demeanor, as though none of this was news to him.

Chief Yang said, Go summon that Mao Zhi woman to come over here.

Mao Zhi, sweat dripping from her face, approached Chief Yang's office. Inside, were a desk and an old-fashioned armchair, and a portrait of Chairman Mao hanging from the wall. Next to the portrait, there was a pistol. As Mao Zhi walked in, Chief Yang was in the process of washing his face with cold water, after which he hung his wash towel on the pine basin stand. He then turned to look at Mao Zhi, and asked, How many blind people are there in your village?

Mao Zhi replied, There are not many who are completely blind. Perhaps five or six.

He asked, How many cripples are there?

She replied, We don't have many cripples either. Perhaps ten or so, but they are all capable of working in the fields.

He asked, How many deaf-mutes do you have?

She replied, There are nine households with deaf people, and eight with mutes.

He asked, Are all their disabilities hereditary?

Mao Zhi replied, There are also some households who arrived in Liven years ago after fleeing famine. No one complained when they settled down in Liven, and we regard them all as disabled.

Chief Yang asked, What proportion of the village is made up of disabled people?

Mao Zhi replied, About two-thirds.

Chief Yang said, While in the district seat, I saw the chiefs of Gaoliu and Dayu counties, and said to myself, Fuck, those two are bad eggs. Take the Dayu chief. He claims that Liven is one hundred and twenty-three li from our county's Boshuzi township, while it is one hundred and sixty-three li from their own Honglianshu township. What he didn't mention, however, is that while it is true that Liven is a hundred and twenty-three li from our Boshuzi township, it is only ninety-three and a half li from their own Chunshugou township, which is to say, thirty li closer. As for the Gaoliu county chief, he is correct when he says that Gaoliu is far from your village, but in the intercalary fifth month of the eleventh year of the Republic—which is to say the renxu Year of the Dog in the lunar calendar—there was a great drought in Henan and many people starved to death, though in the Balou mountains there were several gorges in which the people had more grain than they could eat, including the one where your village is located, and that year Gaoliu sent someone to Liven to collect grain, which they took back to Gaoliu and used to save many people's lives.

Chief Yang said, Look, in strictly geographical terms, Liven is somewhat closer to Dayu's Chunshugou, and technically you should be under their jurisdiction. From a historical perspective, however, Gaoliu once collected grain from you, and one could also argue that you should belong to them. Both of those fuckers sent you over to Shuanghuai, even though we have no connection to you whatsoever. At this point, the sun reached its zenith, and several pagoda trees in the courtyard swayed gently back and forth. The secretary was standing beside the door watering the plants, and Chief Yang pointed outside and said, Secretary Liu, go to the canteen and tell them to *prepare two extra lunches. We want our guests to enjoy a good meal while they're here.*

Mao Zhi stared intently at Chief Yang for a long time, then abruptly stood up and said, Chief Yang, you and I both contributed to the Revolution, and therefore I'd like to just ask you a few questions.

Chief Yang looked slightly startled, but said, Go ahead.

Mao Zhi said, Chief Yang, do you agree that the people of Liven belong to China? He replied, Yes. She continued, Do they not also belong to Henan province? He replied, Yes. She continued, And are they not also from Jiudu? He didn't disagree. She then concluded, In that case, why is it that Shuanghuai, Dayu, and Gaoliu don't want to have us? Aren't you concerned that we'll go down to the district seat to report you?

Chief Yang appeared surprised that a crippled woman from the countryside would have the guts to speak to him like this. He glanced at the revolver hanging from the wall, then snorted and replied, Heavens, would you dare report us to the district? He suddenly stood and said, Fuck, go report us. Go find the Party secretary. When I was in Yan'an, I was the one who initially introduced the Party secretary to the Party. Chief Yang stared coldly at Mao Zhi as he was saying this, as though he wanted to devour her with his eyes.

Mao Zhi, however, was not at all alarmed. She stared back at him for a while, then said, Chief Yang, you've been to Yan'an. I've also been to Yan'an, and if the women's regiment had not been disbanded in the autumn of the bingzi year, I wouldn't be here now asking this of you. As Mao Zhi was saying this, she rested her gaze on the county chief's face. She'd originally planned to wait for him to look at her one more time, then turn around and walk out. To her surprise, however, she noticed he had suddenly gone pale. He gaped at her as if in disbelief, as though he had just recognized her for the first time. He asked, Which women's regiment were you in? Were you really at Yan'an?

Mao Zhi said, You don't believe me, do you? As she was saying this, she turned and hobbled out of his office. She returned to the mill house in front of the county government building, where she asked the stonemason to pass her her bag, which she then took to Chief Yang's office. She opened the bag on his desk and took out two pairs of shoes, placing one shoe at each corner of the desk. Then, she took out a neatly folded white canvas pouch.

151

She untied the pouch and removed an old, faded military uniform, which she spread across Chief Yang's desk. On the jacket's shoulder there was a large patch, which was made not from standard military uniform cloth, but rather from thick black fabric. Beneath the jacket was a pair of neatly folded military-issue trousers, which were as faded and yellowed as the jacket. The edges of the pants had already begun to fray, and it was obvious that this was a very old uniform. After Mao Zhi placed the uniform and travel bag on Chief Yang's desk, she stepped away and said:

Chief Yang, we both suffered in the bingzi year, and if the Fourth Regiment had not been disbanded, I would not be here today asking this of you.

Chief Yang blushed deeply. He looked at the military uniform, and then back at Mao Zhi. He looked again at the uniform, and finally yelled out the door:

Secretary Liu, tell the canteen to prepare those two extra meals. Also, get me a bottle of liquor!

This was the end of the fifth month, and when Mao Zhi and the stonemason returned to Liven, they were accompanied by Secretary Liu, together with Boshuzi's township chief and two soldiers from the township's militia. The latter were carrying rifles, and when they reached the entrance to the village they fired three shots in succession, whereupon all of the villagers—be they blind or crippled—came to the village center to convene the village's first-ever People's Assembly. In this way, Liven was formally brought under the jurisdiction of Shuanghuai's Boshuzi township.

With the sound of those gunshots, a mutual aid team was formed, and the villagers also entered a cooperative society. They thereby began enjoying heavenly days.[3]

CHAPTER 9: FURTHER, FURTHER, FURTHER READING— HEAVENLY DAYS

1) **Foreign cart.** A bicycle. In Henan's Balou mountain region, bicycles used to be called "foreign carts," and later they were called "pedal bikes." After many years of attacks on the Four Olds—old ideas, old culture, old customs, and Maoist old habits—the people of Balou were no longer allowed to utter the word "foreign," and began calling the vehicles "bicycles." Even today, however, there are still some old people who persist in calling them "foreign carts" or "pedal bikes."

3) **Heavenly days.** Heavenly days refers to the unusual period of collectivized labor that followed the institution of the mutual aid teams in Liven in the autumn of the gengwu year, 1960.

Each family's land was combined, and their oxen, plows, hoes, and sowing drills were all collectivized. The families who already had these things obviously lost out, and although they initially wanted to cry and make a scene, after hearing a few gunshots they calmed down and handed over what they owed.

In this way, the mutual aid teams were formed. The township chief and the two militiamen stayed in the countryside for three days, and when they left they took with them one of the guns that they brought, while leaving the other in the village.

They left the gun with Mao Zhi.

Mao Zhi was originally a member of an army contingent. She had fought in battle, and had more experience than any of the militiamen.

She had been a revolutionary since she was young. She had been a leader.

After the oxcart bell was hung from the tree in the middle of the village, whenever Mao Zhi rang the bell the people of Liven would go together to work in the fields. If she told them to go to East Mountain to hoe the soil, they would go to East Mountain to hoe the soil. And if she told them to go to West Mountain to distribute fertilizer, they would go to West Mountain to distribute fertilizer. Originally, the mutual aid teams worked well, but for thousands of years each family in Liven had farmed its own land, plowing and sowing its own fields, with some families at the top of the hills and others down in the gorge, and if they needed anything they would simply give a shout. However, if the household of a cripple wanted to borrow a soil basket from a deaf man, it would not do for him to simply shout out a request, so from the depths of the gorge he would painstakingly trudge to the top of the ridge, and then trudge back down again. But with the establishment of the mutual aid teams, all of this became unnecessary. When Mao Zhi rang the bell in the center of the village and called for everyone to bring their shovels, they simply needed to take their shovels down to the fields. If she told everyone to bring their wicker baskets, they just needed to bring their wicker baskets.

On their way to the fields, the villagers who liked to talk no longer felt lonely, and for those who didn't like to talk, their ears no longer felt lonely.

After they finished in the fields and headed back to the village, those who liked to sing opera arias and Balou and Xiangfu tunes would happily do so, not needing to worry that they might be wasting their voices and talent because no one was around to listen to them.

Winter came and went, and eventually spring arrived. When Mao Zhi rang the bell, everyone—men and women, young and old, with the exception only of the blind and paraplegics—would go down to hoe the wheat fields. First they hoed the largest plot of land to the east of the village. This was more than ten mu in size, and sat catty-corner with the hill, as though it were a piece of sky that had fallen onto the mountain. All those who could carry a hoe—including men and women, young and old, cripples and deaf-mutes—went out to work the fields together. They

154

worked in groups of ten, rhythmically raising and lowering their hoes, as the bright yellow sound of their hoeing echoed through the mountain ridge.

There was a crippled woman who wasn't able to stand, so naturally she couldn't go out to hoe the fields. Mao Zhi, therefore, positioned her at the head of the field and had her sing to everyone while they worked. There was also a blind man who had never known the color of the sky or the earth, but ever since he was young he had liked to listen to people sing, and whenever he heard someone singing he would start singing himself. Mao Zhi had him come along and sing with the crippled woman.

The villagers also sang as they worked. They sang the Xiangfu tunes "A Pair of Jade Swallows" and "Story of a Butterfly," together with the Balou tunes "Story of the Outlaws" and "Two Amorous Women." When they ran out of lyrics, they would make up new ones, such as "I Don't Have a Wife and You Don't Have a Husband":

BLIND MAN SINGS:
*The wheat in the fields is piled into twenty-one
  bundles.
Who would have thought that I would end up without
  a wife?
A single head of garlic cannot be divided into separate
  cloves,
I pity my bachelor self.*

PARAPLEGIC WOMAN SINGS:
*Balou has two bellows,
But I've been left behind as a widow.
At the front of the cart there is a mule, and at the
  back is a horse.
Who knew that I would be left a widow?*

BLIND MAN SINGS:
*I lack a wife, just as my horse lacks a halter.
When the sun sets over the western mountains, where
  is my house?*

When the sun sets over the western mountains gorge,
Who will accept my wifeless self?

PARAPLEGIC WOMAN SINGS:
The stove is full of smoke, and I'm fanning the flame.
Though I, my widowed self, have been left all alone.
The bright moon comes out.
One person sleeps alone.
The door, window, and water jar all shatter,
The wind blows and I am naked,
A lone goose alights on the beach and makes a nest.
It is hard to imagine anyone more brokenhearted
*   than I.*

BLIND MAN SINGS:
The sun sets over the gorge in the western mountain,
Who will accept my wifeless self?
The bellows are empty,
And I, wifeless, am brokenhearted.
I walk halfway up the hill.
Who knows if an unmarried man has been wronged.
My thatched hut has eighteen rafters.
Who knows how I suffer?
If someone plants scallions, I plant garlic.
It is hard to live as an unmarried man.

The villagers sang as they worked the fields. Eventually summer arrived, and everyone spent half a month arduously harvesting the wheat. There was rain when they needed rain, and sun when they needed sun. Who would have thought that the first year Liven entered society, the wheat crop would be so abundant that in all of the village's fields, large and small, the weight of the grain would pull down the wheat stalks? When the villagers were out harvesting the grain, the entire land was filled with the fragrant aroma of wheat. They'd originally planned to harvest wheat all day and then divide

*it so as not to leave it piled up in the field. But this process of apportion-
ment took half a month, and then each family had to carry the wheat home.*

*Each family's jugs and bins were completely filled with wheat. Even
the coffins they had prepared for their parents were filled with wheat, and
the families that didn't have coffins dumped their wheat onto their beds.
In the end, everyone ran out of storage space, as the corners of each house
were filled with bags and bags, and even the foulest latrine was filled with
the sweet fragrance of wheat. They piled the leftover wheat into two storage
houses out in the field, and concluded that, having entered society, they had
genuinely entered the heavenly days. However, along with the heavenly days
there came the great Iron Tragedy.*[1]

Chapter 11: Further, Further, Further, Further Reading— Iron Tragedy

1) **Iron Tragedy.** *Refers to the iron-smelting tragedy that occurred in China during the Great Leap Forward. In the Balou mountains, this was referred to simply as the "Iron Tragedy." But in contrast to natural disasters like floods or fires, the Iron Tragedy was a man-made catastrophe. The problem began in the xinmao year, 1951. At the time, the entire district, including Liven, was enjoying excellent weather. The summer wheat harvest was good, and the autumn corn harvest was also unexpectedly bountiful. Needless to say, food was abundant, which in turn improved everything else. Life was indeed heavenly.*

But in the renchen year, 1952, Mao Zhi went into the township for a meeting that lasted several days, and when she returned she rang the village bell and made two announcements. First, she announced that she had brought a glucose bottle back from the township. It was a clear glass bottle with a rubber stopper, and she used it to distribute sesame oil to every household. Second, she announced that the district government had been transformed into a people's commune, and the collaborative societies and mutual aid teams had been divided into large and small brigades. Because planting was a form of production, they were therefore called large and small production brigades. She announced that the large brigades would not have a Party branch secretary, a district chief, a militia commander, or a production team leader, and the small brigades would not have a production brigade chief, an accountant, or wage workers. She said that because Liven was located in the middle of nowhere, even an independent large production brigade would necessarily be an independent small production brigade. She said that the commune had asked her to assume the responsibilities of the village Party branch secretary, district chief, militia commander, and production team leader.

Before anyone realized it, it was already the wuxu year, 1958, and the country began undergoing major reconstruction to produce more, faster, and more efficiently. Throughout the land, everyone began smelting steel.

All of the trees throughout the country were chopped down.

In Liven, everyone became extraordinarily busy. Mao Zhi finally got pregnant, and her belly started to grow. The commune ordered that every ten days, each village and town must smelt a piece of steel and deliver it to an empty plot in front of the commune. Mao Zhi poked out her belly and went with the other villagers by oxcart to deliver a piece of steel as big as a gob of soybean dregs. It was only then that she realized that the disabled Liven villagers, after working arduously day and night, had managed to produce just half as much steel as those in the other villages. The commune secretary told Mao Zhi and the other villagers to stand in front of the portrait of Chairman Mao with their heads bowed, and to perform a process of self-examination. He said, Mao Zhi, fortunately you were at Yan'an, and it's said that you even saw Chairman Mao, so why don't you pound your chest and consider how you can live up to Chairman Mao.

The secretary said, Beginning today, Liven won't need to smelt any more steel. You are holding us back, and therefore I am hereby expelling Liven from Boshuzi commune, meaning that you should no longer be considered residents of Boshuzi.

Upon returning to the village, Mao Zhi mobilized each household to hand over all of its nonessential iron utensils: old iron pots and buckets, dull hoes, and blunt shovels, together with iron and bronze washbasins, iron fire pokers, iron pegs for hanging things on the wall, and even the iron buckles on the wooden chests that lay at the heads of their beds. After the villagers collected all of these items and handed them over, the commune issued Liven a framed certificate, designating it to be Boshuzi's third model iron-smelting village. But half a month later, the commune sent two more gun-toting militia leaders, who were leading an oxcart and carrying a certificate declaring Liven to be the second model iron-smelting village in Boshuzi. They then hauled away a cartful of iron farming tools. A few days later, another four People's Army soldiers carrying rifles arrived in two oxcarts, bearing a certificate designating Liven to be Boshuzi's first model iron-smelting village. They also brought a handwritten letter from the commune's Secretary Mai. Mao Zhi looked at the letter, and was silent for a long time. Then, with her belly sticking out, she led the visitors from house to house to collect everyone's iron tools.

When they arrived at a blind man's house, he was in the middle of cooking dinner, and his son was squatting beside him. The blind man asked, Who's standing in the doorway? The son responded that it was several wholers, who were all carrying guns. The blind man was startled, and obediently handed over the pot he was using.

As the blind man was serving the food he had been cooking, the People's Army soldiers looked around the courtyard outside. They discovered an iron nail in the wall, which they proceeded to pull out and take away. When they saw two hoes leaning against the wall, they also took the heads of those hoes. At this point, the blind man pulled Mao Zhi aside and said, They even want my pot! What if my family were to not enter society or become a member of society? Would that be okay?

Mao Zhi quickly covered the blind man's mouth with her hand.

When they arrived at the house of the crippled woman who liked to embroider, the woman handed over her pot. She also had a bronze washbasin, but given that the basin was the only dowry she had brought with her when she was married into Liven, she was reluctant to hand it over. The People's Army soldiers proceeded to confiscate all of her remaining pots, ladles, and other iron cooking utensils, and threw them into the cart. Sobbing, the woman dropped her bronze basin and ran outside to grab her iron pot, whereupon the soldiers grabbed the basin as well. The crippled woman hugged Mao Zhi's legs and sobbed, Give me back my pot and my washbasin! If you don't give me back my pot and my basin, my family won't become members of society.

The gun-toting soldiers glared angrily at the crippled woman, who promptly became silent.

They also went to the house of one of the village's deaf men. He was very sharp, and although he couldn't hear, nothing could escape his gaze. The soldiers arrived with their guns, and drove their cart right up to his front door. The deaf man brought out his iron pot and handed it over, together with the iron buckles from his storage chest. He even removed the iron latches from his front door, and threw them into the cart as well. Finally, the soldiers asked if there was anything else made of iron in the house. The deaf man thought for a moment, then removed the iron rings from his shoes and tossed them into the cart.

The cart then drove off.

After the cart's departure, the deaf man tugged Mao Zhi's hand and asked in bewilderment, Stonemason's wife, was this the people's commune? Mao Zhi looked over at the soldiers, who were following the oxcart, then quickly covered the deaf man's mouth with her hand.

The sky began to turn dark red, and the two oxcarts from the commune were full. Each cart was full of the villagers' new and old iron tools—including plows and hoes, pots and ladles, door latches and chest buckles. The carts were so heavy that the oxen were panting with exhaustion as they laboriously hauled them away .

After seeing off the two oxcarts and the rugged soldiers, Mao Zhi turned to go back home. She saw the entire village, including blind men and cripples, old people and children, and particularly women responsible for cooking for their families, all standing, sitting, or lying paralyzed on the ground. They were all glaring at her. Some of them clearly hated her—particularly the young and sturdy women, who were standing in front of the crowd, biting their lips in anger and staring silently at Mao Zhi as she walked toward the village, as if they were prepared to throw themselves onto her and beat her when she approached. Mao Zhi noticed that the stonemason was pale as he waited for her at a house somewhat removed from the village. He waved at her, and she stood still for a while, then walked to her husband's side. Needless to say, a sea of angry gazes followed her. So she walked extremely slowly, one step at a time, and although she tried to avoid their eyes, it was as if she were waiting for the people behind her to call out, to curse her.

However, there was no sound from behind her.

Everything was quiet. Even the sound of their gazes was muffled, as if a window had been slammed shut. The sun began to set behind the mountains, as the iron-smelting furnaces beyond the mountain ridge began to light up. There were a handful of these furnaces in caves behind Liven, and they also lit up. Mao Zhi walked to the two furnaces behind the village, and as she moved farther and farther from the gazes of the blind, deaf, and crippled villagers, it was as if everything was already over.

But suddenly, she heard someone shout out behind her: Mao Zhi, don't leave. Now that we have entered society, our family needs to use a tile basin to cook our food. Would it be okay if we were to withdraw from society?[1]

Mao Zhi, our family has to use an earthenware pot to cook our food. It's all because you led us into society. Could you now lead us back out again?

Hey, my family doesn't even have a tile basin or an earthenware pot. Tomorrow we'll have to use a stone pig trough to cook our meal. I say, Mao Zhi—if you don't pull us out of society, don't expect to have any more pleasant days to look forward to!

Mao Zhi stood under that barrage of cries as if in the middle of a furious river current.

Even Further Reading:

1) **Withdraw from society.** This was a phrase used in reference to Liven's entry into society. Its entry into the mutual aid teams and cooperative societies was called "entering society," and therefore when the village subsequently wished to leave these people's communes, it was referred to as "withdrawing from society."

Book 7: Branches

CHAPTER 1: HOWEVER, THAT EVENT SUDDENLY ERUPTED

Chief Liu was finally going to lead the performance troupe he had organized out of Liven.

Its first stop would be in the city—to do a fund-raiser to purchase Lenin's corpse.

One-Legged Monkey's event was the One-Legged Flying Leap, Deafman Ma's was Firecracker-on-the-Ear, One-Eye's was the One-Eyed-Needle-Threading, Paraplegic Woman's was Leaf-Embroidery, Blind Tonghua's was Acute-Listening, Polio Boy's was Foot-in-a-Bottle, and Mute Uncle's was Spirit-Séance. All of the disabled villagers, as long as they had a special skill, followed Chief Liu into the city. As for Huaihua, because she was pretty and dainty, Secretary Shi said it would be possible for her to come as well, and he had her act as their announcer. An announcer is such a visible role that after Secretary Shi mentioned it, he caressed Huaihua's pretty and delicate face, and she allowed him. She smiled seductively at him, and even let him kiss her on the cheek.

On that day, a large truck drove in from the county seat and stopped at the entrance to the village. Regardless of whether a villager was blind, deaf, crippled, or mute, as long as anyone had a special skill, he or she rushed over to the truck to leave Balou. Chief Liu's car had not yet arrived, and he said that he would save a tank of gas by riding in the truck as well because, after all, wouldn't the driver in the truck's tower[1] take him back to the county seat just the same? He therefore sat in the tower with Secretary Shi, and they all prepared to leave Liven together.

The sun was already several pole-lengths high in the sky, and the villagers had eaten an early breakfast. They prepared to meet at the entrance of the village in order to load their bags into the truck and leave for the city. Tonghua, Huaihua, and Yuhua also hauled their bags to the courtyard, and as the sun began to warm up, the village's bell began to toll. Then, Chief Liu's secretary began shouting an announcement in the morning air:

"All of the members of the special-skills performance troupe must go to the village entrance to board the truck. If you are late and the truck leaves without you, you will no longer be a member of the troupe."

Secretary Shi's voice was as sonorous as a fan, as crisp as an apple pear, and as sweet as sugar. When Huaihua heard him, she immediately blushed bright red. Yuhua glanced at her, and Huaihua said, "What? What are you looking at?" Yuhua didn't reply but rather stared coldly at Huaihua, then picked up her bags.

Yuhua went to grab Tonghua's cane. As they prepared to leave, they first went to bid farewell to their mother, who had been sitting stiffly in the courtyard. Their mother was like a rotten stump, her face ashen and lifeless. She sat there staring out the front gate, then looked at blind Tonghua like someone who has already died but is still grasping a statue of the Buddha.

Yuhua said, "Mother, they are calling for us. We have to go now."

Huaihua said, "Mother, are you concerned? Don't you still have Mothlet to keep you company?" She added, "Don't worry. We'll send you some money in a month. I plan to earn more than anyone, and simply can't imagine that anyone will be able to beat me. In the future, if you don't want to continue farming, you won't have to."

Tonghua knew that their mother was worried. She didn't say anything, but rather knelt down in front of her mother and took her hand. As Tonghua did so, tears began pouring from Jumei's eyes.

Outside, One-Legged Monkey's cadre-like voice rang out, urging them to hurry: "Tonghua and Huaihua, why don't you come? Everyone is waiting for you!" His shout was like a whip, and when Jumei heard it she wiped her eyes and waved her daughters out the door.

They left.

All that remained in the courtyard was solitude. The sun had risen past the building and was now perched just below the wall of the facing house, making the entire courtyard look as though it were covered in bright glass. It was the end of the fifth month, around the time of year when they would normally begin harvesting the wheat, but there wasn't the slightest hint of wheat in the air, only the smell of soil that was soggy from the melted snow. The sparrows were on the roof of the house, chirping loudly, while the crows were in the courtyard trees, carrying twigs to rebuild the nests that had been destroyed by the midsummer blizzard. Jumei was still sitting in the doorway of her house, not moving a muscle. She waved her daughters away. She would have accompanied them to the village entrance, but she was afraid to see a certain someone and, therefore, remained in her courtyard.

She was afraid to see that certain someone, but at the same time very much wanted to see him. Therefore, she kept her front gate tightly shut and sat in her doorway, staring out at the courtyard.

The entourage staying in the temple guest house was about to emerge, and would need to pass by her front door.

Secretary Shi had passed by carrying a large bag and a small one. The sound of the bell tolling was echoing everywhere, but for some reason County Chief Liu Yingque had still not appeared. Jumei was in a state of utter distraction, and thought that perhaps he had already walked by and boarded the truck, and was about to leave the village. The sound of footsteps that had engulfed the village street had already died down, and suitcases full of bedding, clothing, and dishware had already been loaded onto the truck. The joyous and tearful ceremonies of parting had already been performed, and the only sound left in the village street was the chirping of the sparrows. Jumei had stopped watching the front gate when she finally saw him. She stood up to clean a pile of trash her daughters had left behind, but at that moment she saw two legs walking past from the guest house door. Those legs were buried in a pair of reddish brown uniform shorts, and on the feet were a pair of leather sandals and silk socks. The silk socks shimmered in the sun, and the light flashed in Jumei's eyes.

She stared in astonishment from the entranceway. She initially had no intention of saying anything to that person, and instead merely stared silently. But when she saw that he was about to walk away, she suddenly cried out,

"Hey! Hey!"

The sandals immediately paused and turned around.

"What now?"

She pondered for a moment, and it seemed as if it suddenly occurred to her that perhaps she should not have called to him. She said apologetically,

"Nothing. So, I've handed over my daughters to you?"

He glared at her in annoyance:

"You handed over your daughters to the performance troupe, not to me, County Chief Liu."

Astounded, she looked at him helplessly. Then she said softly,

"You should go now."

He turned again and left. He walked quickly, as if he were trying to escape something. A large crowd had gathered at the entrance to the village. All of the villagers, young and old, were there. The disabled villagers with special skills climbed into the back of the truck. They stuffed in their suitcases and bags, and then sat on them. There was also a pile of miscellaneous items, including pots and flour for cooking, steamers for heating buns, earthen pots for making dough, jars for storing water, buckets for carrying water, and sacks of grain and bran.

The entire truckload of people was waiting for Chief Liu. Secretary Shi and the driver were both standing below the truck's tower and peering into the depths of the alley. The people in the truck gazed into the distance, craning their necks in an attempt to see Chief Liu.

Needless to say, the truck couldn't depart until Chief Liu arrived, and the longer it took, the more anxious those who had come to see them off became. Mothers and their children were being separated, and the children outside the truck were trying to climb into their mothers' laps inside the truck—and if they weren't allowed to do so, simply sat there and cried. As for the men in the truck, their wives were giving them countless tasks to do, as if once they departed they would never return. There were some girls in the truck, and the old people outside kept repeating the same things, saying that the girls needed to wash their clothes regularly, because if they didn't the clothes would get moldy. They also told the young woman charged with cooking for the troupe that when she was using flour, she should add some extra baking soda to help the dough rise more quickly, because without it the dough would collapse. They even suggested that when people were thirsty they should drink boiled water—stressing that, regardless of whether they were using a basin or a pot to boil the water, it wasn't safe to drink until it reached a full boil. They went on to say that when it rained, everyone should use an umbrella, and that those who didn't have umbrellas could use the money the troupe issued them at the end of the month to buy a raincoat or something. They said that a raincoat had its benefits, since, unlike an umbrella, it could also be used as a mat to air-dry their grain.

Huaihua was the only person in the truck who wasn't speaking. She repeatedly glanced into the driver's tower, where Secreterary Shi was now sitting, and when no one was paying attention he would peek back at her and smile.

Chief Liu finally appeared, and everyone inside and outside the truck immediately fell silent.

The reason Chief Liu was late was that as he was leaving the temple guest house he suddenly needed to use the restroom. He squatted in a latrine for so long that his feet went numb, and only then did he slowly emerge. As he approached the truck, he surveyed everyone inside and outside the vehicle, and said, "It looks like everyone's here." Secretary Shi answered, "Yes." Chief Liu asked, "Nothing is missing?" Secretary Shi said, "I had everyone make sure they have all the props they need for their performances." Chief Liu therefore turned to the driver and said,

"Let's go."

The driver quickly started the engine.

Along the mountain ridge, there wasn't a cloud in the sky. The sky was so clear you could see more than a hundred *li* in every direction. The sun was shining down brightly, and everyone in the truck was covered in sweat. Huaihua was in the front, and she had picked some tree leaves to fan herself. Other people sat in front of her fan, and soon there was a large group. A sweaty odor wafted over her, and so she tore up the leaves she was holding. The fresh fragrance of corn and millet wafted over from the fields by the road. Everyone was eager to leave. Liven had been turned upside down—but it suddenly occurred to the villagers that, given that they were going to participate in the special-skills troupe, they were, after all, departing. Realizing that they were going to carry out some earth-shattering event, they all suddenly grew silent.

Everything became silent.

Startled by this sudden quiet, the chickens that had been pecking around for food beneath everyone's feet lifted their heads and stared blankly.

The dogs that had been hiding in the shade behind the wall were also startled, and they opened their eyes and looked at the villagers in the truck.

The children stopped crying, and their parents cut off their exhortations. The sound of the engine died down as the truck prepared to depart. The passengers in the truck were ready. Chief Liu was going to ride shotgun, and therefore Secretary Shi climbed into the tower first. Although Huaihua continued gazing at him, he didn't turn around, but rather devoted all his attention to Chief Liu. After Secretary Shi climbed in, he extended his hand to Chief Liu, who accepted it, then grabbed the door handle and hopped in.

The door closed behind him.

The truck started moving.

The truck drove away.

After the truck had proceeded a way down the road, however, *it* happened. Almost as if it had been anticipated, as soon as the truck started moving, *it* happened. Beneath the gable of the blind man's house, *it* happened. This *it* was that Grandma Mao Zhi rushed down to the truck like someone who had just returned from the dead. It was the middle of the summer, but she was wearing the nine-layer silk burial outfit that she had sewn for herself. The inner three layers consisted of what the deceased should be dressed in during hot weather; the middle three layers contained a jacket intended for spring and fall; and the outer three layers included a padded coat, padded pants, and a burial gown that the deceased would wear in winter. The burial gown was made from black silk with gold trim, and in the back there was a gold *homage* character as large as a washbasin. The black silk and yellow embroidery shimmered in the sunlight. Bathed in gold sunlight, Grandma Mao Zhi plunged down from beneath the gable like a comet, landing with a thud in the middle of the street.

She landed right in front of the truck.

The driver shouted, "Hey, woman!" and slammed on the brakes.

The entire village crowded around, shouting, "Mao Zhi, Mao Zhi," "Granny Mao Zhi," "Auntie Mao Zhi."

Actually, Grandma Mao Zhi was quite calm, since the truck's front wheel was still two feet from her. It was two feet away, but she rolled forward until she was directly under it, with the *homage* character on her back facing the sky and shimmering in the sunlight.

The entire village stared at her in astonishment. All of Liven stared at her, transfixed.

Initially, Chief Liu looked simply startled, but upon realizing it was Mao Zhi, he shifted from surprise to fury, which remained frozen on his face.

The driver shouted, "Ma, are you trying to kill yourself?"

Huaihua and Yuhua crowded to the front of the truck, crying, "Grandma, Grandma!" Blind Tonghua shouted with them, "Grandma, what's wrong? . . . Huaihua, what's wrong with our grandma?"

In the midst of these shouts, Secretary Shi opened the truck door and climbed down. At first he looked furious, and wanted to pull Grandma Mao Zhi out from under the tire, but when he realized that she was wearing her burial clothes and saw the *homage* character on her back shimmering in the sunlight, he just stood in front of the truck without moving. The look of fury on his face gradually changed to one of dejection.

"Grandma Mao Zhi," Secretary Shi said, "please come and say what you have to say."

Mao Zhi didn't respond, and grasped the truck's tire with both hands.

Secretary Shi said, "You're our elder; you should be reasonable."

Mao Zhi didn't respond, and continued grasping the truck's tire with both hands.

Secretary Shi said, "If you don't come of your own accord, I'll have to pull you out."

Mao Zhi still didn't respond, as she continued grasping the tire with all her might.

Secretary Shi said, "You're breaking the law by obstructing Chief Liu's truck. I really *will* pull you out!"

Mao Zhi finally spoke, screaming, "Just pull me, then!"

Secretary Shi glanced up at Chief Liu, and as he was leaning down and extending his hand, Mao Zhi brandished a pair of scissors from her burial gown. These were high-quality Wang Mazi–brand scissors, and Mao Zhi held the sharp point to her throat, shouting, "Just *try* to pull me! If anyone so much as touches me, I swear I'll stab myself. I'm seventy-six years old, and have already lost my will to live. My coffin and burial clothes are already prepared."

Secretary Shi stood up, and with a pleading expression looked again at Chief Liu and the truck driver. The driver shouted, "Let's run over her and be done with it." Chief Liu coughed, and the driver added more quietly, "Who would dare to really run over her? I was just trying to scare her."

Chief Liu didn't respond. After considering for a moment, he climbed down from the truck.

The villagers parted to give him room to approach.

Chief Liu walked through the path that had opened in the crowd.

The sun was in front of the truck, and Grandma Mao Zhi's burial clothing sparkled in Chief Liu's eyes. The entire land was quiet, to the point that you could hear the villagers holding their breath. The sun rays rained down like shards of glass falling from the sky. Chief Liu stood in front of the truck, his face as dark as tree bark in the springtime. He was biting his lower lip so hard it looked as though he was going to bite right through it. Holding his hands in front of his chest, he clenched his left hand into a fist and repeatedly cracked the knuckles of his right hand. Then he switched hands, and began cracking the knuckles of his left hand, unleashing another string of popping sounds. In the end, all ten of his knuckles had been cracked, and his teeth had left two rows of indentations in his lower lip, which immediately filled with blood.

He squatted in front of the tire.

"If you have something to say, you should go ahead and say it."

"You must let the people of Liven stay in Liven."

"I'm doing this for their own good."

"Nothing good will come of their leaving Liven."

"You must believe in me, and in the government."

"You must let the people of Liven remain in Liven."

"They are all there of their own free will. Your own three grand-daughters are in the truck."

"You must let the people of Liven remain in Liven."

"Your own three granddaughters are in the truck; everyone is there of their own free will."

"In any event, you should let them stay in Liven. Nothing good will come if the people of Liven leave the Balou region."

"In consideration of the county's eight hundred and ten thousand residents, and in consideration of our Lenin Fund, I have no choice but to create this performance troupe."

"If you want to take them away, you are welcome to, but it will be over my dead body."

"How about this—you let everyone leave, and just state your conditions."

"Even if I gave my conditions, I'm sure you wouldn't agree."

Chief Liu laughed coldly. "Do you forget that I'm the county chief?"

Mao Zhi replied, "I know that you want to raise money in order to buy Lenin's corpse. If you want the villagers to go earn money for you, that's fine. But you must permit Liven to withdraw from society, so that from now on Liven will no longer fall under the jurisdiction of Shuanghuai county and Boshuzi township."

"After so many decades, how can you still be thinking about this?"

"If Liven is allowed to withdraw from society, I won't feel that I've wronged Liven in any way."

Chief Liu pondered for a long time, and then finally stood up and said, "Do you think that Shuanghuai owes you this village? Do you think they owe you these several dozen square kilometers of hilly land? If you come out from under there, I'll agree to this."

Mao Zhi's eyes lit up, becoming several times brighter than her burial garb. She said, "A true agreement can only come in the form of words on paper. If you write this out, I'll let you go."

Chief Liu fetched a notebook from his secretary's bag. Then he lifted his pen and wrote several sentences that took up half the page:

> *I agree that, as of the beginning of next year, the village of Liven will no longer fall under the jurisdiction of Boshuzi township. Representatives of Boshuzi will no longer be permitted to come to Liven on any account. Also, as of the beginning of next year, Liven will no longer fall under the jurisdiction of Shuanghuai county either. Within a year, the county will print a new administrative map, which will no longer include Liven within its borders. At the same time, no one in Liven should use any means to prevent any other villager from voluntarily joining the Shuanghuai County Special-Skills Performance Troupe.*

The final line contained Chief Liu's signature.

After he finished writing, Chief Liu read it out loud to Mao Zhi, then tore out the page from the notebook and handed it to her. He said, "Several decades have passed, and you still think about this every day. To withdraw from society is a major undertaking, and therefore

174

you should give me half a year to explain things to the higher-ups at the district level." Grandma Mao Zhi listened to him and accepted the sheet of paper. She considered for a while, she looked at it for a while, and then suddenly tears began to well up in her eyes.

She held the document in her hand as though an immense burden had, in the blink of an eye, suddenly became as light as that sheet of paper. Though she didn't dare believe it was real, her hand was trembling slightly, causing the paper to shake. She was wearing nine layers of burial garb, but even through those nine layers, you could see that the trembling of her hand was also causing her clothing to shake. Warm sweat had soaked the inner layers of her clothing, and though her face was still as aged as before, without a trace of perspiration, there was a blood red layer buried beneath her yellow pallor. She had already endured more trials and tribulations than there were grains of grass growing on the mountain slope, and therefore when she took the sheet of paper to look at it she uttered only a single sentence. She turned to Chief Liu and said,

"You should stamp this with your county committee and county government stamps."

He replied, "Not only will I stamp it, I will also return to the county seat and issue an official notice notifying each township, each unit, and each board committee."

She asked, "When will this notice be sent out?"

Chief Liu replied, "By the end of the month. In ten days, you can come to the county seat to receive a copy."

She said, "How would I go about receiving this document?"

Chief Liu said, "You could just wear this burial garb and lie down in my house. You could wear this clothing while sleeping in my bed, and then slaughter several blood red roosters[3] and bury them in front of the county committee and county government building."

Grandma Mao Zhi counted the days, and thirteen days before the end of the month she finally crawled out from beneath the truck's tire.

On that day, the truck finally rumbled away, leaving Liven shrouded in solitude.

Further Reading:

1) **Truck's tower.** A truck's cabin.

3) **Blood red rooster.** In Balou and throughout the Shuanghuai and western Hunan region, people often use roosters as sacrificial offerings. Therefore, legend and popular belief hold that if you bury a dead blood red rooster in front of someone's door, that family can expect a catastrophe, and if you bury a blood red chicken in front of a work unit building, the leader of the work unit will be fated to have an unfortunate career and destiny.

Chapter 3: Long after the applause has died down, and the liquor has been drunk

The night was as dark as the bottom of a well, and the moon hung in the sky like a chunk of ice.

When the troupe gave its first informal performance in the county seat, its success vastly exceeded everyone's expectations.

The date had been set for the beginning of the seventh lunar month. Because three, six, and nine are all auspicious numbers, Chief Liu therefore chose the ninth day of the seventh month, and ceremonially wrote the number nine twice in large Chinese characters.

That evening, on the ninth day of the month, was the beginning of the Liven performance troupe's most unforgettable moment. Initially, the county's auditorium was virtually silent, and there were just a handful of people sitting below the stage fanning themselves. It was very hot, and during the day the county's asphalt road became baked into black oil, so that when people walked along the road the heels of their shoes would get stuck and the wheels of their cars would get caught. It was said that at midday people fainted from the heat and recovered only after being given an ice bath at the county hospital, but that some died from the abrupt change in temperature.

Who, therefore, could have expected that the auditorium would end up being filled to capacity—especially since, because this was merely a dress rehearsal, no one had arranged for an audience. Chief Liu had Secretary Shi ask their office to notify only the relevant departments, including the tourism bureau; the culture center and culture bureau, charged with arranging times for performances; and the county committee, county government, and other relevant officials. They originally expected to have just a hundred or so audience members. When Chief Liu sat down at the front of the theater, however, the cadres from the county committee and the county government all crowded behind him, sitting in accordance with their position and status. The auditorium's electric fan was on in consideration of the county chief, and after the room began to cool off, more people began crowding in. Because there was no admission charge, people who were wandering around outside all came pouring into the auditorium to get out of the heat.

The auditorium quickly filled up.

Inside the auditorium, there was a sheet of darkness.

Inside the auditorium, there was a cacophonous hubbub.

Chief Liu had arrived punctually, and as soon as he entered everyone immediately grew quiet, as if the people had come, not to watch the performance or to get out of the heat, but rather to await Chief Liu's arrival. He had a different allure here, and after he entered the arena, everyone in the auditorium broke into loud applause, the way people in Beijing would greet a foreign leader. Actually, here in the county seat Chief Liu was regarded as an emperor or a national president, and it was an ordinary occurrence for people to break into loud applause when they saw him; it had already become a habit. Hearing this applause, Chief Liu walked into the auditorium, blushing deeply, and took his seat in the third row from the front. Then, he turned around, and gestured for everyone to stop applauding and to take their seats. He called Secretary Shi over and whispered something in his ear, whereupon Secretary Shi went backstage to announce that the county chief had arrived. This increased the nervousness of the performers by a factor of ten, or even a hundred, putting increased pressure on the people in charge of overseeing them—professionals formerly affiliated with the Balou tunes opera troupe, who, after that troupe dissolved, had had to rely until recently on performing for family weddings and such.

Days earlier, news had spread that Chief Liu wanted to organize a special-skills performance troupe made up of disabled people—including the blind, the crippled, the deaf, deaf-mutes, those missing a leg, and young polio victims—from that village deep in the Balou mountains that everyone had heard about but no one had seen. Initially, it was said, the villagers hadn't paid much attention to this announcement, but given that it was Chief Liu who made the announcement and invited them to come and perform, they had no choice but to do so.

Secretary Shi had suggested that Huaihua serve as the announcer; he found that although she was on the short side, she was nevertheless attractive. He then said that there would be a dress rehearsal on the ninth day of the seventh month, so it was appropriate to begin preparing right away. He recognized that what the audience was mainly interested in was cooling off under the fan. And sure enough, at first they were not really paying attention, and were therefore startled by the arrival of Chief Liu. He had not been expected to attend, given that this was merely a dress rehearsal and that furthermore he was said to have a cold, with a nose so stuffed it felt as though he had chicken feathers rammed up it. It had been reported that he had gone back to the county seat to take care of some business, and would return to watch the actual performance.

Who would have thought, therefore, that he would suddenly appear to watch a dress rehearsal? When he arrived, the cadres from the county committee and the county government all came with him. As a result, this dress rehearsal was transformed into a formal debut performance. Secretary Shi came backstage and told the fifty-something leader of the Balou tunes opera troupe that Chief Liu had drunk some ginger soup and decided to come after all. He reported that Chief Liu said that his nose was still a little stuffed, so he wouldn't come up on stage to speak. He added that Chief Liu still had to convene a county standing committee meeting that evening to research a construction plan for the Lenin Memorial Hall, and asked the troupe director to hurry up and start the performance.

The troupe director started hustling about. He gathered all of the Liven performers together in a corner of the stage and told them three things: 1) Don't be nervous while performing on stage, but rather be as relaxed as if you were at your own livening festival. 2) Don't look directly at the audience while on stage, because if you do you will become alarmed, so just look at the ceiling instead. 3) After finishing your performance, remember to bow to the audience; Chief Liu will be sitting in the middle of the third row, so when you bow you should be sure to make him feel that you are bowing directly to him, while at the same time making the rest of the audience feel that you are bowing to them. After he finished, the troupe director called Huaihua over, and asked, "Are you nervous?" Huaihua replied, "A little." The troupe director said, "There is no need to be afraid. You are the prettiest girl in the entire troupe. Wait a moment and I'll find someone to apply your makeup, so that when you stand at the front of the stage, you will look as pretty as a peacock. When the audience sees you, they will be astounded by your beauty. You should calmly announce that the performance is about to begin, and what the opening acts will be. That's all."

Huaihua blushed deeply, and nodded to the troupe director.

The troupe director caressed her cheek, and gave her a kiss. Then he asked someone to go apply her makeup.

The performance began. No one anticipated that when Huaihua, this tiny nin, walked onto the stage wearing heels and a blue silk dress, with blush and lipstick, she would look like an oriole fresh out of the nest. Given that she was wearing high heels, she no longer resembled a petite nin, like her sisters Tonghua, Yuhua, and Mothlet. However, since she still wasn't very tall, people felt that she was not seventeen, but rather perhaps eleven or twelve. Her eyes were pits of darkness, and her lips were covered in bright red splendor. Her nose was thin and pointed like a knife. When she stood on stage in the sweltering theater wearing her blue muslin dress, she was like a cool breeze. Her appearance startled the theater audience, and even Chief Liu was utterly spellbound when he saw her. He knew that she was small, but hadn't expected that her voice would be so sweet and delicate, nor that after having been instructed just a couple of times she would have succeeded in shedding her Balou accent and learned to speak with a perfect city accent. She rhythmically uttered one syllable after another, every word flowing like juice from a melon.

Huaihua stood at the front of the stage, and the entire theater fell silent. Then, she said in her sweet, delicate voice, "Our opening act will now begin. The first performance . . . will be the One-Legged Flying Leap."

After finishing her announcement, she stepped off the stage and the troupe director enthusiastically grabbed her hand, as though his own daughter had unexpectedly done something extraordinary. He caressed her face again, patted her, and then gave her another kiss. When Huaihua came off the stage, a wave of applause erupted from the crowd. After it died down, the second red curtain slowly opened, as though the clouds were parting and the sun was coming out. The stage lights came on.

One-Legged Monkey's leap was actually not all that extraordinary in itself. Given that he had been missing a leg ever since he was born, he had needed to learn to walk, carry things, and climb mountains using only one leg. As a result, that one leg had become very strong, allowing him to leap vast distances. However, the troupe director had added his own ideas to the One-Legged Flying Leap performance, making it terrifyingly dangerous. As soon as the curtain was raised, the actor who normally played the part of the clown in traditional opera performances appeared on stage juggling three straw hats. Two people then came onto the stage and scattered mung beans, soybeans, and green peas all over the ground behind him, covering the stage with a red and green sheet the size of three standard floor mats. Then, they had One-Legged Monkey go up on stage and make a one-legged leap over this sea of beans and peas. On the eastern side of the stage, they placed two cushions, so that when Monkey performed his One-Legged Leap, he would land on them. It was Yuhua who brought the cushions over. She was also wearing a theatrical costume, with blush and lipstick, so she looked quite attractive, like an innocent country girl.

On one side of the stage, therefore, a young country girl approached, and on the other side there was a man performing his One-Legged Leap. The resulting contrast was like that between fresh flowers and wilted grass. Needless to say, if One-Legged Monkey didn't manage to complete his leap, he would land spread-eagled on the peas, and quite possibly break his good leg. The theater was filled with the smell of peas. The idea of covering the stage with beans and peas for the opening act was a stroke of genius, and even Chief Liu smiled broadly.

At that point, One-Legged Monkey appeared on stage, his empty pants leg dangling in the air. He was quite handsome, but his face was covered in shiny oil so that you couldn't make out whether he was handsome or ugly. But everyone was astonished by his single leg. Chief Liu already knew about his One-Legged Leap, but the audience hadn't realized that Monkey actually had only one leg. Then, someone on stage announced that he would leap, with his single leg, over the two-meter-wide and three-meter-long pool of peas, and if he didn't make it he would land in the middle of the peas. The person on stage asked the audience to keep their eyes peeled. Accordingly, the audience sweated anxiously on his behalf. As they were watching from below the stage, up on stage the one-legged performer looked small and thin, and when he walked he had to hobble around on crutches.

Huaihua announced that he would leap over that sheet of peas, and that he would leap three meters, or nine feet; this was farther than many wholers could jump, but now *a cripple* was about to attempt this distance. The audience was nervous on his behalf, and One-Legged Monkey himself—either because he was genuinely worried about his ability to clear those three meters, or because he was just putting on an act—went to measure the distance with his hands, as though if it had been even an inch longer than it should have been, he would shift both the pool of peas and the cushions over by an inch. At that point, Yuhua, looking very concerned, gently urged him to be careful. One-Legged Monkey nodded to her.

Finally, he was ready to perform his leap.

The spotlights were as bright as the sun, and the audience were all holding their breath. Even Chief Liu leaned forward in his seat. Then, music and drums started playing, as though he were a brave warrior about to head into battle. One-Legged Monkey ran out from the side of the stage holding his crutch, lurching across like a three-legged deer. His right leg landed with a thud like a wooden mallet striking a board, his left crutch with a thud like a stone hammer hitting a board. After several rounds of this sound, the audience briefly glimpsed the shadow of a figure wearing a green T-shirt and red sweatpants, hopping awkwardly across the stage. His crutch happened to land right in the pool of peas, and seeing that he was about to fall, everyone craned their necks like trees about to topple over. But he suddenly took advantage of his crutch's flexibility to leap into the air, and flew above the pool of peas, landing cleanly on the other side.

The audience was deathly quiet as they watched him leap over the pool of peas and land on the cushion. Then, everyone broke into wild applause. In fact, the applause was so loud that it almost split the building's rafters. Chief Liu was leaning forward, but after One-Legged Monkey completed his leap he sat straight up and led the applause. The applause went on and on, until Yuhua walked out holding a pair of wooden planks, each of which was three feet wide and five feet long. Each of those planks was lined with row upon row of three-inch nails that had been inserted into the boards at one-inch intervals. The audience had not realized that Yuhua was a nin, and it wasn't until she walked to the front of the stage that people noticed she was as tiny as a sparrow. Astounded by her size, they watched as she placed the two wooden boards in the middle of the pool of peas, and realized that when One-Legged Monkey leaped over the pool of peas again, he would also need to leap over this bed of nails. Given that this bed of nails was wider than the original pool of peas, and was covered with sharp spikes, the audience once again fell into stunned silence.

Everyone stared up to the stage in astonishment as One-Legged Monkey succeeded in leaping over the bed of knives.

His third leap, however, was even more amazing. The performance was called "Crossing-a-Sea-of-Fire." On the floor of the stage there were now a pair of thin iron sheets, which were even broader and longer than the bed of nails, and which were covered with kerosene and kerosene-soaked cotton. At the touch of a match, the entire sheet erupted in flames, illuminating the entire theater. In the light of the fire, One-Legged Monkey once again hobbled to the front of the stage. His mouth tightly closed, he bowed to the audience, and after receiving a round of applause he hobbled back. Then, like a three-legged gazelle, he ran out and leaped over the sea of fire.

While he was in midair, however, there was an accident. Because his right leg consisted of merely an empty pants leg, as he was passing over the flames the fabric caught on fire. When he landed on the cushion on the other side, his pants were on fire, and he began to cry in agony. Huaihua and Yuhua, who were observing from the side of the stage, began to scream, and the audience jumped to their feet. Although the fire was quickly extinguished, when One-Legged Monkey came out for his bow, his empty pants leg was now missing, and all that remained was the charred circular opening.

The charred pants leg was clearly visible under the spotlights, permitting the audience to see the stump of Monkey's missing leg poking out. That stumplike appendage clearly had two large blisters, which were shimmering under the lights. One-Legged Monkey thanked the audience and took a bow, and he was enveloped by a wave of breathless applause.

Everyone's hands were red from clapping, and the applause was so loud that white paint started flaking off the walls of the theater.

After One-Legged Monkey took his bow and limped off the stage, the troupe director was waiting for him backstage. Smiling excitedly, he said, "Congratulations on firing the first shot. You will quickly become a sensation. Even Chief Liu was applauding like mad after your performance!"

One-Legged Monkey replied, "Troupe Director, where is the restroom? I peed in my pants."

The troupe director immediately took him to the restroom behind the stage. He told Monkey not to worry, and confessed that when he himself was young, he also had wet his pants the first time he performed on stage.

No matter how you look at it, this opening-night performance was nothing short of an unqualified success. The performance began at dusk, and continued until the sky was full of stars. The entire time, the applause never stopped. Who ever heard of a performance troupe whose members were all blind, deaf, mute, crippled, or paralyzed? Who ever saw someone like Blind Tonghua, who had never known that clouds are white or the sunset is red, but nevertheless could distinguish between willow, tung-oil, pagoda, or chinaberry stakes simply by tapping them with her cane? Who ever saw someone like the Paraplegic Woman, who could take an elm or tung-oil tree leaf, or an even thinner and more brittle pagoda tree leaf—and embroider it with an image of a small bird, a chrysanthemum, or a plum blossom? Who ever saw someone like little Polio Boy, who could curl up his crippled foot and stick it into a bottle and then walk around using the bottle as a shoe, *click-clacking* as he ran back and forth in circles around the stage, and who even turned cartwheels and somersaults? There was One-Eye, who could use a single red thread to thread several needles at once. There was also pretty, petite Tonghua again, completely blind in both eyes, but with an incredibly acute sense of hearing. The entire auditorium became still as she stood in the middle of the stage, and when someone at the east side of the stage dropped a needle, she would say that a wire had fallen to the ground on the east side of the stage. And if someone dropped a white penny onto a rug on the west side of the stage, she would say that a coin had fallen onto a piece of cloth. Some members of the audience couldn't believe she was really blind, and the next time she came onto the stage during her act she covered her eyes with a black blindfold, and when someone tore up a cigarette pack and scattered the pieces, she announced that a tree leaf was blowing around in front of her.

Tonghua's Acute-Listening act was the final event of the troupe's debut performance. Because this event involved audience participation, it functioned as a climax and marked the conclusion of the performance. Huaihua thanked the audience and announced that the performance had run half an hour longer than expected, and that now the performers and the county leaders had to go home and rest.

With that, the performance concluded.

Like guests at a party who are enjoying their dinner only to discover that all the food is gone, or are savoring a fine liquor only to discover that the bottle is empty, the audience had no choice but to get up and walk out of the theater. Chief Liu and the county cadres sitting at the front of the theater all stood and applauded. Each of them had an expression of excitement and amazement. Who would have expected that Chief Liu, after a single trip to the countryside, could manage to bring back this sort of performance troupe, whose every single act was completely unique and unbelievable? No one could believe that all these performers were actually disabled peasants from the remote countryside. But most important, each of the county committee and the county government cadres glimpsed, in the Liven performances, the first hint of Lenin's glory—a money tree from which they would obtain the funds to purchase Lenin's corpse. With the help of this money tree, they would be able to install Lenin's corpse on Spirit Mountain, thereby transforming it into an inexhaustible bank.

The success of the dress rehearsal made Chief Liu's blood boil with excitement. He went backstage to shake hands with each of the performers, urging them to go cook a delicious midnight meal. He said, "The weather is very hot, so for the next performance everyone should bring a paper fan. If you have to buy one, remember to get a receipt and the county will reimburse you. This will count as your first set of fringe benefits." After shaking everyone's hand, Chief Liu left the theater, surrounded by the county cadres, and left for the guest house.

Once there, Secretary Shi and the head of the guest house exchanged a few words, and then Secretary Shi took some stationery and wrote an invitation, which he laid out in front of Chief Liu.

The document read:

> *Invitation to a dinner banquet celebrating the success of the dress rehearsal of the special-skills performance troupe.*
> *County Chief Liu:*
> *In order to celebrate the success of the first dress rehearsal of the Liven performance troupe, we are*

> *presenting the menu of the celebratory dinner below.*
> *Please instruct.*
>
> *Ten cold dishes: cabbage heart, scallion tofu, boiled peanuts, fried peanuts, boiled edamame, shredded ginger and greens, vinegar cucumbers, braised onions, celery sisters, lily brothers.*
>
> *Ten hot dishes: braised hare, pheasant stew, mushroom duck, garlic-flavored entrails, pan-fried beef, carrot lamb, cubed pork with vegetables, chicken liver, jujube grasshopper, and green snake and white dragon.*
>
> *Three soups: three-flavored soup, hot and sour soup, and sweet porridge.*

Chief Liu received the report and examined it carefully. He used a pen to make two corrections, and then wrote "Agreed" at the bottom and signed his name. The report was quickly passed on to the head of the guest house, whereupon ten vegetable dishes and ten meat dishes were immediately brought to the table.

Chief Liu and the county cadres had a celebratory toast in the guest house cafeteria. Under the influence of the alcohol, Chief Liu began spitting out the truth, and proceeded to utter a number of surprising things, and did something that everyone found positively astounding.

The cafeteria had two large tables, and after everyone had eaten and drunk their fill, when it was already pitch-black night and the waiters were dozing outside the room, Chief Liu refilled his glass and lifted it into the air. He looked over the cadres below him, and told them all to raise their glasses as well, explaining that he wanted to ask them a few questions.

The cadres from the county committee and county government all filled their glasses and raised them.

Chief Liu said, "Today it is as if I am hosting a general meeting of the county standing committee, and as the nominal head of the standing committee, I want to ask everyone a question, which is also a request for your opinion. I hope you will express yourselves freely."

Everyone stood up to join the toast and said, "Chief Liu, say what you wish. We will gather around you."

Chief Liu asked them, "Do you think my decision to purchase Lenin's corpse was a wise one?"

Everyone replied that it was a brilliant decision, the most brilliant decision that anyone in Shuanghuai had ever made. The decision would ensure that the eight hundred and ten thousand residents of Shuanghuai would be wealthy for ten thousand generations.

Chief Liu asked, "Do you agree that I've worked hard in making the preparations for the Lenin Forest Park and the Lenin Mausoleum?"

All the cadres replied that he had worked very hard on these projects, and that they had observed this themselves.

Chief Liu asked, "Do you agree that the Liven performance troupe will be Shuanghuai's money tree?"

They all replied that it would not really be a money tree, because with a money tree you still need to go to the trouble of shaking it in order to get the money. Instead, this troupe would be a river of gold, and from it gold would flow into every mouth without anyone needing to do anything.

Chief Liu asked, "Do you see now that we have hope of buying Lenin's corpse?"

Everyone laughed, but didn't reply. When the cadres remembered how they themselves had chuckled at the county chief for being so wildly fanciful, they felt a twinge of guilt. Now, however, Chief Liu looked completely somber, without a trace of a smile on his face. He stood and downed his glass of liquor in a single gulp, then announced brightly,

"Given that this is true, I have a suggestion. If you agree, then down your drink as I just did. If you don't, you can just lower your glass and it will be as if today we just watched a performance and ate a meal, but didn't convene any sort of meeting afterward."

Everyone gazed intently at Chief Liu, waiting for his astonishing pronouncement.

Chief Liu said solemnly, "I suggest that to the right of the Lenin Mausoleum on Spirit Mountain, we dig out a one-room side building, which would be directly adjacent to the great hall of the mausoleum. After we purchase Lenin's corpse and bring it back, we can promote democracy by conducting an anonymous vote to see which of you made the greatest contribution toward creating the Lenin Forest Park and purchasing Lenin's corpse, and who has done the most in the service of the county's residents. This will determine who, after their death, will be buried in this side room next to Lenin, as a gesture of eternal remembrance and appreciation."

When Chief Liu finished speaking, he saw that his table of colleagues appeared flabbergasted by his proposal, and initially were at a loss as to how to respond. The room was filled with the smell of liquor and the cool summer air. The moonlight shining in through the window was blocked by the light inside the room. But from inside, it was possible to see the moon suspended in the Shuanghuai sky, like a thin and bright silk disk in the sky. As Chief Liu stood there with his empty glass watching everyone, his colleagues lifted their glasses and looked at each other. There was a sharp chill in the room. After a long pause, Chief Liu suddenly thought of something. He abruptly threw his liquor glass at the table, and as it shattered a county committee deputy secretary asked him,

"Chief Liu, is it the alcohol that is leading you to say this?"

Chief Liu replied, "I, Liu Yingque, have never been drunk."

"I agree," the deputy secretary said, and drained his glass.

With that, the entire table seemed to awaken from a dream, and one after another they each announced, "I agree," and drained their glasses.

The night was as dark as the bottom of a well. Chief Liu and his colleagues all stumbled out of the guest house and sauntered around in the moonlight. They happened to run into the Liven performers, who were hobbling around, some being led or supported by others. Having straightened up the auditorium following their debut performance and eaten their debut dinner, they were all singing Balou tunes as they made their way back to the west side of town.

They were all staying in a small village to the west of the county seat.

Chapter 5: In front of the door, a bicycle is hung from a tree

It turns out that some people in this world are born merely to perform amazing feats, and it is merely in order to perform amazing feats that they live. Others, meanwhile, live only to observe these feats, and it is through observing these feats that they are able to live an ordinary life. Take Chief Liu, for instance. In the blink of an eye, he managed to establish this performance troupe, which enjoyed such extraordinary success at its first dress rehearsal. Or take the people of this county seat, who that evening were finally able to watch the extraordinary performance for which they had been waiting for centuries.

In the days that followed, everyone in the streets and alleys of the county seat spoke of nothing other than the troupe's performance. The story of One-Legged Monkey leaping over the bed of nails quickly developed into a claim that he had leaped over a mountain of knives, and his vault across the sheet of flames became a vault over a sea of fire. As for One-Eye, his feat of threading seven to nine needles quickly grew into a claim that he could thread seventeen or nineteen needles at once. Deafman Ma's Firecracker-on-the-Ear trick originally consisted of his putting a couple of small firecrackers on each ear, but as the story circulated it gradually developed into a claim that he was using a small cannon. Paraplegic Woman's ability to embroider a cicada or grasshopper on a tung-oil leaf grew into a claim that she could embroider dragons and phoenixes. And then there were Blind Tonghua and the old deaf-mute. Their special-skills performances also became mythologized into something from another world, as though they weren't disabled mortals, but rather had become disabled precisely in order to carry out these amazing feats.

All in all, Liven's performance troupe was truly astounding, and consequently Chief Liu had them perform again in the theater, but this time for actual tickets. An adult's ticket cost five yuan, and a child's cost three. Given that in Shuanghuai tickets to a blockbuster movie cost five yuan, who could have anticipated that the Liven performance troupe, charging the same price per ticket, would sell out in an instant? The line to buy tickets stretched around the block, and became so unruly that the police had to be called in to restore order. But even after things calmed down somewhat, the ticket window remained so crowded that several dozen people ended up losing their shoes. Some people bought tickets, found their shoes, and walked away smiling. Others bought their tickets, decided they didn't want their shoes after all, and walked away barefoot, but smiling. Some children lost their shoes in the tumult, but didn't manage to get tickets, and they proceeded to stand in front of the door of the theater under the hot sun, crying and cursing:

"You fucking sun, you made us kick off our shoes."

"You fucking sun, we're burning up here, and still didn't manage to get a ticket."

By dusk, it was the police who were standing in front of the theater selling tickets. The smart people who had bought fistfuls of three-yuan tickets had already resold them for five yuan each. Those who bought fistfuls of five-yuan tickets, meanwhile, were reselling them for seven or even nine yuan each.

By the next day, ticket prices had risen to between nine and thirteen yuan each.

A day later, ticket prices reached fifteen yuan. While it is true that fifteen yuan a ticket is expensive, the auditorium was nevertheless left with only a few vacant seats.

After the third performance, the focus of the county committee and county government was quietly redirected to the Liven special-skills troupe. They not only released a statement announcing the establishment of the Shuanghuai County Special-Skills Performance Troupe, but also confirmed the appointment of an honorary troupe director, an acting troupe director, a business deputy troupe director, and a publicity officer, together with people in charge of makeup, lights, supervision, and a host of other things that do not need mentioning here. The honorary troupe director was Chief Liu, and the acting troupe director was the director of the Balou tunes opera troupe.

As for the disabled Liven performers, although they were a little nervous at the troupe's debut, by the second performance they were more relaxed, and by the third they were already completely in their element. On stage they were no different from the people who chatted and worked in front of the village, but in view of their efforts the county issued each of them one hundred yuan in compensation. The villagers happily accepted the money, talking and laughing, hopping and jumping. Some of them took the money and immediately went to buy clothes for their parents, which they then entrusted to other people to take back to Liven for them. Some bought toys to take back to their own children. The young men and women bought cigarettes and alcohol.

Huaihua, meanwhile, bought some of the lipstick and face cream that young women in the city use. One night she didn't return to sleep with the rest of the troupe, and when she appeared the next morning she claimed she had gotten lost and spent the entire night wandering around in circles until she eventually ran into Secretary Shi, who took her to the county government's guest house. She described how nice the guest house was, and said that there was running water even when you didn't need it. She also said that all these years she had wanted to marry someone in the city, a respectable wholer like Secretary Shi.

The other villagers laughed at her, and said, "Have you forgotten that you are merely a nin from Liven?"

She replied angrily, "*You're* the nin!" She claimed she was actually growing taller, and that now she was already taller than her sisters.

When the villagers measured her, it turned out that she was indeed a finger taller, and they said happily that Huaihua had begun growing just a few days after leaving Liven. If she started growing furiously, like corn during the growth season, in less than three months she could become a wholer. She continued growing until, a few days later, the performance troupe left the county seat.

The night before the troupe was scheduled to depart, Huaihua once again didn't return to sleep in her own bed, and the next day she claimed that after the performance she had gone to stay at the house of a girlfriend she had just met. Other than Yuhua, no one had ever dared to even spit in her presence, and therefore none of the residents of Liven said anything, and no one could even think of what to say. In this way, the troupe arrived to perform at Jiudu.

The first night in Jiudu was carefully planned out. It would be held on a weekend and they wouldn't sell tickets. Instead, Chief Liu would bring the county's theatrical troupe to accompany the special-skills troupe into the city, where everyone would use the goodwill of friends and family and compete to see who could give away the most tickets and invite the most prominent guests. Therefore, Chief Liu invited Secretary Niu, while others invited friends from the newspaper, radio, and television industries. Because Secretary Niu, who was most directly concerned with Shuanghuai county, came to the theater, the leaders of the various offices in the district all came out as well.

Needless to say, everyone was awestruck after watching the performance, and applause rained down from the rafters. Secretary Niu applauded so hard after every act that his hands became red and swollen. Most important, the next day the district and city newspapers devoted half an acre of newsprint to cover the performance. The newspaper, radio, and television media all declared that each and every resident of Liven was one of the top artists in the world, and that the performance troupe would certainly provide an enormous boost to Shuanghuai's economy, making it more vigorous than an eagle and more beautiful than a phoenix. As a result, the Liven performance troupe became a miraculous story, and news of it spread through the streets and alleys of the entire district. Even three-year-old toddlers knew that a disabled performance troupe had arrived in the city, and they all threw a tantrum in order to be allowed to go.

The schools canceled classes and went en masse to buy tickets and see the performance.

The factories implemented a system of rotating vacations so that each of their workers could take a day off and go watch.

The filial sons of parents who had been lying paralyzed in bed for many years carried their parents to the theater. Afterward, they returned home and complained to their parents, "You've been lying in bed half your lives—why haven't you learned to embroider on a leaf? Why is it that you can't even eat by yourselves?"

Parents with a deaf or mute child took them to watch, and afterward they had their children practice the Feeling-Words-and-Seeing-Color and Firecracker-on-the-Ear routines. As a result, the children's eardrums ruptured and started bleeding. The newspapers immediately reported this, while also devoting several columns of newsprint to warning readers that although they were welcome to enjoy the troupe's performances, they certainly shouldn't force their own disabled parents and children to attempt similar feats.

The performance troupe was a huge sensation in Jiudu, and on the fourth day, when the troupe had its first official performance for which it charged admission, the tickets were priced at forty-nine yuan each, and more than a thousand tickets were sold in less than an hour. It was like the time several decades earlier when the entire county went to Liven in search of grain, and people immediately snatched up everything they could find.

The next day, ticket prices rose to seventy-nine yuan.

By the third performance, prices had risen to a hundred yuan per ticket.

Eventually, prices stabilized at around a hundred and eighty-five yuan for a premium seat, a hundred and sixty-five yuan for a second-tier set, and a hundred and forty-five for a third-tier seat, with the average price hovering around a hundred and sixty-five yuan. These prices vastly exceeded everyone's expectations. On the black market, a one-hundred-and-eighty-five-yuan ticket could easily sell for two hundred and eighty-five yuan, while a two-hundred-and-five-yuan ticket could be resold for two hundred and sixty-five yuan. This was truly a case of a rising tide lifting all boats. The people in the city had gone mad, and it was as though everyone, adults and children alike, had suddenly gone quite mad. At the mere mention of the Shuanghuai County Special-Skills Performance Troupe, everyone would immediately throw down their rice bowls and chopsticks and start panting with excitement. Once it was reported that there was a one-legged performer who could cartwheel over a sea of fire, all the local boys started turning somersaults in the street with their backpacks, making drivers slam on the brakes. When people described how there was a paralyzed women who could embroider a leaf with an image of a bird or a cat, all the girls immediately began drawing pictures of chickens, cats, dragons, and phoenixes in their school textbooks.

Indeed, all of the city's streets and alleys were quite crazed by the troupe's performances. In the factories, there were many workers who for years hadn't been given any work and therefore hadn't been able to draw a salary, and who when the harvest season arrived wanted to return to the countryside to harvest their crops and earn enough to live on. But now they were swayed by the excitement of their neighbors, and acted as though they would have lived in vain if they were to pass up this opportunity. Therefore, they ground their teeth in anguish as they took from under their mattresses the money they had earned from collecting trash and selling recyclable paper and bottles, and then went to buy the cheapest tickets available to see the performance. There were invalids who had lain in bed for months without moving, constantly trying to calculate whether Western or Chinese medicine is cheaper, but who now took out their medicine money and went to buy a ticket to the performance, announcing that no matter how bad the illness and how good the medicine, it was not as important as their happiness. They said that as long as someone is in good spirits, all illnesses could be cured, and therefore they set aside everything and went to watch the performance.

Previously, the bus didn't stop at the Chang'an theater, but now it changed its route so that it would stop right by the front door.

When it did, the vehicle was completely packed with passengers, and consequently the end-of-month bonus awarded to the driver and the ticket seller was much higher than usual. The cars went insane, and the bicycles went insane. The entire area in front of the theater was full of bicycles belonging to people who had come to watch the performance. If someone couldn't find room to park his bike, he would simply lift it up and hang it from a tree, a wall, or even a signpost. The attendant in charge of watching the bicycles discovered that he had run out of little bamboo receipts, and therefore cut up pieces of cardboard and affixed his fingerprint or signed his name, and proceeded to use these pieces of cardboard as receipts for people parking their bikes. Then he used rope to tie together all of the bicycles that were on the ground and hanging from trees and walls.

As the bicycles were going insane, so were the electrical poles. Previously, the city would cut off electricity before midnight, and during the latter half of the night the city would sink into darkness, but now night was as bright as day. Lightbulbs quickly burned out and had to be replaced. Because the troupe performed twice each night, the streetlights needed to illuminate the way for people leaving the theater.

Having arrived in such an insane land, the troupe, though it had originally planned to perform in the Chang'an theater for only a week, ended up performing there for twice that. When it finally moved on to the next theater, the manager of the Chang'-an theater became angry and threw a drinking glass at the stage, exclaiming,

"How have I wronged you? Why do you have to leave now?"

But given that the troupe had already signed a contract with the next theater, they had no choice but to depart.

To the troupe's surprise, they discovered that theaters began competing among themselves for the right to host them, and it was said that a couple of theater managers even got into a fistfight over this. In the end, the troupe turned down theaters with air-conditioning, instead selecting ones equipped at most with electrical fans. This was because lower-quality theaters had comparatively more seats, with a capacity of up to one thousand five hundred and seventy-nine occupants, while the good theaters had a maximum capacity of only a thousand two hundred and one.

The Liven performance troupe's time in Jiudu was insane, absolutely insane—as though a single-stem and single-branch tree from deep in the Balou mountains had suddenly entered the city and within days grew tall enough to scrape the sky. It was as if sickly yellow grass growing under the awnings of a Liven house were to enter the city and, in the blink of an eye, become a luxuriant green lawn with enormous red, yellow, green, and blue blossoms.

This was all simply incomprehensible. By the time Chief Liu returned from the district to the county seat, the performance troupe had already performed thirty-three times in twenty-one days. After arriving in the county seat, Chief Liu didn't go home right away, but rather went directly to the county committee's conference room to convene a meeting of the standing committee. The conference room was on the third floor of the county committee's office building, and had an oval table and more than a dozen wooden chairs. There were several portraits of important figures hanging on the walls, together with an administrative map of the county. The walls were whitewashed, and the floor was made of rough cement. In this simple three-room meeting hall, the mid-morning sun was shining brightly in the sky while clouds were blocking the sunlight from spilling into the room. When Chief Liu opened the window, a refreshing breeze blew in, immediately cooling off the entire room. He had not napped, and instead during the entire hundred-*li* ride he had become increasingly excited by the success of the performance troupe. Now, however, he began to feel a little sleepy, so he removed his shoes, lay down on the meeting room table, and took a nap with his bare feet facing the window, his thunderous snores echoing throughout the room and shaking the maps hanging on the wall.

After a moment, the seven members of the standing committee arrived together.

Chief Liu knew that they had arrived, but he also knew that he was going to sleep a while longer, and therefore he made the standing committee wait for him in the conference room. Nearly an hour later, he was finally able to dispel his drowsiness. He woke up, rubbed his eyes, yawned, and stretched. He felt reinvigorated. Barefoot, he sat in a seat at the center of the conference table, so that everyone else had to sit on either side of him. As was his custom, before the meeting began he spent a while picking his toes. He was doing this not because his toes were swollen, but rather because the spaces between his toes itched. In front of guests who included the deputy secretary of the county committee and the deputy county leader of the standing committee, Chief Liu placidly picked his toes as everyone sat there silently.

When a leader comes to attend a meeting, he must always arrive a little late. Chief Liu, however, was never late, and in fact he would always be the first to arrive. After everyone else showed up he would sit down and get ready for the meeting, but before beginning he would pick at his toes for a while. In this way, the people at the meeting would be reminded of how talented and prestigious he was, together with the fact that they were his subordinates and needed to be deferential in his presence.

Chief Liu didn't pick at his toes for very long—just long enough for the standing committee members to steep some tea. Once he was finished, he slapped the table with both hands, making a sound like the people of Balou when they are hoeing the soil. He removed his feet from the chair in front of him, put his shoes back on, and took a sip of his tea. He laughed and said, "You must excuse me, I am disheveled, and have become a ragged wolf."[1] Then he became serious and announced solemnly, "Everyone take up your pens and notebooks, and help me make a calculation."

The standing committee members all took their pens and notebooks, and then leaned forward to begin recording.

Chief Liu said, "Everyone calculate: A premium ticket costs two hundred and fifty-five yuan, second tier costs two hundred and thirty-five, while third tier costs two hundred and five. If we assume that the tickets on average will cost two hundred and thirty-one yuan each, and if we have one performance a day, and each performance sells an average of a thousand one hundred and five tickets, how much will we earn each day? And, if we have two performances a day, then how much will we earn? Quick, help me calculate these sums."

At this point, Chief Liu paused and glanced around at the standing committee members seated around him. He saw that they were all writing down the numbers he had just given them, and were plugging them into equations. The room sounded like a classroom full of students doing their homework.

Chief Liu cleared his throat and said, "Actually, you don't need to calculate this, since I've already done the math for you. If each performance sells an average of a thousand one hundred and five tickets, and each ticket costs an average of two hundred and thirty-one yuan, then each performance will bring in two hundred fifty-five thousand, two hundred and fifty-five yuan. Fuck, let's be generous—we don't even need those five thousand, two hundred and fifty-five yuan. Even without them we would still earn two hundred and fifty thousand yuan a day, and if we have two performances a day, we would make five hundred thousand yuan. If we could raise five hundred thousand yuan a day, then in two days we could earn one million yuan, in twenty days we could earn ten million, and in two hundred days we could earn a hundred million yuan. How much money is a hundred million yuan? If we took freshly printed hundred-yuan bills and bundled them into bricks of ten thousand yuan each, then a hundred million yuan would be ten thousand of these ten-thousand-yuan cash bricks. If we stacked them up, the pile would reach the roof of this building."

When he mentioned the roof of the building, Chief Liu glanced up at the ceiling. When he looked back down, he saw that the standing committee members were also staring at the ceiling. He noticed that each face was blushed like the eastern sky at dawn and that the eyes were as bright as marbles in the sunlight. He also noticed that, since he was speaking rapidly and his mouth was opened wide, the conference table in front of him was completely covered in spittle.

The nearest deputy committee member, afraid that his face would get soaked in spittle, was leaning as far away from him as possible. Chief Liu was displeased by this and glared at him, whereupon the council member quickly pulled his chair closer, as though waiting to be showered with saliva. As if in retribution, as Chief Liu spoke he oriented himself even more toward this county member, such that all of the spittle that had originally been sprayed onto the table was now landing directly on this committee member's face. Chief Liu deliberately opened his mouth even wider and lifted his head even higher, such that the entire room, the entire building, the entire country, and even the entire world was filled with his soaring voice. It was as if it wasn't just a few county committee members who had come to the meeting, but rather all of the county's eight hundred and ten thousand residents. It was as if this were a mass meeting attended by a hundred thousand or even a million people. Chief Liu fired off his calculations, his voice roaring, resonating through the entire land.

"From this point on, Shuanghuai county will soar. If a performance troupe can earn ten million yuan in two hundred days, then in four hundred days it can earn twenty million. . . . Of course, you can't guarantee that the troupe will be able to have two performances every day. In moving from one theater to another, for instance, after having taken care of the stage sets, the lights, and other assorted hassles, they might well end up losing a day, thereby resulting in five hundred thousand yuan in lost income. Similarly, when they move from one city to another, or from one district to another, they might get sidetracked and lose several days loading the truck or riding the train, resulting in several million more yuan in lost income. Then, there is also the troupe members' salaries and bonuses to consider. Each performer should earn at least half of a hundred-yuan bill for every performance, and therefore a one-hundred-yuan bill for two performances. Accordingly, they could earn a hundred yuan a day, and three thousand yuan a month. Three thousand yuan is actually double the monthly salary of your county chief. But we should calculate these accounts carefully—if one performer earns three thousand yuan, then ten performers will earn thirty thousand, and sixty-seven performers will earn two hundred and one thousand a month. . . . If we calculate it like this, then it becomes clear that in two hundred days we actually won't earn ten million yuan. But could we earn that much in three hundred days? If we can't earn it in three hundred days, could we earn it in a year?"

This last statement was phrased as a question, but it also functioned as an assertion, reassuring everyone that they could definitely earn ten million in a year. Chief Liu excitedly stood up in his chair and began dancing like an eagle soaring through the sky.

"I'm telling you, I calculated these expenses as we were returning from Jiudu. Because all of our performers are disabled, the government doesn't collect taxes from them. If the performers don't pay taxes, every cent they earn counts as income for our county's coffers. The twenty-one days I was away, we performed thirty-three times, and as a result seven million and ten thousand yuan have already been deposited into the county coffers. Knowing this, are you still concerned that we won't earn enough to buy Lenin's corpse? Don't forget that the district government is also going to give us a large donation, but even if they didn't we still wouldn't have to worry about being able to raise this amount of money."

With this last point, Chief Liu threw up his arms, then quickly lowered them again. He leaned over to get his glass and took a sip of water, and proceeded to hop onto the county committee's conference table. The committee members were so startled by this that they pushed back from the table, but Chief Liu paid them no heed. He was, after all, the county chief, and there was no need for him to pay any attention to things like this. He stood on that long red table without looking down at the committee members sitting below him. Because he was standing tall, he could see through the window that the hallway outside the conference room was full of county committee cadres. A dark mass, they were all crowded around the conference room's doors and windows, craning their necks to watch him, like the audience at a performance of the Liven troupe. As for the people assembled outside the building, somehow everyone knew that Chief Liu had brought back good news from the district, and they gathered to hear the speech he gave at the three-story conference hall. As a result, the area in front of the door was full of cadres from the county committee and the county government, along with county-level workers.

The seventh-month sun was blazing hot. Since the ground in front of the county committee building was made of cement, after the sun shone down on it all day long it became hot enough to fry an egg. But all the people stayed, their faces covered in sweat, as they stood on their tiptoes and peered upward, trying to catch a glimpse of Chief Liu's shadow through the third-floor window and to hear his brilliant proclamation.

Chief Liu recited in a booming voice:

"I assure you that by the end of this year or the beginning of the next, Shuanghuai will no longer be the same county you know now, because by that time we will have brought back Lenin's corpse and installed it in the mausoleum in the Lenin Forest Park. At that point, thousands of tourists will come pouring in every day. Tickets will sell for a hundred yuan each, with ten people paying a thousand yuan, a hundred people paying ten thousand yuan, a thousand people paying a hundred thousand yuan, and ten thousand people paying a million yuan!"

Chief Liu stood on the conference table hollering and shouting, his voice sounding like a thunderstorm, and it left the entire building and courtyard completely soaked. He was calculating so furiously that he cracked his knuckles. As he was explaining how much money this would be, and specifically how much they would raise from admission tickets to the Lenin Park each day after they succeeded at bringing in Lenin's corpse, he paused and brought his fists to his chest, like an eagle soaring in the sky that folds its wings as it glides toward the earth. He peered down at every committee member so that each could hear his oration more clearly. For their part, the committee members leaned even farther back in their seats so as to see more clearly his gestures and facial expressions. He noticed that people in the hallway had left the door to the conference room ajar, and their faces were all pressed flat as they tried to watch him through the cracks in the door and the window. He saw that not only was the field in front of the courtyard full of people, but there were people standing along the border of the fountain in the middle of the courtyard, while some had even climbed onto the fountain itself. He saw that everyone's face was glowing with amazement, and their eyes were as bright as the sun and the moon. He raised his voice to the point that it enveloped the mountains and the clouds.

He roared: "One million a day, ten million in ten days, a hundred million in three months, and three hundred and seventy million in a year. Three hundred and seventy million—and this would be just from the sale of admissions tickets. In addition to the Lenin Mausoleum, the Lenin Forest Park will also have a Nine Dragon Cataract, a Thousand *Mu* Pine and Cypress Forest, and a Ten Thousand *Mu* Wildlife Mountain. You can climb the mountain to watch the sunrise, and come back down to see the Heavenly Lake, the Deer Looking-Back Stone, the Fairy Pond, the Cave of the Green and White Serpents, and the Hundred Herb Garden. . . . Spirit Mountain will have endless scenery for you to enjoy. If you climb the mountain to visit the Lenin Mausoleum, you will need to purchase a constant stream of admission tickets, to the point that it will even be necessary to remain up on the mountain for a night or two. This, in turn, will involve paying for a hotel room and for meals. Even a box of tissues will cost two yuan. . . . Just think, a tourist visiting the mountain will, at the very least, need to spend five hundred yuan. How much money would ten thousand tourists spend? They would give us five million yuan! And what if each of them were to spend a thousand yuan, or even thirteen or fifteen hundred yuan? And what if, during the peak tourist season in the spring, we don't have ten thousand tourists a day, but rather fifteen, twenty-five, or even thirty thousand?"

Chief Liu looked around at the cadres and spectators inside and outside the building, took a sip of water, and cleared his throat. Then, acting as though he were reaching the conclusion of a meeting, he smiled helplessly and said,

"It's such a large amount of money, I can't even calculate it. Please, help me figure out how much money Shuanghuai would earn in a year. . . . By that time, the question will not be how much money we can earn, but rather how we could possibly spend all the money that we do earn. Our primary challenge will be finding ways to spend all that money."

He once again gazed at his audience, who were all listening attentively and with bright faces. Then, he announced at the top of his voice,

"Spending the money we earn will be our most difficult challenge. Whether you are shopping or constructing buildings, how much money can you possibly spend? Even if we extend the county committee and county government buildings halfway to the sky, and build separate office buildings for each department and board committee, and even if you were to paint the walls and pave the streets in gold, the endless flow of money would continue pouring into the government's coffers, like a river of gold. How much can you possibly eat? How much can you possibly spend? Even if all of the county's peasants were to stop farming while continuing to receive a paycheck from the county every month for just sitting there, you would still end up with more money than you can spend. If you become anxious about not farming, you could plant your fields with flowers and grass, so that they would be colorful and fragrant all year round, thereby attracting more tourists. If you have more tourists, however, you will end up bringing in more money. . . . Shuanghuai will become a county in which it is ridiculously easy to make money, but excruciatingly difficult to spend it. What do you propose to do once we reach that point? What will we do? Even I, as county chief, don't know what we'll do. All I know is that if we bring back Lenin's corpse and install it in the Lenin Forest Park, we will end up with more money than we can spend—money that will be as abundant as autumn leaves on the ground. By that point, every family and every household will have so much money that their food will no longer taste fragrant, and they won't even be able to sleep at night. Each household will undergo extreme hardship in their attempts to spend the money. However, this is not my concern as county chief, but is rather an issue each of you must face, since it is a new problem encountered by Shuanghuai's revolution and reconstruction. It would take a much more capable county chief than I to solve this problem. The district or province would need to send someone down to investigate the situation for ten days to two weeks, or even three to six months, before we can hope to solve this difficult problem. . . ."

Further Reading:

1) **Ragged wolf.** DIAL. Refers to those people who, like cubs in a wolf den, don't know how to take care of themselves.

CHAPTER 7: ESTABLISHING TWO SPECIAL-SKILLS TROUPES, AND IN NO TIME AT ALL THERE IS A SHEET OF SNOW ON THE ROOF

The sun was in the western part of the sky by the time the county's standing committee meeting concluded. In the courtyard, things had already started to quiet down, and everyone departed, brimming with excitement. The offices in the buildings with electric fans all turned off their fans, and also locked their cabinets and the doors to the offices. The hallways were quiet except for the part-time workers sweeping the floor and emptying the trash. At this point, Chief Liu—stepping carefully as though he were walking on cotton—emerged from his office.

He had to return home—he had to go to his Hall of Devotion.[1] He had to return home and sleep with his wife.

It had been ever so long since he had been home and entered his Hall of Devotion.

Given the success of the Liven troupe's performances, and given that he had just been talking nonstop at the standing committee meeting, Chief Liu felt exhausted. He returned to his office and, after sending out Secretary Shi and the other office workers, sat there for a while drinking water. He savored the memory of the excitement

206

of his speech, together with the anticipation of each segment of the preparations for purchasing Lenin's corpse. Eventually, as the setting sun passed his window like a silk disk silently being pulled away, he began to rest from his excitement and fatigue.

The sky outside the window was overcast, and the streets were now quiet. He could vaguely see and hear the bats flying around in front of the buildings as they waited for dusk. It occurred to him that it had been almost two months since he'd last returned home. At the time, he had told his wife in a fit of anger that he wouldn't be back for three months. But that, after all, had been said merely in anger. How could he have really meant that he wouldn't come home? He would go back to check on things, and retreat to his Hall of Devotion and offer a prayer for his efforts over the preceding two months to establish the performance troupe and take it on tour. Then, he would have dinner, watch some television, and sleep with his wife.

He thought dispassionately about enlivening with his wife.

It occurred to him that it had been several months since he had enlivened with her. He was like a child craving a candy, but who can't bring himself to eat it and therefore hides it somewhere and forgets about it. Therefore, with a smile, Chief Liu got up from the stool, drank the rest of his water, and headed home.

But then, but then . . . in a coincidence like the kind you find in operas, just as he was opening the door to leave he happened to run into the one person he least wanted to see. This was Liven's Grandma Mao Zhi, who was leaning on her dusty crutch in his doorway and holding a bundle. He stared at her in dismay. He knew the reason she was waiting there was that she wanted to discuss the prospect of allowing Liven to withdraw from society. He realized that a month earlier he had written her a document agreeing that in ten days or two weeks he would go to the county seat to take care of the relevant paperwork. His desire to return home and enliven with his wife immediately faded, as though he had had a bucket of cold water poured over his head. Nevertheless, he merely smiled and said with surprise, "Oh, Grandma Mao Zhi, please come in."

Grandma Mao Zhi walked into the office. The office was not entirely unfamiliar to her. In the *renchen* year, she and her stonemason husband first arrived in this courtyard looking for that county clerk from the Fourth Red Army to help Liven enter society, and ever since her husband passed away in the *gengzi* year, she'd never stopped wanting to return to this courtyard to get Chief Liu and the Party secretary to help her arrange for Liven to withdraw from society. She had been struggling for more than thirty years to withdraw from society, and during that time the county committee had exchanged its red-tiled building for office buildings, but these office buildings were dilapidated and run-down. The county committee's building was so brightly illuminated that people cast shadows on the cement floor, which was so worn away that it was full of holes, and the whitewash on the walls had already begun to turn yellow and peel off. There was an electric light hanging from the ceiling, and when she first saw the room more than a decade earlier, it had been as white as snow, but now it was covered with cobwebs. Even when the light was turned on it didn't seem very bright, given that two of the fluorescent bulbs had already burned out, though the middle one still worked.

Grandma Mao Zhi walked in and looked around. Eventually, her gaze came to rest on the Shuanghuai county map on the wall next to Chief Liu's desk. Then she took the note that Chief Liu had written urging that Liven be permitted to withdraw from the jurisdiction of Shuanghuai county and Boshuzi township, and placed it on the desk. She said, "I've been waiting here for you for two weeks now. I hear that you took the people of Liven to perform at the district seat. Did the performance go well?"

Chief Liu smiled and said,

"Guess how much each villager can earn each month."

Mao Zhi placed her bundle on the ground, then sat down in front of Chief Liu and said,

"I don't care how much they can earn. I've come to get our paperwork signed."

Chief Liu took the document he had written and glanced at it, then said,

"Each of them can earn two to three thousand yuan a month. With two thousand yuan you can build a large tile-roofed house. After performing for three months, each of them could return to Liven and build a house."

Mao Zhi picked up the bundle and hugged it to her chest, as though she were afraid someone might steal it. Then, she looked disdainfully at Chief Liu and said,

"You can give me your empty words if you like; I've come to fill out the forms permitting us to withdraw from society."

Chief Liu straightened his neck and said,

"Really, everyone who watches the Liven troupe perform goes crazy. Every performance is completely packed. If you were to join the troupe, I guarantee that you would also earn two or three thousand yuan a month."

Mao Zhi again waved the blue bundle she was holding, and replied, "I won't go."

Chief Liu asked, "How about if I were to offer you five thousand yuan?"

Mao Zhi replied, "I wouldn't join even if you gave me ten thousand yuan."

Chief Liu asked, "Are those your burial clothes you are carrying in that bundle?"

Mao Zhi replied, "I thought about it, and eventually decided that if you don't sign the documents authorizing us to withdraw from society, I'll put on these clothes and die right in your house or office."

Chief Liu replied seriously,

"We just convened a standing committee meeting to discuss the issue. The committee members all agree with me that between the end of this year and the beginning of the next, we should definitely allow Liven to withdraw from Shuanghuai county and Boshuzi township. As of the first day of next year, Liven will no longer fall under their jurisdiction."

Mao Zhi just gazed at Chief Liu, looking as though she couldn't believe her ears. Then she quickly asked, "Chief Liu, you won't change your mind?"

Chief Liu replied, "I have always been a man of my word."

She asked, "Today it is already dark, but tomorrow could you fill out the paperwork so that I can take home a copy?"

Chief Liu said, "In the next official document that we send to the county committee and county bureau, as well as to each of the township and village committees, I will print the forms and include them. Today, however, one of the members of the standing committee raised a question."

Grandma Mao Zhi stared at him intently.

Chief Liu said, "The committee member suggested a condition. He pointed out that there are a hundred and sixty-nine disabled villagers in Liven, but that we are only using sixty-seven of them for the current troupe. Liven, therefore, could actually establish a second troupe—having other deaf people practice the Firecracker-on-the-Ear routine or something of the sort, other cripples learn the Leaping-Over-a-Mountain-of-Knives-and-Crossing-a-Sea-of-Fire routine, and other blind people learn the Acute-Listening routine. The member of the standing committee said that as long as you establish a second performance troupe, then by the end of the year the county would be sure to send down an official document, and by the beginning of next year you would no longer belong to Shuanghuai county or Boshuzi township. You would be completely free. Neither earth nor the heavens would pay you any mind, and all of you could enjoy your heavenly days."

Having said this, Chief Liu stared intently at Grandma Mao Zhi. They were separated by only a few feet of table. The sun had already begun to set in the west, and dusk began to fall. Bats continued to fly around outside. It had become a little darker in the room, but Chief Liu could clearly see the corner of Grandma Mao Zhi's mouth twitching anxiously. Her original bright but skeptical expression had been replaced by a pallor that blended in with the dusk.

Chief Liu said, "The county committee and the county government are both acting in Liven's best interests. If you establish two performance troupes and recruit someone from every household, then by the end of the year every household in the village will be earning a high salary. By next year, each family will be able to build themselves a tile-roofed house. By that point, the entire village will be a sea of red-tile roofs and snow-white walls."

Chief Liu added, "But think about it. If you withdraw from society next year, then Liven won't have its own seal, and each family won't have its own residence permit booklet. They would be living in today's world, while at the same time not even belonging to this world. If you wish to go to the market you could certainly do so, but without a seal you won't have any letters of introduction, and without letters of introduction you won't be able to go out on business, and you certainly won't be able to have the two special-skills performance troupes tour under the name of Shuanghuai county."

Chief Liu said, "Consider this carefully, and if you agree, then we can sign a contract right here and now. If you agree to establish another performance troupe for the county, and have these two troupes perform until the end of the year, then I guarantee that each performer will earn at least three thousand yuan a month, and that at the end of the year I will send out a document stating that as of the beginning of next year Liven will be completely independent of Boshuzi township and Shuanghuai county."

Chief Liu concluded, "From Liberation up to the present day, Shuanghuai county has had seven county chiefs and nine Party secretaries. You have spent the past thirty-seven years trying to withdraw from society, and I have just agreed to all of your requests."

He added, "If I help you, you should also help me. Everything has its own complement. If you agree to establish a second performance troupe, I agree that as of the beginning of next year, Liven will be permitted to withdraw from society. This is a perfectly reasonable arrangement, and should be mutually agreeable to both parties."

He asked, "Do you agree? It is almost dark."

He continued, "Please consider this carefully. This is something I would like to do for Liven before it withdraws from society. Once I have purchased Lenin's corpse from Russia and installed it at Spirit

Mountain, the county won't have to worry about not having enough money, and instead will merely worry about not being able to spend all of the money. By that point, however, Liven may well become so poor that you won't even have enough money to buy salt or vinegar. The question then would be how to rejoin the district and the county. Therefore, you should establish a second performance troupe, so that every household in Liven can earn a lot of money. In that way, you will not only be helping me, you will also at the same time be helping yourself and Liven."

He continued, "So, please consider carefully. You should give me an answer by the time I leave for work tomorrow."

He added, "Look, the sun has already set. Where are you staying? I'll have someone escort you back, and arrange for your meals and lodging."

He said, "Go. You should go now."

As he was saying this, he stood up. Through the window, the sun obeyed his order and fully slipped behind the wall of the building. The lights in the room seemed to brighten. At this point, Grandma Mao Zhi just looked at Chief Liu, and then placed her bundle of burial clothes next to one of the legs of the chair. The corner of her black silk burial gown was sticking out of an opening in the bundle, and because the gown had a bright yellow silk border, it looked like a blooming black funerary flower with a yellow stamen.

Chief Liu gazed at the black flower.

Grandma Mao Zhi asked, "How many more people would we need to recruit to go touring with the second troupe?"

Chief Liu looked up from the black funerary flower and said,

"If we are speaking of blind, deaf, crippled, and paraplegic villagers, then thirty to fifty more would be enough."

Grandma Mao Zhi said, "But what if they don't have any special skills?

Chief Liu laughed lightly. "As long as they have something, it'll be fine."

Grandma Mao Zhi raised her voice and said,

"In that case, I'll pick out a few for you, but you must put what you said today into writing and stamp it with the official county committee and county government stamps, together with your own fingerprint. Regardless of whether or not you ultimately succeed in purchasing Lenin's corpse and bringing it back, the people of Liven will only perform until the end of the year. As of the beginning of next year, we will no longer fall under the county's and the district's jurisdiction. Also, no matter what, you must give each Liven performer a monthly salary of three thousand yuan."

In this way, they quickly reached an agreement. Grandma Mao Zhi had no reason not to agree, so she simply acceded to all of Chief Liu's conditions. Chief Liu also agreed to everything Grandma Mao Zhi asked for.

All of the lights in the building had gone dark, and even the cleaning staff had disappeared, but Chief Liu opened the door to his office and shouted into the hallway, "Is anyone there?" With this, someone suddenly appeared out of nowhere, and Chief Liu instructed him to tell the people remaining to immediately drop their rice bowls and come running to his office. In this way, Grandma Mao Zhi managed in a single night to sign a contract with the county committee, the county government, and Chief Liu, who was in charge of overseeing all of the county's work. Each clause in the contract was clearly written, and every word was legally binding.

The two-page contract read as follows:

Party A: The village of Liven, deep in the Balou mountains.

Party B: The Shuanghuai county committee and county government.

 For historical reasons, over the past several decades the village of Liven has been requesting permission to be allowed to withdraw from society and return to the so-called free and enlivened existence that it formerly enjoyed. With the mutual agreement of both parties, therefore, the county committee and county government have reached the following agreement with respect to Liven's proposed withdrawal from society:

1) *Liven must establish two special-skills performance troupes, known as the First and Second Shuanghuai County Special-Skills Performance Troupes, respectively, and each troupe must have at least fifty performers. The first of these troupes has already been established, and the second must be established within ten days.*

2) *The two troupes' administrative and performance rights will be controlled by Shuanghuai county. Shuanghuai, furthermore, will guarantee that each Liven performer will earn at least three thousand yuan a month in salary.*

3) *The two troupes will perform only until the final day of this lunar year, which is to say the thirtieth day of the twelfth month. After that point, the troupes will no longer have any administrative or economic relationship with Shuanghuai county.*

4) *As of the final day of this year, Liven will no longer fall under the administrative jurisdiction of Shuanghuai county and Boshuzi township, but rather it will once again become an independent village. All of the village's people, plants, rivers, territory, and other aspects will thereby have no relation to the county or district. Similarly, no one from the county or district shall interfere with any of the village's affairs. But if Liven were to experience a natural disaster, Shuanghuai county and Boshuzi township would still have a responsibility to offer uncompensated assistance.*

5) *As the final date specified in the performance troupes' contracts approaches, the county must, before the end*

of the year, submit the formal document affirming that
"Liven will no longer fall under the jurisdiction of any
county or township" to each department and board com-
mittee in the county, as well as to the township govern-
ment and every village committee in the entire county.

Naturally, the final page of the agreement contained the bright red seal of the county committee and county government, together with the signatures of both Grandma Mao Zhi and Chief Liu, in their respective capacities as the representatives of the two parties. Not only did they both sign the document, but furthermore Chief Liu, at Grandma Mao Zhi's urging, placed his private seal and his fingerprint below his signature, and Mao Zhi added her own fingerprint. In this way, the last white page of the document was marked with a red seal, looking as the snowcapped mountains of Balou might if they were abloom with red roses.

After everything was filled out and Grandma Mao Zhi had been accompanied back to the county guest house to rest, it was agreed that the next day she would be escorted back to Liven, where she would establish the second performance troupe. Given that the number of troupes had been doubled, the amount of time needed to raise enough money to purchase Lenin's corpse would be cut in half. As a result, it was now projected that by the end of the year Shuanghuai county would be able to purchase Lenin's corpse and install it on Spirit Mountain.

With everything arranged satisfactorily, Chief Liu had no choice but to retreat to his Hall of Devotion.

CHAPTER 9: FURTHER READING— HALL OF DEVOTION

1) **Hall of Devotion.** *Also known as a Divine Hall. To explain the origins of this term, we must go back to the* xinchou *and* renyin *years, or 1961 and 1962—the period of famine and natural disaster when the infant Liu Yingque was left abandoned in front of the soc-school. Liu Yingque ended up becoming the adopted son of Teacher Liu at the soc-school, and in the process truly became a child of the soc-school—which is to say, a soc-school babe. At mealtimes he would carry his rice bowl to the canteen, and at class times he would carry his stool into the classroom along with the other cadres and Party members. He would listen as the teacher read aloud from official documents, newspapers, or editorials. He would glance through large books written by national leaders. Some of the Party members and cadres would smoke or doze off in class, but Liu Yingque would always listen attentively as the teacher lectured and read aloud. He would watch as his adopted father carefully wrote one line of block letters after another on the blackboard.*

Given that this was a soc-school, the lessons naturally all concerned Great Man theory, addressing topics such as Marxist-Leninist economics, politics, and philosophy. Yingque didn't understand Great Man theory, but as he listened he gradually learned to read and write, and before he turned ten he was able to make his way through an entire newspaper article. After the teacher's wife ran away with a cadre from a neighboring county when

Liu Yingque was twelve, he was formally promoted from the status of soc-school babe to that of the teacher's adopted son, whereupon he began his formal studies.

However, it was precisely around this time that the unprecedented Cultural Revolution began. The Cultural Revolution regarded this teacher at this rural soc-school as a rich peasant, and therefore a class enemy—an enemy who spent every day on stage reading from great books. A notice bearing the county committee red seal arrived at the soc-school, which relieved Teacher Liu of his teaching duties and assigned him to sweep the floor and watch the school gate. Teacher Liu fell into a depression, and constantly needed to take Chinese medicine.

One day several years later—when Yingque was sixteen, his sister was nine, and Teacher Liu was fifty-six—Teacher Liu suddenly began to feel chest pains. He lay down in bed, his head covered in sweat and his sheets completely soaked. This happened to be the period of the fall harvest, and the school was in intersession. All of the cadres had returned home, and Yingque's sister, Liu Xu, had gone to visit a classmate in the city, so the only people left at the school were Yingque and his foster father. It was muggy, the tree leaves were drooping in a sickly manner, and the cries of the cicadas were as long as a whip. Squatting down in front of his bed, Teacher Liu grasped his shirt, then repeatedly pounded his chest, his face completely pale. At this point, Yingque returned home and shouted, Father, Father! He was prepared to run to the county hospital with his foster father in his arms.

Teacher Liu waved him away. He examined Yingque for a moment, then said, Yingque, you are sixteen and already are taller than I. If I entrust your sister, Liu Xu, to you, would you be able to raise her?

Liu Yingque suddenly realized the severity of the situation, and nodded solemnly. What his father said next, however, left Yingque completely bewildered. Teacher Liu asked if Yingque was willing to look after Liu Xu for the rest of her life. He explained, I'm concerned that once she grows up she will come to resemble her mother, becoming skittish and unreliable. But you, ever since you were young, have grown up in the soc-school, and by the age of thirteen you could fill out the school's examination booklets as well as the cadres themselves. I am convinced that you will go on to have great success in life. If you do, then your sister won't end up like her mother. Her

217

mother resented my lack of success, and because of it ran off with someone else. If you have success, and are willing to marry your step-sister, then I will die content. I will know that it wasn't in vain that I took care of you and Liu Xu for the past ten years. When Yingque's foster father reached this point, a tear appeared in his eye—though it was unclear whether this tear appeared because he was suffering from chest pain, or because he was struck by the tragedy of human existence. His face was pale and sallow, and as the tear ran down his cheek, it was as if it were rolling down a creased piece of paper.

As Yingque gazed at his foster father, he nodded and asked, But what kind of success can I achieve?

The school courtyard was completely silent. The sound of the crows in the trees outside the door echoed through the darkness. When Yingque nodded, his foster father smiled, as though a thin beam of fluorescent lights had been illuminated in the summer night. Then, his father edged over to the side of the bed, sat up, and wiped the sweat from his brow. He took Yingque's hand and placed a key in his palm, saying, Use this to open the door on the east side of the school warehouse. Once you go look at that room, you will be guaranteed to have success in life. You will know what you need to do. Whether you have modest or great success will depend on you, on fate, and on luck, but if you visit that room, then even if you only go on to become a commune secretary, I will feel that I've done all that I could to help you achieve success. After having been addressed as "teacher" by cadres my entire life, I will feel that I succeeded in raising my son to enter the government and become a cadre.

Yingque gripped that sweat-covered key and stood in front of his father's divine[1] bed, as though he had suddenly found a road to a holy place but didn't dare take the first step.

His foster father said, My entire life earnings are in that warehouse. Go look, and after you see it you will strive for success your entire life.

In his father's bedroom, Liu Yingque could barely see anything, but at the same time it was as if he could see a path through the darkness, and a flickering light. The sun was bright outside, lighting up all corners of the soc-school. As Yingque entered through the school gate and crossed the courtyard, then arrived at that storage room on the east side of the school, he didn't have any idea what he would find inside. He opened the door, quietly went over to the easternmost warehouse, then stopped and pulled himself together. He unlocked the door and opened it, and the first thing he saw was that the sunlight that had been shining on the outer wall now poured into the dark room.

It turned out that this was also a storage room, the only difference being that while the other three rooms were full of the school's bikes, cart wheels, old ladders, old blackboards, stools, chairs, and desks, together with the pots, bowls, chopsticks, and serving dishes that the Party officials and cadres left behind when they were not at the school, in this particular storage room there weren't any of those sorts of random objects. Instead, the room was full of the school's textbooks and other documents. This room was in fact like a large library or a book depository, except that the books were not arranged on shelves; they were all piled high on a round table against the wall. The walls of the room were covered with old newspapers, and the ground was paved with bricks, while the ceiling was made from thatched straw. The room had a strong mildew odor. Liu Yingque stood in the doorway, looking as though he had taken a wrong turn. Initially he didn't notice anything different about this room—didn't see anything that would guarantee him success in life, as his foster father had promised.

The room was extraordinarily quiet, but it was into this silence that Yingque walked. He first looked at the tables, and noticed that the arrangement of books on each table was actually completely different from what you would find in a library or reference room. Each author's works were grouped together and arranged into piles. The first level covered half the table, the second level was positioned two inches back, the third level two inches beyond that, up to the top level, which was like the top of a tower, with only a few volumes arranged there. Because this was a soc-school, the books were not recreational novels; rather, they were all on politics, economics, or philosophy. There was a complete clothbound set of Marx's and Engels's collected works, together with individual volumes of their respective titles. There were the complete works of Lenin and Stalin, and also works by Hegel,[3] Kant,[5] Feuerbach,[7] Saint-Simon,[9] Fourier,[11] Ho Chi Minh,[13] Dimitrov,[15] Tito,[17] Kim Il Sung,[19] and so forth. There were multiple copies of some titles, such as The Communist Manifesto, Capital, Discourse on Surplus Value, and

Lenin's Complete Works, *but there were also single copies of some titles, such as Holbach's*[21] Christianity Has Been Exposed, *Feuerbach's* Future Philosophy, *Locke's*[23] Essay Concerning Human Understanding, *and Adam Smith's*[25] The Wealth of Nations.

There was one particular volume amid that enormous pile of books, like a leaf in the middle of a forest. This was a volume that Yingque's foster father had pulled out from the pile and placed on top, so that it now stuck out. Needless to say, the majority of books in the room were by Mao Zedong and included the four-volume set of his Collected Works, *together with his* Collected Sayings, *also known as his "Little Red Book," of which there were at the very least several hundred, or even several thousand, copies. Chairman Mao's books alone took up three of the eight tables in the room and were arranged into piles, with each progressively higher pile being only an inch behind the preceding one, such that the final pile nearly touched the ceiling.*

Of course, if the books had been merely arranged into piles then Teacher Liu, who had spent half his life teaching in a soc-school and the other half working in the fields, could hardly have claimed that this represented the sum of his life's achievements. Yingque looked over the first table, and saw that the books in the first pile were all by Marx, those in the second pile were all by Engels, and those in the third were all by Lenin. The fourth pile was all by Stalin, the fifth all by Mao Zedong, the sixth all by Dimitrov, the seventh all by Ho Chi Minh, the eighth all by Tito, and after that there were books by Hegel, Kant, and Feuerbach. He noticed that following this order, between the pages of the book at the top of each pile, there was a sheet of paper. He removed the paper from the volume at the top of the pile of Marx's books, and saw that it contained a drawing of a pile of books, each of which carried a caption.

The caption on the first row read: Marx was born in the wuyin *Year of the Tiger, in the Prussian city of Trier.*

The second row read: In the gengyin *year of the Tiger, when Marx was eleven, he and his family moved to Trier's Wilhelm Center.*

The third row read: In the yiwei *Year of the Goat, when Marx was seventeen, he enrolled in law school at the University of Bonn, and joined the Hegelian "Doctoral Club."*

The fourth row read: In the renyin *Year of the Tiger, when Marx turned twenty-three, he wrote his first thesis, "On Prussian Censorship," and became the editor of the* Rheinische Post. *The following year, he married Jenny von Westphalen.*

The seventh row read: In the yisi *Year of the Serpent, when Marx was twenty-seven, he was expelled from France and relocated to Brussels.*

The seventeenth row read: In the renxu *Year of the Dog, when Marx was forty-three, he began writing* Capital.

The thirtieth row read: In the guiwei *Year of the Goat, when Marx was seventy-three, he passed away between the second and third solar terms, having become one of the great leaders of the world proletarian revolution.*

Yingque removed the sheet of paper from the pile of Engels's books.

He removed the sheet from the pile of Stalin's books.

He removed the sheet from the pile of Chairman Mao's books. . . .

Yingque noticed that in the first stack of books from Engels's pile, there was a sheet of paper that said Engels was born in the guichen *Year of the Dragon* to a small capitalist family in Barmen, on the Rhine. Below this, there was a line drawn in red pencil.

He noticed that in the first stack of Lenin's books there was a sheet of paper saying that Lenin was born in the gengwu *Year of the Horse* to an ordinary working-class family; below this there was a red line. He noticed that the paper from the thirty-fifth stack said that in the dingsi *Year of the Serpent*, the Soviet Union's October Revolution succeeded and the forty-seven-year-old Lenin became the general secretary of the Soviet Union's Communist Party; below this there appeared two red lines.

Yingque noticed that at the bottom of the Stalin pile, there was a sheet of paper that said that in the jimao *Year of the Hare*, Stalin was born to a poor family in Georgia. His parents were both serfs, and the entire family relied on income from the father's work as a cobbler. Below this there were three red lines. On the top level of the pile, it said that in the jiazi *Year of the Rat*, which is to say in the thirteenth *Year of the Republic*, Lenin passed away from illness, and Stalin become the general secretary of the Soviet Union's Communist Party. Below this there were three red lines.

Yingque noticed that in the bottom level of the Mao Zedong pile, there was a sheet of paper that said that in the guisi *Year of the Serpent*,

Chairman Mao was born to a peasant family in Shaoshan. Below this there were two red lines. On the ninth level, it said that in the dingmao Year of the Hare, Chiang Kai-Shek initiated a counterrevolutionary coup d'état, and the entire country was engulfed in a White Terror. The Communist Party held its First Party Congress in Hankou, where Mao Zedong was elected as an alternate member of the Central Political Bureau. Below this there were two red lines. On the tenth level the paper contained the two words "Autumn Uprising," below which there were three red lines. In the yiyou year, Chairman Mao had just turned fifty-one, and at the Zunyi Conference he confirmed his status as the key leader. Below this, there were five red lines. From the top level the paper said that in the renzi year Mao was named chairman of the Party, chairman of the nation, and chairman of the armed forces. Below this, there were nine red lines.

The final pile contained works by a variety of authors. From the top stack Yingque removed another sheet of paper, on which there also appeared several dozen rows. These rows, however, didn't contain the names and birth dates of important figures, as did the other papers, but rather had been left blank—as barren as a field after the autumn harvest. Yingque didn't know what his foster father had been planning to put in these empty rows. The entries in each row were fairly unremarkable, with the first containing only the innocuous words "commune messenger."

The second row said "soc-school employee."

The third row said "national cadre," the fifth said "commune secretary," the eighth said "deputy county chief," and the ninth said "county chief." Below this were merely empty rows without any text. In particular, there didn't appear a row for district commissioner or for provincial chief. Perhaps Yingque's foster father thought the county chief was an almost celestial position, and if you were appointed county chief, that was all you needed. Perhaps he thought the county chief was already like an emperor and there wasn't any need to continue moving up the chain of command, and this was why the lines after that of the county chief were left blank. Yingque counted carefully, and found that there were an additional nineteen blank rows. The nineteenth was the final one, and it should have contained a title such as "chairman of the Party," "chair of the nation," or "chair of the armed forces," but instead it was simply blank. Although these nineteen rows were not filled in, each nevertheless had one or more red lines beneath it, and the final row contained so many red lines that it became a solid block of red.

What else did he see in that room? Nothing. Only books, piles of books, and sheets of paper wedged into those piles. Each sheet was marked with graph squares, in which were written the birth date and accomplishments of a famous leader. There were also the red underlinings, which were more numerous when the person in question had humble origins, and were particularly numerous when underscoring the extraordinary achievements he would subsequently come to attain.

What else did Yingque discover? There really wasn't anything else. As he gazed at those piles of books, and at those sheets of papers filled with the biographies of important leaders, it was as if he already knew about those books, those people, and those events—as if he had already heard about all of them in the soc-school classroom. The only thing that came as a surprise to him was that such a great man as Engels came from a capitalist family. He hadn't expected that the child of a capitalist family would dedicate his life to speaking and working on behalf of poor workers. He also hadn't expected that Lenin would have come from an ordinary working family, nor that the family of such a great man would be as ordinary as a solitary tree in a mountain forest. He was surprised to learn that Stalin came from a family of serfs, and that his father was a cobbler. He was surprised to learn that the son of a cobbler would go on to become someone whom the entire world would view with amazement. He was further surprised to learn that Chairman Mao, who ultimately became greater than everyone else, came from a family of peasants who worked in the fields for a living.

Yingque sat quietly in that room, as sunlight shone in through the door and windows, and for the longest time he gazed silently at those piles of books and at the biographies and red lines on those sheets of paper. It was if he had finally realized what his foster father had meant when he said that once Yingque saw this, he would strive for greatness. At the same time, however, it was also as if he hadn't discovered anything at all, but instead had just felt a breeze blowing past his face—which would disappear without a trace. He struggled to remember what he had gained from that breeze, and quietly pondered this until he heard a dull thud coming from the school courtyard.

It was like a dead tree suddenly toppling over.

It was like a large sack of cotton or bran falling to the ground

Yingque paused for a moment, then ran out of the room. He flew across the quiet courtyard, not stopping until he arrived in front of the main gate.

It was his foster father who had fallen out of bed.

His father had died.

Before dying, he had gripped the front of his own shirt tightly with both hands.

Yingque's foster father was the school's oldest teacher, and even the county chief and the secretary had studied under him at the soc-school. The day Yingque buried his foster father, the county chief came and said that three days earlier he had received a letter from him, saying that Teacher Liu had struggled his entire life to instill Marxist-Leninist theory in all of the county's cadres and Party members, and now was asking the county chief to help his daughter finish her studies, and to help his son, Liu Yingque, secure a job, ideally in his old home in the Boshuzi commune. But Yingque was still young, so perhaps it would be best to appoint him as a messenger, the letter added, so that in another couple of years he could go to the countryside to carry out socialist education. If he did well, he could then be made a cadre.

The county therefore arranged to have him sent to the Boshuzi commune, to work as a messenger.

At that point, the young Liu Yingque finally understood why his foster father had drawn those charts without titles—it had been in order to plan out a chart of Yingque's own future. His father had been so optimistic about Yingque's prospects that he'd placed Yingque's life chart alongside those of great men. He had used those red lines to remind Yingque that great men started out as ordinary people, and that as long as he worked hard and struggled, he could become a great man like them.

The day that Yingque left the soc-school and went to the Boshuzi commune, he returned to that book room and pulled out all of those sheets of paper wedged between those piles of books. He took particular note of the sheet that had "commune messenger" on its bottom row, while the second row said "soc-school member," the fifth row said "commune secretary," the ninth said "county chief," and the tenth through the nineteenth rows had all been left blank.

As he gazed at that chart, his heart began to pound. He felt a surge of energy coursing from the soles of his feet up though his bones and his viscera. At that instant, the memory of his foster father's death swept over him; it was as if the sun had suddenly emerged and shone on everything before him, making him feel as though he had now grown up, as if sixteen was even older than twenty-six. He felt that his foster father's death had opened up a door for him, and that as he walked out through that door, he was stepping onto a road leading directly to heaven.

So, he went to work in the Boshuzi commune as a messenger boy, delivering newspapers and mail, boiling water, and sweeping the grounds.

Ten years later, the day that he was appointed commune secretary, when he felt as powerful as an emperor, he requested an extra room in the commune guest house and proceeded to set it up as a precise replica of the book room his foster father had created in the commune. On the wall, he hung portraits of the ten great international leaders, including Marx, Engels, Lenin, Stalin, Chairman Mao, Tito, Ho Chi Minh, and Kim Il Sung, and below them he hung portraits of ten great Chinese military leaders: Zhu De, Chen Yi, Jia Long, Liu Bocheng, Lin Biao, Peng Dehuai, Yi Jianying, Xu Xiangqian, Luo Ronghuan, and Nie Rongzhen. Below those portraits there were charts containing the biographies and professional accomplishments of each individual. On the wall in front of this double row of twenty portraits, there was an enlarged and framed portrait of his foster father. Right next to the frame there was a sheet of graph paper as big as the frame and with nineteen rows. The bottom row was filled with writing: Liu Yingque, born in Shuanghuai county in the gengzi year of the famine. When he was one year old, his parents abandoned him in a field. His foster father was a teacher at the Shuanghuai county soc-school. Yingque was bright and precocious, and could already read a newspaper and write a letter before even having started school. He even had a general grasp of Marxist-Leninist theory.

The second level had two rows of text: In the yimao Year of the Hare, when Liu Yingque was sixteen, his foster father passed away. Yingque's life

plans thus became difficult, and he began working for the Revolution, work-
ing as a messenger for the Boshuzi commune.

The third level said: In the gengshen Year of the Monkey, when Liu
Yingque turned twenty-one, he officially became a national cadre, and was
named the most advanced soc-school worker in the county.

The fifth level said: In the wuchen Year of the Dragon, when Liu
Yingque turned twenty-nine, he was appointed Party secretary of Liulin
township, and was the top fund-raiser in the county.

Beginning with the sixth level, up to the top, all of the rows had been
left blank, waiting for the future.

In this room decorated with the portraits of great men and charts
detailing their biographies and accomplishments, there was also his foster
father's portrait, together with a chart detailing Liu Yingque's biography.
This room had followed Liu Yingque throughout his various promotions, as
he was relocated from the township to the town, and from the town to this
pair of rooms on the south side of the courtyard of the Shuanghuai county
committee and county government building. This pair of rooms was very
solemn and sacred, and therefore Liu Yingque, in his heart, regarded it as
a Hall of Devotion.

Further, Further Reading:

1) **Divine.** *Sacred and dignified.*

3) **Hegel.** *Georg Wilhelm Friedrich Hegel, German philosopher*
(1770–1831).

5) **Kant.** *Immanuel Kant, German philosopher, founder of philosophical*
idealism (1724–1804).

7) **Feuerbach.** *Ludwig Andreas von Feuerbach, German materialist phi-*
losopher (1804–1872).

9) **Saint-Simon.** *Henri de Saint-Simon, French socialist visionary*
(1760–1825).

*11) **Fourier.** François Marie Charles Fourier, French socialist visionary (1772–1837).*

*13) **Ho Chi Minh.** Chairman of the People's Republic of Vietnam (1890–1969).*

*15) **Dimitrov.** Georgi Dimitrov, Communist secretary and chairman of the Council of Ministers of Socialist Bulgaria (1882–1949).*

*17) **Tito.** Josip Broz Tito, Premier of the Communist Party of Socialist Yugoslavia (1892–1980).*

*19) **Kim Il Sung.** Premier of the Communist Party of Socialist Democratic North Korea (1912–1994).*

*21) **Holbach.** Paul Holbach, French materialist philosopher and atheist (1723–1789).*

*23) **Locke.** John Locke, English philosopher and political theorist (1632–1704).*

*25) **Adam Smith.** English capitalist economist, and the founder of the discipline of traditional political economy (1723–1790).*

CHAPTER 11: FACING A ROW OF GREAT MEN'S PORTRAITS, AND WITH THE PORTRAIT OF HIS FOSTER FATHER BEHIND HIM

Whenever Chief Liu had a major success, he naturally wanted to retreat to his Hall of Devotion.

The night had already begun to enter its darkest hour. The moon was gone, the stars were barely visible, and clouds enveloped the county seat like fog. It seemed as if it was about to rain. The dense humidity surrounded Chief Liu like a wall of moisture. A few of the streetlights were lit, but most of them were dark—either because the bulbs were burned out or because the electrical line had been cut. Although the Shuanghuai county seat was bigger than before, and although Chief Liu, after assuming office, borrowed a bit of money from his Lenin Fund to expand some of the roads and add some more intersections, the city still appeared as run-down and dilapidated as before. Only the new road in front of the entrance to the county committee and county government building had all its streetlights illuminated.

Chief Liu, however, didn't want to walk along that new street, as there were likely to be many old people and children out enjoying the evening. Of those people, there wouldn't be any who wouldn't recognize their county chief, just as after the Cultural Revolution broke out in the *bingwu* Year of the Horse everyone throughout the land knew who Chairman Mao was. Ever since Liu Yingque was appointed Shuanghuai county chief, and resolved to purchase Lenin's corpse and establish the Spirit Mountain Forest Park and Lenin Mausoleum—from that point on there wasn't a single child in the city's back alleyways who didn't know what he looked like. As he said in a document that he wrote out by hand and sent to all eight hundred and ten thousand residents of the county, as long as he was able to purchase Lenin's corpse and install it on Spirit Mountain, Shuanghuai county would become so rich that its peasants wouldn't need to pay to see the doctor or to get on the bus to go the market in town, children wouldn't need to pay for books, and city-dwellers wouldn't need to pay for their electricity or water. He said that within two years of the opening of the memorial hall, he would give every family in the county its own house.

Copies of this document rained down into every courtyard of every house in the county, and entered the heart of every resident. Naturally, everyone began to regard Chief Liu as a deity, and even peasants in the countryside somehow managed to buy copies of his photograph and hang it up on their walls. They hung his photograph alongside the pictures of the bodhisattvas, the stove god, and Chairman Mao. In the county seat, there were even some people who, when they posted pictures of door gods on New Year's, would post a picture of Lord Guan on one side and of Chief Liu on the other, or they would post a picture of Chief Liu on one side and a painting by Zhao Ziyun on the other.

Once when Chief Liu went down to the countryside and came across a small restaurant called Sojourner's Home, he wrote an inscription, and business immediately took off and the restaurant had a constant stream of customers. Another time, Chief Liu spent half the night in a roadside inn, and afterward the innkeeper collected the face basin, washcloth, and soap box that Chief Liu had used, wrapped them in red cloth, and placed them in a box to serve as relics.[1] The innkeeper hung a wooden placard above the room where Chief Liu had slept, on which it said that on such-and-such month of such-and-such year, County Chief Liu Yingque spent the night here. The innkeeper had previously rented that room for twelve yuan a night, but now he increased the rent to twenty yuan, and whereas previously he didn't have many guests, after Chief Liu's visit he found he had a constant stream of customers who all wanted to lie in the bed where Chief Liu had slept and sit in the chair where Chief Liu had sat. Truck drivers in the middle of long hauls would go hundreds of *li* out of their way to spend the night at the inn where Chief Liu had stayed.

In Shuanghuai, Chief Liu was regarded as an extraordinary figure, comparable to the legendary Qing dynasty emperors Qianlong and Kangxi, or the founders of the Ming and Song dynasties, emperors Zhu Yuanzhang and Song Taizu.

Chief Liu couldn't walk casually down the street, because whenever he appeared people would immediately crowd around, trying to ask him questions and shake his hand. They would pass him their babies and get him to kiss them, then would parade their offspring about telling everyone that on such-and-such month and such-and-such day, the county chief kissed my baby.

By now, everyone knew that the Liven troupe was raking in money as easily as it might rake autumn leaves, and that Lenin's corpse would soon be purchased and brought back to Shuanghuai, so the good days could not be far off. Chief Liu was already regarded as a divinity in Shuanghuai, and was worshiped by each of the county's eight hundred and ten thousand residents. Naturally, he couldn't walk alone through the streets. Fortunately, however, on this particular night the sky was completely dark, and when Chief Liu, bearing a heavy emotional load, made his way back to the residential compound of the county government, he wasn't detained by anyone or anything.

This residential compound was inside a courtyard to the north of the county government building, and Chief Liu's Hall of Devotion was located in that courtyard. His family lived in a building in the innermost area of the courtyard, and his Hall of Devotion was in a large three-room building in the southernmost section of the compound. That building had originally been a conference hall for one of the county offices, but after that office moved out Chief Liu had appropriated the room for his Hall of Devotion. By this point the night had reached its darkest hour, and people who were out getting some fresh air had already begun making their way back home. When Chief Liu walked in through the main gate of the residential compound, the sixty-three-year-old gatekeeper hadn't yet gone to sleep, and when he saw Chief Liu through the window he quickly rushed out and bowed to him.

Chief Liu asked him, "You haven't gone to bed?"

The old man replied, "After I heard the talk you gave in the county committee building, I became so excited by the thought that we are about to enter a period of having more money than we'll be able to spend that I found myself unable to sleep."

With a broad smile, the county chief nodded to the old man, and added a few words of encouragement. Then, he turned and headed toward the southernmost building, the sound of his footsteps echoing through the quiet night. When he arrived at the door, he looked around, then pulled a key out from a crevice in the door frame. He opened the door, walked in, and closed it behind him. Then, he flipped on the light switch.

Instantly, the room became as bright as windswept snow. The three fluorescent bulbs hanging from the ceiling bathed the three-room building in bright light. The walls were whitewashed, and the door and windows were tightly sealed, so that not even a speck of dust could make its way into the room. Apart from a table and a chair, there wasn't any other furniture. If you looked up at the walls, however, you would see the portraits of great men hanging there. The top row had ten portraits of great leaders, including Mao, Engels, Lenin, Stalin, Mao, Tito, Ho Chi Minh, and Kim Il Sung, while the bottom row had portraits of ten of China's great military leaders. But in this bottom row there were actually eleven portraits, with the eleventh being that of County Chief Liu Yingque himself. As for the wall behind him, there was only one portrait, which was that of his foster father, and below it there was an inscription by Chief Liu: *Shuanghuai county's disseminator of Marxist Leninism.*

Below each portrait frame, there were captions detailing the men's biographies and accomplishments, including the ages at which they had assumed their respective positions. Chief Liu had underlined the important points in red, just as his foster father had done. For instance, Lin Biao had just turned twenty-three when he was appointed corps commander; Jia Long was only thirty-one when he was appointed army commander; Zhu De was nineteen when, in the *yisi* Year of the Serpent, he participated in an uprising protesting Yuan Shikai's rule, and in the *bingwu* Year of the Horse he participated in the National Protection War opposing the warlord Duan Qirui; and so forth. These details were all underlined in red.

This underlining was intended to serve as a caution for Chief Liu, so that every time he entered the Hall of Devotion he would feel even more reverential toward the great men whose portraits hung on the wall, and would therefore strive even harder for excellence in his own life. Every time he saw the caption explaining that when Lin Biao had just turned twenty-three he successfully organized the shocking military victory at Pingxing Pass, Chief Liu was reminded of how he himself was appointed soc-school teacher in the Boshuzi commune at the age of twenty-one, and every year he would go down to the countryside to help wake up the peasants and encourage them to read newspaper articles and urge them to sharpen their sickles at harvest-time and to plow the fields at sowing time.

He would feel a bit sorrowful even as a surge of energy would spring up from his feet, such that he would always be willing to work harder. Not only could he help them bring the grain into the warehouse before the summer rains, but in winter he could get the sprouts out of the ground before the first frost. He would let the peasants know that in Beijing in such-and-such year and such-and-such month there was such-and-such meeting that was being held. He would report which official documents were being sent down, and even cite the important points in each one. Some people in the village had relatives in Taiwan and Singapore, and Chief Liu would help them stay in touch and do everything he could to encourage their relatives to visit their hometowns. When those Overseas Chinese returned to Shuanghuai, they would arrive with broad smiles on their faces, but would immediately start crying their eyes out and have no choice but to donate their entire life savings to their hometowns, to help pave the roads, erect electrical lines, and build factories.

In the end, the rural areas where Chief Liu stayed ended up becoming more affluent than the neighboring regions, and consequently he was promoted from soc-school cadre to the position of deputy Party secretary of the commune, and then promoted again to Party committee member. Able at a young age to manage cadres who were ten or even twenty years his senior, Chief Liu was able to draw a red line under his occupation at the age of twenty-three.

Three years after the commune was converted into a township, Liu Yingque was transferred from Boshuzi commune to Chunshu township. Although he was only the deputy township chief, the township chief had been hospitalized and therefore Chief Liu was responsible for the township's business. He convened a meeting with all of the village heads, and told them that every village should have ten men stay behind to lead a group of women and the elderly in working the fields, while the rest of the village's young men and women should go out to find work. They could steal and loot if they had to, but no matter what, they couldn't remain at home working the land. He gave each young person a letter of introduction to the township, and then used several trucks to haul the boys and girls, the men and women, to the district and provincial bus stop. After they got out of the truck, however, he wouldn't pay them any heed, telling them that even if they were starving to death, they shouldn't return home in less than three to six months. He said he would fine any residents a hundred yuan if they went home early for reasons other than sickness or disaster, and if they didn't have any money he would confiscate their pigs and sheep until the residents, no doubt screaming and hollering, left home again.

A year later, Chunshu township had one group of young people and children after another go to work in the city—even if they were merely washing dishes, cooking, or collecting garbage—so that every town and village would have money to buy salt and coal. One house after another was rebuilt into a tile-roofed residence. In Huangli village, there was a household in which all of the children were girls, so Liu

Yingque sent the two eldest daughters to the provincial capital to find work. Within half a month, however, they had used up all their money and were famished, and started selling their flesh.[3] Within half a year, the family was able to build a new house, and Yingque led all of the cadres in the township to their home to host an impromptu meeting, bringing the parents flowers and hanging a plaque on the wall of the house. The officials even issued congratulatory letters, stamped with the township's seal, to those two girls who were out selling their flesh. Although Yingque spit on the ground upon walking out of the house of those two flesh-selling girls, afterward all the village boys and girls competed to leave the township to go look for work, and the township enjoyed some of the best days it had ever seen.

A year after that, when the township chief was released from the hospital, the county didn't allow him to keep his position, and instead promoted Liu Yingque from deputy township chief to township chief.

After Liu Yingque was promoted, he began speaking and acting like an emperor.

One day, one of the men from the township who had gone out to find work was escorted home by one of the city dwellers. When he returned, Chief Liu asked, "What's wrong?" The man from the city replied, "He's stolen from others! How is it that people from this district are sent out to steal?" Chief Liu slapped the thief's face, and shouted, "Tie him up!" Someone from the police station got a rope to tie his hands, and then accompanied the accuser into the township to eat. After their meal, Chief Liu walked the accuser back to his car, but as soon as he departed he had his officers release the thief.

Chief Liu asked, "What did you steal?"

The thief lowered his head.

Chief Liu hollered, "I said, what did you steal?"

The thief replied, "I stole a motor from the factory."

Chief Liu said sharply, "Get out of here! Your punishment is that within three years you need to set up a factory in your village. If you can't do so, then if someone else brings you in for stealing, I'll send you to jail."

The thief left. He didn't go back to his village to see his mother and father, but immediately returned to the city. Or he went to the provincial capital or to cities in the south to develop his skills. Soon, he did in fact manage to establish a small factory in his hometown—either a flour, rope, or nail factory.

Another day, someone called from the district asking Liu Yingque to go into the city to fetch someone, and he had no choice but to go. He took a ride into the city, where he visited the district's Public Security Bureau, and found more than a dozen seventeen- to nineteen-year-old women who had all been selling their flesh in the entertainment district. The women were squatting at the base of the wall half-naked and clutching their clothes. When the person at the Public Security Bureau saw Chief Liu, he asked, "Are you the township chief?" Chief Liu replied, "I am." The officer squinted at Chief Liu, then spit at him, saying, "Fuck, do the factories in your township churn out whores rather than grain?" Chief Liu stared in amazement, then lowered his head and wiped away the spittle while cursing the officer under his breath. Then he looked up with a smile, and said, "I'll take them away, and when we get back I'll make them parade around the village carrying old shoes. Would that be okay?"

He led the women out of the bureau, but as soon as they were outside he addressed them, saying, "You have the ability to make a Public Security Bureau Officer divorce his wife, disrupting his family so much that his wife and children leave him. You have the ability to become a madam and teach other women to follow in your footsteps. You have the ability to send money home, enabling your family to build a tile-roofed house and permitting the entire village to have electricity and running water, such that the village will erect a good-merit stela celebrating your good deeds." He then spit repeatedly on them before turning around and heading back to the bus station.

The women stared after him in shock, then started giggling and dispersed throughout the city.

Afterward, some of the villagers did in fact set up hairdressing shops and massage parlors in the city. They served as managers, and had young women from the countryside come and work for them.

Others went from collecting trash to setting up a recycling center. Someone else went from helping cart around bricks and cement to eventually helping the city-dwellers build kitchens, repair their walls, and construct chicken coops. Eventually, he began advising people on new buildings. For instance, he would point out how between the first and second floors the outer wall of the new building leaned to the east, but from the second to the third floors it straightened out and leaned back to the west, and by the time it got to the fifth or sixth floors it was perfectly straight. In the end, he became a labor contractor, and on his ID card he was listed as the manager of a construction team.

Three or four years passed, and Chunshu township gradually began to acquire an air of prosperity. All of the roads leading to the village were paved, and electrical lines were installed. In front of each family's newly constructed house there was a stone lion. Chunshu became a model for the entire county, and the Party secretary personally came to the village to give a talk. Liu Yingque drew a red line under his lifeline for the age of twenty-seven, and wrote that he was promoted from township chief to township secretary. When he was thirty-three, that red line was extended upward, as he was again promoted, from township secretary to deputy county chief, becoming the youngest deputy county chief in the entire district.

Now Liu Yingque was thirty-seven years old, and his life achievement chart was already marked in bright red. His Hall of Devotion was extraordinarily quiet, to the point that you could hear the air entering through the crack beneath the door. The night was as dark as the bottom of a well, and people who'd been out for an evening stroll had all returned home to sleep. The old man guarding the gate to the residential compound for government employees had long since locked up. Chief Liu sat at a table in the center of this Divine Hall, looking repeatedly at each of the portraits on the wall. Over and over he read out loud the underlined descriptions of their significant achievements. Eventually, his gaze came to rest on his own portrait, positioned last in the row of ten great military marshals.

In the picture, Chief Liu appeared with a flattop, a square head, and a red face. Although he was smiling brightly, his eyes carried an unmistakable trace of sorrow and anxiety, as though something truly difficult to accept had just been revealed. His gray suit was very elegant, and he was wearing a bright red tie. But if you looked closely, you noticed that the suit looked awkward on him, as though he had not actually been wearing it when the photograph was taken, but rather had it painted in afterward. As Chief Liu looked at the portrait, the portrait gazed back at him. When he looked excited, however, the portrait retained its melancholy expression.

Chief Liu's excitement immediately faded.

He continued staring at the portrait, though, and as he did so the soles of his feet began to itch and feel hot. He knew that he was about to have another burst of energy. Each time he was promoted he would always come alone to his Hall of Devotion and look at the portraits on the wall. When his gaze finally came to rest on his own, he would invariably feel a burst of energy start at his feet and work its way up through his body, as a wave of blood surged to his head. Needless to say, this meant he had to do something—walk up to the portrait and write down his age and the rank to which he had been promoted, and then draw a thick red line under the row specifying that in such-and-such year and such-and-such month he had been promoted to such-and-such rank. Afterward, he would burn three incense sticks in front of his foster father's portrait, meditate for a while, and bow. Then he would go back home, locking the door behind him.

However, this time when Chief Liu came to his Hall of Devotion, it was not because he had just been promoted, but rather because of the success of the village's performance troupe, and because he and Grandma Mao Zhi had just signed a contract agreeing that she would establish another performance troupe, and because by the end of the year they would have raised far more money than was needed to purchase Lenin's corpse. Chief Liu had never expected that even now he would feel this surge of energy emanating from the soles of his feet, as though he were standing on a brazier on a cold day. Suddenly, his palms got sweaty and he felt an overwhelming urge to go up to his chart and write down a new promotion, underlining it in red. He knew that if he didn't write something, he wouldn't be able to sleep.

He hesitated, the sweat from his palm soaking his fingers. His head was pounding, and as the blood filled his veins, he felt as though a herd of wild horses was galloping through him.

He stood up.

He abruptly pulled a pen out of his pocket, then carried a stool over to his portrait. Counting from the bottom, he carefully wrote a line of text on the tenth empty line:

> *In the* jimao *Year of the Hare, when Liu Yingque turned thirty-nine, he was promoted to deputy district commissioner.*

Chief Liu had originally intended to write that that in the *wuyin* Year of the Tiger he had been promoted to the position of district commissioner, but when he took up his pen he felt a jolt of modesty, so he pushed the date back a year and assigned himself a lower position. He revised it to read that in the *jimao* Year of the Hare, when Liu Yingque turned thirty-nine, he was promoted to the position of deputy district commissioner. After all, Lenin's corpse had not been purchased yet, and it wouldn't be until the following year that the people would begin to have so much money that they couldn't spend it all, and the question of whether he would be promoted first to deputy district commissioner or whether he would skip right over the position of deputy commissioner and be promoted directly to district commissioner had not yet been decided. Chief Liu knew that it was inappropriate for him to preemptively claim something he had not yet achieved, and that even his own wife wouldn't let him do this, but he still wrote it down and then underlined it in red.

The earlier red lines had all turned dark over time, and seemed to be waiting impatiently for a new one. After Chief Liu drew the bright red line, he jumped up from his stool and took a step back. He gazed at that new line of text and that new thick red line, and his face lit up in a bright smile. He felt a wave of peace flow over him, and the energy and warm blood that had been surging through his body began to subside.

He had to return home. It was already the middle of the night.

But just as he was about to leave, his hand began to shake as he grasped the door handle, and he suddenly had a nagging feeling that he had neglected to do something. He initially thought that it was because he had forgotten to burn incense for his foster father, so he removed three incense sticks from one drawer and a sand-filled incense holder from another. He lit the incense sticks and stuck them in the holder, then pushed the table over to his father's portrait. He watched as the three columns of smoke spiraled up into the air. He recognized that since he was already a county chief and almost like an emperor, it would be entirely unbefitting for him to kneel down and kowtow before his foster father's portrait. But he still solemnly gazed at the portrait, and bowed down three times while holding his hands to his chest, intoning: "Father, you can rest easy: Next year I will buy Lenin's corpse and bring it to Spirit Mountain. Within two or three years I will be promoted to district commissioner."

Once he finished, Chief Liu felt he had done everything he needed to do, and could leave at ease. Just as he was preparing to depart, however, he again had a nagging feeling that there was something he had failed to do. When he considered it carefully he realized that what he had found in his travels was not what he had originally been looking for. It was only then that it occurred to him that the task he felt he needed to finish was not that of burning incense in front of his foster father's portrait. Instead, he turned around and looked at the two rows of portraits. He examined each image in turn, and when he reached the fifth one on the second row, the portrait of Lin Biao, he hesitantly took down his own portrait and hung it where Lin Biao's had been.

After Chief Liu finished rehanging his portrait, he felt completely at ease, as though he had finally succeeded in doing something he had been trying to accomplish for decades. He suddenly felt as though the unspeakable envy he felt toward Lin Biao for being promoted to corps commander at the tender age of twenty-three had subsided somewhat. Chief Liu stood in the same spot where he used to stand while examining Lin Biao's portrait, though now he was looking instead at his own image. It seemed to him that the portrait was hanging perfectly straight, and that the trace of melancholy in his eyes had been replaced with a look of unconcealed joy. After having gazed with infatuation at his official portrait, hanging right next to Liu Bocheng's, he smiled for a long time, then wiped the dust off his hands and walked out of the Hall of Devotion.

Chief Liu noticed that the lights in his house were still on and the window was as bright as the daytime sun. Chief Liu stared at that light in stupefaction, then began making his way home.

Further Reading:

1) **Relics.** DIAL. *Refers to souvenirs.*

3) **Selling flesh.** DIAL. *Refers to prostitution, but the phrase doesn't carry any pejorative connotations.*

Chapter 13: Hey, who was that who just walked out of our home?

"Fuck! I've been knocking for hours. Why didn't you open up?"

"Oh, it's you! I thought you were a thief."

"Stand right there. Tell me, who the hell was it that just left our house?"

"If you saw him yourself, then why are you asking me?"

"I just saw his shadow. Tell me who the hell it was."

"Secretary Shi."

"What the hell was he doing here at three o'clock in the morning?"

"I asked him to come over, to bring me some cold medicine. You were the one who told him that when you weren't here, he should be diligent and come whenever he was called."

"I'm telling you, you shouldn't be having people bring you stuff at three o'clock in the morning."

"Are you suspicious? If so, you should just go ask him about it yourself."

"I can fire him with a single word."

"Go ahead."

"With a single word, I can have the police arrest him."

"Go right ahead. Do it."

"With a single word, I can have the courts send him to jail for years. I can make it so that he would never get out of jail alive."

"Do it, then."

". . ."

"Okay, then. Didn't you just go away for three months without returning home?"

"This is my home. I can return whenever I want."

"So now you remember it's your home. . . . Why didn't you just endure another month before coming back?"

"I couldn't resist. You know how much I've done for the county this past month? Whenever anyone sees me in the street, they should all bow down and kowtow to me as though I were an emperor."

"I know that you established a special-skills performance troupe, and that next year you plan to purchase Lenin's corpse from Russia and bring it back. I know that within two or three years you hope to be promoted to deputy district commissioner. But do you know how our daughter has been this past month? Do you know how I've been?"

"Where is our daughter?"

"She's at her godmother's."

"How have the two of you been?"

"We both came down with bad colds. Our daughter had a fever of thirty-nine degrees, and had to spend three days in the hospital having shots."

"Oh, I thought it was something important. At any rate, I also want you to know that I signed a contract with Liven's Grandma Mao Zhi, agreeing that within a couple of weeks she will establish a second special-skills performance troupe. The proceeds from the admissions tickets from the two sets of performances will flow into the county's coffers like a river. By the end of the year we will have enough money to buy Lenin's corpse from Russia. As soon as we bring the corpse back and install it on Spirit Mountain, the county's coffers will be so full that money will pour out through the doors and windows, and everyone in the county will be able to enjoy the good life. Their only worry will be that they have more money than they can spend. By that point, when winter comes I'll give everyone in the county a free imported flu shot, so that no one in the county will ever catch the flu again. Hey, why have you fallen asleep?"

"Do you realize what time it is?"

"Okay. If you want to sleep, then sleep. I won't take a bath tonight."

"You can sleep in the other room."

"Where are you going to sleep?"

"I'll sleep right here."

"Do you want to do it?"

"I have my period."

"I'm telling you, your husband is not the same Boshuzi commune soc-school teacher you originally married. He's not the same turnip-head cadre he once was. He is now the county chief, the emperor of Shuanghuai county, with eight hundred and ten thousand subjects under his command, including tens—or even hundreds—of thousands of women who are younger and prettier than you. He could sleep with any of them, if he wanted."

"Mr. Liu, I also want tell you that you shouldn't forget where you grew up and who raised you. Do you think that you got to where you are today simply by relying on your own efforts? Don't forget that it was the secretary of the Boshuzi commune who promoted you to the position of the commune's Party committee member, and it was because the secretary was one of my father's students. And don't forget that the reason you were appointed Chunshu township chief was that the director of the Organization Department was also one of my father's students. And don't forget that the reason you were able to become the youngest deputy county chief in the entire district is because the district's Secretary Niu was formerly the principal of the commune soc-school, and was also close to my father. Fuck this! Get out! Go get your stuff from the bedroom and smash it! If you can, you should take all of our spoons, ladles, pots, and pans to a relative's courtyard and smash them. This will let everyone in the county know that you, the county chief, can also smash dishes."

"Hey, you can go on and on about this, but I never betrayed your father. I am now the county chief, and perhaps in another two or three years I'll be promoted to the position of district commissioner. Although your father was only my foster father, I still burn incense for him every month like a filial son."

"Where do you burn it?"

"In my heart."

"Asshole. Are you going to go sleep in the other room? Because if you won't, then I will."

"I won't sleep in that room, or in this one. The entire county is my home, and therefore I can sleep anywhere I want. Do you think that, as the county chief, if I leave these two rooms I won't have anywhere to sleep? Let me tell you something: I'll sleep better anywhere else but here. If your father hadn't taken my hand before he died and asked me to look after you, then I could easily go three months without returning home, or even thinking about you."

"If you want, then you really should go three months without returning home. You should go three months without touching me."

"Do you think I can't live without you?"

"Go, go to Spirit Mountain to build your Lenin Mausoleum. Go to Russia to buy Lenin's corpse. If during the following three months you find that you can't resist coming home again, then you shouldn't be county chief! You shouldn't even *think* about being promoted to district commissioner. Even if you are promoted to district commissioner, you should be sent to jail."

"Huh? You mean if I buy Lenin's corpse and bring it back, I won't be able to resist returning home? Why don't you calculate for yourself. When we last agreed I wouldn't return home for half a month, I ended up staying away for a month and three days. This time we agreed that I would stay away for three months, but because I lacked resolve I ended up returning after only two. Now I'm telling you, I, County Chief Liu Yingque, won't return home for at least half a year. After bringing Lenin's corpse back, I won't return home again for at least six, or maybe even twelve, months."

"Okay then, why don't you go. If you really do go for half a year without returning home, I'll wait on you however you like. If you want me to kowtow to you like a maid kowtowing to the emperor as I back my way out of the room, I would be happy to do so."

"That's fine. What if you don't kowtow to me?"

"Then you can go to my father's tomb at the soc-school and dig up his remains."

"Deal."

"And what if *you* can't resist returning in less than half a year to touch and caress me?"

"I would agree to transfer your father's remains to the Lenin Mausoleum on Spirit Mountain."

"Agreed. If you go back on your word, may you be struck dead by a car, choke to death while drinking water, die from infection as a result of a splinter in your foot, or be poisoned in broad daylight."

"You don't need to curse me like that. Just say that I won't succeed in bringing back Lenin's corpse—which, for me, would be a fate worse than death."

". . ."

"Bam!" The door to Chief Liu's house slammed shut.

Book 9: Leaves

CHAPTER 1: EVERYONE RAISES THEIR HANDS, CREATING A FOREST OF ARMS

Liven became a virtual ghost town, since most of its disabled residents left to perform with the troupe. Even if someone's only disability was that he had six fingers rather than five, as long as he could use his extra digit to help him pick up two bowl-sized balls, he could perform a six-fingered bowl-lifting event.

Even the sixty-one-year-old Cripple joined the troupe. Because Cripple had a younger brother whom he physically resembled, the deputy leader of the Balou tunes opera troupe decided to modify Cripple's residency papers, changing his birth date from the twenty-first year of the Republic to the same year in the preceding sixty-year *jiazi* cycle, thereby making him a hundred and twenty-one years old. The decision to change his age to a hundred and twenty-one, rather than a nice round number, was deliberate on the part of the wholers, who thought this way the age would appear more realistic.

But if Cripple was now a hundred and twenty-one years old, what about his younger brother? Given that the brother was originally three years younger, now that Cripple had sixty years added to his age, that meant he was now sixty-three years older than his younger brother.

The younger man, therefore, could no longer call Cripple "Brother," but rather should begin calling him "Grandpa." The younger brother pushed Cripple onto the stage in a wheelchair and showed the audience Cripple's residence permit and identity card stating that he was a hundred and twenty-one years old. Standing before the audience of more than a thousand, the fifty-eight-year-old man called his elder brother "Grandpa." The audience was amazed that a hundred-and-twenty-one-year-old man's eyesight and hearing were still reasonably good, and that he looked so much like his sixty-something-year-old grandson. In fact, apart from having lost a few teeth and needing to be pushed around in a wheelchair, Cripple didn't seem to be much worse for the wear. The performance was a sensation, and someone in the audience shouted in amazement,

"Hey, what does the old man normally eat?"

The hundred-and-twenty-one-year-old Cripple pretended he couldn't hear very well, and therefore his fifty-eight-year-old grandson responded in a Balou accent:

"What does he eat? He eats mixed grains."

"Does he exercise?"

"He worked in the fields his entire life. Working in the fields is a kind of exercise."

"How did your grandfather become crippled?"

"Earlier this year he was climbing down a mountain after having gone to cut some kindling, and he fell into a ravine."

"Heavens. A hundred-and-twenty-one-year-old man still climbing mountains to cut kindling? How old is your father, and is he still able to work?"

"My father is ninety-seven. He is back home supporting us by raising cattle and plowing the land."

The audience became increasingly animated, asking an additional series of questions. This Guess-the-Age-of-the-Old-Man routine was a sensation, and was rewarded with energetic cheers. In this way, the Second Shuanghuai County Special-Skills Performance Troupe got under way and began touring the region beyond the Balou mountains. To everyone's surprise, this second troupe turned out to be as successful as the first. The second troupe consisted of forty-nine Liven villagers, all of whom had been selected by Grandma Mao Zhi. Of these forty-nine villagers, there were also, in addition to Mothlet, nine nins ranging from thirteen to seventeen years old. All nine of these nins were under four feet tall and weighed under fifty-seven pounds, and therefore the county had the three youngest nins dress up and put on makeup, so that from a distance they would all resemble each other. They were then given a single residency permit booklet, which claimed that they were an exceedingly rare set of nonuplets and that it took their mother a full three days to give birth to them.

The audience stared in amazement when they stood there without moving, and their performance came to be known as Nine Mothlets. This was the second troupe's pièce de résistance. They used it as their opening act, and it tugged at the audience's heartstrings. The performance then went on to a series of acts similar to those popularized by the first troupe, including Blind-Person-Listening, Deaf-Person-Setting-Off-Fireworks, and Cripple-Leaping. The audience gave off gasps of amazement, as their attention was riveted on the stage.

The troupe also added the Six-Fingered-Handprint, accompanied by a local Balou tune, followed by a Guess-the-Age-of-the-Old-Man routine that lifted the audience's mood even further, like an autumn breeze of wheat fragrance that wafts over from distant fields. The second troupe, like the first, also performed Leaf-Embroidery and Foot-in-a-Bottle routines, although the new Leaf-Embroidery performer could not embroider a sparrow, as the one in the first troupe could. The act still consisted of a paralyzed woman embroidering a tree leaf, but the woman in the second troupe could embroider only peony and chrysanthemum blossoms. However, given a leaf from a wood-oil or poplar tree, she could embroider it with blossoms in less time than it takes to smoke a cigarette or eat a piece of candy. This was a very unusual ability. Although the boy responsible for the Foot-in-a-Bottle performance had a rather large foot and his polio-stricken leg was thicker than a cane, so that he could insert his foot only into a bottle that had an opening as big as a jar's, he was nevertheless willing to turn somersaults on stage while wearing this bottle-shoe, and even if the bottle didn't shatter when he landed the audience would still roar in appreciation. While these performances were not as good as those of the first troupe, at least the Nine Mothlets routine was an inimitable act that the first troupe couldn't duplicate.

Nonuplets. Who had ever heard of someone giving birth to nonuplets? And for all of them to survive? The very fact that the girls were all nins made the claim that they were nonuplets seem all the more convincing.

Although the girls in the Nine Mothlets routine were all performing as nins, they were nevertheless still human beings. But who had ever heard of someone giving birth to nine infants at once? Before every Nine Mothlets performance, the announcer would say many moving things, and then would ask for anyone in the audience who had twins to stand up and come onto the stage. Over the course of ten performances, on only one or two occasions did anyone ever report having had twins—whereupon the red-faced mother would lead her twins onto the stage, and the audience would stare enviously at them. Then, the announcer would call out,

"Does anyone have triplets?"

The audience would look around expectantly, thinking that someone might in fact have triplets, but they would be disappointed.

The announcer would then call out,

"Does anyone have quadruplets?"

Some people would still turn and look around, but relatively few. She would then call out, "Any quintuplets?"

No one turned around, as they were beginning to get tired of her questions. She, however, continued calling out,

"Any sextuplets?"

"Any septuplets?"

"Any octuplets?"

Finally, screaming at the top of her lungs, she would shout, "Any nonuplets?"

At this point, the nonuplets would run onto the stage holding hands, looking like a preschool class from the city. They were all the same height, weight, and body type, and after applying makeup they even had a child's red cheeks. They were all wearing the sort of red cotton shirts and green silk pants that normally only preteen girls wear, and they all had their hair braided into two pigtails.

Most important, they were all dwarfs, which is to say nins.

These nine little nins stood together on stage like nine mothlets, as the audience stared in amazement. The entire theater fell silent, and when the spotlight shone on the face of someone in the audience, everyone could hear the sound of the light shining down, as though it were possible to hear a shadow passing over the person's face.

At this point, the announcer began to introduce the girls one after the other. He said the first was called Mothlet, was fifteen years old, and weighed fifty-seven pounds. The second was called Second Mothlet, was fifteen years old, and weighed fifty-seven and a half pounds. The third was called Third Mothlet, was fifteen years old, and weighed fifty-seven and three-tenths pounds. And so on until the last one, who was called Little Mothlet and was also fifteen years old and also weighed fifty-seven and three-tenths pounds.

After the introductions were complete, the girls began their performance.

The nonuplets' opening act was very different from those of the other disabled performers. Because they were so tiny, they began with a mothlet dance. How tiny were they? One crippled man wearing a performance costume climbed onto the stage and announced that his family's chickens had gone missing. He started looking for the chickens on stage, and each time he found one he would stuff it into his bag. By the time he found the ninth one, he had filled two large bags. He then carried the bags around the stage. Eventually, one of the bags ripped open and a tiny mottled chick fell out of the hole, followed by two white ones and a black one. All together, nine black, white, and mottled chicks tumbled out of the bag and began dancing around the stage. They were all singing a Balou tune.

As might be expected, however, the little nins were in fact as tiny as chicks, and when they opened their mouths they could produce only a high-pitched squeal, like a knife being sharpened. The girls sang together, their voices as sharp as daggers flying toward the audience from the stage, making a noise that threw the entire auditorium into a commotion. The sound exploded through the windows and doors, shaking the lights back and forth and knocking the dust off the walls, and the audience covered their ears in terror.

But the more the audience members tried to cover their ears, the louder the nine little nins sang:

Brother, you left the Balou mountains.
At home, my sisters and I are waiting anxiously.

Leaving one village, and looking back at another,
I am waiting here anxiously.

Climbing a mountain and fording a river,
I've nearly gone insane searching for my brother.

Advance one step, and retreat one step,
We don't know which family's daughter has entangled
     our brother.
Advance two steps, and retreat two steps,
We don't know which mother has led our brother
     away.

Advance three steps and retreat three steps,
We don't know which family's daughter has stolen our
     brother's heart.

Advance seven steps, and retreat seven steps,
We don't know if our hearts will be able to pull
     brother's soul back.

The end of the song marked the conclusion of the routine and the show.

The city-dwellers watched this unexpectedly dazzling performance, and for days they couldn't stop talking about the blind man who could hear a pin drop, the paralyzed woman who could embroider a leaf, the

254

hundred-and-twenty-one-year-old man, and the nonuplets who were able to sing with such vigor that they nearly brought down the roof. Their stories grew and grew, and each time the troupe arrived at a new location newspapers and television stations would invariably give them a lot of free publicity. Therefore, at each new location, everyone would be certain to get tickets. As expected, the performances of the second troupe that Grandma Mao Zhi selected were as astonishing as those of the first, and at each new site they would need to put on at least three or five performances. The county arranged it so that one troupe would perform in the entire eastern part of the district and the other throughout the western part, and then they would switch. After they had performed in all of the cities throughout the province, one of the troupes would proceed to Hunan and Hubei, Guangdong and Guangxi, concentrating on the area along the railroad and the highway linking the respective provinces, while the other troupe would proceed to Shandong, Anhui, Zhejiang, and Shanghai.

The Southeast is one of the most prosperous regions in the world, and the area along the coast is particularly wealthy. Some families are so wealthy that when their kids take a shit, if they don't happen to have any toilet paper on hand they'll simply use a ten-yuan bill or two instead. When they heard that there was this sort of disabled performance troupe, they initially couldn't believe their ears, but eventually they started flocking to the theater to watch the second troupe in amazement.

Sometimes, the troupe wouldn't stop at one performance a day, but rather would give two or even three. The money from the ticket sales started pouring in, flowing along the banks' channels and into the county coffers. Every day, the county-appointed accountant would rush to the bank, going as often as he did the restroom.

As the original troupe made its way from Hubei to Hunan, and on to Guangdong, it goes without saying that it too often performed two or three times a day, and the money from ticket sales piled up high enough to touch the sky. Some people claimed that as the troupe continued its tour, Huaihua kept growing taller until she could no longer be considered a nin. Even without high heels, she was taller than many wholers, and with heels she was one of the tallest girls around. Not only did she grow like crazy over the course of those several months, but her appearance changed dramatically. It was said that while Huaihua was touring, she would always sleep with the troupe director, during which time she began growing at an incredible pace and soon became an extraordinarily beautiful wholer. It was said that when Secretary Shi heard that Huaihua and the troupe director were sleeping together, he made a special trip to visit the troupe, bringing with him a letter from Chief Liu, and then beat the troupe director until he knelt down before Secretary Shi and begged for mercy.

Who knows whether any of this was true, but what was known was that Huaihua grew into a wholer. Afterward, her sisters Tonghua and Yuhua refused to speak to her. It was also said that when she stood at the front of the stage as the announcer, the audience would cry out upon seeing her beauty. Many people went to the troupe's performances simply to see her, and as a result ticket prices kept rising and the county's coffers became increasingly swollen with bills.

By autumn, the money in the county's coffers had reached the ten-figure range—a sum so large that even a pair of abaci weren't enough to calculate it, and instead five or six would be needed to figure out how much money the two troupes had succeeded in bringing in, and how much of a bonus each of the bank employees should receive.

In virtually no time they succeeded in raising essentially all the money they needed for the Lenin Fund.

It was already almost the end of the year, and while it was bitterly cold in the north there were some areas in the south where it remained nearly as hot as a northern summer. By this point, the first troupe had already reached Guangdong, while the second was in northern Jiangsu, in one of the leading cities in northern China, where the skyscrapers were so tall they disappeared into the clouds and the houses were clustered as thick as trees in a forest. It was said that some of the rich people there were capable of gambling an entire night and losing a hundred thousand—or even eight hundred thousand—yuan. Therefore, after the villagers selected by Grandma Mao Zhi had given several performances, they found that they simply couldn't stop.

Everyone went crazy.

No one could believe there was a performance troupe consisting entirely of blind and deaf people, cripples and mutes, together with people who were missing a limb or had an extra finger, and little nins less than three feet tall. No one could believe that these disabled performers were all from the same village. No one could believe that in this village there was a mother who had given birth to nine girls at once. No one could believe that there was a child who was completely blind yet could hear a tree leaf or a sheet of paper fall to the ground. No one could believe there was a middle-aged deaf man who, because he was deaf, dared to hang a string of firecrackers around his neck, separated from his face by only a thick board, and proceed to ignite them. No one could believe that the nonuplet girls could sing their northern mountain songs so shrilly that if you threw a balloon into the air above them, their voices would cause it to pop.

There was not a single event in the entire performance that people could believe.

The more unbelievable the performances seemed, the more audiences flocked to see them, to the point that every home, factory, and office closed its doors and its inhabitants or workers went to watch. The price of an admission ticket rose from three hundred to five hundred yuan, and if the troupe hadn't raised the ticket prices the scalpers working out front would have ended up making a fortune. Local newspapers, radio, and television stations suddenly had lots of new material. It reached the point that even after holding twenty-nine performances in a certain city the troupe still wasn't able to pack up and move on to its next destination.

Eventually, however, the end of the year arrived and the troupes, in accordance with their agreement with Shuanghuai county, needed to conclude their tour. Liven had almost reached the date when it would withdraw from society.

On one particular day it started to rain, and the entire city was engulfed in water. Cars and trucks all came to a halt, and even motorcycles found themselves unable to move. It became difficult for people to get around, and the members of the troupe looked up at the sky and sighed. When they arrived at a new location, they would invariably sleep in the auditorium behind the stage, this being a common practice among northern theatrical troupes. After laying out their bedrolls, the men would sleep on one side of the room and the women on the other. The young people would then play cards, and the paralyzed women would fold everyone's performance costumes, while five of the nine little nins sat in a corner washing their costumes. The older performers, meanwhile, would retreat to quiet areas and count the money they had earned over the preceding five months. Grandma Mao Zhi had gone to considerable effort to revise the terms of the county contract so that the villagers would no longer simply be guaranteed a minimum of three thousand yuan a month in salary; instead the contract now clearly stated that each time one of the villagers performed, he or she would earn a "seat." In theatrical lingo, a "seat" refers to the price of an admission ticket. If tickets were selling for three hundred yuan apiece, each villager would therefore receive three hundred yuan for each performance. If ticket prices rose to five hundred yuan, each villager would receive five hundred yuan for each performance.

Calculated in this way, from Henan and Anhui provinces to Shandong's Heze and Yantan cities, on to Jiangsu's Nanjing, Suzhou, and Yangzhou, together with the northern Jiangsu star city, ticket prices for each performance averaged around three hundred yuan, and since the villagers would give at least thirty-five performances a month, each villager was able to earn thirty-five seats a month, or ten thousand and five hundred yuan. From this the villagers would have to discount the cost of food and overhead—though, to tell the truth, there was no real overhead, since each performer was given one seat a month to buy food, and consequently they all had more fish, meat, rice, and noodles than they could possibly eat. Speaking of overhead, the men went out to buy several packs of cigarettes, while the women and girls would buy lipstick and foreign soap for washing clothes and washing their faces, but when everything was added together each person spent less than a hundred yuan a month. For them to be able to earn more than ten thousand yuan a month was so astounding that it was enough to make their ancestors turn over in their graves.

What can you do with ten thousand yuan? If you are building a dwelling, ten thousand yuan is more or less enough to build a three-room house. If you are getting married, it is more or less enough to pay the fiancée's family her bride's price, in return for permission to marry her. If you spend ten thousand yuan on someone's funeral, this would be enough to transform an ordinary earthen grave into an imperial tomb.

The first month the villagers received their salaries, they were all so excited their hands trembled. They stuffed the money into their underwear, and then wouldn't take off their clothes even to go to bed. Some of them sewed an extra pocket onto their inner clothing, and then stuffed the money into it, and when they went out to perform the money would pound against their bodies like a brick. Although it wasn't very convenient for them to perform with all that cash, they would nevertheless do so even more enthusiastically because the money was there. When performing Firecracker-on-the-Ear, the deaf man would use two hundred firecrackers rather than one hundred; and when performing the Acute-Listening act, the blind man, in order to prove that he was really completely blind, would let someone shine a hundred-watt spotlight directly in his face, followed by a five-hundred-watt or even a thousand-watt light.

By the following month, everyone was being given more than ten thousand yuan in salary. They found that there wasn't anything to be afraid of on stage. When the little Polio Boy inserted his foot into the bottle and did a somersault, he wasn't trying to break the bottle but rather waited until the end so that the bottle could shatter under his feet. He would then stand on the glass shards while taking his bow, and the audience could clearly see the blood flowing out from under his foot.

The audience would break into loud applause.

The Polio Boy became even less concerned with the pain in his foot.

He subsequently began to earn more and more money each month.

By the end of the year, after five months of performances, everyone had earned several tens of thousands of yuan, and households with two or three performers could earn more than a hundred thousand yuan. Because almost all of Liven was out performing, the village itself became a virtual ghost town, and when the performers wanted to wire money home, they found that there was no one reliable in town to receive it. Consequently, they sewed thick wads of cash into every pillow and comforter, and also stuffed them into the chests that each performer had to keep. In this way, the money piled up like autumn leaves, to the point that the villagers didn't even dare go outside except to perform. Even when it was time to eat, they would take turns so that there was always someone backstage keeping guard. When it rained, all of the villagers crowded together on their bedrolls, and some of them would hide in a corner, claiming that their comforter was ripped and needed to be mended, whereupon they would rip the comforter open at the seams and stuff it full with their recent earnings.

They would claim that their performance chest was broken and needed to be nailed back together, whereupon they would add several more layers of cash to the chest, reinforcing it with several more nails and a larger lock.

They would complain that their pillows were no longer comfortable, and needed to be fluffed up, whereupon they would dump out the wheat and bran from inside the pillow, and then fill it with their carefully folded clothes, now stuffed with wad upon wad of brand-new hundred-yuan bills. As a result, the pillow would be as hard as a board or a brick from all that cash.

When it rained, they all looked after their money, and once they had put it all away they called out, "Hey, have you finished sewing your comforter?"

"Almost."

"Do you want to play cards when you're done?"

"Sure. Why don't you come over here to play."

"Why don't you come over here instead. You can bring your comforter."

So, they nodded and, watching each other, broke into broad smiles.

It was pouring rain outside, while inside the theater a thick layer of fog hovered over the ground. The theater seats were all covered in droplets, and even the curtain on stage looked as though it had just been washed and hung out to dry. The wholers from Shuanghuai county who had come to organize the two special-skills troupes took advantage of the rain to go shopping in the city, and only the disabled performers were left behind in the theater, which was called the Emperor and Concubine.

It was at this point that Grandma Mao Zhi shared with everyone an unforgettable memory that was weighing on her. It was as if this matter had taken root in her heart, and over the preceding five months and three days—a total of one hundred and fifty-three days since the troupe's debut performance in Jiudu—this matter in her heart had grown a thick trunk, started to sprout leaves, and recently begun to bloom. No one ever expected, however, that long after the villagers had forgotten about this matter, they would suddenly remember it with surprise. It was as if they had been hurtling forward from one day to the next and then saw the opening of a deep well, and just as they were about to fall in they came to their senses.

Each family had dug its own hole.

Each family had fallen into its own trap.

Each family had put poison into its own rice bowls.

Grandma Mao Zhi asked, "Hey, does everyone remember what day today is?"

The villagers all stared at her.

Grandma Mao Zhi said, "Today is the winter solstice, and in another nine days, on the thirteenth day of the lunar month, it will be the last day of the year in the Western calendar."

The villagers continued staring at her, not knowing what was significant about its being the last day of the year.

Grandma Mao Zhi explained with a bright smile, "On that day, our contract with Shuanghuai county will expire, and Liven will formally withdraw from society. Shuanghuai county and Boshuzi township will no longer have any jurisdiction over us."

At this point, everyone suddenly remembered the performance contracts that had been signed five months earlier when the troupes were established, and realized there were only nine days left until those contracts expired. The expiration had been anticipated, but as the villagers performed day after day, earning piles and piles of money, they completely forgot that the last day of the performances was approaching. As the rain fell, the fog was so thick that you couldn't even move your hand through it. There was a bright spotlight shining down on the stage, as bright as if it were the sun itself hanging from the ceiling. Grandma Mao Zhi sat next to her comforter mending several performance costumes. At that point, the villagers focused their gaze on her, as though there were a dark cloud enveloping her face.

"The time has come? So the troupes will have to disband?"

"The time has come, and we'll have to return to Liven."

The person asking the question was the little Polio Boy. He was playing cards, and abruptly lifted up the card he was holding, as though he had suddenly thought of something of monumental importance. Staring intently at Grandma Mao Zhi, he asked carefully,

"What happens after we withdraw from society?"

"After we withdraw from society, no one will have any more authority over us."

"And what will happen once they have no authority over us?"

"Once they have no authority over us, you will be as free and enlivened as a wild hare."

"If no one has authority over us, will we still be able to perform our special skills?"

"This is not a question of our special skills, but rather of our exploited dignity."

The boy threw the card he was holding onto the table.

"I am willing to have my dignity exploited," he announced. "If withdrawal from society means that the performance troupes have to disband, then my family will fight the withdrawal tooth and nail."

Grandma Mao Zhi was startled by this outburst, and looked as though someone had thrown a bucket of cold water on her head. She looked closely at the little Polio Boy for a moment, then shifted her gaze to the crippled woman who embroidered leaves. She gazed at the deaf man who exploded firecrackers next to his ears, and the blind man with acute hearing. She gazed at the six-fingered man and the other cripples and mutes, together with the two wholers responsible for carrying the troupe's suitcases and bags. She asked for those who weren't willing to withdraw from society to raise their hands—and suggested that if it turned out everyone wanted to withdraw, then the Polio Boy could stand alone outside performing his Foot-in-the-Bottle routine day after day. After saying this, she looked over at the moth-like little nins, then let her gaze come to rest on a group of villagers in the back of the theater, thinking that everything had been resolved and that the Polio Boy's comments had been addressed.

What she hadn't expected, however, was that at that moment the forty-odd members of the troupe would all look at one another as though trying to discover something in their neighbors' faces. They continued staring at one another for the longest time, then eventually looked to the two wholers.

Without glancing at Grandma Mao Zhi and staring instead at the red curtain, one of the wholers said, "If we withdraw from society and Shuanghuai ceases to have any jurisdiction over us, then we will not be able to perform and earn money. But if we can't continue earning money, then what would be the point of withdrawing from society?" As he was saying this, he tentatively raised his hand.

Seeing the first wholer raise his hand, a second wholer also raised his, saying, "Everyone knows that Shuanghuai county will soon bring Lenin's corpse back from Russia and install it on Spirit Mountain, and that afterward everyone in the county will become incredibly anxious about not even being able to spend all of the money they earn. They say there are already many people from neighboring counties who are secretly shifting their residency permits to Shuanghuai. Wouldn't it be the ultimate in stupidity if we were to withdraw from society now?"

It was as if he were asking the other villagers. He cast his gaze over their faces, silently urging each of them to quickly raise a hand.

Sure enough, the deaf man raised his hand.

The blind man also raised his.

The paralyzed woman also raised hers.

Under the bright light that illuminated the room, a forest of hands were raised in the air.

Grandma Mao Zhi turned pale, as though all those hands were slapping her in the face. All the villagers—with the exception of her granddaughter Mothlet—were sitting there, their faces red with excitement, raising their hands so high that their sleeves rolled down their arms, revealing a forest of forearms.

The chill from the rain outside was oppressive, and the light from the ceiling shone down like fire.

On stage, everything was perfectly still—so much so that everyone's breath became as coarse as a rope. Seeing that forest of arms, Grandma Mao Zhi felt her throat become dry, and she began to feel somewhat dizzy. She wanted to curse them all, but when she turned around and saw that even Mothlet, standing next to her, was raising her delicate hand, Mao Zhi felt as though she had been struck by something inside her chest—struck so hard that it tore her open. She could smell a foul, bloody odor emanating from inside her chest, and immediately had an urge to vomit up a mouthful of bloody phlegm and use it to scare that forest of naked arms back to their original positions. She coughed loudly, but didn't pull up anything except that bloody odor. In the end, she simply cast her gaze over the villagers, and it eventually came to rest on the old deaf man, the paralyzed woman, and several forty-something-year-old wholers and semi-wholers. Then she snorted and asked them coldly,

"The children may not know about the Year of the Great Plunder[1] and the construction of the terrace fields, but is it possible that even you have forgotten?"

She continued, "Have you also completely forgotten about how, during the Year of the Great Plunder, the entire village was in an uproar wanting to withdraw from society? Do you not have the slightest aurality?"[3]

She added, "Withdrawing from society is a debt that I owe you, your parents, and your grandparents. It is a debt I will repay even if it kills me. If you do not wish to withdraw from society, you are welcome to rejoin it afterward. Entering society is as easy as going shopping, but withdrawing is as difficult as being reincarnated after death."

As she was saying this, Mao Zhi's voice began to grow hoarse, as though something had gotten lodged in her throat. Her words were forceful, but her pain and sorrow nevertheless came through loud and clear. When she finished speaking, Mothlet immediately pulled her hand down and peered at her grandmother's face, as though she owed her something. But Mao Zhi didn't look at her granddaughter, and neither did she look at the other villagers who immediately followed suit and lowered their hands.

Instead, she stood up and straightened her back like a tree that had been bent over by the wind. Grasping the wall, she hobbled slowly off the stage.

Grandma Mao Zhi walked out through the empty theater. Because she hadn't brought her crutch, each time she took a step her stick-thin body lurched to the left and then pushed toward the right, and in this way she awkwardly propelled herself forward, making a concerted effort not to fall. She arduously traversed the auditorium, like an old sheep struggling to ford a river. Rising and falling as she moved forward, she exited the theater and stood alone outside in the rain.

CHAPTER 3: FURTHER READING— THE YEAR OF THE GREAT PLUNDER

1) **The Year of the Great Plunder.** *The Great Plunder is a historical term for what has also been referred to as the Iron Smelting Disaster.*

After the Great Leap Forward, which began in the wuxu year, 1958, thoroughly swept through the Balou region like a tornado, the Great Iron Smelting Campaign resulted in all of the trees on the mountain being cut down and the fields being burned to the ground. As a result, the mountain range was left completely barren. By winter of the following year, everything was dry and without snow, and the next summer there was only a single drizzle, followed by a hundred-day drought. That autumn, however, it rained continuously, resulting in a historic locust plague. In Balou, locusts are called grasshoppers. These "grasshoppers" had flown in from outside the mountain, blanketing the sky and obscuring the sun. From miles away, you could hear the stormlike sound.

The sky was completely blanketed by the grasshoppers, and the bean fields were left barren.

The sesame fields were also left barren.

The golden blossoms of the rape plants disappeared.

By evening, after the grasshoppers had flown over, the sun was dark red. The dying grasshoppers covered the village streets like a red veil.

Mao Zhi was in the process of smelting steel when she gave birth to her daughter. Because her beautiful and whole-bodied daughter was born during the transition from autumn to winter, and since ju *bloom in autumn and* mei *bloom in winter, Mao Zhi named her daughter Jumei, after the terms for chrysanthemums and plums. That evening, Mao Zhi walked out of the house carrying her daughter, and saw the grasshopper plague. She immediately put Jumei down and shouted into the village of Liven,*

"There is an autumn tragedy, which means that next winter there won't be enough to eat, and each family will have to economize. . . ."

"There is an autumn tragedy, which means we need to set aside food for the winter, to prepare for the possibility of a famine. . . ."

In the end, that is how things turned out, and a year of famine resulted.

Autumn was almost over, and winter was about to arrive. It was bitterly cold in the mountains, and even the water at the bottom of the wells was frozen solid. The new bark on the tung-oil and willow trees that had grown after the steel- and iron-smelting campaigns was also frozen solid. The villagers who went to the commune to shop at the market all hurried home and exclaimed, God! This has truly been an act of God. Not only are our wheat fields lying fallow, but wheat throughout the region beyond the Balou mountains has also failed to sprout. After another couple of weeks, a villager hurried back from the market, and as soon as he reentered the village he told everyone, with a look of terror on his face, This is disastrous! Even in the commune, no one has any grain to eat. They can only serve one meal a day, and they report that they are all starving. Some people have even stripped the elm trees of their bark and used it to make soup. Everyone, is as pale as a ghost, and their legs are as swollen as ripe radishes.

Mao Zhi left her daughter at home and went down the mountain. She walked thirty-something li until she encountered a small procession carrying a corpse.

She asked, What disease did he die from?

They replied, He didn't die from disease; he died from hunger.

When she saw another procession carrying a corpse, she again asked, What did disease did he die from?

No disease; he starved to death.

She encountered yet another funeral procession. This time the corpse was not in a coffin, but rather was wrapped in a mat. She asked,

Did he starve to death as well?

No, he didn't starve to death. He died of constipation.

What did he eat?

He ate dirt, and drank water soaked in the bark of an elm tree.

The people described the man's death as coldly as they would that of a chicken, duck, ox, or dog. They evinced no trace of sorrow, as though the deceased were not a relative or neighbor from their own village. The children of the deceased followed the procession, but without tears, acting as though the deceased was not their parent. The weather was unusually frigid, and the wind cut like a knife. Mao Zhi continued on her way until she arrived at a small village where she noticed a cluster of new graves, like a clump of newly sprouted mushrooms. The graves were haphazardly arranged, and there were several dozen—or even several hundred—of them, each of which had several sheets of blank paper hanging from it, like white chrysanthemums and peonies.

Mao Zhi stood in front of the graves for a while, then turned around and hurried back to Liven before dark. Upon arriving at the first blind man's house, she saw that his family was sitting around a fire eating noodles—white garlic-flavored noodles seasoned with grinding oil. She stood at their door and asked in a sharp voice, How dare you eat noodles? People throughout the land are starving to death, to the point that it is no more remarkable for a person to die of hunger than it would be for a chicken to do so. And yet, you still dare fill your bellies with noodles? When she arrived at the next house, she found that the family was not eating noodles, but when she saw their pot of corn soup, and that it was thick enough to hold a spoon erect, she poured a ladle of cold water into it and yelled, There is famine throughout the land, and people are starving to death like chickens. Don't you know you need to ration? At the next household, the children were horsing around and eating oil buns. Before the rest of the buns were fully cooked, she took the griddle out of the fire and used a ladle of water to douse the flames. She shouted, Go outside and take a look. People are starving to death like dogs, yet your family dares to cook oil buns behind closed doors! She roared, Do you not want to live? Are you prepared to have your family starve to death next winter?

Mao Zhi reached the home of Crippled Bo at the back of the village. Although Crippled Bo's family was sitting around a fire, they were merely *having diluted noodle soup and buns made from a mixture of black and white grain. They had only a single bowl of pickled cabbage.*

Mao Zhi stood in the doorway to their house.

Crippled Bo asked, What's wrong?

Mao Zhi replied, Crippled Bo, there really is going to be a grain shortage. Throughout the land people are starving to death like dogs.

Crippled Bo pondered quietly for a moment, then suggested that every family dig a pit in front of the village, in which the family could bury one or two jugs of grain.

Mao Zhi convened a meeting and instructed each family to dig a pit and bury grain.

After they all did so, she established three rules for the village to follow. First, no family was permitted to eat noodles. Second, no family was permitted to eat baked oil buns. Third, no one was permitted to wake up in the middle of the night and fix a midnight snack. Mao Zhi wrote down these rules and distributed a copy to every household in the village, telling everyone to post them next to the family's picture of the kitchen god. Furthermore, she established a local militia consisting of several young wholers in their twenties armed with guns, and told them to patrol the village day after day. Particularly before mealtimes, they would instruct each family to carry their bowls outside to eat, as they had in the past. No family was permitted to eat behind closed doors. If anyone disobeyed the first two rules the wholer militia would take the family's noodles and oil buns and carry them to the entrance to the village, where they would permit the family with the thinnest gruel to eat the noodles and oil buns, while the first family had to drink the gruel.

One day followed the next, and after the twelfth month came the first month of the new lunar year. A major event took place in that first month. The commune's Secretary Mai led several stout wholers to the village in a steel-wheeled horse cart. After saying a few words, they departed with two bundles of wheat from the village's grain warehouse. Secretary Mai sought out Mao Zhi and requested that she come to the village entrance, where he asked her, Why is it that there isn't a single new grave in your village's graveyard?

Mao Zhi replied, Isn't it a good thing that there aren't any new graves?

He said, Yes, it is a good thing. How many meals do the villagers eat each day?

Mao Zhi replied, The same three meals as always.

The secretary said, People are enduring hellish conditions throughout the land, and only the village of Liven is enjoying a heavenly existence. It has already been half a year since the wheat harvest season ended, and now we are in the dead of winter, yet when we walked past your village we noticed a sweet fragrance of wheat coming from your fields. When we followed this fragrance, we discovered that in your warehouse there are several bins of undistributed wheat.

The secretary then exclaimed, My god! Throughout the land entire families are starving to death, yet you have more grain than you can eat.

The secretary gazed at a group of villagers, and said, Tell me, can you bear to watch as people from the same commune starve to death one after another? Can you bear to watch famine refugees come begging at your door, while you refuse to give them food? Are we not all living under the Communist Party? Are we not all class brothers and sisters?

The wholers thereupon seized Liven's three to five remaining bins of wheat, loaded them onto a cart, and hauled them away, not leaving a single grain behind.

They carted everything away. But three days later, several more wholers arrived, each with a carrying pole and a letter written by the secretary. It said:

> Mao Zhi,
>
> One hundred and thirteen out of the four hundred and twenty-seven people of the Huaishugou production brigade have already starved to death. There isn't any bark left on any of the trees in the village, and even all the soil has been eaten. After reading this letter, you must collect a quart of grain from every home in the village. Don't forget that you and the people of Liven are all members of the socialist family, and are each other's class brothers and sisters.

Mao Zhi, carrying the secretary's letter, led the visitors to every home in the village, in order to collect a quart of grain from each family. The visitors left, and several days later someone else brought a letter from the secretary, and this person too went door-to-door to collect two bundles of wheat. Before the first month of the year was over, three to five groups of people had come to Liven demanding grain and bearing a carrying pole, a travel sack, and a letter with the commune's seal and the secretary's signature. If the villagers didn't give them any grain, the visitors would plant themselves at the entrance to the village or in front of Mao Zhi's house and refuse to leave. In the end, the villagers had to give them a quart of grain from the blind man's household and a bowl from the crippled man's household. In this way, Liven came to function as a granary for the entire commune, until eventually every family's vats were empty. When the villagers used a bowl or ladle to scoop grain out of the vat, they would hear it strike the sides of the container, and every head of household would shudder, feeling a chill rise up from his or her heart.

On the final day of the first month, two more young people from the county arrived in the village. Their attire, however, was completely unlike that of the commune visitors, and instead they were wearing Mao suits with several pens sticking out of their shirt pockets. Mao Zhi immediately recognized one of them as County Chief Yang's former secretary, who was now known as Teacher Liu at the county soc-school. Teacher Liu had a handwritten letter from the county chief himself. It said:

> Mao Zhi,
>
> We are both veterans of the Fourth Red Army. Currently, the socialist revolution has reached another pivotal turning point, and even the members of the county council and the county government are starving. After receiving this letter, please send us some of the village's grain as quickly as possible, in order to help address this pressing matter.

The letter was written on a sheet of yellow grass paper, and the writing was crooked and uneven, as though a clump of weeds was growing on the paper. At the end of the letter, there was not only the county chief's signature but also his fingerprint in red ink. Next to the fingerprint, there was the red badge from Chief Yang's cap, which he had preserved from his time in the

Fourth Red Army. The fingerprint was as red as fresh blood, with round and oval ridges, while the cap insignia was so old it resembled dried blood, and all five corners had faded to the color of lead. Mao Zhi looked at the letter, then removed the five-star insignia and held it in her hand. Without saying a word, she led the visitors to a spot beneath the eaves of her house, where she removed the lids of two large vats and announced that there was wheat in one and corn in the other. She told the visitors that they could take as much as they wanted.

Teacher Liu said, Mao Zhi, how much do you think we can carry by ourselves? Tomorrow a horse cart will come to the village.

Mao Zhi said, Let them come. When they come I will lead you to each home in the village to collect grain.

The next day, a horse cart did in fact arrive in the village, together with not one but two large carts with rubber tires. They stopped in the middle of the village, and the village children, who had never seen rubber tires before, all crowded around, touching and smelling the tires and hitting them with sticks. They noticed that the rubber had a peculiar odor, and that it had the same texture as ox hide. They hit the tires with hammers and sticks, but found that they simply bounced back. Then, a cripple and a deaf person who had never ventured far from home came over to look at the carts, as a blind person stood nearby listening intently to what other people were saying. While the villagers were looking and asking questions, Mao Zhi led the cadres from one home to another to collect grain.

When they arrived at the eastern end of the village, Mao Zhi said, Third Blind Uncle, they have come from the county to collect grain, and they have a signed letter from the county chief. Please open your grain vat and let the cadres help themselves to what they need. It is said that even the county chief is so famished that his legs are all swollen.

When they arrived at the western end of the village, Mao Zhi said, Fourth Auntie, is Fourth Uncle home? These visitors have come from the county seat. This is the first time in a century that people have come from the county to collect grain. You should open your vat and let them take as much as they want.

Fourth Auntie asked, After this, will they come again to collect more?

Mao Zhi said, This will be the last time.

Crippled Fourth Auntie removed the lid of the family's grain vat, permitting the visitors from the county to take what was inside. The visitors then proceeded to the next family, the head of which had only one arm. He was Mao Zhi's brother-in-law, which is to say the younger brother of her husband, and the first thing he said when he saw her was, Auntie, you've brought more people to collect grain? Mao Zhi replied, Please open the grain vat; this will be the final time.

Her brother-in-law led the visitors into the main room of his home, and allowed them to help themselves to his grain. The visitors' two carts were filled to the brim with large and small bags, and in the end they carted away all of the village's grain. It was already the first lunar month, and spring was not far away. It was agreed that the commune and the county wouldn't send anyone else to demand grain, and every family was exuberant. But after the county committee and the county government hauled away the grain they had collected, a representative from the county agricultural ministry arrived with a letter from the county committee demanding even more, and a representative from the Organization Bureau arrived with a similar letter. A representative from the armed forces department not only brought a letter, but arrived in a car and bearing guns.

Following the first lunar month, after the announcement from the county was distributed, the families in Liven were no longer exuberant, and at most they would provide their visitors with only a single meal. But even so, people came from dozens of li away for the sole purpose of asking Liven for food. Ordinarily, you wouldn't find beggars anywhere in the village, but at mealtime they would arrive from who knows where—leading their children by the hand to every home in Liven, passing their bowls through every doorway and up to every pot.

From the end of the gengzi year to the beginning of the following year, Liven experienced a severe grain shortage and the crisis became even more severe. There were refugees from other villages outside every home in Liven. These refugees were all wholers. Under the eaves of the front of houses and everywhere the sun was shining, families of beggars could be seen. At nightfall, they would sleep in people's doorways, behind their houses, or even in shielded areas of the street itself. When it was so cold that they couldn't sleep, they would go into the streets and stomp their feet, run around, and generally make such a commotion that all night long the village echoed with the sound of their footsteps.

One night, Mao Zhi walked out of her house and found several men secretly stripping the bark from the village's elm trees, so she went over and told them that if they did that, the trees would die. One man stopped and looked at her, and asked if she was a Liven cadre. She replied, Yes, I am. The man said, I have a fifteen-year-old daughter at home. Please help her find a husband in Liven. Even a blind man or a cripple will do, as long as he can give us a quart of grain. Mao Zhi then went to the center of the village, where a family was sitting around a fire. She asked, Why are you still in Liven? Our village doesn't have any food left. The father looked at her and said, I see that you are a cadre; is it true that anyone who is blind or crippled can stay and live here in Liven? Mao Zhi replied, It is true that this is a village of the blind, the deaf, and the crippled. There are no wholers who can live out their lives here in the depths of the Balou mountains. The man said, If that is the case, then by tomorrow my entire family of wholers will be missing either an arm or a leg, at which point you should certainly give us a bite to eat.

Mao Zhi didn't dare continue forward. Every time she took a few steps, someone would kneel down in front of her and beg for food. People would kneel down and, sobbing, hug her legs. That night it was bitterly cold, and the moonlight was like ice. The people sleeping outside all went to the fields and pulled up the wheat straw, which they then brought back and spread out in the streets. They took the thatched roofs of the huts in the wheat fields, and spread them out on the ground in the village. Some people even slept in the ox shed at the front of town, and because it was so cold they pressed their bodies against the ox's belly. If the ox was well behaved, the parents would let their children hug its legs while they slept.

There was also Seventh Cripple's pigsty, near the entrance to the village. The pigs were half-grown, and on the floor of the pigsty there was a fresh layer of new straw. A family was sleeping on the ground with the pigs, the children hugging the piglets, and the entire family eating out of the pig trough.

When Mao Zhi visited the family that was sleeping with the pigs, she asked the parents if they weren't afraid the pigs might bite their children. They replied that pigs were better behaved than humans, and the risk was not so much that the pigs might bite the humans, but rather that the humans might bite the pigs. They said that in their village, there had even been a case of cannibalism.

Mao Zhi didn't dare say anything else. The next day, she notified all the families in the village that at each meal they should each prepare two extra bowls, which they would then take to the village entrance to give to the famine refugees.

Afterward, the situation simply got worse, as even more famine refugees poured into the village, making it seem as though Liven were hosting a major convention. When the people of Liven ate their meals, they no longer gathered together in the dining area at the front of the village but rather, for better or worse, would close their doors and lock themselves in their houses. However, Liven did have food, and the village's cemetery didn't have a single new gravestone. This was something that people could see for themselves. The news spread like wildfire that all you needed when you arrived in the village of Liven was a letter marked with a seal from the commune or the county and you would be able to collect some grain, and if you brought out your rice bowl you would be able to receive a bowl of food.

People from throughout the Balou mountain region and beyond surged like the tide toward this village in the depths of the mountains. In Liven, the number of famine refugees vastly exceeded that of the original villagers. Some were from the same township or the same county, while others came from other provinces, including Anhui, Shandong, and Hebei. Overnight, Liven became known far and wide. Dayu and Gaoliu counties sent people to Liven with certified letters and, emphasizing either the village's history or its geographic environment, claimed that they previously belonged to the same canton or county as Liven, and at the very least were either currently neighboring counties or belonged to the same district, and therefore hoped Liven could give them some grain.

By the middle of the month, Liven stopped giving out food to everyone who requested it. Families behaved as though they were confronting an implacable enemy, and kept their doors tightly shut all day long. They would eat at home, shit at home, and not speak or have any other interaction with anyone outside their own family. Even if they heard old men and women in the streets crying their hearts out, they remained unwilling to open their doors and give them any rice or steamed buns.

Mao Zhi was a cadre, and as such she was expected to behave differently from the other villagers. Therefore, at mealtime, she would always keep her door wide open. She would prepare a pot of sweet potato soup, and after everyone in her family had a bowl, she would leave the remainder outside her door. After three days, however, her husband stopped preparing an entire pot of soup, and instead would make only half a pot, and after another three days he began making only half of a small pot. Mao Zhi stared at him and said sharply, Stonemason, don't you have a conscience? He replied abjectly, Go look in the jar yourself, and see how little flour we have left.

Mao Zhi didn't reply.

After another three days, Mao Zhi's household had no more grain, and had to borrow a bit here and there from the neighbors, and some of those begging for food ended up starving to death in Liven.

They were buried along the village's mountain ridge road.

More people starved to death, and were buried at the entrance to the village.

In Liven, there came to be a cluster of graves belonging to outsiders.

One night, something momentous took place. It was as if an explosion had rocked the village of Liven to its core. At the end of the first month of every year, there are always a few days in the Balou mountains that are as cold as hell. If this year had been as cold as in the past, the refugees in the streets would have been stomping around trying to keep warm. On this particular night, however, there was no sound of footsteps or of a bonfire. The village was so quiet it seemed as though there wasn't a single refugee around. Occasionally a child in one of the village homes would cry out in hunger, but he or she would stop after one or two cries and the silence would return.

Mao Zhi didn't realize that buried within this silence there was an imminent explosion, and therefore she, as usual, cooked a pot of sweet potato soup to give to the refugees outside her door. When she returned, her husband had already warmed up her bedding for her, so she took off her clothes and said, Stonemason, in the future you needn't warm my bed for me. Given that you are not getting enough to eat yourself, your body doesn't have any excess warmth. Her husband laughed, and then sat at the head of the bed and said, Mao Zhi, the chisel, hammer, and apron that I cleaned today were all hanging on the wall, and they fell to the ground of their own accord. I'm

afraid this is an omen that something calamitous will happen to us, which
will mean I won't be able to continue warming your bed for much longer.

    Stonemason, how can you still be superstitious under the new society?

    Mao Zhi, Tell me the truth—do you regret marrying me?

    Why in the world do you ask that?

    Please, just tell me the truth.

    Mao Zhi didn't answer, and instead gazed silently into the distance.

    Her husband asked, Why are you afraid to answer?

    Do you really want me to answer?

    Yes, go ahead.

    Okay, then I will.

    Then answer.

    I always do feel a little regret.

    The stonemason immediately turned pale, and stared at her in shock.
He saw that though she was still very young, only thirty-something years
old, she looked as though she were almost fifty.

    He asked,

    Is it because I'm so old?

    She replied,

    I regret that Liven is so isolated and is full of blind, deaf, and crippled
people. If it weren't for you, when we joined the commune I would have
moved to the county seat to become the chair of the local women's federa-
tion, or even the county chief. But now, I am still in Liven directing people to
farm the land, and don't even know if this counts as part of the Revolution
or not. If it doesn't, I will always regret that I spent the latter half of my
life here in Liven without having a chance to contribute to the Revolution.

    When she got to this point, the situation erupted. First, someone
began knocking on the gate, and after a while someone else climbed over
the wall. The stonemason asked, Who's there? The footsteps came up to
the door of the house. Mao Zhi asked, Who are you? Are you starving?
If so, we'll cook you a bowl of soup. The person didn't say a word, and
instead pushed open Mao Zhi's door, and in rushed five or six burly whol-
ers. They were all carrying clubs and shovels, and once they entered they
immediately stood in front of the bed, waving their clubs and shovels at
the stonemason's head and at Mao Zhi's face. They said, We are sorry for

this; heaven is not fair. But we are all starving to death, while no one in this village of one-armed, one-legged, blind, deaf, and crippled villagers has experienced hunger, to the point that there isn't a new gravestone in the entire village cemetery.

The speaker took out a letter of introduction from the county—stamped by both the county committee and the county government—directing him to collect grain from Liven. He thrust the letter, which was written with a brush on grass paper, onto the bed in front of Mao Zhi and said, You have already seen this sort of letter, yet you don't permit Liven to distribute any more grain? You leave us with no choice but to take matters into our own hands. This is not stealing, but rather simply collecting what the government says is already rightfully ours. As he was saying this, he signaled to the men behind him, and immediately two middle-aged men took a cloth sack and went into another room to look for flour. They peered into the kitchen pot for something to eat.

By this point, the stonemason had already gotten down from the bed. He grabbed his cleaning sack from the bedpost and pulled out a hammer. But at that moment, someone waved a hoe at his head and shouted, Don't forget that you come from a crippled family! The stonemason glanced at Mao Zhi, then stood motionless. Another man waved a club at her head and said, Be smart. Given that you fought in the Red Army and contributed to the Revolution, how is it that you don't know that you should distribute grain to the masses? At this point, Mao Zhi's daughter Jumei was awakened by all the commotion, and started howling as she tried to crawl into Mao Zhi's lap. Mao Zhi stopped her, then stared at the burly young man who was now holding her hair. She recognized him as the father of the children to whom she would give a bowl of soup every day. She looked at him coldly and said, You, how can you be so lacking in compassion?

The man said, We have no choice. We have to find a way to help our families survive.

Mao Zhi replied, You are willing to steal to survive? Have you no principles?

The man said, What do you mean by principles? We are your principles! How can you speak of principles when people are starving to death? I've also fought in the Red Army, with the Eighth Regiment.

The sound of a bowl could be heard coming from the kitchen. Needless to say, this was the sound of a bowl shattering on the ground. The sound of jars and vats could be heard from another room, as the men searched desperately for food. Looking over the outer wall, the stonemason could see that one of the men had found their corn and poured it into his bag, and was now stuffing a handful into his own mouth. The stonemason said, You should eat more slowly; that jar had rat poison in it. The other man replied, I'd be happy to die of poisoning; at least it would be more pleasant than slowly starving to death. The stonemason said, In that case, you should just put the poison inside a baked bun, so that you don't also poison your wife and children. The other man then held the light up to the opening of his cloth sack, and from inside he pulled out a dried bun and tossed it behind the door.

In the house, everything was in tumult. Jumei was in Mao Zhi's lap, her shrill sobs reverberating throughout the room. Mao Zhi opened her shirt and stuck her nipple in Jumei's mouth, immediately stanching her cries. The only sounds that remained in the room were those of footsteps and the sound of drawers being opened and closed. One man didn't find any grain, or anything else, and walked disappointedly out of the kitchen. He stood in front of Mao Zhi and, with knife in hand, said, I didn't find anything, and didn't take anything. My child is only three years old, and is cold and hungry. You must give me something. Mao Zhi picked up Jumei's padded jacket from the bed, handed it to him, and asked, Is this jacket too small?

He replied that it was fine if it was a little small.

Mao Zhi said that it was a girl's jacket.

He said it was fine that it was for girls.

At this point there was a pause. Everything in the room that could be eaten or worn had been taken, and the men returned to Mao Zhi's bedside. One of them was somewhat older, and he looked first at Mao Zhi and then at the stonemason. He bowed down before them, and said, Forgive me, I'm just borrowing this. Then, he led the other wholers out the door.

It was as if a tornado had blown through the house.

The room was quiet. The stonemason looked at the wall where his gun had been mounted, and remarked that it was a good thing the militiamen had not taken it. Mao Zhi turned around and glanced at the empty wall behind the bed, then placed Jumei down, whereupon she and her husband *proceeded to get dressed. When they stepped out into the courtyard, they discovered that the men had latched the gate from the outside, leaving the entire family locked inside the house.*

Mao Zhi and her husband stood alone in the courtyard. They could hear people shouting in the street, saying, They've buried their grain beneath the bed, their grain is beneath the bed! Then, they heard some wholers next door looking for pickaxes, shovels, and hoes, together with the sound of them digging a hole and refilling it. They heard one house after another being ransacked, as though there was a war going on. The stonemason saw Mao Zhi growing increasingly anxious, as she kept asking, What are we going to do? How can the wholers be so heartless? What are we going to do? How can the wholers be so heartless? He brought a stool over and placed it at the foot of the courtyard wall, then climbed over the wall to open the gate from the outside.

The moon was bright, and you could see halfway across the village. In the fields, there were many clusters of shadowy figures moving busily about. It was unclear what they were carrying. Some of the people were rushing into the village, while others hurried out, their footsteps resounding. Several wholers were leading oxen, while two strong ones were carrying a pig and some young ones were carrying chickens. The entire area was filled with the sound of chickens squawking, pigs oinking, and whips striking the backs of the pigs and oxen. Some of the wholers were rushing around urgently, and as a result the things they were carrying often fell off their backs and rolled over to the side of the road, at which point they would put down their things and go look for what had fallen. Then, other wholers passing by would pick up the things the first wholers had put down, and carry them off. In the resulting chaos, it seemed as though the entire world was in tumult.

Every family in Liven was sobbing. Under the bright moon, you could see the villagers' shouts and cries flying around the village like dried-up blood clots. The blind man whose home had been robbed was standing under the eaves of his house, hugging his wife and child, who were also blind. He sobbed as he pleaded, Our entire family is blind; please leave us at least a handful of grain. A wholer walking out the door with a sack of grain asked, How is it that you blind people are living better than us? Who ever heard of disabled people leading better lives than able-bodied ones? He added, We haven't come to steal your grain; we were sent by the government. There was nothing the blind family could say, as the three stared darkly at the wholers carrying off all of their grain.

One of the deaf people was quite strong, but since he couldn't hear the footsteps of wholers entering his courtyard, they were able to catch him and tie him up to the legs of his bed. The deaf-mute couldn't hear, but he could sense what was going on, so the wholers knocked him out with a stick. A seventy-seven-year-old crippled man wanted to go stop the wholers, but they said, If you move, we'll break your good leg. The cripple suddenly re-membered that he was disabled, and therefore had no option but to watch helplessly as the wholers took all of his family's belongings.

A wholer asked, Where is there a lamp?

The woman lifted her only arm and pointed, It is there, on the corner of the table.

The wholer said, Go light it.

So she went to light the lamp, and handed it to him. She said, Fam-ine is sweeping the land, and I know you are hungry. But my own child is only one year old. Could you at least leave him a quart of mixed grain flour? The wholer said, We are also from Boshuzi commune, and have a letter from the people's commune instructing us to come collect grain. The letter is stamped by the county government, and if you don't believe me I can fetch it. There isn't a single person in your village who has had to go hungry, while four people out of our family of seven have already starved to death. On what grounds could you refuse to give us grain, given that we have a letter from the commune? As he was speaking, he pulled out the jar of grain that was hidden beneath the bed, ladled out the last quart of mixed grain flour, and carried it off.

When he reached the end of the courtyard, he turned and said,

Just think, who ever heard of disabled people being better off than able-bodied ones?

Every household was robbed.

The street was filled with the sound of footsteps.

The entire village was filled with cries and sobs.

The entire Balou region was in tumult.

Mao Zhi and the stonemason stood in their doorway in the moonlight, watching as the thieves disappeared into the night like water flowing through your fingers. They saw that there were four or five people leading the village's yellow ox, and as they walked past Mao Zhi she hobbled out to the middle of the street and grabbed the ox's reins, saying, Leave the ox here! Tomorrow, the big brigade and production brigade will still need to plow the fields! One of the people looked at her, then kicked her good leg, knocking her over. She crawled forward and hugged his leg, saying, You can't treat us like this; we are all members of the Boshuzi commune! The person responded, What do we care about being members of the commune? When people are starving to death, what does it matter whether or not you are a member? Then he led the ox away, even as Mao Zhi continued grasping his leg. So he stopped and kicked her good leg again. At this point, Mao Zhi's husband ran over from the doorway and knelt down before the wholer, clasping his hands and bowing. He pleaded, Please don't beat her. She is crippled, and only has that one good leg. If you want to beat someone, then beat me.

The man said, Is she your wife? Tell your wife to let go of my leg.

The stonemason kowtowed to the man and said, Please leave us the ox. If we don't have an ox, then how will we plow the fields next year?

The man kicked Mao Zhi's good leg again.

Mao Zhi screamed in pain, and grasped his leg even more tightly than before. The stonemason kowtowed more quickly and more urgently, and begged, Could you please beat me instead? Could you please beat me? My wife was at Yan'an, and contributed to the Revolution. She helped establish the new society. The wholer looked at the stonemason, then back at Mao Zhi. Grinding his teeth, he said, Blast your grandmother. It is all your fault that society has gotten messed up. If it hadn't been for the Revolution, our family would still have our ox and two mu of land. Thanks to your Revolution, we were designated as a rich peasant family and consequently lost both our ox and our land. During the famine, three out of the five members of my family starved to death. As he was saying this, he kicked Mao Zhi a couple of times more and said, You woman, you weren't content to lead your own life, and instead had to carry out your fucking Revolution. I'll revolutionize you, that's what I'll do. I'll submit you to the Revolution! Saying this, he kicked Mao Zhi several more times in the belly.

Mao Zhi stared in shock, then loosened her grip on his leg.

The wholer snorted, then led the ox away with the other men. After they had proceeded several steps, he turned around and said, Granny, if you all hadn't carried out your Revolution, we wouldn't be having this famine. After saying this, he angrily left the village and went back up the mountain ridge.

The village gradually settled down.

The last group of wholers to leave the village were despondently muttering to themselves, saying: I didn't manage to get anything. Fuck her grandmother, I didn't manage to get anything. It was unclear, however, whether they were cursing the people of Liven or the other wholers, who had not left them any grain to steal.

The sun rose.

The village was quiet. There were no cocks crowing, oxen lowing, or ducks squawking.

Throughout the village there were empty baskets and sacks, and the ground was covered with corn and wheat, together with stamped and signed letters of introduction from the commune.

The sun came up just as it always had, shining down on the mountain ridge, on the village, and on each courtyard. The sparkling red government stamps that adorned those letters of introduction were like beautiful flowers. Someone came out of his house and stood in his doorway, and immediately the other villagers—young and old, including the blind, deaf, mute, and crippled, as well as wholers—all came out of their homes and stood silently in their respective doorways, gazing at one another. Their faces were calm, without a trace of sorrow or grief. Instead, they were all completely impassive as they regarded one another with frozen expressions.

After a while, one of the deaf men said, My family doesn't have a single handful of grain. We are starving to death, and even the jar of millet we had hidden beneath the bed was taken away. One of the blind men said to the deaf man, Someone said that our family didn't need light, and therefore they even took our oil lamp. That lamp was made of bronze, and the next time there is a steel shortage, our family won't have anything to contribute.

At this point, the villagers noticed Mao Zhi walking, her limp even more pronounced than before. She grasped her crutch, and with every step it looked as though she was about to collapse. Her face was ashen and her hair looked as though she hadn't combed it for eight hundred years. She had aged visibly overnight, her face as wrinkled as a spiderweb and her hair having turned gray. She stood beneath the honey locust tree, beneath where the oxcart wheel bell used to hang, and gazed at the people who lined both sides of the street. The villagers began walking toward her, as they had done when she used to hold meetings there. They crowded around and waited.

At this point, the voice of the daughter of that seventy-seven-year-old crippled man rang out from the back of the village. Her hoarse voice sounded like the wind blowing unevenly through the branches of a tree. She jumped up and down, slapping her thighs and shouting,

"Come quickly! My grandfather has died, and is lying in the grain pit beneath the bed! . . . Come quickly, My grandfather has died of anger, and is lying in the grain pit under the bed!"

That seventy-seven-year-old man had died. He died inside the pit where his family stored its grain. Next to the pit there was a letter demanding grain, which bore a stamp from the people's commune, together with another from the People's committee. Mao Zhi led the villagers to the side of the pit, where she picked up the letter. It turned out the old man was actually still alive, and he used his last breath to say,

"Mao Zhi, let the people of Liven withdraw from society. Liven should never have been part of this commune, or this province."

After saying this, the old man finally died.

After he died, he was buried.

After he was buried, the people of Liven began to endure a full-fledged famine.

For the first few days, families didn't leave their homes. Instead, they conserved their energy so as to retard the starvation process. A few days later, some people began going out—heading up the mountain to look for roots. Later, they started stripping bark from the trees to eat, as the people beyond the mountain did. After stripping off the outer layer of dry bark, they would remove the inner layer of living bark and take it home to boil into a glutinous soup. They continued like this for half a month, until all of the grass roots on the mountain had been dug up and the elm trees were all stripped of their bark, and then some people began eating dirt from the mountain itself.

People began starving to death.

One person died after another.

New graves began to appear in the village cemetery. After another half a month, those graves began sprouting like bamboo shoots after a spring shower, and eventually an array of graves as vast as a wheat field appeared in the front of the village. When unmarried young people died, they could not be buried in the ancestral plots, and therefore were buried at the head of the village.

When children under the age of five or so starved to death, it wasn't deemed worthwhile to buy them a coffin, and instead they were wrapped in a reed mat and placed in a bamboo basket, which would then either be thrown into the ravine beyond the village or placed next to a pile of rocks along the mountain ridge.

The sky was an expanse of blue and the mountain was perfectly still. The village of Liven was left behind in that expanse of blue, like a pile of grass or some historical relic. Eagles were screeching overhead, and would swoop down and stand in front of those bamboo baskets with children's corpses inside. The children's parents would initially watch over the baskets, and would strike the eagles with bamboo sticks. After a few days, however, they stopped guarding the baskets, since they were so hungry they couldn't leave the house. As a result, the eagles and wild dogs became very busy. A few days later, even the children's own parents went somewhere else to look for food, leaving behind the baskets on an expanse of wild grass.

Afterward, these empty basket was joined by many others. The area became a barren field, an amusement park for eagles, wild dogs, wolves, and foxes.

The sound of sobbing from Liven did not increase, but the gravestones and empty baskets on the mountain did. As winter ended and spring approached, the weather became warmer, and in the village some people slowly started to emerge from their houses, standing in the sunlight in front of their front doors. They would say a few words to their neighbors, and would talk about only one thing. They would mention how, in the past, life in the village had been one of livening and comfort, and how it was only after Mao Zhi led them to join the co-op, and then led them to join the people's commune, that they encountered this once-in-a-millennium disaster. They said that since it had been Mao Zhi who arranged for the village to enter society, she must now help them withdraw, so they might once again return to the life that they had been enjoying. They said that if the village hadn't entered society, people from outside wouldn't have even known there was this gorge in the Balou mountains, in which there was a village where disabled people lived a happy and carefree life all year long, with plenty of clothing and abundant grain. To the extent that the outside world had known about the existence of this village, Shuanghuai county believed that Liven belonged to Dayu county, Dayu believed it belonged to Gaoliu, and Gaoliu believed it belonged to Shuanghuai.

If they were permitted to withdraw from society, they said, they would never again fall under the jurisdiction of another county or commune, and would live carefree and enlivened lives. Who, under those circumstances, would be able to bring a letter of introduction and demand grain? Who would have ever thought to go plunder Liven? They said that all of this was Mao Zhi's fault, and it was because she brought the village into the commune and into the county, that they were now suffering from the present famine.

They resolved to go together to her house.

The called out at her door, and when it opened they saw her unsteadily emerge. Like everyone else's, her face was swollen and had a greenish tint. They saw that in the courtyard in front of her kitchen, there was a basin half-filled with water, in which was soaking the bag the stonemason used to carry his hammer and chisel. The stonemason's bag was made from cowhide, and after being soaked in water it could be boiled and eaten. Every day Mao Zhi would cut several strips from the cloth, soak them in water, dip them in salt, boil them, and then feed them to her daughter.

Mao Zhi stood there, seeing the villagers angrily assembled in front of her. Even the stonemason's own cousin was in the crowd. She realized something was about to happen, and the greenish tint in her face immediately turned ashen. She asked, You have all come? What do you want?

The villagers calmed down. Speaking on behalf of the crowd, the stonemason's cousin said, Sister, every family in the village has someone that has starved to death. They are concerned about you and your family, so they came to see you.

A smile came to Mao Zhi's lips, as she said, Thank you, thank you for thinking of our family.

The cousin then said, Sister, there is another thing I should mention. Everyone remembers the livened life we used to lead. Sister, if you are still able to walk, could you go down to the commune and county seat and arrange it so that Liven might return to the way things used to be, when we didn't have to listen to any commune or county?

Mao Zhi continued smiling, but began to look uncomfortable.

The cripple who was forced to hand over his ox at gunpoint when Liven joined the cooperative society asked, Why shouldn't we be able to do this? When we originally entered society none of the three surrounding counties even wanted us.

The one-eyed woman whose plow was confiscated under the angry command of the district chief when they joined the commune said, Sister, when we entered society you had said that this would allow the people of Liven to enjoy a heavenly existence, such that they wouldn't need oxen to plow the fields or oil to light their lamps. Please explain to us where those heavenly days are now?

Several dozen wholers and disabled women all started shouting, saying, Mao Zhi, you should go to the cemetery and the area in front of the village, and see how many villagers have died and how many new graves there are. You should go to the mountain and the gorge, and count how many baskets there are into which people have thrown their dead children. They asked, Is this the heavenly existence you spoke of? Is this the heaven you promised us once we joined the commune? One after another, the blind, deaf, and crippled villagers complained angrily, like a torrential downpour. The deaf-mutes pointed at Mao Zhi and signed angrily.

Mao Zhi's complexion turned sallow, and sweat ran down her face. The winter sun was shining brightly. There was no wind, and the entire village was filled with silent sunlight and leafless trees. The oxen had been led away, the pigs had been carted away, the chickens and ducks had been carried away. The village was like a ghost town, and apart from the people who were desperate from hunger, the others showed scant signs of life. Mao Zhi gazed out at the crowd assembled at her door; some were standing while others were kneeling on the ground. Some of the women were sitting and holding their children, who were so hungry they couldn't even cry.

Mao Zhi examined that crowd of villagers, glancing at the barren mountains and empty sky beyond the village, and began feeling faint. She felt as though the ground was spinning. She leaned her hand against the door frame to support herself, then let her body slide down to the ground. She ended up kneeling in front of the villagers, and said,

Uncles, aunties, brothers, and sisters. Everyone should relax. As long as I, Mao Zhi, am alive, just as we originally found a way to enter society, we will similarly find a way to withdraw. Two weeks ago Jumei's father, the stonemason, starved to death in his bed. He refused to eat this leather bag. He said that he had been a stonemason his entire life, but never imagined that this bag would be the most valuable possession he would be able to leave behind for his wife and daughter. Uncles, aunties, brothers, and sisters, half of the leather bag is still left, and I'll go and cut everyone a strip. However, I'll also ask everyone to lend me a hand, to help me dig a hole in the back of the village, so that I may bury my husband. The weather is getting warmer, and therefore he must be buried. I, Mao Zhi, have let you all down. I've let you all down. My husband, however, was a good man, and I beg that, in honor of his memory, you please help me.

Mao Zhi knelt in front of the villagers as she said this, and when she was finished she bowed her head and kowtowed three times. Afterward, she leaned against the door frame to pull herself up, and invited the villagers into her house.

The villagers stared at each other in disbelief.

Mao Zhi said, I am begging you. You have my word that, because I let you down, I haven't dared leave my house for two weeks for fear of seeing anyone. Today you have all come here, and you ask why I don't permit Liven to withdraw from society and return to the carefree life that the village once enjoyed. I accept responsibility for what has happened. If I don't have grain, may I starve to death; and if I have grain may I die from overeating, and after my death, may my corpse be eaten by maggots, devoured by dogs, torn apart by wolves, and pecked by vultures. But if this famine happens to spare my life, I vow to you that I, Mao Zhi, will ensure that Liven withdraws from the commune and from Boshuzi township. Now, though, I beg you to help me carry the body of my husband out of the village and bury it. Jumei is still too small, and she is terrified of his dead body lying there.

Mao Zhi's cousin was the first to enter her house, followed by a wholer. Inside, they saw that the tall stonemason was in fact lying stiffly on the bed, his body covered by a sheet, while on the ground there was a door plank on which Mao Zhi and her daughter had arranged their beddig. Jumei was lying on this makeshift bed, chewing a strip of boiled leather. As she was chewing, she saw the villagers walk in, whereupon her emaciated and sallow face broke into a grin.

The villagers took the corpse and buried it, and while Mao Zhi was thanking them she stood in front of the grave and once again knelt down toward the villagers and swore, Uncles, aunts, and brothers, I will no longer contribute to the Revolution. I, Mao Zhi, just want to live. Given that it was I who arranged for our village to enter society, I will therefore do everything I can to make sure that we withdraw again.

These were the events of the Year of the Great Plunder.

3) **Aurality.** DIAL. Means "memory." To say that someone lacks aurality is to say that he or she forgets that which shouldn't be forgotten.

CHAPTER 5: EVERYONE KNELT DOWN IN FRONT OF HER, AND THE ENTIRE WORLD WAS FULL OF TEARS

Grandma Mao Zhi never expected that things would get twisted around like this, like a dead-end path through the mountains that might lead deep into a forest or to a moonlit riverbank, but could also lead right up to the edge of a precipice. This mid-sized city in Subei was no different from the other cities she had seen. The buildings were tall enough to reach the clouds, and in many cases their walls were made entirely of glass. When you walked up to one of those buildings in the middle of the day, it was as though you were standing next to a fire so hot it could bake the oil right out of your body, and you could smell the noxious smell of everyone's hair. The street was very wide, and if it were being used to air-dry grain, it would be able to hold enough wheat or corn to feed the entire world.

But the entire street didn't contain a single grain of wheat, and instead was completely full of people and cars. The gasoline smelled even worse than the manure in Liven's pigsties and ox sheds, which was a very familiar and distinctive odor. The odor of Liven's pigsties and ox sheds circulated through the village as individual strands. The stench of gasoline, however, was even fouler, and could be smelled blanketing the main street, in the back alleys, and everywhere in between. Fortunately, it was raining that day, and consequently the sticky odor was not as intense as usual, having been partially washed away by the rain.

The entire city had been washed clean.

Grandma Mao Zhi walked alone out of the theater, and walked alone down the street. She hadn't expected that the people of Liven would abruptly decide they didn't want to withdraw from society after all, nor that they wouldn't want to leave the performance troupe. She also hadn't expected that after she left the theater and stood beneath the building's awning, sheets of rain would pour down on the theater's roof and onto the steps in front of the theater, and that she would suddenly see the troupe director and several wholers from the county standing in the rain, looking like chickens soaking in a pot. When they saw Mao Zhi, they all looked excited, as though they had suddenly stumbled onto a bonfire in the dead of winter. Grandma Mao Zhi didn't know where they had gone on their stroll, but upon seeing them she immediately realized they were on their way back from somewhere, and they were standing in the rain discussing something. When they saw Grandma Mao Zhi, they appeared to reach some sort of agreement and began walking toward her.

They said, "Grandma Mao Zhi, it's good that you happened to come out, since there is actually something we would like to discuss with you. Chief Liu just called and said that the Lenin Fund is almost complete. At the end of the month the contractual term of your traveling troupe will have expired, and therefore the county has agreed that as of the first day of next year Liven will no longer fall under its jurisdiction.

"But," they added, "Chief Liu said that everything should proceed in accordance with the will of the people, and before we take you back to Shuanghuai, he wants us to take a poll. He said that the people of Liven should all vote, to see how many of them wish to remain in Shuanghuai and under the administrative jurisdiction of Boshuzi, and how many of them wish for the village to remove itself from the county's jurisdiction and enjoy a carefree existence."

The rain was coming down harder than ever, but everyone continued standing on the steps in front of the theater. Some had umbrellas, while others simply let the rain pour down on their heads. One way or another, everyone's face was completely soaked, and the smell of water smothered everybody's own odors. You couldn't tell what the group had been discussing, or what those discussions foretold. It was as though they had just received Chief Liu's phone call when they ran into Grandma Mao Zhi, and had immediately proceeded to tell her about it.

Grandma Mao Zhi's heart started pounding, as though a heavy instrument was slamming into her chest. This group didn't know that the other troupe had just voted behind the stage, and that the vast majority of them indicated that, after having been part of the traveling troupe over the past five months, they no longer desired to withdraw from society, but rather wished to remain under the jurisdiction of Shuanghuai county. Grandma Mao Zhi didn't mention the vote, and instead asked the wholers,

"What about the other performance group?"

The wholers asked, "Which other group?" They immediately added, "Do you mean the other traveling troupe? They already voted in Guangdong, and out of the entire troupe of sixty-seven people, not a single person wished to withdraw from society. Instead, all of them indicated that they hoped their troupe would never disband, and instead would continue traveling and performing forever."

Grandma Mao Zhi felt a knot in her throat. She wanted to say something, but nothing came out.

Appearing to understand Grandma Mao Zhi's reaction, the county cadres who came to supervise the two troupes took advantage of the situation to announce their decision, and proceeded to describe the plan they had formulated while standing in the rain. They said, "Grandma Mao Zhi, we have a proposition we would like to present to you. We know you have struggled your entire life to help the village of Liven maintain its independence and that now, to borrow your own expression, you wish to have the village withdraw from society and enjoy a carefree existence. We also know, however, that the people of Liven who have gone out with the traveling troupes have all earned a large bundle of cash, and are concerned that if they withdraw from society they won't be able to continue performing and earning money. If you want to withdraw from society, you just need to agree to one thing, and if you do, then we'll report to the county that the people of Liven have voted and unanimously agreed to withdraw from society. This way, when you return to Shuanghuai next year, you will no longer fall under the jurisdiction of Shuanghuai county and Boshuzi township, and indeed will have completely withdrawn from society."

Grandma Mao Zhi cast her gaze over those county cadres, and waited for them to tell her what they wanted her to agree to do.

"Actually, what we are requesting is not anything particularly extraordinary," one of them said. "We have been leading the traveling troupes for the past five months, and are exhausted. We want to divide the ticket revenue from these final few days among ourselves, and all we need is for you to sign your approval on the registration form, stating that because it was raining each of the final ten days, the troupe had no way of performing."

They added, "We have already discussed this with the other troupe, and they agreed to do the same thing. Everyone knows that it rains heavily in the south, and no one would doubt that bad weather prevented them from performing."

They added, "For the remaining shows, we could increase the ticket price from five hundred to seven hundred yuan per ticket, and each time you perform we will receive two seats, meaning that each of us would be able to earn more than a thousand yuan a day."

They added, "For seven hundred yuan a ticket, though, we should add a new event, one that everyone would feel they absolutely have to see."

They added, "Tonight, we will pack up and prepare to move on to the next city—Wenzhou. It hasn't rained there recently, and the sun is shining bright. The people of Wenzhou are even richer than the people here, and families, when their children get married, paste brand-new hundred-yuan bills together on a sheet of red paper to form an auspicious double *happiness* character, and then take these enormous characters and post them on walls throughout the city. In fact, many families don't even burn fake money after someone dies, but instead burn one bundle of real money after another."

They added, "It wouldn't be hard at all to add a new event to the program. You, Mao Zhi, could also perform something. You could contribute the closing act."

They added, "We could move the act featuring the hundred-and-twenty-one-year-old man to the end, and after the audience has expressed their astonishment, we could then wheel you out in a wheelchair and announce that you are two hundred and forty-one years old, and that the nonuplet girls are your great-great-great-granddaughters. We could say that they are your family's ninth-generation descendants. This event could be called Nine-Generations-Beneath-One-Roof.'"

They said, "We should think of a way of bringing up your residential permit and your identification card. Actually, it doesn't really make a difference whether you perform or not. In fact, it doesn't matter whether or not you agree to write on the performance record that the final shows were canceled on account of rain. It doesn't even matter whether or not we are able to keep the proceeds from the final performances. The important thing is whether or not you will permit the people of Liven to withdraw from society. *That* is the crucial question."

They said, "Just think, if you agree to have the troupe move on to Wenzhou, then tomorrow night they will start performing there."

They said, "With each performance, you can earn three hundred seats. If that is not enough, we could increase your share to four hundred seats."

Mao Zhi listened to all of this and thought it over, then said,

"I don't want money."

One of the men asked, "What do you want, then?"

She said, "I need some time to think."

He said, "Then take some time. It will take us the better part of the night to relocate to Wenzhou. And furthermore, it is raining, so the roads will be slick."

The group walked away and entered the theater. Meanwhile, Grandma Mao Zhi hobbled along the street outside the theater, not looking to either side, but occasionally glancing at the cars and at the streaming rain behind her. Because of the rain, all of the residents of the city were inside, leaving the street completely empty, like a cemetery without any visitors. The rainwater flowed into crevices in the ground, and along the side of the road there were many silvery puddles. The buildings in front of her resounded with the pouring rain, just as, in midsummer along the Balou mountain ridge, the poplar grove resounds with the wind. Farther away, the houses and buildings disappeared into the mist as though they were frozen in the rain. They looked gray and black, but there was a shimmering, watery vapor emanating from them and slowly wafting overhead.

Grandma Mao Zhi truly believed that there was an enormous expanse of water in front of her. She stood there examining it carefully, but realized that it was actually not water, but rather the asphalt road and the gray ground merging together in the rain. She noticed that not far off there was an intersection where two cars had collided. She couldn't hear what the drivers were saying to each other, but after a while they got back into their respective cars and drove off into the rain. Grandma Mao Zhi started walking toward the intersection where the accident had taken place, and when she arrived she noticed that not only was the ground covered with shattered glass, but there was a half-grown mottled dog that had been struck by one of the cars and was lying motionless in the rain. The dog's blood was mixed with the rainwater, becoming gradually more diluted as it went from dark crimson to bright red to light pink and finally dissolved altogether.

As the raindrops fell into the pool of blood, they emitted a sharp sound. Red bubbles emerged from the pool, like the red paper parasols that dot the streets of that city on sunny days. When the bubbles burst, it was as if the parasols were closed up, and even the sound was similar, though parasols make a longer popping sound than the bubbles did. When the bubbles popped, a faint odor would emanate from them, then quickly dissipate. Grandma Mao Zhi stood next to the shattered glass from the car accident, next to that cacophony of odors, and gazed silently at the wounded dog. The dog stared back at her, as though begging her to hold it in her arms.

She was reminded of the disabled dogs she had at home.

She squatted down and patted the wounded animal's head, then stroked its blood-soaked hind legs. It occurred to her that if a ticket could really sell for seven hundred yuan, then ten tickets could sell for seven thousand, a hundred tickets could sell for seventy thousand, and a thousand tickets for seven hundred thousand. But during their performances over the preceding two months, the troupe had always sold at least thirteen hundred tickets per performance. Thirteen hundred tickets would be equivalent to nine hundred and ten thousand yuan, and even if you were to subtract the proceeds that the wholers had promised to give the performers, they would still be left with at least eight hundred and fifty thousand yuan, to be distributed among these eight county cadres, together with the troupe's accountant, cashier, ticket seller, and guards. In all, in addition to the forty-five disabled performers, the troupe included about fifteen wholers, and for every performance these fifteen wholers could collectively earn eight hundred and fifty thousand yuan.

That is to say, each of the villagers could earn two seats for each day's performance, while the wholers could earn, at the very least, an average of fifty thousand yuan a day.

That is to say, if Grandma Mao Zhi didn't sign the form stating that the performances had been canceled on account of the rain, then each of the wholers would lose the opportunity to earn five hundred thousand yuan.

That is to say, everything hinged on her.

The rain was coming down harder and harder. Grandma Mao Zhi squatted there in the rain next to the injured dog and began to feel cold, as though she weren't wearing any clothing at all. At the same time, however, she began to feel rather hot. She remembered that if she declined to add her fingerprint to the box on that form, the wholers would not receive a single cent in compensation. She felt a wave of warmth surging up from her lower regions, and when it reached her head it felt as if her entire body was warm. Her chill immediately disappeared without a trace.

Grandma Mao Zhi caressed the dog's head again. She wiped the raindrops from the animal's face as though wiping tears from a child's eyes. Then, she gently moved the dog to a safe spot on the side of the road. She watched it for a while, then turned around and walked back. She looked as though she had just made a decision, and although certainly her leg was still crippled, her pace was brisker than before. She took a deep step followed by a shallow one, and each time her good right foot hit the ground she had to use more strength to move her crippled left leg, thereby making a much bigger splash. After only a few steps, her left pants leg was completely soaked.

There wasn't anyone else in the street.

Grandma Mao Zhi trudged through the rain like an old peasant passing through the city. But she noticed a tiny sound behind her, as though a lost child were calling her mother.

When she looked over her shoulder, she saw that the dog was crawling after her, dragging its hind legs. When the dog saw her turn around, it started energetically crawling forward like a child discovering her mother, gazing at her with a baleful expression.

This was one of the city's wild dogs. She hesitated a moment, then hobbled back a few steps and picked it up, hugging it tight to her chest. She held the dog as though it were a water-soaked sack of flour, and immediately felt it trembling, both from the cold and from gratitude. Then, as she was walking back to the theater with this dog that had had its legs broken by the car, she noticed that a group of three to five other dogs had appeared out of nowhere and were following her as well. Some were black and others were white, but each was old and ugly. The rain had plastered their fur to their bodies, revealing their bones, as if they were emaciated people during the Year of the Great Plunder.

Mao Zhi stood there without moving.

The dogs stared at her intently, like street beggars staring at a charitable-looking person with food.

She said, "I'm an old woman. You can't follow me like this."

The dogs didn't make a sound, and instead continued staring at her.

She said, "I don't know why you are following me, since I don't have anything to give you."

297

They stared at her still.

She walked away, and they followed her.

She stopped, and they also came to a halt behind her.

She gently kicked the dog in front, and it let out a yelp as the others retreated a few steps. But when she continued toward the theater, the dogs again followed her as though they were her tail.

She stopped worrying about whether or not they were following her, and instead focused on hobbling forward. When she brought that half-grown mottled dog to the front of the theater, she looked back and saw that the handful of dogs had now grown to a pack of more than a dozen. These old and filthy dogs were all animals abandoned by the residents of the city. Like the people of Liven, the dogs included animals that were blind in both eyes and whose eyes were full of mucus and oozing yellow pus. There were dogs who had broken one of their legs, and had to stand on three legs like a crippled person leaning on a crutch. There was also a dog that looked like it had roamed back and forth in front of the city's various restaurants searching for something to eat, until someone from the restaurant threw a pot of boiling soup onto its back, and its body gave off a smell of putrid meat, as if it were an amusement park for flies and mosquitoes.

By this point the rain had started to taper off, and the sky was covered in a bright light.

Grandma Mao Zhi was engulfed by the dogs' nauseating stench. She stood in front of the theater and was about to urge the dogs to leave when the dog at the front of the pack—an old, crippled animal that walked unsteadily—suddenly came forward and knelt down in front of her. Mao Zhi felt her own crippled leg begin to tremble, as though someone were pinching her nerves. She gazed intently at the crippled dog's front leg, and noticed that when the animal knelt down it appeared to topple over as it splashed into water on the ground. In order to distinguish between the acts of kneeling and lying down, the dog kept its rear legs erect so that its body inclined upward from the front to the rear, tail and rear end sticking straight up in the air. At the same time, however, it kept its head erect as it watched Mao Zhi, thereby granting itself a very peculiar posture.

She asked, "What do you want?"

She looked down at the dog she was carrying in her arms. "Is this your pup? If so, I'll return it to you."

She then proceeded to put down the mottled dog. As she did, it immediately turned and looked the older dog in the eye, then turned again and dragged itself forward toward Mao Zhi.

She therefore picked it up again.

As she did, the older dog suddenly looked back, then barked several times, as though telling the other dogs something. Then, all the other dogs knelt down in front of Mao Zhi as well. They all began crawling toward her, gazing both at her and at the dog she was holding. They gazed at her with a pleading expression, and at the dog in her arms with a look of envy. They were all hoping she would hold them as well, hoping she would carry them somewhere. It was as though they all knew she wouldn't abandon them, and instead would take them back to that village in the Balou mountains where almost all of the residents were disabled. It was as if they knew that in Liven, she already had more than a dozen disabled dogs living with her. It was as if they had finally found their master, their mother, and their wet nurse. And as they knelt down before her, their eyes were filled with tears.

The air was filled with the smell of tears.

The entire world was filled with the bitter smell of the dogs' tears. They wept as they entreated her, their throats emitting a peculiar growl of pain. They were heartbroken, having reached the point where they had no choice but to beg someone for help. Grandma Mao Zhi heard their whimpering, which sounded like crying. She saw their whimpers floating around her like clouds. She smelled the salty odor of their tears, like the aroma of a salty soup. She knew what they were begging her to do. Her heart was as soggy as a clump of sand in a puddle of water, but eventually it began to settle in her chest, a mound of dry sand.

The dogs could not but accompany her back to Liven, Grandma Mao Zhi thought as she stared at that pack of old and disabled dogs.

The rain finally stopped, and the sky and earth were illuminated by a bright light. That pack of more than a dozen dogs kneeling down in the rainwater let out a pathetic, muddy bark. Mao Zhi wasn't sure what to do, so she put down the dog she was holding. She thought that if she didn't carry the dog back behind the theater to feed it and bandage its leg, then maybe this pack of dogs wouldn't keep begging for her help. After she put the dog down, however, it crawled abjectly up to her feet while making whimpering sounds, as tears flowed from its red eyes and down its melon-shaped face into its mouth.

Grandma Mao Zhi was at a loss as to what to do.

It turned out that those able-bodied cadres affiliated with the performance troupe had not returned to the theater, but rather had been waiting for her at the theater entrance, or perhaps had left, changed—Grandma Mao Zhi noticed they were all wearing dry clothing—and then returned. As she was standing there not knowing what to do, one of the cadres walked over to her. He looked curiously at the enormous pack of dogs, then back at her.

He asked, "Have you decided? We have already told the stagehands to begin preparing for the move to the new site tonight."

He said, "We have decided to pay each of the performers five seats for each performance, which is to say, three or four thousand yuan."

He said, "If you agree to do one performance, however, we would pay you ten seats, which is to say roughly seven thousand yuan." He added, "Of course, the most important thing is not the actual proceeds, but rather that we need to call up the county and report to the county chief that the residents of Liven want to withdraw from society and leave the jurisdiction of Shuanghuai. Once you return home, you can take that withdrawal certificate and never have to return to the jurisdiction of Shuanghuai and Boshuzi. Never again will anyone be able to tell you what to do, and should you ever choose to perform again, you will be able to keep a hundred percent of the proceeds."

He said, "Tell us your decision, Grandma Mao Zhi. Whether or not Liven withdraws from society hinges on a single word from you."

He said, "Tell us. One way or the other, you should say something."

Grandma Mao Zhi looked at the wholers standing in front of her, these cadres who had come to lead the performance troupe. Eventually, she let her gaze come to rest on the cadre who had done most of the talking.

She said, "Go tell Chief Liu that in Liven there isn't a single person who does not wish to withdraw from society."

The wholer gave a sigh of relief. "That's good to hear."

She said, "There's another thing. For each performance, we won't receive five seats, but rather ten, though I, Grandma Mao Zhi, don't want a single cent. The remaining money from these final performances can all go to you, but first you must provide a car and help me take these dogs back to Liven tonight."

The wholers stared at her in confusion, then laughingly agreed. They each started working on their respective assignments. One of them went to call the other performance troupe, instructing them to report to the county that all of the Liven residents affiliated with their troupe also wished to withdraw from society; another went to arrange for a car to send this pack of more than a dozen dogs back to Balou; another went to arrange for crates and vehicles to transport the troupe to Wenzhou; and someone else hurriedly went out to buy Grandma Mao Zhi a costume and props for her performance.

Given that Grandma Mao Zhi was going to appear as someone who was two hundred and forty-one years old, her residence permit and identity card both had to be replaced, and the person responsible for making new ones needed some time to work. The person responsible for making her new costume also needed at least a full night to finish the task.

Two hundred and forty-one years ago, it had been the Hongli reign of the Qing dynasty, more specifically the twenty-first year of the Qianlong emperor's reign. Between then and now, China had undergone the rise and fall of the Qing dynasty, the United Army of the Eight Nations, Yuan Shikai's presidency, the Xinhai Revolution, and the Republican period, together with the new government following the War of resistance against Japan and the ensuing Liberation.

For someone to have survived from the Qianlong reign up to the present day, she naturally would have needed some special techniques. For Grandma Mao Zhi to have lived to be two hundred and forty-one years old, her secret must have been not merely keeping to a vegetarian diet, but going to work in the fields every day. Most important, when she became ill in the seventeenth year of the Daoguang reign, at the age of eighty-one, she preemptively put on her burial garb, but somehow managed to survive. It was as though Grandma Mao Zhi had already died once, and that therefore from that point on never again feared death. She wore her burial clothes three hundred and sixty-five days a year—wearing them to eat and work in the fields, and at night even wearing them to bed. In this way, she was always prepared for the possibility that she might not wake up the next morning, but each morning she did wake up after all.

In the third year of the Guangxu reign, when she was a hundred and twenty-one years old, she suffered another illness. But after being on the brink of death for three days, she again managed to survive. Afterward, she was doubly prepared to die at any time, and therefore continued to wear her burial clothing day and night. She wore it while eating, while working in the fields, and particularly at night while sleeping.

Year after year, month after month, she wore her burial clothing day in and day out, ready to pass away at any moment. In this way, she lived to be two hundred and forty-one years old, surviving from the Qianlong reign up to the present day. In the process, she witnessed countless historical events, from the Jiaqing to the Daoguang, Xianfeng, Tongzhi, Guangxu, and Xuantong imperial reigns, together with the Republican period. Over two hundred and forty-one years, she witnessed nine imperial reigns. It was during the Daoguang reign that she began wearing burial clothing, and during the third year of the Guangxu reign that she switched to wearing it both day and night. During the following century or so, she must have worn out countless sets of burial clothing, and therefore in order to have her two-hundred-and-forty-one-year-old self perform on stage, it would be necessary to prepare at least eight or ten sets of clothing. That clothing, moreover, had to appear old and tattered, so as to convince the audience that it really was on account of wearing these clothes that she had been able to survive an additional hundred and sixty years up to the present day.

The wholers hustled about getting everything together, and by early morning, they had succeeded in relocating the troupe to the new city, where they would soon begin their magnificent performance.

CHAPTER 7: LENIN'S MAUSOLEUM IS COMPLETED, AND THE INAUGURATION PERFORMANCE BEGINS

Chief Liu had to go to the district and provincial seat to attend an important meeting for a few days.

Grandma Mao Zhi and the disabled performers in her special-skills troupe had returned from the south by train and by car. Before they even had a chance to spend the night with their children, houses, trees, and streets and alleys, together with their chickens, pigs, dogs, ducks, sheep, and oxen, Chief Liu urgently sent them up to Spirit Mountain to do one final performance to help celebrate the opening of the mausoleum.

The Lenin Mausoleum was complete, and even the latrines lining the road up to the mausoleum were finished. The red *Men* and *Women* signs over the door to the latrines had been dry for several days. Everything was ready, and all that was missing was the final touch.

The delegation responsible for purchasing Lenin's remains had been away from Shuanghuai for seven or eight days, and it was said they had completed all of the requisite paperwork to travel to Russia. They had been delayed another day or so in Beijing, after which they would fly to Russia and initiate negotiations for purchasing the corpse. These so-called negotiations were really simply a process of haggling over the price, in which the people on one side would say they would pay only ten million yuan for the remains, while the other side would insist on getting a hundred million. The first side would then offer fifteen million, whereupon the other side would repeat that they wouldn't even consider an offer of less than a hundred million. The first side would offer twenty million, and the other side would reply that if the first side really wanted to buy the remains, they should offer a realistic price.

At this point, the leader of the first delegation would furrow his skybrows,[1] one set of wrinkles after another appearing on his shiny sun panel,[3] as though he had encountered an incredibly difficult dilemma. And to tell the truth, this *was* in fact an incredibly difficult dilemma. If he offered too low a price, his counterpart might refuse to sell the corpse at all, but if he offered too high a price, he might end up unnecessarily giving away millions—or even tens or hundreds of millions—of yuan. During the six months the two troupes had been performing, they'd earned the county a vast profit, while the district had also donated an enormous sum to the fund. In the end, however, this money was not like tap water, and after it was spent it would be gone forever. The higher-ups would not disburse any more money to Shuanghuai for at least the next three years.

The contract between Shuanghuai and the performance troupes had expired, and this seven-day celebration of the opening of the Lenin Mausoleum was intended to serve as Chief Liu's threat and promise to Grandma Mao Zhi, and it was only with this that she offered her support. After seven days, not only would the troupes not be able to continue performing on behalf of Shuanghuai county, but even the performers themselves would no longer belong to Shuanghuai. On the map of Shuanghuai, the village of Liven would no longer exist.

It was essential that they purchase Lenin's remains.

It was also essential that they somehow find a way to bargain down the price. In order to do so, Chief Liu would need to personally take a team to Russia to negotiate. The district and the province called an extraordinarily urgent meeting, and said that every county chief and county secretary was required to attend. Because the meeting had implications for the election of both the district commissioner and the provincial governor, the announcement specified that even if the county chiefs and county secretaries were in the hospital, as long as they didn't have cancer they were obligated to leave the hospital and come to the district and provincial seat to attend the meeting. And if they were in fact suffering from cancer, if the cancer was still in its early stages they were still expected to attend the meeting.

Chief Liu therefore had no choice but to appoint his most trusted, and most capable, deputy county chief to lead a delegation to negotiate in his place. In this deputy chief's family hall there was an enlarged portrait of Chief Liu himself. The deputy chief's primary responsibility, furthermore, was the tourism industry. Once he found himself chatting at dinner with a Taiwan businessman who happened to be passing through Shuanghuai on his way to the provincial capital to invest some funds. Despite the fact that they had different surnames, they nevertheless promptly declared themselves to be blood brothers and thereby became instant relatives, even agreeing to share an ancestral grave site.

In this way, they became extremely close. They discussed the details of their respective families, to the point that the visitor from Taiwan began bawling his eyes out, and suddenly decided to leave Shuanghuai the several tens of million yuan that he was originally planning to invest in the city. He donated money for the county to build an electrical generator, as a result of which every household in Shuanghuai came to have electricity. Chief Liu promoted the deputy county chief to the position of managing deputy county chief, and upon being named to the county standing committee, he was allowed to attend all important meetings, large or small, and to hold a crucial vote.

This deputy chief was an excellent choice to lead the expedition to Russia, given that he was a superb negotiator. He was accompanied by an expensive interpreter, who had studied in Russia for many years and knew the country as intimately as Chief Liu knew his own Shuanghuai county.

Chief Liu was not concerned about their trip to purchase Lenin's corpse, since he had prepared for every eventuality. If the other side asked them to propose a realistic price, the deputy chief, needless to say, would not immediately offer a specific figure, even if the price had already been discussed countless times at home and they had agreed what the upper limit would be. Even if they couldn't agree to that price, however, they understood that they absolutely had to complete this purchase, allowing them to bring Lenin's corpse back to Shuanghuai and install it in Balou's Spirit Mountain. At this point, the situation would become difficult for the negotiating team, and they would have to rely on the patience of the deputy chief, who had it in abundance.

Perhaps the negotiations would take place in the room next to Lenin's remains, the reception room to the west of Lenin's crystal coffin. That room was far smaller than the underground reception room Shuanghuai had constructed. The walls were made of brick, the inside was whitewashed with a special powder, and the outside was styled as a traditional Chinese tomb. On one side of Moscow's Red Square there was a stone stage on an elevated piece of land, and twenty feet below the stage there was a square pit, in which there was a stone wall as big as two or three houses. In the center, shielded from the cold of winter or the heat of summer, was Lenin's crystal coffin. This was truly disrespectful to Lenin, since his mausoleum was not even as large as the ones that some of the wealthy inhabitants of Wenzhou built for themselves, the only difference being that the pit in Lenin's tomb was deeper than most of our houses are tall. Because Russians are generally taller than we are, it was only natural that their ceilings would be higher and the tomb taller. The walls inside the mausoleum were painted with a special water-resistant and anticorrosive whitewash, and in this white expanse lay the crystal coffin. Even though seventy-five years had elapsed since Lenin's death, the coffin had hardly changed at all, nor had the walls of the mausoleum been repainted.

Despite the fact that carefully selected administrators spent the entire day meticulously polishing the coffin with a feather duster and a flannel cloth, its surface was not as resplendent as it had been three-quarters of a century earlier. Viewed from outside, Lenin's corpse was also not as translucent as it had been several decades earlier. In the large underground reception hall, the salaried managers wiped it down every day, and every month they stood on the back of a chair or a couch and swept away the dust and cobwebs from the walls and ceiling. But in the end, that whitewashed wall had been there for seventy-five years, and the white paint could no longer cover the yellow grime underneath. In some places the wall had become a sheet of deep yellow, like the yellow paper the people of Balou, Shuanghuai, and western Hunan burn every year during the Qingming festival.

As for the small waiting room next to the room holding Lenin's corpse, after one went through the ornately carved door frame, the first thing one might see would be an oil painting in a white birch frame above an old wooden couch, though it might not be clear what kind of wood it was. Over time, that wood would become only more and more resplendent, though the cover on the couch would not age well and might have started to fade and peel. There would be holes in the armrest, through which several metal springs might be visible. It would be on this couch—and, naturally, it had to be on this couch—that the deputy county chief would politely discuss his business. After a long conversation, the two negotiators would finally agree on a time to ship Lenin's corpse, whereupon the deputy county chief would announce that if the price of the corpse were to exceed a certain amount, his group wouldn't buy it even if their lives depended on it. His Russian counterpart would respond that if the Chinese delegation didn't offer more than such-and-such a price, the Russians wouldn't sell the corpse even if *their* lives depended on it.

The deputy county chief would say, "Don't forget that our country is the only one that has any interest in purchasing Lenin's remains."

His counterpart would reply, "That's not necessarily true."

The deputy chief would say, "It is true that there are other countries willing to buy the remains, but you need to consider their poverty and whether or not they would be able to actually pay the enormous price you are demanding."

His counterpart would say, "If we can't sell the remains, then we won't."

"If you don't sell the remains, then you won't even have enough money to maintain them. You don't even have funds to repair the mausoleum, or to pay the salaries of your managers." He would add, "If you don't sell the corpse, then you'll have no choice but to watch it deteriorate day after day, as it becomes deformed to the point of becoming completely unrecognizable."

The deputy chief would be sitting in one of the rooms adjacent to the mausoleum. Eventually, he would take what the Russians had said to heart and agree on a price that the delegation felt was the lowest they could get, and that their counterparts felt was the highest *they* could get. Once they had all agreed on a price, they would begin drawing up a contract.

Of course, there were many things that needed to be done before the contract could be signed. The managers of the mausoleum would have to write their superiors a report, and their superiors would have to write *their* superiors a report, and so forth, until finally a report would be sent to the country's highest, highest levels of government. Everything would have to go through multiple rounds of discussion and study. And then, nothing. Perhaps the Russian leaders who participated in these discussions would turn down the proposal for undisclosed reasons, refusing to allow China's Shuanghuai county to purchase Lenin's corpse. Perhaps they would feel that if Lenin were to go to China, it would amount to his going to a foreign land. In order for the nation to save face, and in order to have an explanation they might offer, perhaps they might agree to lease the corpse for a thirty- or fifty-year period, or even just ten or twenty years. Once they agreed on an appropriate time frame, they would specify that the corpse would need to be returned in its original condition. Chief Liu had already anticipated all of these additional stipulations, and instructed his deputy chief on how to proceed. He said that as long as they could bring the corpse back as quickly as possible, he would approve any conditions that his deputy chief was able to negotiate.

Chief Liu said, "Just think—the sooner you bring the corpse back, the sooner the county can start earning tons of money."

There was nothing to worry about. They simply *had* to bring Lenin's corpse back, irrespective of the cost. They had considered everything they needed to consider, and done everything they needed to do. Although the delegation had started out in the *wuyin* Year of the Tiger, 1998, by now it would already be the end of the lunar year, or the beginning of the following year by the Western calendar. The new Lenin Mausoleum would already be complete, and Liven's two special-skills troupes would have already returned from Wenzhou in the south to pass the winter in the Balou mountains. Seven or eight days would have already elapsed from the date they had originally agreed Liven would be released from the jurisdiction of Shuanghuai county.

In theory, once the delegation returned from abroad Chief Liu should have sent the document certifying that the village of Liven had been released from the jurisdiction of Shuanghuai, and distributed the document to every council, office, township, town, and village committee. Then, he should have taken it and personally placed it directly in Grandma Mao Zhi's hands.

But he did not send the document down, and instead wanted Grandma Mao Zhi and the performance troupe to help him one final time. In the banquet hall where they were holding a welcome dinner for the special-skills troupes, Chief Liu brought over a cup of liquor to Grandma Mao Zhi and, with a plaintive expression, said, "The documents that would completely release Liven from the jurisdiction of Shuanghuai county have been printed out, are ninety-nine percent ready, having been stamped by the county committee and the county government. But before Liven can completely withdraw from society and remove itself from the jurisdiction of Shuanghuai county and Boshuzi township, I must first ask something of you."

Grandma Mao Zhi stood in the middle of the dining hall of the county's guest house looking at Chief Liu.

Chief Liu said, "My entire life, I have never begged anyone for anything. This is the first time."

He said, "Construction of the Lenin Mausoleum is already complete, and the new crystal coffin has already been placed inside. We therefore need to host a ceremony celebrating the completion of the mausoleum, and I would like your special-skills troupes to offer seven days of performances on Spirit Mountain."

He said, "You have traveled thousands of miles, and you shouldn't mind taking one more step. If you feel that seven days of performances is too much, then you can do three instead. After you have performed for three days, I will personally read aloud the document certifying Liven's withdrawal from the jurisdiction of Shuanghuai county."

He said, "Lenin's corpse will be shipped back, and before that happens I want to create some momentum for Spirit Mountain. We cannot have momentum without a performance by your special-skills troupe." He said, "If you perform at Spirit Mountain, if won't be for nothing. Whoever climbs the mountain to visit the memorial hall will also watch your troupe's performance, and for each they will have to buy a ticket. For people from the county, the tickets will cost five yuan, and for outsiders they will also cost five yuan. One-third of the proceeds will go to the performance troupe, one-third will go to the Spirit Mountain Office of Recreation Management, and the remainder will go to the county treasury."

Chief Liu said, "Let's agree that before the first performance I will go to the memorial hall to cut the ceremonial ribbon, and then I will proceed to the district seat to attend a meeting. After the full-day meeting, I will return, and immediately following the third performance, I will read from the stage the document announcing Liven's withdrawal from society, so that the entire county will know. From that point on, you will have officially withdrawn from society, and will no longer fall under the jurisdiction of Shuanghuai, Boshuzi, or any other county or township in the country."

In this way, things were decided. At dawn the next day, Grandma Mao Zhi and the residents of Liven sat on the troupe's fully loaded truck and rode to Spirit Mountain to perform for the ceremony celebrating the completion of the Lenin Memorial Hall.

Further Reading:

1) **Skybrows.** DIAL. Means "eyebrows." Because one's eyebrows are above the face, they are called skybrows.

3) **Sun panel.** DIAL. Means "forehead." The origin of the term is comparable to that of "skybrows."

Chapter 9: They have countless skills, as well as a purple aura

Originally it had been agreed that the troupe would give three more performances, whereupon Chief Liu would come back and read aloud on stage the document certifying Liven's withdrawal from society. But only a day after he cut the ceremonial ribbon, Chief Liu abruptly had to go back down the mountain, and afterward there was no trace of him.

It was already the twelfth month of the Western calendar, and the final day of the month had quietly sneaked up on them. While it was still very warm down south, where the trees were green and the flowers blooming, here in the north winter was already approaching. It was unbearably cold in some regions, and while it hadn't snowed yet, in the early morning the entire mountain was covered in frost, which would freeze into a thin layer of ice. If water vats were left half-filled overnight, by the next morning they would be frozen solid. Similarly, if a wet bucket was left in the kitchen doorway, by morning it would be frozen to the ground and impossible to move, to the point that you would need a brick to dislodge it. If people were worried that the brick might break the bucket, they could instead first light a fire to melt the ice.

The trees also withered; their leaves had fallen off even before the twelfth month arrived. In the mountain and the village, all of the trees were barren. Sparrows could no longer hide amidst the branches, and instead as soon as one made a sound, you could turn around and see it sitting there, then throw a rock and hit its frozen body.

In the Balou mountains, usually the only trace that could be seen of the wild hares, chickens, weasels, and elusive foxes in winter were the openings of their burrows. If you were to roll a stone down the mountain, the clever foxes might remain hidden in their burrows, but the wild hares, chickens, and weasels would all come running out, whereupon the sound of a hunter's gun would go off behind them.

In both the daytime and the evening, you would see countless hunters going into the fields and proudly walking back to the village with a few wild chickens or hares dangling from the barrels of their rifles.

Occasionally, they might have a fox.

However, in this winter of the *wuyin* Year of the Tiger, these scenes were entirely absent along the mountain ridge. Instead, everyone went up Spirit Mountain to watch the village of Liven's troupes perform, and to visit that rarely seen Lenin Palace. Crowds of people along the mountain ridge were all walking toward the mountain, and as they crowded in they were all beaming as though they were attending a temple festival. Adults brought their children, and middle-aged people used a cart to haul their elderly parents. People coming from afar brought not only baked and steamed buns, but also bedding, pots, bowls, and chopsticks, so that they could eat and sleep on the road. The sound of people talking along the mountain path, together with the rumbling of their carts and the sound of footsteps that increased steadily from one day to the next, all left the path to the top of the Balou mountains covered in flying dust that came raining down like water. At midday, the weather would warm up, and the sparrows became increasingly animated, following people's footsteps and calling out, flying from one tree to another as though they were migrating south. The wild hares were startled out of their burrows and ran down to the bottom of the gully, but upon hearing gunshots they returned to their burrows and watched uneasily as the crowds of villagers and city folk surged up the mountain.

All of the villages throughout the Balou mountain region were left empty.

All of the villages outside of the Balou mountain region were also left empty.

Even people in the city took vacations from work and came by train to Spirit Mountain.

First, it was the people from the towns and townships closest to Spirit Mountain who came, including Shuanghuai's Boshuzi, Lianshuzi, Xiaoliu, Daliu, Yushu, Lishu, and Xinghuaying townships, Gaoliu's Shihezi, Qingshanzi, Caojiaying, Caoma, and Shisanli Puzi townships, together with Shangyu's Taoshuzi, Taozi, Xiaohuai, and Lianzi townships. The residents of each of the three surrounding counties all climbed the mountain to watch the performance, visit the mausoleum, and enjoy the scenery. The winter happened to be a period of rest from agricultural work, when people would go in search of entertainment, and it was precisely at this point that the Lenin Memorial Hall was going to hold its opening ceremony and the village of Liven's special-skills troupes were going to perform on the mountain.

One man who went to visit the mausoleum remarked upon his return, "Heavens, the trees there are already budding, and the memorial hall is even more stunning than a throne room. There is a girl named Huaihua who is even more beautiful than the memorial hall itself." As for what Huaihua and the throne room really looked like, the man couldn't say, since in fact he'd never even seen them—though he did see that there was fresh grass and green trees, even in the northern winter. This was very unusual, and it was said that a fairy had appeared in Liven.

A woman who visited the mausoleum returned and said, "Quick, go see for yourselves. It really is springtime there. They have already installed the crystal coffin in the memorial hall. There is a girl named Huaihua who is as white as the coffin, which is itself brighter than glass, and, like crystal eyeglasses, if you touch it you will leave your fingerprints. Under a two-inch-thick crystal board, you can see the dust on the bottom of the coffin, and even this dust glows."

Although she said this, she had not necessarily seen for herself the dust inside the coffin. She had not necessarily touched the coffin herself. Yet, it was only by speaking like this that she could prove she not only had gone to the memorial hall, but had seen the crystal coffin that had been prepared to receive Lenin's corpse.

Old people who had been carted up the mountain by their children encountered other people on their way back down who said enthusiastically, "Go see, go see. And if you do, then even if you were to die tomorrow, you wouldn't have lived in vain. Lenin was such an important person that once his corpse arrives, winter will become spring."

Someone asked, "Really?"

He said, "The throne room is so tall that it brushes the clouds. How could they have transported all of those bricks and stones up there?"

The person responded, "That's not a throne room, that's a memorial hall."

She said, "In any event, it's the same thing as a throne room." She added, "That crystal coffin is as white and bright as jade. I heard that that single crystal coffin alone is so expensive that even if we were to sell our entire county we still wouldn't have enough money to pay for it."

The person said, "How could it not be enough? The people of Liven went on a performance tour, and in just a few days they earned enough money to buy the coffin."

Upon turning to the topic of the troupe's performances, one man sighed and said,

"Heavens, I wish I were disabled. If only I were deaf, then I too would dare to explode a firecracker right next to my ear."

Sitting on the cart, his wife added,

"If I were blind, I too would be able to embroider flowers on paper or a leaf."

An old man walked past and said,

"I still can't understand this. I'm fifty-three years old and am losing my eyesight, and have lost all my teeth. That crippled old woman is a hundred and seven, so how is she still able to chew fried corn and thread a needle?"

His daughter, who was accompanying him, said, "Father, it's because she wears her burial clothes every day, even when eating or sleeping. I would never want you to wear your burial clothes around the house."

At this point, a group of excited children between the ages of seven and nine were dragged down the mountain by their parents. They saw many fellow villagers heading up the mountain, and while they didn't specify what they had seen up there, the children just shouted to their parents,

"I want to go back! . . . I want to go back!"

As for what they wanted to see, they themselves couldn't say. But even though they couldn't say, their cries resounded through the heavens. In the end they were beaten, whereupon the more obedient children quieted down while the more insistent ones went back up the mountain with relatives or friends.

Spirit Mountain was extremely crowded and tumultuous. The ten-meter-wide cement path leading up the peak was like an anthill, full of people from dawn to dusk. The formerly clean path became covered in wastepaper, rags, kindling, chunks of steamed bun, empty cigarette packs, shoes, socks, hats, and all sorts of debris, as though it were a road to a recently ended temple festival. There were also chopsticks, bowls, vegetables, drinking glasses, garlic and scallions, boiled eggshells, and sweet potato cakes scattered all about, as though it were a theater just after a performance. Lining both sides of the path were countless small stoves made of bricks or rocks. People would take a few branches from the trees alongside the road and use them to start a fire. After they used the stove to cook some soup or steamed buns, those bricks and rocks would be black on one side, and the ground next to the stove would be covered with charred kindling, leftover food, and stones that had been brought over to serve as seats, together with used matches, lighters, clothes that children had taken off and left behind, and old pots and pans that people for some reason didn't want to take back with them. Scattered about everywhere there were also books, newspapers, magazines, toys, tobacco pouches, wooden guns, paper airplanes, paper wallets, aluminum necklaces, and glass bracelets that people no longer wanted.

The road was completely filled with people.

The road was completely filled with debris.

The road was filled with ashes left over from cooking. With a smoldering bush here and a smoking shrub there, the mountain looked as though a forest fire had just swept through. There were many *Beware of Fire* signs, yet the fires continued to spread unchecked.

That winter, it had snowed heavily in many of the areas outside the Balou region, and in some villages the sheep, pigs, and plow oxen had all frozen to death. Visitors from Gaoliu and Shangyu counties reported that not only had it snowed back home, it had snowed so much that people couldn't get out their front doors, that when they woke up in the morning they were not even able to open their courtyard gates. But if they walked a few dozen or a hundred *li* over a mountain to the Balou region, it no longer seemed like winter. The trees along the mountain ridge were all still leafless, but the alpine rush, fountain grass, and twitch grass on the lower slope were turning green as if with the arrival of spring, their winter dormancy having ended in the blink of an eye. Below that layer of dry vegetation, flowers were beginning to bud, and the pagoda and elm trees along the mountain were already producing new leaves. Even the pine trees, which had not lost their original green color, began displaying their new verdure within just a few days.

The areas with wheat fields were also perfused with this light green color.

Lenin was coming, and spring had arrived a step early. Really, this was heaven's decree. The ceremony celebrating the completion of the memorial hall was upon them, and winter here had begun to assume some of the characteristics of spring, or even early summer. The yellow sun was shining down brightly on the mountaintop and a gentle warmth enveloped the entire region. Thin clouds were hanging in the sky like balls of cotton. People surged up the mountain, and the commotion they made echoed throughout the valley like a thunderstorm.

A humid scent of early summer hung in the air.

There was also the sound of firecrackers everywhere, as at a New Year's festival.

The memorial hall emerged out of this cacophony of sound and shadows, and could be seen from miles away. The visitors who came to observe the excitement would not have gotten halfway up the mountain before they would see the memorial hall waiting for them up at the top. Under this winter sun—which was actually warmer than in either spring or fall—the yellow tiles that covered the memorial hall's roof sparkled, revealing a splendor comparable to that of a legendary palace throne room. The distant mountain ridge, meanwhile, appeared as still as the back of an ox or camel. The trees were light green, as were the ridge and the gorge. In fact, the entire world was light green. In this green land, the memorial hall rose up out of nowhere, a palace that suddenly appeared out of thin air, making people's eyes light up in excitement. You could clearly see the flash of gold in the light reflected from the roof tiles, together with the heavy lead in the light reflected from the marble walls.

You could also see the Hanbai jade railing on either side of the fifty-four kowtow steps[1] leading up to the memorial hall, its light containing many silvery traces of green. As the marble kowtow steps sparkled in the sunlight, they gave off glimmers of gold, aluminum lead, and silver jade, with traces of bronze, all blurring together to produce a heavy and powerful mercury-like light resembling a strip of wet white silk that stretched into the sky, or the mysterious purple lightning that often appears in the sky. When people saw the palace and the purple light, they gasped in amazement.

They said, "Heavens, it's purple lightning."

They said, "Heavens, how did they ever find such beautiful scenery?"

They said, "Heavens, this is truly the kind of place where someone like an emperor would rest."

With all of this oohing and ahhing, everyone unconsciously picked up their pace.

Upon reaching the memorial hall, the visitors saw a large sign under the eaves of the entrance. Just as there is a sign in clerical script in front of Mao Zedong's mausoleum that reads, *May the Great Leader, Chairman Mao, Be Eternally Remembered by Posterity,* this one read, *May the Great Teacher of the World's People, Lenin, Be Eternally Remembered by Posterity.* The visitors saw that this memorial hall on top of the mountain was as large as a wheat field, while below it there was a public square as big as two wheat fields. The square was paved entirely with cement bricks, and if you wanted, you could use it to sun-dry a whole village's worth of sorghum, millet, and wheat. You could dry a village's entire year's harvest. On either side of the square, it was like any other tourist area, with two rows of small buildings selling a variety of local products such as tree fungus, gingko, and mushrooms, together with imported products such as low-quality jade that is purchased cheaply from the south and then resold up north at a higher price. These trinkets include jade bracelets, pendants, horses, sheep, knives, swords, figurines of the twelve animals of the zodiac, jade pagodas, and incense burners. Everything looked both new and familiar.

People who had come from afar knew that not a single one of these products was authentic. When the seller roared like a lion, asking for a hundred yuan, a visitor would reply as meekly as a mouse and offer instead ten yuan, and then the seller would in fact accept ten yuan, and still make a substantial profit. And when naïve people who enjoyed a comfortable existence and spent all their time at home would hear someone announce that a jade pendant was selling for ten yuan, their first thought would be that ten yuan was really too cheap, and in order to demonstrate to the seller that they were in fact well-off and not lacking in money they would offer nine yuan for it. The seller would pretend to consider for a while, and then reply disappointedly, "I'll sell it to you, because for the opening ceremony of Lenin's memorial hall, I'm not trying to make a profit, but rather merely trying to produce some good fortune."

Many visitors started to file up to the memorial hall carrying assorted tourist trinkets. One person said, "Lenin died young, departing the world at the tender age of fifty-four. If you carefully count the kowtow steps beneath your feet, you will find that there are precisely fifty-four of them." Furthermore, when everyone counted, they found that the railing on either side of the steps had exactly twenty-seven columns—which, when added together, also totaled fifty-four. All those walking up these steps, including men and women, young and old, all counted out loud like schoolchildren: one, two, three, four, five . . . all the way either to fifty-four or to halfway to fifty-four, which is to say twenty-seven. When the total came out as expected, their faces would break into broad smiles, as though they found this extremely amusing.

Then, they would arrive at the door to the memorial hall. Some people would bound into the hall, while others with somewhat more experience, who might have been to Beijing and visited Mao's mausoleum, might proceed more deliberately, wanting to appreciate the similarities and differences between Mao's and Lenin's mausoleums. From a distance, of course, they primarily noted the similarities between the two structures, which were roughly the same size and height, with stone walls and a flat, square roof covered in yellow tiles.

In fact, it turned out that the architecture of the two edifices was identical. Everyone knew that when the Lenin Mausoleum was first conceived, Chief Liu took his workers to Beijing, where they spent an entire day visiting Mao's mausoleum, going in and out at least seven or eight times. They not only memorized the mausoleum's layout, but furthermore managed, while avoiding the notice of the police stationed all around the site, to measure the structure's precise length, width, and height. They also took countless photographs, calculating hundreds of measurements of the mausoleum's location and the distances between its various components. Given this, why *wouldn't* the Lenin mausoleum be identical to Chairman Mao's?

Strictly speaking, the only salient difference between the two structures was precisely that Mao's mausoleum was in Beijing while Lenin's was located in Shuanghuai, in northern China. Or, to be more precise, Mao's mausoleum was located in Beijing's Tiananmen Square, while Lenin's was at the top of Spirit Mountain, in the depths of the Balou mountain region.

What other differences were there between the two halls? None to speak of. But some experienced people were nevertheless able to notice some interesting details. Lenin lived to be fifty-four years old, and the stairs in front of his mausoleum had fifty-four steps, and the railing fifty-four columns. At Mao Zedong's mausoleum, there were four columns on either side, for a total of sixteen, while the Lenin Mausoleum had four columns in front and ten in back, with none on either side, making fourteen in all, which is two less than sixteen. Why is this? Educated people who had attended the country's soc-schools and Party schools, and who always memorized their lessons, would tell you that the four columns in front of the Lenin Mausoleum and the ten in back were in recognition of Lenin's birth date. Under the old lunar calendar, Lenin was born on the tenth day of the fourth month of the *gengwu* Year of the Horse. These four and ten columns, therefore, foretold that Lenin would receive a new life in the mausoleum, and would never grow old.

In addition, there were no columns on either side of the mausoleum, but there were twelve mid-sized pine trees on the left and sixteen midsize cypresses on the right. All of the trees were several dozen feet high, and their canopies blocked out the sky. The numbers twelve and sixteen, meanwhile, correspond to the date of Lenin's death. Given that Lenin passed away on the sixteenth day of the twelfth month of the first year of the preceding sixty-year *jiazi* cycle, these twelve and sixteen trees symbolized his eternal life. Why didn't they plant newly sprouted saplings or, conversely, why didn't they simply transplant full-grown trees? Full-grown trees would have completely blocked out the sun, as though they had been growing there for several centuries, or even millennia.

If the person in charge of the mausoleum happened to be a friend of yours, you might hear a masterful story about how these midsize trees were precisely the same age as Lenin when he passed away, and accordingly that they each had fifty-four growth rings. When these trees were transplanted, they were inspected by forestry experts from the county, who drilled a hole in the trunk of each tree, from which they were able to confirm that they were all precisely fifty-four years old. If the forestry experts determined that the age of a tree did not match Lenin's age when he passed away, but rather was a little older or younger, then irrespective of how straight and tall the tree might be, or how dense its canopy, it would not be transplanted. The mausoleum manager said that in order to find twelve pine trees and sixteen cypresses that were each precisely fifty-four years old, forestry experts spent half a year digging up trees on Spirit Mountain, and for each tree that was the desired age they had to dig up five others that weren't. On the entire mountainside, however, there were only about a hundred pines and cypresses in all. Out of every hundred or so trees, therefore, there might be only one pine or cypress, and furthermore there was no telling whether or not that particular tree would prove to be precisely fifty-four years old.

After they had finished searching several mountainsides through-out the county, and had dug up several forests' worth of trees, they finally managed to find twelve pines and sixteen cypresses that were the requisite age.

Naturally, these twelve pines were called Lenin pines, and the sixteen cypresses were called Lenin cypresses. Planted on either side of the Lenin Mausoleum, these trees became the structure's masterpiece. In order to verify the ages, a hole had been drilled in the trunk of each tree, and even after these holes were plugged with cement, sap continued to ooze like glue from around the cement ring.

There was a pungent odor of pine sap everywhere.

Of course, it was only in these technical details that the Lenin Mausoleum differed from its counterpart in Beijing. But if you were to see those trees and follow the crowds into the mausoleum, you would learn something even more mysterious, such as the fact that in the memorial hall there are precisely thirteen marble pillars and columns. Why is this? It is because Lenin's original name was Vladimir Ilyich Ulyanov, which in Chinese is written with thirteen characters. Therefore, these thirteen pillars and columns represent Lenin's name. If you were to know all this, you might very well wonder about other details, and therefore would have to visit it again and again.

Inside the mausoleum there was a main hall that was twenty feet high, which would make you feel very solemn. The lights embedded in the walls were as soft as milk, and beneath this milky light the crowds slowly made their way forward, following the rope railings. Although the main hall was half as large as a typical wheat field, or as big as a wealthy man's courtyard, the path leading up to it was as narrow as a back alley. While Lenin's corpse had not yet been brought in, the newly constructed coffin was already installed in the center of the main hall. The hall was already extremely solemn, and no talking was permitted.

If you had a crying baby, you would be immediately asked to leave.

And if you tried to smoke or take photographs, you would be immediately asked to leave, and would be fined.

Everyone crowded around the front and back doors as though they were lining up to cross a bridge. In this slow movement, it was as though they were walking through a narrow alley, and everyone, young or old, keenly felt a chill in the memorial hall. It was as if they'd suddenly entered a deep gorge in the middle of summer, and everyone at once felt as though their breath had been taken away, because they immediately saw the crystal coffin sitting on a platform in the center of the hall. The platform was made from large slabs of marble, and it was rectangular in shape, and as large as a reed mat. The coffin rested right on top of the marble platform, like a translucent shard of aquamarine glass, or a milky white piece of transparent crystal jade. A nylon rope marked a perimeter of about five or six feet around the coffin, keeping the tourists outside the roped area and ensuring that they would merely observe, and not touch, it.

Given that the coffin could not be touched, it appeared even more mysterious, leading people to want to examine it even more carefully. The more carefully they examined it, however, the more confused they would become. The coffin was the same shape as every other coffin, with a wide section for the head and a narrower one for the feet. It seemed as though the middle section was like that of typical rural coffins—about two feet seven inches wide and two feet seven inches high. But the section for the head was much wider and taller than that of a typical blackwood rural coffin, just as the section for the feet was slightly taller and wider than that of a conventional rural coffin. The overall coffin, meanwhile, was about half a foot longer than a typical rural one.

In sum, you felt that the coffin's ratios were somewhat out of sync. But this was a crystal coffin, and in a few days the body of a great man would be lying in it. The coffin was for an enormous foreign figure who was admired by half the world. So, you didn't dare ask why the coffin was constructed that way, but rather had no choice but to silently file past with everyone else, slowly moving forward as though walking along a balance beam. When you came up next to the coffin, you would feel a cold breeze, and you might even see several strands of hair on the transparent base of the coffin. These would be gray hairs, and they would make you suddenly start shivering again.

There was barely any noise in the enormous main hall, and everyone's footsteps sounded like falling leaves. You could hear people breathing, like white strands of wool floating in the air. You could also see the flickering of the milky white lights, like winter fog along the mountain ridge. One person couldn't restrain himself and coughed with his hand over his mouth, his dry cough resonating through the hall like a stone falling from the sky, shattering the silence. Everyone immediately stopped gazing at the coffin and instead turned to look in the direction of the cough.

The person bowed his head, as though he had just committed an unpardonable crime.

Everyone, young or old, was still trudging forward along the rope line, and by the time you brought your gaze back from the person who coughed, you would have already reached the coffin.

Even though you hadn't seen enough of that crystal coffin, the people behind you would be already pushing you forward and out the back door of the hall.

Even after viewing the coffin, everyone felt as though they hadn't seen anything. They therefore filed out of the hall and stood around morosely, feeling that it hadn't been worth it and they hadn't gained anything. It was as though they had traveled thousands of miles to go to the market, only to find that the market was closed, or as though they had traveled night and day to attend an opera, only to find that the opera had already concluded.

The sun was bright and the weather was warm. Everyone seemed rather bewildered, and you would stand there feeling somewhat lost, hearing people around you express their disappointment and discuss what was worth seeing and what wasn't. At this point, you would notice several people crowded around a white-haired figure in his forties, who was perhaps the manager of the memorial hall. He would say that he personally placed the crystal coffin there, and that the memorial hall was constructed under his supervision. He would ask, "Do you know why the main hall of the mausoleum has three side rooms, rather than two, four, or six? It's because when Chief Liu went to visit Lenin's former residence, he reported that the house consisted of a main hall with three side rooms."

He would ask, "Do you know why the crystal coffin is not seven Chinese feet long, but rather seven feet five inches? Do you know why the height, width, and depth of the head of the coffin are all two feet nine inches, rather than the more conventional two feet seven inches? And why the height, width, and depth of the foot of the coffin are all one foot five inches, rather than the more conventional one foot nine inches? Why is this? Does anyone know?"

He said, "Given that I'm sure none of you knows the answer, I'll just tell you. The reason why the coffin was constructed to these precise dimensions is because when Chief Liu traveled to Russia he carefully measured Lenin's tomb. The coffin is precisely one-tenth the size of Lenin's tomb. Chief Liu said that the tomb was long and narrow—twenty-two and a half steps long. Three of Chief Liu's steps are precisely ten feet, and therefore those twenty-two and a half steps are equivalent to seventy-five feet, ten percent of which is seven and a half feet. Lenin's tomb was twenty-nine feet wide, and therefore the head of the coffin is two-point-nine feet wide. Lenin's tomb is fifteen feet tall, and consequently the crystal coffin is one and a half feet tall."

He said, "Lenin's Mausoleum contains countless marvelous details, and enough stories to fill a book." He said, "Do you know why the portrait of Lenin you see when you walk in is five feet one inch tall? Or why the portrait's base is two feet one inch wide, three feet eight inches long, and three inches high? That is because Chief Liu had been intimately familiar with all of Lenin's works ever since he was a young boy in the soc-school. The reason he said Lenin's portrait should be five feet one inch tall is because this is equivalent to one-point-seven meters, and Lenin's collected works is comprised of seventeen volumes. The reason why the portrait's base width is two feet one inch is because that is equivalent to seventy centimeters, and Lenin's selected works are comprised of his most influential seventy essays. The reason why the portrait's base is three-point-eight feet long is because in China there happen to be thirty-eight different editions of Lenin's works. Finally, the reason why the base of the portrait is six feet off the ground is because if Lenin's books were all stacked up one on top of the other, they too would be six feet tall."

That person stood in front of the back door of the memorial hall, rambling on as people crowded around him. The more people crowded around him, the more extravagant his descriptions became, until eventually it seemed as though every single brick in the memorial hall had its own story, and every stone was directly linked in some way to Lenin's life. He said, "When you initially walked in, you probably didn't notice that the stones in the floor of the memorial hall form a semicircular image, in which there appear countless crickets and grasshoppers. This is because in the courtyard of Lenin's former residence, there was also a semicircular pond, and when Lenin was a child he would often go to the edge of the pond to catch grasshoppers for cricket fights. This image on the floor of the memorial hall symbolizes the notion that when Lenin's corpse arrives it will be as if he has finally returned home, while also returning to his own childhood."

He added, "When great people age, it is as though they are returning to their childhood, which amounts to their receiving a new life. In the great hall there are six large columns, on three of which appear engraved images of Chinese dragons, together with images of Tiananmen Gate and Tiananmen Square. On the other three, there are engravings of various foreign churches, foreign architecture, and scenes of laboring masses, together with images of Lenin's own books. There are also images of our own sickles, axes, Chairman Mao's works, and a chronology of the Revolution, as well as pictures of that other country's October Revolution, the overthrow of the czar, people cheering the defeat of Hitler during World War Two, and so forth."

With the sun about to set, the white-haired person had been speaking until he was hoarse, until the mausoleum was full of allusions and significance. Finally, he concluded, "This illustrates the principle that those who are able to observe will see things the way they are, while those who can't observe will instead see everything in confusion. Given that it is still early, I urge you to go back inside the memorial hall and examine it all again. Otherwise, you will have wasted a trip, because once Lenin's corpse is installed, you will have to purchase a ticket each time you want to go in."

When he finished, he set off toward the area below the mausoleum. At this point, it suddenly occurred to someone that the speaker was in fact the Boshuzi township chief, and he remarked in amazement that whereas the township chief had originally been a coarse fellow, now that the memorial hall had been constructed he'd suddenly become a learned intellectual. The person had wanted to ask the township chief a few more questions, but someone else had called him over. So the township chief had walked away, leaving villagers who'd originally felt as though they had gained nothing from visiting the memorial hall staring at his departing shadow as they praised his knowledge and experience, while lamenting their own ignorance and shortsightedness.

By this point, the mountain ridge had turned crimson. The sun was about to go down, and under the setting sun the memorial hall appeared calm and serene. Because the sun was about to set, some people hurried back to enter the hall a second time, while others decided that it would be dark soon and there was still a lot more to see on the mountain.

Most important, none of them had had a chance to see Liven's special-skills troupe perform. If they weren't able to see that performance, they would truly have come to Balou for nothing,[3] and would truly have climbed Spirit Mountain for nothing.

Further Reading:

1) **Kowtow steps.** *In old times Buddhist temples always had steps in front of them. When people entered a temple they had to kowtow, and therefore the people of Balou call these steps "kowtow" steps.*

3) **For nothing.** *For no direct compensation. The phrase means "to do something in vain."*

CHAPTER 11: THE WEATHER IS INCREASINGLY WARM, AS WINTER BECOMES A SWELTERING SUMMER

Liven's two special-skills troupes had never before performed together. The first time they did so was during the inauguration of the Lenin Mausoleum, just before Chief Liu was scheduled to cut the ribbon. Liven's special-skills troupes perfunctorily performed in the square in front of the mausoleum, and then dispersed to show off their skills at various sites throughout the area. One-Legged Monkey led little Polio Boy, who inserted his foot into a bottle, to perform at the Black Dragon Pool, while someone else led Deafman Ma, who exploded firecrackers next to his ear, to perform at the Silver Apricot Forest. Paraplegic Woman, who could embroider a leaf, went with Blind Tonghua, who could listen acutely, to perform at the Deer Looking-Back Riverbank. Grandma Mao Zhi and her nine little mothlets took their performance to another mountainside, where they could watch the sunset and the sunrise.

After visiting the mausoleum, you could proceed to the Nine Dragon Cataract, the Stone Cliffs, the Mountain-Top Stone Forest, and the Cave of the Green and White Serpent. If you still had some free time, there was also the old legend, invented by the town's lite-rati, about the monstrous black python that emerged from the Black

Dragon Pool. These sites were all located along a path beside the creek, and the performances took place along the same path. Perhaps these mountains and streams were not particularly interesting, but Liven's performances were truly extraordinary, and you couldn't help going to watch them.

Everyone knew that the money used to purchase Lenin's corpse was raised by Liven's performance troupes. They knew that when the troupes were performing down south, they would charge up to a thousand yuan per ticket. Balou families, however, typically couldn't even earn eight hundred yuan a year. Needless to say, for them to be willing to spend the equivalent of their entire annual salary in order to watch some blind, deaf, mute, and crippled performers, the performances had to be really extraordinary, consisting of something that wholers would never dare try to do themselves.

There was a moment of quiet just before dusk, as the sun was slipping behind the mountain. In the distance, the mountain creeks fell silent, as though the entire land had fallen into an old well.

Previously, you couldn't find anyone carrying anything. Now, however, when everyone went to the square in front of the mausoleum to watch Liven's troupes perform, they were all holding something to eat—including cold steamed buns, bags of peanuts, fava beans, baked buns, and shop cookies and cakes, together with the tea-eggs that peddlers were hawking, and as a result the entire area was filled with the sound of people munching away on their food and sipping their drinks.

The villagers who sold food and drink struck pay dirt, and proceeded to sell even their families' years-old grain, which had already gone bad. The villagers who didn't have anything to sell would take a large pot normally used for slaughtering pigs and use it to boil water, which they would then haul up the mountain in buckets, where it would become liquid gold.

It was the middle of winter, yet here it felt like a summer evening. Even in the middle of summer, though, it remained cool in the mountains, and in this particular region it could get quite chilly. This summerlike evening, therefore, signaled a respite not so much from the midday heat, but rather from the bitter chill typically associated with a midwinter night. Everyone—villagers and urbanites, old and young, men and women—were either standing in the square or sitting on the fifty-four kowtow steps leading from the square to the mausoleum. Those kowtow steps provided an ideal position to watch the performance, while the stone railing on either side of the steps offered the young people a perfect perch from which to view the festivities.

A stage was set up on the side of the square in front of the mausoleum. It was surrounded on three sides by new yellow canvas, and the top of the stage was also covered in new canvas. The canvas's odor of fresh paint was as thick as the fragrance of summer wheat, moistening people's hearts. The leader and deputy leader of the Balou tunes opera troupe were attending the villagers' performances and, having learned from Chief Liu's example, they were several times more respectful of Grandma Mao Zhi's performances than he had been. What they were most certain of, however, was how much extra money Shuanghuai could earn from each of these additional performances and, by extension, how much extra money their own families might receive.

Earlier that day, Chief Liu had said, "Soon, Liven will no longer fall under our jurisdiction. Do you not realize this?"

The troupe director added, "Grandma Mao Zhi, during the day everyone will perform separately, and at night everyone will come together for a collective performance. But no matter what, you absolutely must give us some additional performances."

Grandma Mao Zhi said, "Chief Liu, we agreed that at our final performance, you would read aloud from the stage the document affirming our withdrawal from society."

Chief Liu said, "Let's agree that you will first perform continuously, drawing everyone up to Spirit Mountain, where our influence is as vast as the earth and sky."

Grandma Mao Zhi said, "Chief Liu, you agreed that one-third of the proceeds from the Spirit Mountain performances would go to Liven."

One-Legged Monkey added, "The county authorities said that the ticket revenues must be distributed immediately following the performance."

Now, meanwhile, the troupe director said, "Quick, quick. Go summon the villagers and Grandma Mao Zhi. The audience is growing impatient, and if they have to wait any longer, they may very well tear down the stage."

The performance was delayed half an hour.

This was the troupe's final performance, at which Chief Liu had agreed to read aloud the document permitting Liven to withdraw from society. But when it was time to begin the performance, Chief Liu still had not appeared. Grandma Mao Zhi asked, "Will he come or not?" The county official replied, "Chief Liu has never gone back on his word. The organizers of a meeting sometimes may wait before starting the meeting without him, but he would invariably arrive at the very last moment, just as the meeting was about to adjourn."

The county official added, "There is no way that Chief Liu wouldn't come for this."

The performance, therefore, got under way. The program was one that the troupers had already performed hundreds, or even thousands, of times while touring the country, and they were as familiar with it as rural women are with preparing rice, rolling dough, tying thread, and mending shoes. The only difference was that they had previously been touring as two separate troupes, while now they were united into a single troupe, and they had to eliminate the duplicated acts and rearrange the order of the overall performance.

Chief Liu had said, "Go perform. Perform all the special-skills routines that people haven't seen yet, and I'll give a bonus of a thousand yuan to whoever performs well."

Grandma Mao Zhi had said, "Certainly. At any rate, this will be our final performance."

This final performance did, in fact, turn out to be unlike any of the preceding ones. From the very beginning, it was different. The beauty of Huaihua was absolutely out of this world. She was now a goddess among wholers, with a slender physique, a moonlike face, and limpid white skin that looked as though she had been doused in milk. When she stood in front of the stage in her role as announcer, she wore a clear dress, and up on stage she appeared like a moon hanging from a willow branch. Her hair was so black it looked as though all of the spotlights were shining directly on her head. Her lips were as red as ripe persimmons, and her teeth were as white as agate jade.

Everyone knew that when she left Liven she had been a tiny nin like her sisters Tonghua, Yuhua, and Mothlet. While out performing over the preceding half year, however, she had developed into a wholer. Her performance troupe had watched as she'd become increasingly radiant, but, like parents observing their children grow up, they did not find her transformation extraordinary, having watched it unfold day after day. Once she returned to Shuanghuai and encountered the villagers from the other performance troupe, however, those who hadn't seen her for several months were left speechless. The trash collector stood in amazement and ceased collecting trash, the porters stopped in their tracks, and people who had been squatting around all stood up and stared at her, to the point that the fairylike Huaihua began to feel rather discomfited, as if she had somehow wronged them by taking something from them.

When the Paraplegic Woman saw Huaihua, she suddenly leaped into the air. When she fell back to the ground, she exclaimed in amazement,

"Heavens! My heavens! Huaihua, how you have grown!"

Grandma Mao Zhi had been quietly watching her granddaughter from a distance. She stared in astonishment, but eventually laughed and said, "It has been worth it then. These past six months of touring and performing have certainly been worth it." She said this as though the villagers' touring and performing had taken place not to enable the village to withdraw from society, but rather to enable Huaihua to grow into an extraordinary wholer. As for Mothlet, she stood there with a look of surprise and envy, then eventually pulled Huaihua aside and asked, "Sis, how did you manage to grow so tall?"

After first glancing around furtively, Huaihuai whispered,

"Mothlet, if I tell you, will you still listen to me?"

Mothlet said, "Why wouldn't I?"

Huaihua replied, "Tonghua and Yuhua no longer listen to me. They act as though, in becoming a wholer, I've somehow taken something from them."

Mothlet said, "Tell me, Sis. I won't be like them."

Huaihua said, "You're already seventeen years old. It's time you were with a man. And it should be a wholer. You should sleep with a wholer." Mothlet stared at her whole and beautiful sister in astonishment. It seemed as though she was about to say something, but she suddenly noticed someone walk into the theater. It was Secretary Shi, and when Huaihua saw him she laughed and immediately rushed over.

After a while, Huaihua announced that she was going to accompany Secretary Shi back to the county government building to take care of some affairs, and then walked out with him. She retired to his room, and remained there until the two troupes were about to ascend Spirit Mountain. As the trucks carrying the troupes were ready to leave the county, she suddenly hurried back to rejoin them.

The moon rose at the usual time, and the stars also appeared in the sky as scheduled. For tens or hundreds of *li* outside the mountain region, everything was still frozen in the dead of winter, but here in Balou the weather was unusually warm. The evening was like the middle of summer, and the sky was so indigo it seemed fake, as though it had been artificially dyed. The night was extremely tranquil, without a trace of wind, and the milky white moonglow flowed over the mountain and the gorges, looking as though water were flowing over the landscape.

The entire land was in a state of peace, and it was only in the memorial hall that there were lights and the sound of human voices. It was as if everyone in the world had suddenly vanished, and the only survivors were the people in the memorial hall, who were celebrating their survival. Huaihua walked leisurely up to the front of the stage, her waterlike dress complementing her moonlike face. At that moment, the thousands of people in the audience were astonished by Huaihua's beauty and instantly fell silent, like a mountain sparrow suddenly glimpsing a phoenix. Everyone's gaze was riveted on Huaihua, on her body and her face, and everyone was waiting for her to speak. As she continued to stand there silently, a faint smile on her face, the audience became increasingly anxious, and finally she said softly,

"Comrades, friends, village elders. To celebrate the completion of the Spirit Mountain Lenin Memorial Hall, and to celebrate the impending arrival, in two or three days, of Lenin's corpse, the village of Liven's two special-skills troupes have arranged tonight's performance.

"This special-skills performance is one that people simply can't believe when they hear about it, or even when they see it with their own eyes. You are welcome to believe it or not. Seeing is believing. Now, the performance will begin, and the first event will be . . . Firecracker-on-the-Ear."

Who could have imagined that not only would Liven's Huaihua be transformed from a tiny nin into a beautiful wholer, but furthermore that her stage voice would become soft and smooth, such that she now sounded just like a professional announcer? In fact, watching her was like watching a performance in itself. Nevertheless, she looked as though she could hardly bear to talk, and instead merely offered a few brief comments, then bowed to the audience, took a couple of steps back, and walked off the stage—like a sparrow that happened to fly onto the stage and then immediately flew away again. Everyone's eyes and hearts were left empty, as though they had lost something they truly loved.

Fortunately, as soon as Huaihua stepped off stage, the actual performance began.

The opening act was no longer One-Legged Monkey's Leaping-Over-a-Mountain-of-Knives-and-Crossing-a-Sea-of-Fire routine, but rather Deafman Ma's Firecracker-on-the-Ear. Because in the mountains they performed out in the open, the troupes didn't have to follow the same order as they did in the city, but rather they needed to immediately quiet down the rambunctious audience so that everyone would fall into a stupefied daze. Therefore, they decided to use Deafman Ma's Firecracker-on-the-Ear as their opening act, and he left the audience so astonished that they didn't know what to do. Tonight, he was wearing the sort of white silk lantern outfit that an acrobat might wear. Whereas in the beginning he had been paralyzed by stage fright, now he was a seasoned performer. All of the disabled residents of the village of Liven had become seasoned performers. Deafman Ma slowly walked onto the stage, bowing deeply to the audience. Then, someone wrapped a string of two hundred firecrackers over his ears.

The audience immediately calmed down, as though they were seeing someone about to leap to his death from a precipice or a tall building.

Huaihua reappeared and stood in a corner of the stage. Speaking in a normal voice, she explained that Deafman Ma was forty-three years old this year, and since he had been fond of setting off fireworks ever since he was small, he had perfected his Firecracker-on-the-Ear technique. Huaihua did not claim that Deafman Ma had been deaf since infancy; rather, she said that he began setting off fireworks at the age of seven, and after practicing his technique had reached the point where he wasn't afraid of *any* sound next to his ear. Later, Huaihua took a raincoat from the corner of the stage and had Deafman Ma put it on in order to protect his lantern outfit. Then, she told him to stand at the front of the stage, placing a thin iron sheet between the firecrackers and his face.

She then lit the fireworks herself.

These two hundred red firecrackers emitted a cloud of smoke as they began exploding around the left side of his face. The audience was petrified with shock, and everyone—adults as well as children—immediately turned pale. In order to prove that he really wasn't afraid of the firecrackers, Deafman Ma turned his head so the audience could see the left side of his face, and so that the fireworks were now exploding in their direction. This stunned everyone into silence.

After all of the fireworks had been detonated, Deafman Ma calmly removed the iron sheet from his face and struck it a couple of times, as though he were striking a drum. He then picked up a firecracker that had failed to detonate and placed it on the sheet. He lit it, and it sounded as though an explosive were being detonated on the surface of a drum. Afterward, he showed the audience the blackened left-hand side of his face, convincing everyone that although his face was completely blackened, he was unharmed. Finally, he smiled blankly at the audience.

With this, the audience seemed to awake from their stupor and erupted into a flood of applause. The sound echoed through the quiet mountain region, the white applause mixing with the purple sound of people's voices. The sound flew out from the square, resonating within the memorial hall and throughout the valley. The sound reverberated through the quiet night, to the point that the entire region was enveloped in hot white applause and purple chatter. The calm night absorbed this sound, as if one were waking up from a dream to find the entire land filled with cries of enjoyment.

The audience called out, shouted, applauded, and waved their fists toward the stage as they hollered,

"Hang a gong from your face! . . . Hang a gong from your face!"

How could the audience have known that Deafman Ma was deaf from birth, and consequently his entire life had never been able to hear any shouts, explosions, or thunder? He had seen lightning countless times in his life, but had never heard the accompanying thunder. Accordingly, he hung a bright yellow bronze gong shaped like the lid of a small pot over his ear, and then placed a string of five hundred firecrackers on it and lit them. As the audience shouted in amazement, he threw the gong to the ground and smiled stupidly, hitting his own face as though he were striking a stone. As he lay on the canvas covering the stage, he removed an explosive as big as a turnip from his pocket and placed it on the upward-facing side of his head, then gestured to the audience to indicate that he wished for someone to come up on stage to help him light it.

At this point, the audience became deathly silent. The shouts and applause had all ceased, and the entire land seemed as if it had been pushed into a valley of death. Everyone could hear the sound of the light striking the stage. They saw one another's eyes, which were riveted on the stage like moths drawn to a flame.

Deafman Ma was still gesturing to them.

At this point, Huaihua emerged, smiling, from a corner of the stage, and announced, "Young people, friends, please come up on stage to light the firecracker. When we were touring down south, we didn't perform this routine even for people paying a thousand yuan per ticket. Instead, it is one that we prepared specifically for our fellow villagers today."

With this, a young man from the audience hopped up onto the stage.

He struck a match, then squatted down and lit the explosive.

It exploded.

The sound of the explosion rang out, and was followed by a cloud of light and smoke. The lights hanging from above waved back and forth. Deafman Ma, however, continued lying there calmly as though nothing had happened. Then he clambered to his feet and shook the ashes from his body. He touched his cheek and discovered that it was covered in blood and ash, so he accepted a white handkerchief from Huaihua and wiped his face. Finally, he bowed to the audience and walked off the stage.

After a period of stupefied silence, the audience once again broke into wild applause and cheers of approval.

Grandma Mao Zhi was standing on the side of the stage.

Deafman Ma wiped the blood off his face and asked, "Will this earn me a big bonus from Chief Liu?"

Before Grandma Mao Zhi could respond, the troupe director laughed and said, "Absolutely, you'll definitely get your thousand-yuan bonus."

Deafman Ma smiled as he went to find someone to bandage his face.

Then, the troupe's second act went on. The first act had been extremely raucous, but the second one was extraordinarily peaceful—consisting of One-Eye threading a needle. In the past, when One-Eye threaded a needle, he would take eight to ten large needles used for mending shoes and hold them in his left hand between his thumb and index finger, while in his right hand he would hold a strand of thread.

339

He would then twist the thread with his fingers, aim carefully, and align the eyes of all the needles in a row. Finally, he would pass the end of the thread through the eyes of the needles as though it were an arrow flying down an alley.

This time, however, he reached into a cardboard box and took out a handful of embroidery needles, inserting more than a hundred of them into the cracks between the fingers of his left hand. Then, with his palm facing downward, he lightly knocked on a wooden board, as those hundred-odd large-eyed needles lined up one against the other. He turned his hand over so that his palm was now facing upward, toward the light, whereupon he proceeded to open his own eye wide and, using the index finger and thumb of his right hand, rolled up the four rows of needles in his left hand, such that the eyes of the needles were all aligned toward his own. Through those four rows of needle eyes, he could see the bright splendor of the lights overhead. He took a strand of thread that had been twisted as straight as a metal wire, and proceeded to thread it through each of those rows of needles. In the blink of an eye, all four rows of needles were suddenly hanging from a red thread.

Initially, he was able to thread eight to ten needles in the time it took to swallow a gulp of saliva, and he could thread forty-seven to seventy-seven large acupuncture needles in less time than it would take to eat a steamed bun. This night, he managed to thread one hundred and twenty-seven embroidery needles almost instantly, needing no more time than it takes to chew and swallow a bite of steamed bun. Moreover, he was able to repeat this performance three times, threading two hundred and ninety-seven embroidery needles in all.

He asked, "Can I receive the bonus that the county chief referred to?"

The troupe director replied, "Yes, certainly."

The Leaf-Embroidery performance was also different from usual. Not only was Paraplegic Woman able to embroider images of grass, flowers, grasshoppers, and butterflies on a sheet of thin, brittle paper; she could even embroider an image of a tiny moth on a cicada shell hanging from a tree in the middle of winter. To give the tiny moth a colorful highlight, she didn't use red thread but rather pricked her hand with the needle, producing a tiny drop of blood. With this, the tiny moth was transformed into a flower red butterfly.

Little Polio Boy's performance was also different from usual. Wearing a glass bottle on his foot, he hobbled around the stage three times, backward and forward. Then, he suddenly stopped and gazed out at the audience, and energetically stomped on the bottle, shattering it. He lifted his foot, and the audience watched as he deliberately stepped on the shattered glass with his shriveled appendage. The glass was white and clear, and was covered in bright red blood.

By this point the audience had reached the point where they couldn't shout and applaud anymore. When they saw Polio Boy lift his tiny foot into the air, blood dripping like rain onto the canvas, they noticed that his face was yellowish white, like a translucent sheet of paper. Someone in the audience suddenly shouted, "Does it hurt?"

The boy replied, "I can bear it."

Someone else said, "I dare you to get up and walk around the stage!"

Polio Boy therefore stood up and, with his forehead covered in sweat and a trace of a smile on his lips, lowered the foot that had been cut by the shattered glass. He then leaned on that leg, which was as thin as a stick, and proceeded to walk around the stage three times.

It was pitch dark outside, as though the sun had fallen into a deep, dark hole. Chief Liu had agreed that it would be at this performance that he would announce his decision to permit the village of Liven to leave the jurisdiction of Shuanghuai, and that he would read the corresponding document aloud to the audience. At the end of this final act, however, he still had not appeared. Pacing nervously backstage, Grandma Mao Zhi didn't see any headlights in the street or hear the sound of a car approaching. She asked, "Chief Liu couldn't fail to show up, could he?" A county cadre replied, "How could he?" He added, "Perhaps his car broke down, or he was delayed by another emergency." He said, "Why don't you go up and perform as well. You could perform several more acts while waiting for Chief Liu. He is certain to come; he said he would read the withdrawal-from-society document."

Grandma Mao Zhi agreed to perform several additional acts while waiting for Chief Liu to arrive.

She called out to the bloody Polio Boy, saying, "Boy, if you can, please walk around the stage several more times."

The moon was already directly above the mountains, and people to the north had already gone to watch the sunrise over the mountaintop. The moon seemed to be suspended from a giant tree on the mountain. It was in its final quarter, and in the shape of a crescent, as it hung there between the branches. The stars were fading and the air was now as cool as a midsummer's night. But it was, after all, still winter, and there was a chill in the air. Some people in the audience put their padded jackets on, together with the sweaters and sweatshirts they were holding in the crooks of their arms. In the past, everyone would be sound asleep by this time, but the audience in front of the memorial hall were not sleepy at all, and instead continued watching the performance with wide eyes.

Polio Boy had already started walking around the stage again on his bloody and deformed foot. Alternating between walking and running, he hobbled around the stage three times and back. He left the stage covered in a thick pool of blood, and every few feet the canvas was marked with one of his bloody footprints. These sticky footprints were initially bright red, but they quickly faded to deep purple, and then to black. Polio Boy's forehead was still covered in sweat, but he maintained a sweet and bright smile on his face, as though he had finally conquered himself. After he finished making six loops, he went to the front of the stage to take a bow, and even lifted his leaflike deformed foot to show the audience. They saw that the glass bottle in which he had originally inserted his foot was gone, and that instead the shards of glass were now embedded in the sole of his foot, such that he left a trail of bloody footprints everywhere he went, as though he were walking not on a foot but rather on one of those water faucets that city-dwellers use.

Finally, it was Grandma Mao Zhi and Mothlet's turn to perform. By this point the moon was on the other side of the mountain, and the humid peacefulness of the mountain range extended throughout the entire region. In the pauses in the audience's commotion, it was possible to hear the wind in the trees, together with an occasional birdsong emanating from somewhere deep in the mountains. The stage lights pierced the sky like an arrow. There was a winter chill in the air, combined with a refreshing summer-night scent.

Grandma Mao Zhi had said, "When you return, you must remember to bring the document certifying our withdrawal from society."

Before he left, Chief Liu had said, "Grandma Mao Zhi, even if they tried to beat me to death, I would still return to read out the document certifying Liven's withdrawal from society."

One of the higher-ups now said, "Grandma Mao Zhi, you should hurry and perform. I can hear a car coming up the mountain."

Grandma Mao Zhi therefore went on stage. This was her special finale, and as soon as she appeared the audience would gasp in astonishment. First, however, her granddaughter, who had already become a wholer, went to the front of the stage and directed a series of questions to the audience, including, Is there anyone in your family who is eighty years old? Anyone who is ninety? Anyone who is over a hundred? And, if so, have their teeth already fallen out? Has their vision faded? Can they still eat peanuts and walnuts, and chew soybeans? Can they still thread a needle and sew shoes?

Huaihua then got down from the stage and Grandma Mao Zhi was pushed on stage in a wheelchair. It was announced that she was a hundred and nine years old. Because she was already over a hundred, they dressed her in the sort of dark blue double-breasted jacket that women used to wear during the Republican period. Her hair was gray and she appeared old and decrepit, as though she had just been pulled out of a coffin. But precisely for this reason, she appeared very striking. Because it had already been announced that she was a hundred and nine years old, and that she had been crippled her entire life, it was natural that she was pushed out by a wholer. More specifically, the person pushing her was the middle-aged man who, when the troupe was touring down south, had performed as a hundred-and-twenty-one-year-old man, though now he was appearing as the *son* of a hundred-and-nine-year-old woman. Every time he opened his mouth, he had to call her "Mother."

The decision to have Grandma Mao Zhi be a hundred and nine years old—rather than two hundred and forty-one, and her great-grandchildren a hundred and twenty-one—was the result of a careful calculation on the part of the wholers. Everyone in the Balou mountain region knew about Liven, and the wholers couldn't very well claim that Grandma Mao Zhi was two hundred and forty-one, but if they said she was a hundred and nine most people would probably believe it. There were already a few centenarians in the district, and although they were rare, it was not as though they were completely unheard of. If the wholers claimed Mao Zhi was a hundred and nine, even people from Liven's neighboring villages wouldn't be inclined to doubt it. Given that most of the residents of Liven were disabled, the residents of these neighboring villages never thought of coming over to visit and never took any interest in Liven's affairs, and therefore had no way of knowing whether or not Liven really did have a resident who was over a hundred.

The "son" who was pushing Grandma Mao Zhi onto the stage explained, with an old villager's honest expression, that his mother was born a hundred and nine years earlier, in the *xinmao* Year of the Rabbit of the preceding *jiazi* cycle—meaning that she had lived through the fall of the Qing and the subsequent Republican era. To prove his mother's age, the son took out their family's residence permit and his mother's identification card and passed them around. He showed everyone the framed birth certificate that Chief Liu had personally engraved, signed, and stamped. Given that Grandma Mao Zhi had Chief Liu's signature and stamp, the audience would have no grounds to doubt that she was indeed a hundred and nine years old, rather than merely seventy-one.

At this point, her son announced that it was actually not that remarkable for someone to live past a hundred; the important thing was that his mother still had all of her teeth and that her hearing and eyesight remained sharp. The only effect of her advanced age was that she walked somewhat unsteadily. In order to prove that his mother's teeth were still strong, he handed Grandma Mao Zhi two walnuts, which she cracked with them. In order to prove that her eyesight was still good, he handed her a needle and a piece of black thread, and then turned off the floodlights, leaving the stage in shadows, like the oil-lamp-illuminated houses people have in the countryside. Grandma Mao Zhi held up the needle in the dim light and, after several attempts, eventually succeeded in threading it.

Everyone was astonished by her ability to thread the needle, crack the walnut, and chew peanuts and fried beans. After all, whose parents or grandparents could be expected, under normal circumstances, to live past a hundred? And who could live to a hundred and nine with hearing, eyesight, and teeth intact? As the audience was still reeling in amazement, Grandma Mao Zhi's son disclosed the secret of her longevity. He removed his mother's big-collared jacket and her oversized pants, both of which had been fashionable during the Republican era, and revealed that underneath she was wearing sparkling black burial clothing.

The audience gasped in astonishment, then erupted into shouts as everyone's gaze was suddenly riveted on Grandma Mao Zhi, standing up on stage. After all, even at a hundred and nine years old, she was still a living person who had just been cracking walnuts. As she'd been threading her needle, she had smiled and said, "I'm old, and in a few days I'll no longer be able to do this." And now they found her wearing burial clothing like a dead person!

The burial garb was made of high-quality black satin with subtle sparkles that shimmered under the stage lights. The bottom of the outfit had a florid border the width of a belt, which was stitched entirely with gold and white thread, and this border shimmered differently from the black satin. The black satin and florid border shimmered under the lights like pure silver and gold, like the light from the morning sun shining directly into people's eyes just after it has emerged from behind the eastern mountains. The burial outfit's oversized dress, meanwhile, appeared even more unusual up on stage. Not only were the arm and neck openings adorned with a gold border, but the front lapel was decorated with a carefully embroidered image of a phoenix. On the left lapel there was an image of a serpent that looked like a live dragon soaring and seemed as though, if fully extended, it would be more than ten feet long. The dragon undulated and stretched all the way from the bottom of the dress to the shoulder, with each claw and scale embroidered with minute precision, so realistic that it seemed as though it might leap off the stage at any moment. The phoenix on the right lapel, meanwhile, was a combination of crimson, purple, scarlet, pink, and a variety of other shades of red, making it look as though an actual flaming phoenix had alighted on her lapel. Against this juxtaposition of red and yellow, the black appeared to emit a white light, the red emitted a purplish light, and the yellow had a golden bronze luster.

This resplendent burial outfit shocked the thousands of people in the audience into silence. As everyone was staring in astonishment, the man playing Grandma Mao Zhi's son turned her around, such that the large *libation* character inscribed on her back sparkled in the light. This character originally should have been in the shape of a square, but whoever made the clothing had embroidered the character in the shape of a circle. The tailor had used platinum-colored silk thread, and each of the stitches was at least an inch wide, while the gaps between them were as narrow as incense sticks, thereby making the character resemble a rising or setting sun. In the two circles surrounding the character, there appeared an array of little *longevity* characters nestled against one other, giving the *libation* character even more of an aura of death, revealing a threatening *yin* quality.

With this, like a climber who finally scales a mountain, the act reached its climax, as did the troupe's performance as a whole. The able-bodied members of the troupe were somewhat smarter than the disabled ones, and wiser in the ways of the world. They knew that the goal of each act was to astound and amaze, and that once the performance reached its climax it was not necessary for the audience to shout madly and applaud until their hands bled. Instead, by this point they would already be hoarse from shouting, their hands would be in agony, and they would be generally exhausted and drowsy. Therefore, anything short of a decapitation would probably not be able to arouse their interest.

The wholers understood the principle of moving when one should move, and resting when one should rest, together with the inverse principle of moving from excitement to calm, and from calm to excitement. The Firecracker-on-the-Ear performer's face was black with blood, One-Eye had threaded almost three hundred needles at once, One-Legged Monkey had deliberately set his shirt on fire, and the blind performer had reached the point where she could distinguish between the sound of a strand of hair from the body of a pig and one from a horse's mane. The troupers naturally couldn't come up with anything more extraordinary, and they had no choice but to conclude with an act that would bring the audience back down to earth, leaving everyone speechless. Grandma Mao Zhi's appearance in her burial clothing had had the desired effect: The audience simply couldn't understand why a living person should be wearing her burial clothing around the clock.

It was the middle of the night, and outside it was as dark as the bottom of a well. The entire world was as silent as a dream, as everyone seemed to be hovering at the boundary between life and death. Upon seeing a hundred-and-nine-year-old woman appear before them on stage wearing burial clothing, everyone had turned as pale as the moonlight, as though all of the blood had suddenly drained from their faces, making them look as though they had just returned from the dead. The audience was deathly quiet, so quiet that it was as if there weren't anyone there at all. Up on stage, you could hear the snoring of an infant nestled at its mother's breast, the sound of a boy calling out to his mother.

The sixty-one-year-old man playing the part of Grandma Mao Zhi's ninety-year-old-son then told the audience two very ordinary things, which they had no choice but to believe. He said,

"For several decades now, my mother has never taken off her burial clothes. She has been eating and sleeping in these clothes for more than half her life."

He further explained that in the *wuzi* Year of the Rat of the preceding *jiazi* cycle, which is to say the thirty-seventh year of the

347

Republic, 1948, his mother fell into a ravine while collecting kindling on the mountain. She broke her leg, and the scare brought on a major illness. She was in a coma for seven days and seven nights, during which time he dressed her in her burial clothes in preparation for her imminent demise and ascent to heaven. As he was preparing for her death, she suddenly woke up and proceeded to take off her burial clothes. After doing so, however, she became even sicker and eventually lapsed back into a coma; but as soon as she was dressed again in her burial clothes, she immediately regained consciousness. They went through this cycle several more times, until eventually she decided not to remove the burial clothes, and instead her son prepared several additional sets so that she could rotate between them. She proceeded to wear these burial clothes day in and day out, wearing them to eat, to work the fields, to haul manure, to harvest the crops, and even to sleep.

The son said that his mother had been wearing these burial clothes for fifty-one years.

He said that during those fifty-one years, his mother had never once fallen ill.

He said that Chinese doctors in the Balou mountain region had reported this, and that when she was touring with the performance troupe, the city doctors had also confirmed it. They all claimed that the reason she had never gotten sick over the preceding fifty-one years was precisely that she had been wearing her burial clothing the entire time. They said that everyone fears death, and that nine out of ten illnesses could be attributed to an accumulated fear of dying, which had the result of transforming minor illnesses into major ones, and major illnesses into life-threatening crises. They said that as long as people don't fear death, and instead views death the way they would view the act of returning home or going to bed, their body wouldn't suffer from stagnating *qi*, and their blood would continue to circulate freely day after day, and year after year. This, in turn, would be why for ten, twenty, fifty, or even a hundred years, they would never have gotten sick. And if they never got sick, they would naturally live a very long time and be extraordinarily healthy.

How healthy was Grandma Mao Zhi? At a hundred and nine years old, not only could she still sew a comforter, resole a shoe, cook, and do laundry for her children and great-grandchildren; she could even go into the fields to help harvest the wheat, pounding it with a wooden club like all the other villagers. And even now she not only was able to lift a carrying pole weighing one hundred or two hundred pounds, but could even, while leaning on her crutch, lift nine people off the ground.

At this point, four young men emerged from backstage with two bulging canvas sacks. They placed a carrying pole between the two sacks, and Grandma Mao Zhi, after a couple of attempts, was in fact able to lift the sacks a little bit off the ground.

After she put the sacks down, nine live girls proceeded to leap out of them.

Nine tiny girls, like mothlets or butterflies.

These were The Nine Mothlets, who were said to have all emerged from the same womb. Once on stage, they proceeded to sing, dance, and fly around like countless tiny butterflies.

Book 11: Flowers

Chapter 1: A sheet of white cloth covered by a myriad of red dots

To everyone's surprise, Chief Liu had still not returned by the end of the performance. As the villagers of Liven were going to sleep, however, something extraordinary took place.

The villagers were all in one of the memorial hall's side rooms. Just as they had been doing while traveling through China with their troupe over the preceding six months, they had laid out their bedrolls and were sleeping together, grouped by family, with the men and women in separate rooms. But this evening, on the winter solstice of the *wuyin* Year of the Tiger, as everyone was returning to the memorial hall to sleep after having cleaned up the clothing left on stage, the villagers noticed that neither their comforters nor their pillows were where they had left them at the heads of their beds. The cotton inside their bedding and mattresses had been ripped out and scattered everywhere, and the clothes in their travel bags had similarly been strewn about.

The money they had earned while performing over the preceding six months was no longer hidden inside their bedding, mattresses, and pillows, and neither was it in their travel chests or anywhere else.

Their money had been stolen.

It had all been stolen by the wholers.

By this point, the thousands of people who'd come to watch the performance had all dispersed to locations along Spirit Mountain, and the sound of their footsteps had already faded. Throughout the rest of the land it was a bitterly cold winter, but here spring had arrived early, and the trees were all putting out new buds. The grass was green, and in the warm air there was a light aroma. In this warm weather, you could stop anywhere for the night. You could sleep under the eaves of a house, next to a ditch, under a tree, or on a stone.

The wholers escorting the troupe had all disappeared without a trace. As for those visitors from nearby towns and villages, they could pay two yuan to rent a mat for the night, or four yuan to rent a rug. Standing on the kowtow steps in front of the Lenin Memorial Hall, a wholer was calling out loudly:

"Who wants to borrow[1] a mat? . . . Only two yuan each . . ."

"Who wants to borrow a sheet? . . . Only five yuan each . . ."

As he continued shouting, his voice was drowned out by the villagers' cries of alarm. It was as though a thunderstorm had completely smothered the light breeze that had preceded it. These shouts were originating from the side room of the memorial hall, reverberating throughout the land like explosions.

"My god, where has my money gone?"

"My god, someone has cut up my pillow and bedding."

"My god, we've been robbed! Everything has been stolen! How will we ever manage?!"

The first person to return to the side room was One-Legged Monkey, since he walked quickly. He wasn't carrying any clothing or props, and as soon as he stepped into the memorial hall he went to the room directly across from the crystal coffin. He opened the door and turned on the light, and the scene of the robbery immediately struck him between the eyes. The side rooms in the mausoleum were arranged in suites, one adjacent to another, and in all there were more than ten individual rooms. As soon as One-Legged Monkey walked into the room he saw that the villager who had stayed behind to watch over their stuff was tied up and covered in blood. The villager had a pants leg stuffed into his mouth and had been tossed into a corner of the room like a discarded ball. One-Legged Monkey immediately rushed over to the entrance of the second room and saw that his bedding, which had been carefully folded and left at the foot of the wall, had been ripped open. The clothes he had stuffed into his pillow were strewn about everywhere. Deafman Ma, One-Eye, and Lame Carpenter, together with Six-Finger and Mute, who were usually charged with helping to carry and unload boxes, all slept on the floor, but their chests, bags, and bedding had also been scattered about. The stuffing from someone's bedding had been thrown into the doorway, and Deafman Ma's red underwear had been tossed up onto the windowsill.

One-Legged Monkey immediately realized that this was a grave catastrophe, and threw down his crutch and leaped forward on one leg, as though he were on stage leaping over a sea of fire. He grabbed his bedding, and saw that someone had cut it open with a pair of scissors, and that the ten thousand yuan in brand-new hundred-yuan bills that he had stuffed inside was missing. He then checked on the money he had stuffed into his mattress, and found that the mattress had also been ripped open and left with a gaping hole.

He knelt down and started to wail,

"Where has my money gone? . . . Where has my money gone?"

That wailing quickly became a wave of sound that echoed throughout the mountains and valleys. Crippled Woman, Lame Carpenter, Blind Woman, Six-Finger, the Mute, One-Leg, Tonghua, Mothlet, Huaihua, and Yuhua, together with the wholers who had come along to cook for the troupe—more than a hundred of Liven's villagers in all—began wailing and sobbing inside the Lenin Memorial Hall. Some of them leaned against a door frame and stomped their feet, while others sat on the floor hugging their empty cloth bundles, sobbing and abjectly beating themselves. Those who had sewn their money inside their bedding found that their bedding had been ripped open, while those who had stuffed it inside their pillows found that all that was left was wheat and bran. Those who had stuffed their money into the cotton inside their mattresses found the cotton scattered all over the floor. Those who had put their money inside a wooden chest found that the lock of the chest had been forced, or else that the chest had simply been smashed open. Huaihua, who had bought the sort of embossed leather chest that city-dwellers often use and had locked her money and valuables inside, found that the entire chest had disappeared.

Some of the older villagers had placed their money inside metal pails, and wherever they went to perform they would dig a hole beneath their bedding and bury the pail inside, and then would place their sleeping mat and pillow over it. Those villagers had assumed that no one else knew where they had buried their money, but at this point—and precisely at this point—they found their empty pails lying discarded next to Lenin's crystal coffin.

The people of Liven had been the victims of a devastating robbery.

In the main hall of the mausoleum, next to Lenin's crystal coffin, there were blind people, deaf people, mutes, and cripples sitting on the ground of the three side rooms. Men and women, young and old—the sounds of their shouts and curses cut through the air like a sharp blade through bamboo. Their voices were alternately hoarse and piercing, and it seemed as though the sheer sound of their cries would be enough to knock over the memorial hall.

Quite a few wholers entered the hall. They had been sleeping in the area around the mausoleum after watching the performance, and upon seeing the villagers cursing the heavens and wiping tears from their eyes, the wholers tried to console them.

They said, "Don't cry. You can always earn back the money you lost."

They said, "As long as there is a verdant mountain, how can you be worried about not having enough wood for kindling?"

They said, "The fact that over the past few months you've been able to earn so much money despite being disabled is simply breathtaking."

After reassuring the villagers in this way, the wholers began to feel drowsy, and retired to go back to sleep.

Under the blazing white light, the crystal coffin emitted a bluish glow. It was as if the coffin were made not of crystal, but rather of cold, hard jade. After shouting and wailing for a long time, the villagers eventually stopped. They stood in the main hall of the mausoleum, a few on the left and a cluster on the right, and this dark crowd of people all directed their gaze at Grandma Mao Zhi.

Grandma Mao Zhi's face was covered in a thick layer of dust, but beneath it she was as pale as death. She stood woodenly at the head of the coffin, her crutch resting on the middle of it. Her black satin burial clothes lay in a bundle on top of the bluish crystal coffin, as naturally as a needle and thread in a needle basket or a candle in a candleholder. The blue glow from the coffin was like a cloudless sky, while the black silk burial clothes looked like a sheet of black glass. Both were incomparably bright and powerfully silent.

After Grandma Mao Zhi had finished cleaning the things on stage following the performance, she'd looked at the memorial hall for a while before returning there. After deciding that Chief Liu would probably not arrive that night, she sighed and limped back.

It was already so late that the moon had begun to set and the stars had begun to fade. The memorial hall was high in the mountains, and it was as if the mountain ridge were lifting it up into the sky. Everything was extremely peaceful, and the wind blowing under the eves of the building produced a quiet whisper.

It was at this point that Grandma Mao Zhi heard the cries and wails inside the memorial hall. Limping, she rushed to the side room where she and her four granddaughters had been staying, but all she found was Yuhua sitting on her reed mat grasping her bedding and sobbing, "I couldn't even bring myself to spend money to buy a single piece of clothing! . . . I couldn't even bring myself to spend money to buy a single piece of clothing!" Mothlet was also sitting on her mat, grasping her pillow and saying, "After dinner it was all still here, and before I left to perform I could still feel it here!" Huaihua and Tonghua were standing on their respective mats, but the blind Tonghua was just staring darkly ahead, without saying a word, as though she had already foreseen the theft. Huaihua, meanwhile, wasn't crying, and instead merely stomped her feet and complained, "Great, this is just great! Now you don't need to complain that I can't bring myself to spend any of my money. You don't need to say that I treat buying a cotton shirt as though I were being asked to purchase an entire wheat field."

Grandma Mao Zhi stood in the doorway looking at her four granddaughters, immediately realizing what had happened. Then, she hobbled over to the door of the second side room and peered inside.

She hobbled over to the door of the third side room and peered inside.

She hobbled over to the door of the fourth side room and peered inside.

After she had looked inside seven of the side rooms, she abruptly turned around. It occurred to her that she should look for one of the higher-ups—one of the wholers from the county—to tell them what had happened.

However, when she ran to the side room behind the coffin, she opened the door and immediately noticed that the wholers' clothing and bedding were no longer there. The room had been left completely bare.

There wasn't a trace of anyone.

Grandma Mao Zhi's heart lurched, and she felt as though there were a heavy chunk of ice pressing down on her chest. She rushed outside and over to the front of the stage, at which point she noticed that the two trucks that had been shuttling them around for the preceding six months were both gone. Instead, there was only a set of tire tracks and some kindling.

Standing in the entrance to the memorial hall, Grandma Mao Zhi leaned her hand against the cool redwood door frame, then collapsed.

She didn't shout or cry, but rather just sat there on the stone floor without moving. After a long pause, after the people who had come to check out the scene had walked past her and gone back to sleep, she returned to the crystal coffin, and called to all of Liven's villagers to come over. She also summoned the young man who had stayed behind in the main hall to supervise the villagers' things.

Compared with the other villagers who had gone on tour, the young man was virtually a wholer. He was neither blind, crippled, nor mute, and his only disability was that the fingers on his left hand were permanently stuck together, like a duck's foot. His hand had been this way since birth, and ten years later it remained unchanged. He squatted down in front of Grandma Mao Zhi, pale as death, as though the villagers' tragedy was all his fault. He had been beaten repeatedly, to the point that half his face was swollen, his mouth and nose were misshapen, and his normally thin left hand was so engorged that it now resembled that of a normal person. He looked at Grandma Mao Zhi, and then over at the Liven villagers. He felt so guilty that he bowed his head, tears pouring down his face like cobblestones smashing against the marble floor.

Grandma Mao Zhi asked,

"Who did it?"

He replied, "It was a pile[3] of people."

Grandma Mao Zhi said, "But *who* precisely?"

He said,

"They were all higher-ups—the wholers who traveled with us when we went to perform in the south. It was a big group, at least ten or twenty of them."

Grandma Mao Zhi asked,

"Why didn't you call out?"

He said, "They tied me up as soon as soon as they arrived, and stationed someone at the door to serve as a sentry.[5] Someone else went through the room turning over the bedding and prying open the chests. They knew exactly where everyone hid their money—it was almost as if they were taking their own belongings."

Grandma Mao Zhi asked again,

"Why didn't you call out?"

He said,

"They were all wholers, and they said that if I uttered a word they would beat me to death. Then they taped my mouth shut."

Grandma Mao Zhi asked,

"What did they say?"

He replied,

"They didn't say anything. They just said that the world was turned upside down, and now the entire world belonged to you blind men and cripples."

She asked, "What else did they say?"

He considered for a while, and then replied, "They said that you are all waiting here, but even if you wait until you die, Chief Liu still won't return."

After that there were no more questions, and no more replies. The main hall became deathly quiet—so quiet it seemed as if it were completely empty, except for the coffin. In this stillness, the villagers gazed at Grandma Mao Zhi, but to their surprise her anxious expression gradually disappeared, and her pale face regained its normal color. It was as if the winter ice were finally thawing, and beginning to develop a lively atmosphere. There was a hint of flexibility in her expression, but in that flexibility it seemed as though she had suddenly thought of something. It was as if she suddenly had something very important to say.

She said, "Now you know what the wholers are capable of. I'd like to ask you all one thing: Do you or do you not wish to withdraw from society? Do you or do you not want to return to the livening life that we used to enjoy?" After asking this, she didn't use her gaze to force the villagers to respond, as she might have done in the past, but rather simply turned and opened the bundle of burial clothes that was lying on the crystal coffin. She then used her teeth to rip a strip of the white lining, ripping it again and again until it was a perfect square, like one of those sheets of paper used for steaming buns. She placed it on top of Lenin's coffin, and then walked to the side room to look for a pair of scissors. When she returned, she stood in front of everyone and used the point of the scissors to prick the middle finger of her left hand, letting the blood form a coin-sized pool on top of the coffin. Next, she dipped her right index finger in the blood and pressed it onto the white cloth, leaving a scarlet fingerprint. Finally, she turned to the villagers and said,

"Everyone who now recognizes the wholers' true nature and wishes to withdraw from society, come leave your fingerprints on this cloth. If you disagree, you are welcome to remain there and suffer the black disasters[7] and red difficulties[9] that the wholers will give you."

Grandma Mao Zhi spoke in a soft voice, but her words were extremely powerful. Only after she finished speaking did she look at everyone's face. Under the hall light, the faces had a somewhat wooden appearance. Everyone seemed embarrassed, as though they didn't know what to say or what to do. It was as if the theft had left everyone paralyzed. After Grandma Mao Zhi brought up the topic of withdrawing from society, the villagers found themselves unable to react appropriately, like horses stuck in a narrow alleyway with no way to turn their heads. As they stood there silent and petrified, time flowed as slowly as tree sap. Their resentment at having been robbed gradually faded, but it was only after they had endured countless black crimes[11] and red crimes[13] that they eventually shifted their attention to other matters, such as whether or not to withdraw from society.

There was no one else left in the enormous hall. Even the people sent down by the county to oversee the memorial hall had all disappeared. Perhaps they had left with the higher-up wholers, or perhaps they were still sleeping peacefully in their own beds. The floor and walls of the enormous hall were made of bright marble, and in the center of the hall there was a portrait of Lenin and his crystal coffin. There was a crowd of villagers sitting around the coffin, including blind men, deaf men, mutes, and cripples, together with people suffering from a variety of other disabilities. Others were sitting or standing elsewhere, or leaning against door frames or one of those cold marble walls. The hall was absolutely silent, and this silence made the scene appear all the more solemn. It was as if they were facing a life-or-death decision of whether or not to leave their fingerprints on that white sheet.

They looked at one another, everyone waiting for someone else to make the first move.

Finally, One-Legged Monkey said, "Will we still be able to go on performance tours even after withdrawing from society?"

Grandma Mao Zhi did not respond, and instead just gazed at him coldly.

At that point, the young man who had stayed behind to watch the villagers' things exclaimed, "Fuck, I want to withdraw from society even if it kills me. I live in fear now, and living in fear is worse than death."

He was the first to go up to the coffin and stick his finger into the pool of Grandma Mao Zhi's blood, and leave his fingerprint on the sheet.

The leaf-embroidering Paraplegic Woman crawled forward and said she would rather die than perform again, and was willing to die in order to return to their former way of life. As she spoke she continued to drag herself along, and when she was directly below the coffin she removed a needle from her hair and used it to poke one of the fingers of her right hand, which she then pressed against the white cloth.

Some of the older villagers began coming forward to leave their fingerprints, gradually transforming that white cloth into a sea of red dots. Eventually, however, it reached the point that no one else wanted to leave his or her fingerprints. The atmosphere in the hall became rather oppressive, as though muddy water were flowing through the air. Originally everyone had been grief-stricken over having been robbed, but Grandma Mao Zhi hadn't told the villagers what they should do to address this problem, and had instead forced them, at this moment of hardship, to decide whether or not to withdraw from society. This didn't seem to be the best time to decide—it was as if after someone falls into a well, you then take advantage of the situation by demanding something of him. In any event, none of the young villagers came forward, but rather they all kept their gaze riveted on One-Legged Monkey. Even Grandma Mao Zhi's granddaughters stood behind her without moving, Yuhua and Mothlet peeking at their grandmother's face, Huaihua staring, like the other young villagers, at One-Legged Monkey, as though urging him not to leave his fingerprint on the cloth. If he were to leave his fingerprint, they would have no choice but to do the same; and if he didn't, they certainly wouldn't either.

One-Legged Monkey became the de facto leader of the young villagers.

Grandma Mao Zhi directed her gaze at him.

One-Legged Monkey, however, turned away and muttered,

"If we withdraw from society, then eventually things will reach the point that we won't even have our own shadows,[15] and if we don't have our shadows how will we be able to perform? Now that our money has been stolen, how can we not go perform?" As he shouted this, it was as if he were explaining something, or as if he were trying to remind the villagers of something. When he finished, he hobbled back to the side room where he had been sleeping.

Huaihua glanced over at her grandmother, then followed One-Legged Monkey.

The other young people followed them into the side room, one after another, their footsteps making it sound as if an evening village meeting had just adjourned.

Only a few villagers were left standing next to Grandma Mao Zhi—perhaps ten or twenty in all, and each of them more than forty or fifty years old. They looked silently at one another, then directed their gaze back to Grandma Mao Zhi. She then said calmly, "Go back and sleep; at dawn we will return to Liven." When she finished speaking, she turned and slowly dragged herself back to the side room. She walked extremely slowly, and it seemed as though if she were to move any slower she would topple over.

Chapter 3: Further Reading —Black disasters, red difficulties, black crimes, and red crimes

1) **To borrow.** Means "to rent." There are many situations in which the people of Balou use "to borrow" in place of "to rent," in order to add a level of intimacy to the relationship between renter and rentee.

3) **Pile.** Originally used to refer to a pile of dirt, but here refers to a large group of people.

5) **Sentry.** Means a sentinel. To be a sentry means to stand guard.

7) **Black disasters,** 9) **red difficulties,** 11) **black crimes,** 13) **red crimes.** These four terms are all equivalent. Only the people of Liven regularly use these words, and only villagers over the age of forty understand their historical meaning.

   The black and red crimes are not merely allusions, but rather they each have their own etymologies. The terms have their origins in events that took place more than twenty years earlier, in the bingwu Year of the Horse, 1966. At that point the Revolution was enveloping the nation like a storm, from the mountains to the seas, from the cities to the countryside. Throughout the land, everyone was busy destroying the old and erecting the new, parading through the streets, and subjecting people to struggle sessions. Everyone was busy taking down old portraits of the god of longevity, the kitchen god, Lord Guan, Zhong Kui the demon chaser, the Tagathe Buddha, and various bodhisattvas, and replacing them all with portraits of Chairman Mao.

By the following year, these struggles had turned on the people themselves. As if feeding the Revolution's limitless appetite, every two weeks each large brigade in a commune had to take turns sending the county seat a landlord, a rich peasant, a counterrevolutionary, or a bad egg or rightist, who would then be publically humiliated and tortured in mass struggle sessions; and if such people weren't struggled against, they would at least be made to wear a dunce hat and sweep the streets, improving society's political landscape and its revolutionary atmosphere. In every large brigade this period was treated like a festival, and everyone approached these struggle sessions like holiday concerts designed for the people's enjoyment.

Over time, however, Boshuzi commune discovered that they didn't have enough landlords and rich peasants, and it occurred to them that the Revolution had already lasted from the bingwu Year of the Horse to the jiyou Year of the Cock, and that during that three-year period they had completely forgotten about the village of Liven deep in the Balou mountains. It occurred to them that during these three years, they had not struggled against a single landlord or rich peasant from Liven. They therefore sent revolutionaries to notify Mao Zhi that by the beginning of the following month she needed to send over a landlord for them to struggle against.

Grandma Mao Zhi said, Our village doesn't have any landlords.

The revolutionary asked, What about rich peasants?

Mao Zhi said, We don't have any rich peasants, either.

The revolutionary said, If you don't have landlords or rich peasants, then why don't you just send us an upper-middle peasant?

Mao Zhi said, We don't have upper-middle peasants, middle peasants, lower-middle peasants, poor peasants, or even hired peasants. Every household in the village contains only revolutionaries.

The revolutionary said, You blasted woman! Not only are you not willing to contribute to the Revolution, you even dare to spout nonsense in front of an actual revolutionary.

Mao Zhi replied, Liven didn't come under the jurisdiction of the county and the commune until the collectivization movement had already concluded, and so our residents were never classified as landlords, rich peasants, and so forth. No one in the village has ever known that their household was a landlord, rich-peasant, or lower- or middle-peasant household.

The revolutionary stared at her in shock. Upon realizing that the village's revolutionary history was lacking something, he decided it was necessary to give Liven a critical lesson, adding a new page to its history books. He sent a work team and an investigation team to Liven, and ordered that by autumn of that year they divide the villagers into landlords, rich peasants, and lower and middle peasants.

Mao Zhi said, Liven has sent the county committee a request for permission to withdraw from society, and therefore it is not necessary to divide our residents into different classes.

The revolutionary said, We realize that you know the county committee's Secretary Yang, and that you and he both were at Yan'an. But now Secretary Yang is a counterrevolutionary, and is afraid of being hanged. Let's see now which other counterrevolutionaries would agree to allow you to withdraw from society.

Mao Zhi said, Then I'll ask you, okay?

The revolutionary said, Fuck, do you want to die?

Mao Zhi said, Liven originally didn't have landlords and rich peasants, and if we are going to make class divisions now, everyone should be poor and lower-middle peasants.

The revolutionary said, If you don't have landlords, rich peasants, and evil tyrants, then you, Grandma Mao Zhi, will need to go to the commune every day to be struggled against. You will need to wear a dunce cap and sweep the streets every day.

Mao Zhi was stunned into silence.

By that point the corn sprouts were as tall as a chopstick and the mountain ridge was full of the fresh aroma of grass and crops. The work team arrived in Liven and held a meeting for the villagers, at which they asked each household to report how much land, how many oxen, and how many horses it had before the Revolution, together with how much millet, wheat, sorghum, and soybeans it could harvest each year. Households were also asked to report whether or not they were able to eat bran, oatmeal, buckwheat, and wild vegetables on a daily basis; whether or not they went begging during famines; whether or not they worked for other people on a long-term or short-term basis; and whether, when they worked in the home of a landlord, they had to massage his back, wash his dishes, eat the dregs left over from his meals, and permit the landlord's wife to beat their face and hands with an iron awl.

At the meeting, Mao Zhi instructed the villagers to tell the visitors the truth, and report how much land they had twenty years earlier. She warned them not to exaggerate, because if they did they'd risk being branded rich landlords. At the same time, however, they also shouldn't underreport how much they had, because if they did they would be classified as poor peasants. Every household included some blind and crippled members, and consequently if a family was classified as a poor-peasant household it would mean that another family would need to be classified as a landlord household, and the members of the first family would have that on their consciences for the rest of their lives.

The members of the work unit set up a square table in the middle of the village, where they recorded the amount of land and property that each household had owned before Liberation. Everyone gave reports orally, while the work team members wrote everything down. But after they finished recording everything, they discovered to their surprise that before Liberation, every household in the village of Liven had had more than ten mu of land and more grain than they could eat, and that if a household didn't have an ox, it would share its plow, hoe, or metal-wheeled cart.

Someone asked a blind man whether his family had enough grain during that period.

The blind man answered, How could we eat it all?

On New Year's, were you able to eat a white bun and half a bowl of dumplings?

Normally, we could eat whatever we wanted. Those were considered to be delicacies.

You are blind, so how did you manage to work the fields?

I would help other villagers build bamboo fences, and when they were done plowing and sowing their own fields they would come help me with mine.

They asked a cripple, How much land did your household own?

More than ten mu.

You are a cripple, so how did you work the fields?

We had an ox, which we would lend out to others to use, and after they finished working their own fields they would help us with ours.

Did you live well?

Better than now.

How well did you live?

We had more grain and vegetables than we could eat.

Finally, they loudly asked a deaf man, Given that your family had so much land, did you hire farmhands to help you?

No, we didn't.

Then how did you work all that land?

Our household didn't have an ox, but we did have a cart that our neighbors would often use. After the neighbors finished working their own fields they would come help us with ours.

In the end, it proved impossible to divide the villagers into poor peasants, rich peasants, and landlords. They all had more land than they could manage, and every family had more grain than they could eat. Everyone asked others to help them out, while at the same time helping their neighbors. During that period, a cripple might use a blind man's legs, a deaf man might use a mute's ears, and a mute might use a deaf man's mouth. The entire village behaved like a large family—peaceful and prosperous, and with no struggles or conflicts. In the end, the visitors issued each family a black booklet the size of a man's fist. On the cover was written the name of the head of household, and inside there were just two pages—on one there was a quote from Chairman Mao, and on the other there was a passage asking you to be law-abiding and serve the people.

The visitors left Liven and, after returning to the commune, sent Liven a notice instructing all the villagers to line up at the head of the village every two weeks and to then have one household send someone—whether blind, crippled, or deaf and mute—to the commune with that black booklet. While there, the villager had to wear a tall dunce hat and parade through the

368

streets, or else appear on stage during a rally and allow people to struggle against him.

The first villager sent was asked: Are your family landlords?

No.

Are they rich peasants?

No.

If you are neither a landlord nor a rich peasant, then why do you have a black booklet?

Several people slapped the villager in the face and kicked him in the groin, whereupon the villager grunted and knelt down on the stage in front of the hundreds or even thousands of people who had come to attend the meeting.

He was asked, What have you stolen?

I haven't stolen anything. The people of Liven have never been thieves.

Even when you didn't have enough to eat, you didn't steal any sorghum or sweet potatoes?

If it hadn't been for all the wholers in the county coming to the village to steal our grain over the past several years, every household would have had enough grain saved up to last a decade or more.

The people then beat the villager some more, saying, Regardless of whether someone is disabled or not, a bad person is still a bad person. After all, just look at how much grain this household has stored up. The people asked for their grain back, but the villager replied that other people had already come to his house to confiscate it. They therefore beat him even more severely than before, their fists raining down on his nose, mouth, and eyes, and their clubs striking his head and legs. When they punched his nose, it started bleeding, and when they hit his mouth, his teeth were knocked loose. They hit his face so hard that they left him with a huge black eye, and struck his legs so violently that he would have been left a cripple if he hadn't already been one.

When he returned home half a month later to recuperate, it was some-one else's turn to take that black booklet and endure this black crime and black disaster. The person who returned home to recover from his wounds would run into Mao Zhi in the village, and stare furiously at her. When he saw her household's pigs, he viciously kicked them, and when he saw her household's chickens, he would throw a rock at them. When he saw the squat melons[1] and beans she and her family had planted behind their house, he would pull them and throw them to the ground, and then stomp on them, grinding them into paste, which he would use to feed his own pigs and goats.

One morning when Mao Zhi got out of bed, she saw that her family's pig, which they had raised from when it was a mere piglet, had been poisoned and was lying dead on the floor of the pigsty. The chicken that they had for laying fresh eggs had eaten some of the poisoned pig's slop and was also lying dead in the courtyard. Mao Zhi stared in shock, then opened the courtyard gate and saw that all of the villagers—the ones who had been sent to the commune to be struggled against as well as those who had not—were standing at the door to her house. Each of them was holding a black booklet, and when they saw her, they stared at her coldly. Then, someone suddenly spit at her and hit her with the black booklet, saying that she was the one who had instructed them to tell the truth to the higher-ups, after which all the families in the village had been deemed to be landlords and rich peasants, and had to be struggled against. They said, Go look, yesterday Blind Man Lin went into town and was beaten to death. People asked him if he was a landlord or a rich peasant, and he replied, I am neither a landlord nor a rich peasant. Then, they beat him over the head with a stick, and before they had finished venting their anger, he died right there on stage.

Mao Zhi immediately hurried over to Blind Man Lin's house, where she found that Lin had, in fact, passed away. His corpse was laid out on a door plank, and his family was standing around it weeping inconsolably.

She didn't say anything else.

Mao Zhi returned to her house, where she picked up a black booklet that was lying on the ground in front of her door. Then, leaning on her crutch, she proceeded to the Boshuzi commune. It was almost dark by the time she arrived at the revolutionary committee. She found one of the people who had distributed the black booklets to the residents of Liven, and knelt down before him and asked, How is it possible for everyone in Liven to be a landlord? How can there possibly be a village in which every single family is a landlord?

The revolutionary replied, It is also impossible for there to be a village in which there are no landlords.

Mao Zhi said, I'll tell you the truth. Before Liberation, my family had several dozen mu of land, together with several long- and short-term hired hands. Our entire family enjoyed a life in which they only had to reach out to get their clothes, and open their mouths to get food. You should classify my family as landlords.

The revolutionary stared at her in delight. He asked her many questions, then took the black booklet she was holding and returned to the office to exchange it for a red one. The red booklets were the same size as the black ones, and also had only a few pages. The cover was printed with the names of the heads of household of each family in Liven, while inside one page was printed with Chairman Mao's sayings while the other contained a statement regarding the nation's policies and future path. The revolutionary handed her a pile of red booklets, saying, You should go now. We haven't mistreated the people of Liven. According to the land reform policies and ratios specified in the land redistribution program, before Liberation Liven must have had at least one landlord and at least one rich peasant. Therefore, now that we have identified you as a landlord, we are set. You should go back to the village tonight, and return tomorrow with your bedding. The following day, the commune will host a mass rally, at which everyone must struggle against you.

Mao Zhi returned to Liven that night and distributed the red booklets to every household in the village, explaining that they were indicators of revolutionary status. She explained that everyone was classified as a poor lower-middle peasant, and the village had only one landlord, which was her. She said that afterward, if the village had anything that needed to be done by a landlord or a rich peasant, she would take responsibility for it. After she finished distributing the red booklets, she collected her bags and bedding, then cooked a pot of food and steamed some buns for her daughter Jumei, who was already nine years old. After she fed Jumei and put her back to bed, Mao Zhi took the village's only black booklet and, carrying her bedding, returned to the commune to receive the black crime.

The sorghum was already ripe, and its sweet fragrance enveloped the entire mountain region. Moonlight streamed over the village, and as Mao Zhi was about to leave for the commune, the residents of Liven all came out to see her off. They said, Go on, we'll look after Jumei while you are *away. They said, Go on, even revolutionaries are good, honest people, and if they tell you to say something, you should just say it. That way, they won't viciously hit and kick you.*

She said, You should all go back inside. While I'm away, separate the sorghum. Everyone should continue doing what should be done. After you have separated the sorghum, you should plow the fields, and after plowing the fields you should quickly sow the wheat.

Then she left.

The mass rally the next day was held along the riverbank on the east end of Boshuzi Street. This area had previously been full of running water, but several days earlier the commune had altered the course of the river so that the sandy bottom could be used as a meeting place. The main attraction of the rally was the public trial of a counterrevolutionary who, after teaching school for only three days, was writing the phrase Long Live Chairman Mao on the blackboard when he accidentally wrote Long Live Shi Jingshan instead. "Shi Jingshan" was the teacher's own adult name, and his infant name was Shi Heidou. Before he had an adult name, he'd had only a child's name, but after being appointed as a teacher he felt that the name "Heidou," or "black bean," was not very appropriate, and therefore, inspired by the revolutionary site of Mount Jinggang, gave himself the name "Shi Jingshan" instead. He had intended to tell his students that his name was Shi Jingshan, but as he was writing his name on the blackboard he instead accidentally wrote the phrase Long Live Shi Jingshan.

Needless to say, in doing so he committed a grievous transgression, and when the revolutionaries seized him, he immediately confessed.

The revolutionary asked, Do you know what crime you have committed?

I do.

What crime?

I wrote "Long Live Shi Jingshan." on the blackboard.

The revolutionary pounded the table and said, You must not utter the words that you wrote on the blackboard. Each time you repeat them, you are committing another crime.

Then what should I say?

You should tell the truth, and if you have something to say, then say it.

He therefore bowed his head and reflected.

The revolutionary asked again, Do you know what crime you have committed?

I do.

What crime?

I wrote four words on the blackboard.

What words?

He looked up at the revolutionary and replied, "Long Live Shi Jingshan."

The revolutionary started trembling with fury, and proceeded to smash the trial record and ink pot against Shi Jingshan's face, saying,

If you dare say those words one more time, I'll shoot you.

Then what should I say?

Figure it out for yourself.

He once again bowed his head and reflected.

The revolutionary asked, Do you know what crime you've committed?

I do.

What crime?

I wrote four words on the blackboard.

What words?

The teacher again looked up at the revolutionary, but didn't answer, and instead he wrote the words Long Live Shi Jingshan on the ground with his finger. The revolutionary became so angry that his face turned purple and his entire body started trembling. He said, Fuck you, for you to write this out is even worse than saying it. It is another level of crime.

With the teacher's initial crime having been compounded with another and another, eventually he would be executed. This happened to be a market day before the autumn harvest, and more than fifty thousand people were attending the mass rally to judge him at the river basin. The river basin was one li wide and two li long, and the audience's heads resembled a field of black beans. Furthermore, in front of each person's head there was a red booklet proving that person's revolutionary status. The autumn sun was shining down brightly, as warm as a small flame. The people on the sand had come from villages located up to dozens of li away, and now they were all crowded into this river basin until it was nearly overflowing, the booklets hanging from their necks appearing as red as a sea of fire. This was unlike anything anyone in attendance had ever seen before, and there wouldn't be a comparably tumultuous scene in the district until thirty years later, when Liven's special-skills troupes began touring. Everyone crowded in, standing shoulder to shoulder, like ten thousand horses all neighing together.

It was precisely in these final moments before everything was to begin that Grandma Mao Zhi was tied up by the revolutionaries and carried to the front of the stage. She was not only a woman but a cripple, and they didn't permit her to bring her crutch. As a result, even though there were two people supporting her, she still walked very unsteadily, like a three-legged grasshopper trying to hop across the stage. As she hopped along, the sign hanging from her neck waved back and forth, and the string holding it rubbed her neck raw. She had just turned forty and her hair was still jet black. She was wearing a dark blue double-breasted coat, and her unkempt hair hung over her shoulders like grass floating on the surface of a pond. On the white sign hanging from her neck were written the words counterrevolutionary and female landowner and, as though to confirm the accuracy of those labels, the black booklet she had recently received was also hanging there.

As soon as she arrived on stage, the audience was abruptly silenced, as if they had been struck by a club.

Who could have expected that a woman would be brought up on stage, and moreover a cripple?

The interrogation began.

When she was forced to kneel down on the stage, her face was as pale as death and her lips were blue and purple, like two colorful lines drawn on a sheet of white paper. Then, a torrent of questions and answers began streaming from the loudspeakers into the river shoal:

What is your status?

I'm a large landowner.

What crime have you committed?

I am a practicing counterrevolutionary.

Tell us the truth again.

I'm not a Red Army soldier, but I still insist that I was at the revolutionary site of Yan'an. I'm not a descendant of the Revolution, but insist that my parents both participated in the Great Railroad Construction of the dingmao Year of the Hare. I'm not a Party member, but insist that when I was in the Red Army I joined the Party. I say that I was in the Red Army, although it is true that I don't have a Red Army certificate. I say that I was a Party member, though I don't have a Party certificate. Actually, I am a practicing counterrevolutionary, a large landowner who has hidden in the Balou mountains. Before Liberation, my family owned several dozen mu of land, together with several oxen and oxcarts. We also employed many short- and long-term workers. We enjoyed a life in which all we had to do was reach out to get clothing, and open our mouths to get food. As for the Revolution, comrades, look here, I should be executed for my crimes. I should be executed along with Shi Jingshan.

The person then asked her, What did your family eat before Liberation?

We ate whatever we wanted. We had so many steamed buns and dumplings that we fed our pigs with our own leftovers. We wouldn't even let our workers eat them.

What did you wear?

Silk and gauze. Even the curtains of our horse shed were made not of millet stalks, but rather of the finest silk.

What have you been doing during these years since Liberation?

Day in and day out, I've been trying to bring about a restoration, to return to that life of ease that we enjoyed before Liberation.

He didn't ask her any more questions, but rather shouted to the thousands of people in the audience, saying: What do you say we do about this practicing counterrevolutionary and female landlord?!

The crowd lifted their arms like a forest and shouted in response,

Execute her! . . . Execute her!

That raucous response determined the path of her fate.[3] After interrogating the teacher named Shi Heidou or Shi Jingshan, who had been teaching at the school for only three days, they dragged him to the riverside to execute him, at which point they dragged her away as well. Mao Zhi was told to kneel down next to him in front of a fresh grave, their backs supported by the sort of wooden placards normally used by people facing execution. The sun was shining down brightly. The sky was an endless expanse of blue, without a trace of clouds. The corn planted on the riverbank should have already been separated and laid out to dry. The air was full of the bright fragrance of corn, together with the smell of sweat from the crowds.

When it came time for the revolutionaries to open fire, Teacher Shi Jingshan, who was only twenty-two, was so terrified he collapsed next to the pit like a pile of mud, the stench of feces and urine emanating from his body. As for the middle-aged Mao Zhi, her pallor suddenly disappeared, as did the green and purple tint of her lips. She knelt there as calmly as someone tired from walking who had decided to rest for a while.

The revolutionary approached the young man who was about to die and asked, Do you have any final requests?

He trembled and replied, I do.

The revolutionary said, Tell me.

He replied, My wife is about to give birth. Could you give her a message? Tell her that after the child is born, she should be sure to render it either deaf or crippled. Then, she should take the child to a village deep in the Balou mountains, where it is said that everyone is disabled, and consequently there is no district, county, or commune that wants this village or pays any attention to it. The people of this village eat what they sow, enjoying a heavenly life of relaxation and livening. Please tell my wife and child to go there.

The revolutionary standing behind him laughed coldly.

Mao Zhi gazed at the young man, and wanted to say something to him, but the revolutionary walked up to her and asked, Do you have anything you'd like to say?

She replied, Yes.

The revolutionary said, Then spit it out.

She said, After I die, please go to the village of Liven deep in the Balou mountains and tell the disabled villagers living there that they can forget anything else they want, but they mustn't forget about the need to withdraw from society and return to a life where no one has any control over us.

After she finished, the young man kneeling beside her turned and stared at her in amazement. Just as he was about to ask her something, however, the gun went off behind him and he fell into the pit like a sackful of grain. Drops of blood splattered onto Mao Zhi's face and all over the ground.

As for Mao Zhi, she of course survived. It turned out that she had merely been brought over to kneel next to the young man. After the gun went off, she shuddered as if someone had shoved her from behind, and for a moment she seemed as though she were about to fall into the pit as well. But the shove was fairly light, and in the end she merely swayed back and forth while remaining in a kneeling position.

Mao Zhi spent the next half month sweeping the streets in front of the commune. By the time she was given permission to return to the village, it had gained two new members—a young woman and the infant to whom she'd just given birth a few days earlier. The child was born a wholer, but somehow had become paralyzed. The woman had explained that no matter what, she simply had to come live in Liven, to become a resident of the village. She said that ever since she was a child she had known how to embroider, and could embroider a flower on a sheet made from cowhide. She said that if she was allowed to stay, she would be happy to embroider whatever other families needed.

The woman settled down in Liven, and Mao Zhi gave her a red booklet, which she hung from her neck every day like an amulet.

However, this red booklet brought a disaster of its own. Although this disaster was different from that of the black booklets, the suffering it induced was in no way inferior. One day followed the next, and Mao Zhi could often be seen sweeping the streets of Boshuzi and being struggled against. But in the village they continued to assign her the same number of work points and issue her the same number of daily grain rations as before. When Mao Zhi returned to the village, she was respected by everyone. When her neighbors—including the families of the deaf man and the blind man, together with the wholers in the families of the deaf-mute and the idiot—saw that she had returned, they all wanted to come over to her house to pay their regards, and to take away her tasty buns and rice. They provided earnuts[5] that they were originally going to use as seeds, and somehow managed to come up with some peaches and chestnuts that had been hidden away.

On behalf of the other villagers, Mao Zhi voluntarily assumed the consequences of the black disasters and black crimes. As a result, everyone else was able to enjoy a good fortune, and came to regard her as an even more important personage. But two or three years later, the entire land needed to be divided into lattice fields,[7] and the commune sent everyone who had been issued a red booklet to a ridge outside the Balou mountain range. There, they were assigned to different hills based on which village they belonged to. All of the residents of Liven were naturally sent to the same hill. The Revolution didn't care whether or not you were disabled; all it cared about was how many red booklets you had accepted from the revolutionaries. People with one red booklet had to build, in the course of a single winter, two mu of lattice fields. Liven had thirty-nine households that each had a single red booklet, and therefore they were expected to build at least thirty-nine mu of lattice fields.

In this way, the forced labor of the red disaster and red crime began. It seemed as though every hill throughout the land had villagers living on it, and they were all planting their red flags and posting their red slogans. The entire land became as red as if it were ablaze, and everywhere there was the sound of pickaxes striking the ground and shovels leveling the dirt, and everywhere there was the sound of iron being pounded in furnaces used to make more shovels and pickaxes.

Needless to say, every household in Liven dispatched people to live and work on that barren slope. Because the land was distributed based on red booklets, which in turn were distributed based on household status, each household was given two mu of land to be converted into lattice fields by the end of winter. Each household was responsible for figuring out a way of accomplishing this, and this was true regardless of how disabled the household might be—whether the household had five members of whom three were blind, or seven members of whom five were crippled, or three members of whom the only wholer was merely a child.

What kind of solutions did the villagers come up with? While everyone was in the process of dividing the land into lattice fields, there was a blind man's household in which the father took a pickax in the middle of a snowstorm and began digging. He caressed his fourteen-year-old blind son's face, then took the hand of his wife—who was paralyzed, but not blind—and told her he needed to go to the latrine. His wife followed him, directing him to turn east. He, however, deliberately turned west and plunged into the ravine, taking his own life.

As a result, the revolutionary exempted the woman and her family from having to build more lattice fields, and told them to return to the Balou mountains to bury the father.

There was another household in which the entire family suffered from polio. There were five family members in all, and the legs of all three children were shriveled from the disease. One day, their father went to an ironworks shop on the hillside to forge a pickax, and on his way there he hanged himself by the side of the road. The revolutionary also permitted his family to return to the village to bury him.

There was a family of wholers who were assigned to build lattice fields. The family didn't have a man in the household, and instead there was only a mother with her thirteen- and fifteen-year-old daughters. One day the mother smiled and asked her daughters,

Do you want to return to the village to rest?

Yes.

Then get ready to return home tomorrow.

The daughters thought she was joking. That night they slept in the lattice fields, in an area shielded from the wind, and when they woke up the next morning they discovered that their mother had drunk rat poison and died in her sleep. The revolutionary cursed her, but still let her daughters return their mother's corpse to the village for burial.

That winter, there were thirty-nine households in Liven who, with their red booklets, went to build lattice fields, but thirteen heads of household died holding those same red booklets. In the end, the revolutionary became enraged. He told all of the disabled villagers to return to Liven, but instructed all of the wholer households to stay behind. However, when he went out to conduct a survey, he discovered that there wasn't a single household consisting entirely of wholers, and consequently he had no choice but to deploy his revolutionary humanism and allow them all to return to Liven.

These were the black disasters and red difficulties that were brought on by the black and red booklets. Many years later, only the older villagers understood what Grandma Mao Zhi was referring to when she spoke of the black disasters, the red difficulties, or the black and red crimes. As a result, *it was only those older villagers with a good memory who, in the Lenin Memorial Hall, left their fingerprints on that white cloth.*

15) Shadows. *DIAL. These refer not to people's actual shadows, but rather to people who, after withdrawing from society, no longer have any status or certification, no proof of existence.*

Further, Further Reading

1) Squat melons. *DIAL. Refers to pumpkins.*

3) Path of fate. *DIAL. Refers to one's fate.*

5) Earnuts. *DIAL. Refers to peanuts.*

7) Lattice fields. *The term is not from the local dialect, but rather is a specialized historical term. On one hand, the term refers to a series of flat fields that, like a latticework, are each one level higher than the previous one. On the other hand, the term may also be used to refer to that special period during the "Learn from Dazhai" Movement, in which a revolutionary style was expressed through labor.*

Chapter 5: Summer reverts back to winter, and spring is right around the corner

Not only did Chief Liu fail to arrive, and not only did the villagers discover that they had been the victims of a great theft, but in the final days of the *wuyin* Year of the Tiger, an earth-shattering event took place.

In theory, this should have been the dead of winter, but the summer heat skipped right over the spring and arrived all of a sudden in the Balou mountains. The seasons were truly in a state of mad confusion. Although it had been warm on the mountain ridge during the preceding half month, this could still be regarded as merely a winter warmth; but after that night the sun went from pale yellow to searing white. The forest had begun to turn green, but had not yet fully burst into bud. The fields also turned dark green, and between the branches and leaves there was the sound of countless cicadas, together with the chirping of sparrows. Up on the mountain, between the distant peaks and the nearby ridges, a cloud of white mist billowed forth.

Summer had arrived.

It arrived silently, but with a bang. The first person in Liven to wake up was little Polio Boy. The previous night, after he'd pulled the smashed bottle from his foot, he wiped off the blood, bandaged his foot, then whimpered in pain half the night. Eventually he was able to fall asleep, but as soon as he woke, he found himself extremely thirsty, and his lips were as dry as summer sand. And that's why he woke up before everyone else.

There was a buzzing sound in the room. It was a mosquito that, right on schedule, was flying in from somewhere into summer.

The boy rubbed his eyes, and felt a jolt of pain in his shriveled leg, as though he had been stung. The initial pain was followed by numbness, but this was more or less normal for him. Feeling very thirsty, he wanted to get some water, but when he lowered his hand from his eyes, he saw the sun shining in through the glass window, making the entire room appear as though it were on fire. The walls were painted white, but now looked as though they were covered in smoke. The air was full of the sort of dust that you normally see only under the summer sun, and there was a faint burning odor that you normally smell only in the summer.

The boy was confused. The previous night, the villagers in the side rooms had been sitting in a daze, bewailing their stolen money and cursing the theatrical higher-ups—saying that they would definitely go complain to the political higher-ups and to the county chief. They were all deeply discomfited and unable to sleep. But now when the boy looked around, he saw that the room was full of naked villagers, all sleeping soundly. The sun was already high in the sky, but they were still snoring loudly, as though they had stones wedged in their throats. Furthermore, they had all thrown off their covers and were lying there buck-naked. Some of them were covered by a thin sheet, while others just had a shirt draped across the stomach, covering the belly so as not to catch a chill.

Summer had really arrived. The boy was so thirsty he felt as though his throat was burning. He got out of bed and went to fetch some water from a side room where there was a pump. He brought the lever down to its lowermost position, but discovered that there wasn't a single drop inside.

He tried a different pump, but found that there wasn't a drop left in that one either.

He came out of the side room, and just as he was about to go into the main hall to look for some water, he discovered that the massive red doors were locked. Normally they would be latched from the inside, and once you unlatched and pulled them, they would immediately swing open. This time, however, he tried pulling the pair of doors several times, but couldn't get them to budge. He was just a child, and didn't realize that not only had winter disappeared and summer skipped right over spring, but furthermore everything was upside down, as if there had been a change of dynasties. He pounded on the door and shouted angrily,

"Open the door! I'm dying of thirst in here! . . . Open the door! I'm dying of thirst in here!"

An adult wholer standing outside kicked the door and shouted into the room,

"Who's awake in there?"

The boy replied, "I'm dying of thirst."

The man outside asked, "Is anyone else awake?"

The boy replied, "Not yet. Open the door, I'm dying of thirst!"

The man asked, "You're just thirsty? You're not hungry?"

The man laughed coldly. He had a hoarse voice, and sounded like that husky driver who drove the truck carrying the troupe's performance props. The driver had a rocklike physique, with virtually no fat and shoulders as broad as a door. He could pick up one of the truck's tires with a single hand, and could kick a box of theatrical props out of the trunk with his foot. Once the boy recognized the driver's voice, he said, "Uncle, I'm thirsty. Please open the door."

The driver said, "You want some water? Go call Grandma Mao Zhi."

The boy went to the second side room across from the crystal coffin to look for Grandma Mao Zhi. She had also just woken up, while her four granddaughters, together with the paralyzed woman who helped cook for the troupe, were all still sleeping soundly, just like the men in the other room. They had kicked off their sheets and were lying there uncovered. The boy saw that Grandma Mao Zhi's body looked like a bundle of kindling, and the paralyzed woman was so fat that as she slept she looked like a big clump of weeds. He saw Tonghua, Yuhua, and Mothlet all lying in a row, their budding breasts like buns straight out of the steamer. He suddenly understood why breasts were sometimes called "sweet buns," and immediately felt his throat go dry with hunger and thirst. He had a sudden urge to crawl onto those breasts and drink passionately from them.

More important, he saw that Huaihua was sleeping beneath the window, at the end of the room and apart from everyone else, as though she were afraid someone would get too close to her. Her bedroll was covered in a bright red sheet, and she was lying in the sunlight that was streaming in through the window. She was wearing just a pair of underpants and the kind of pointy, curved white bra that only city girls wore. Apart from that, she was completely naked, displaying her fish- and snakelike body for everyone to see. The boy could smell her willowy fragrance, and saw that her legs, belly, and face were all as white as jade and as tender as an oriole that had just emerged from the nest. He had an urge to caress and kiss her pale body. He wanted to call her "sister" and hold her hand, but then Grandma Mao Zhi sat up and looked around the bed for her summer dress as she mumbled, "This weather, this weather!" She pulled a green shirt out from under her pillow and put it on, whereupon she suddenly noticed the boy standing by the door.

She asked, "Your leg doesn't hurt?"

"I'm very thirsty."

"Drink some water."

"The door is locked from the outside. The driver asked for you to go over—he's waiting outside the door."

When Grandma Mao Zhi heard this, she appeared confused. She squinted at the boy, then appeared to remember something. She abruptly turned pale, as though something had just been confirmed to her. She got up and followed the boy through the main hall containing the crystal coffin, then she pulled at the big red doors, her face as white as a cloudy sky.

She shouted through the crack in the door, "Hey, who are you? If you have something to say, then open the door and say it."

Hearing no response, she called out again, "I am Grandma Mao Zhi. Please open this door."

Eventually, they heard movements outside the door. First, there were footsteps of people walking up the kowtow steps, followed by several people waiting quietly on the other side of the door, and finally the gruff voice of the driver of the troupe's props truck. He said, "Grandma Mao Zhi, do you know who I am? I believe in doing everything aboveboard. I am the driver who has been traveling with you and the troupe for the past six months, and with me are the managers of the memorial hall." He said, "I'll be frank—we've locked the door from the outside because we want the troupe's money." He said, "I know about how the troupe was robbed, but that was done by some blasted higher-up cadres and motherfucking cadres working for the theater. Just as you were in the middle of your next-to-last act, they went into action, and before you left the theater they took advantage of the confusion to ask me to drive the truck down the mountain. They thought I didn't know what was going on, and therefore when they were dividing up the money they didn't give me a cent; Grandma Mao Zhi, I assure you, I really didn't get a cent from them. As we were heading down the road, I told them that the truck was having engine problems and I had to stop and get it fixed. As soon as they left, however, I immediately drove back here. We won't be as greedy as they were, and instead we just ask that you give each of us eight or ten thousand yuan. So that it won't be in vain that I've been your driver for the past six months, or that my buddies have been watching over the memorial hall this entire time, not leaving it unattended for even an instant."

At this point, someone else in the memorial hall woke up—Deafman Ma. He couldn't hear any of what was going on, and when he went to the latrine he washed up, then peeked over and returned to the side room. Perhaps it was already almost noon. The sunlight that streamed into the hall through that enormous window appeared dark red, like hot coals. In the summer, this massive hall would stay quite cool, but because this year summer had followed immediately after winter, all of the windows remained tightly shut, leaving the hall so hot and stuffy that the villagers felt as though they were locked inside a tightly sealed chest.

Grandma Mao Zhi turned around to look at those glass windows, each of which was more than ten feet tall. This memorial hall was deep in the mountains, and all of the windows were positioned two person-heights from the floor, or three, four, or even five person-heights from the ground below—so high that it was as if they were at the level of a normal building's second or third floor. If the villagers couldn't get the door open, it would be completely impossible for them to leave the memorial hall. All of them were disabled, of course, but even if they had been wholers there would have been no way for them to escape if they were to manage to make it up to the window in the first place.

Grandma Mao Zhi looked away from the windows.

The people outside became impatient waiting for her response. They kicked the door and shouted,

"Have you decided yet? Grandma Mao Zhi, we don't want much of your money. There are only eight of us, and all we ask is that you give us ten thousand yuan each. Or, if you don't have that much, eight thousand would also suffice."

Grandma Mao Zhi said, "We don't have any money, we really don't. All our money was stolen."

The people outside kicked the door again, saying, "If you don't have any money, then forget it. But when you do manage to come up with some, then call us. If we don't answer, you can knock at this door three times."

Having said this, the people left, and the villagers inside the memorial hall could hear their footsteps as they walked away to somewhere beneath the kowtow steps. The memorial hall suddenly fell silent, and when Grandma Mao Zhi turned around, she saw that the villagers had all gotten up and were standing quietly behind her, the dark mass of people looking as though they were attending a meeting. Because it was so hot, the men were all topless, and some of them had draped their shirts over their shoulders. The women were not topless, and instead were wearing their summer shirts. It had been summertime when they'd all left the Balou mountains to embark on their performance tour, and when they'd returned they didn't go back to the village but rather came directly to this mountain, so fortunately they still had their summer clothes in their suitcases.

The villagers understood the situation—each of the wholers outside wanted eight thousand to ten thousand yuan from them, and since there were eight wholers, that meant they were demanding at the very least about sixty thousand yuan. But where would those sixty thousand yuan come from? The villagers who filled half of the main hall of the memorial hall all looked at one another as the room fell silent.

The strange thing was that, by this point, the villagers were not as indignant as they had been the previous evening, nor were they as distraught. It was as if they had known all along that this kind of thing might eventually happen. No one said a word, and instead they stood behind the door or leaned against the hall pillars. The women looked at the men, while the men squatted on the ground smoking their cigarettes as though nothing had happened. Huaihua was still wearing her transparent dress, and like everyone else hadn't yet washed her face, but nevertheless she was still seductive and ravishingly beautiful. She glanced at One-Legged Monkey, and saw that he was just standing there silently with his arms crossed, not saying a word. He would rub his upper lip against his lower teeth, and his lower lip against his upper teeth. When he realized there was nothing new to be seen, he snorted and shifted his gaze to somewhere else.

The room was filled with an interminable silence.

Grandma Mao Zhi looked over at One-Legged Monkey. It was as though she were testing him, but also genuinely wanted to ask him something.

She asked, "What are we going to do?"

One-Legged Monkey turned his head and said, "How would I know? If I still had any money, I would hand it over."

Grandma Mao Zhi turned to a deaf man.

The deaf man had been standing, but then squatted down and loudly announced, "I don't have a cent! All my money was stolen."

She turned to two young wholers, who said, "We definitely don't earn as much as you do. For each performance, you receive two seats, while the two of us combined don't even earn the equivalent of a single chair leg. Everything we do earn we put under our pillow, and now it is nowhere to be found."

It became clear that there was no point in discussing things further. Grandma Mao Zhi considered for a moment, then returned to the side room where she had been sleeping. After a while, she appeared with a large bundle of cash. It was not clear where the money had come from, but it was all in crisp, new hundred-yuan bills, all bound together into bundles that were each as thick as a brick. Her four granddaughters stared at her in astonishment. Huaihua stood in a corner of the room with a wooden expression, but blushed bright red as she waited for Grandma Mao Zhi to walk by her. She suddenly swooped down to her grandmother's side and grabbed the hand in which Grandma Mao Zhi was holding the money, yanking her so hard that she almost toppled over.

Fortunately, Grandma Mao Zhi managed to keep her balance. She stared at Huaihua in astonishment, then slapped her across the face. Grandma Mao Zhi appeared to have aged considerably overnight, and while that slap was not very hard, it was nevertheless still a slap. Huaihua's cheek immediately turned brighter red.

"That's my money!" Huaihua shouted. "I can't even afford to buy a single dress."

Grandma Mao Zhi replied, "You've already bought enough!" She stared angrily at her granddaughter, who was grasping her hand, and then went over to the door and knocked on it. An excited response was heard outside, as the wholers said, "Exactly, all you people of Liven have your special skills, and each time you go out to perform you earn a huge profit. Why should you begrudge us a little bit?" As they were saying this, they shouted to the people below the kowtow steps, "Hey, come up quickly."

Then, they instructed her, "Pass the money under the door. Once you have done so, we'll open it for you."

Grandma Mao Zhi passed the bundle of cash under the door, and the person on the other side accepted it. As he did so, he called out to Grandma Mao Zhi,

"Quick, keep it coming."

Grandma Mao Zhi said, "I really don't have any more. This eight thousand yuan is all I have. Everything else was stolen last night."

The person replied unhappily, "You are welcome to try to fool ghosts and swine, but we are neither ghosts nor swine and therefore won't let you fool us." He added, "This is only one bundle of eight thousand yuan; you are still missing the other seven. If you don't pass over the remainder, I'll let you all die of hunger and thirst."

He fell silent, and they heard the driver outside muttering something to somebody. Then he led some people down the kowtow steps. Grandma Mao Zhi called out to the departing footsteps,

"Hey, I really don't have any more. Those eight thousand yuan were pooled together from everything we have on us."

The person responded, "Don't 'hey' me, and stop giving me your farting excuses."

"If you don't believe me, then open the door and come inside to search us."

"Go fuck yourself. Do you really think that you disabled people could overpower us wholers?"

"Don't you fear the law?"

"We wholers *are* your law."

"Are you not afraid of Chief Liu?"

The person laughed.

"To tell you the truth, Chief Liu is in big trouble. If he wasn't, do you think those scoundrels from the county would have dared steal your money in the first place? If Chief Liu weren't in trouble, I would never have dared to lock you inside the Lenin Memorial Hall."

Grandma Mao Zhi was dumbfounded, as the person walked away while talking to the people at the bottom of the kowtow steps. Then, the only sound that remained was the echo of his footsteps against the stone steps, as they reverberated against the brick walls of the memorial hall and inside the villagers' hearts.

The air inside the hall had gotten so warm that it became difficult even to breathe. The villagers grew agitated, their mouths dry and their bodies covered in sweat. They were all parched and famished. The boy who had originally woken up because he was thirsty, then realized that the door of the memorial hall was locked from the outside, was by this point so thirsty he didn't even have a voice with which to ask for water. The deaf man mumbled, "Fuck your grandmother, go get us some water from somewhere." The mute gestured toward his throat and stomped his feet. There was no water in the pump, but people kept going up to try it.

Grandma Mao Zhi suddenly remembered the boy, and turned to look for him. She saw that he and his uncle were huddled together in a corner. The boy was lying in his uncle's lap, like a baby in its mother's bosom. His uncle was sixty-three years old, and had been acompanying the troupe to serve as their cook. He caressed the boy's head and patted his waist, and said to Grandma Mao Zhi as she approached,

"We must find some water, the boy is running a fever. . . . We must find some water; the boy is running a fever."

Grandma Mao Zhi felt the boy's forehead, and found it burning hot. She waved her hand to cool it off, and felt his forehead again. Then, she went to knock on the memorial hall door.

The person outside said, "Pass the money under the door."

Grandma Mao Zhi said, "A boy in here has a raging fever. I'm begging you to give us a bowl of water."

The person outside called to someone else and said, "We need water. . . ."

The driver, who was off to the side, responded, "Make them pay for it. . . ."

The person said to the villagers inside the memorial hall, "Do you want water? Then pass us the money."

Shocked, Grandma Mao Zhi asked, "Do you have even a trace of conscience left?"

The person outside said, "You can act as though we've fed our conscience to the dogs."

Grandma Mao Zhi considered for a moment, then asked, "How much money for a bowl of water?"

"One hundred yuan."

"Do you really not have a trace of conscience left?"

"I already told you, you can act as though we've fed our conscience to the dogs."

He didn't say anything else, and everyone inside watched Grandma Mao Zhi. She looked helplessly over at the corner of the room, where the boy's uncle appeared so perplexed it seemed his head was about to fall off. The villagers fell into a dead silence, as though everyone had plunged into an open grave. One-Legged Monkey went up to the door and shouted at to the person on the other side:

"How can a bowl of water cost one hundred yuan?"

"You are all going to die. You have to do something."

"How about one yuan for a bowl?"

"Go fuck your mother."

"How about ten yuan?"

"Go fuck your mother."

"Twenty yuan?"

"Go fuck your mother. I won't even take fifty."

One-Legged Monkey didn't say anything else. At this point, Grandma Mao Zhi went back to the side room where she slept and collected several ten-yuan bills and a pile of smaller bills. Then, she shouted to the person on the other side of the door, "How about eighty yuan?" The person replied, "One hundred yuan for a bowl of well water,[1] two hundred for a bowl of white noodles, and five hundred for a steamed bun. If you want them you can have them, and if you don't, you are perfectly welcome to starve to death in there." Without saying a word, Grandma Mao Zhi slipped a hundred-yuan bill under the door. After a while, the villagers heard some rustling outside. They initially assumed the people outside would open the door and pass them a bowl of water, but instead the wholers leaned a ladder against the door, climbed up, and knocked on the glass window above the door, asking someone inside to open it and take the water. The person who did so was One-Legged Monkey, standing on the Mute's shoulder. He saw that on the other side of the window there was a twenty-something-year-old with a flattop and a red face. One-Legged Monkey said quickly, "If you leave this ladder here tonight, I'll give you a thousand yuan. Deal?" The red-faced guy immediately turned pale, and replied, "I value my life." Then, he quickly descended, moving the ladder to one side.

By this point it was past noon. The intense sun was suspended directly overhead. The weather was already so hot that the fields felt as though they would scald anyone who tried to work in them. Like withered grass, the people of Liven went back to their respective side rooms to lie down. Because One-Legged Monkey had accepted the water through the window, he felt somewhat awakened. He and several of the wholers found a couple of empty boxes and an old table tucked away in the corners of the memorial hall, and when they stacked them one on top of the other, they could just reach the window.

One-Legged Monkey quietly climbed up, and saw that the mountain ridge outside was empty and silent. He had no idea where all the tourists who had covered the mountainside the previous day had gone, or why now there wasn't even a single tourist to be seen. The truck that had been used to haul around the stage props was parked under a big tree in front of the memorial hall, and those wholers—and there were about seven or eight of them—were all lying in the shade next to the truck. They had already eaten lunch, and their bowls and chopsticks were strewn about. Under the tree, some of the men were playing cards, while others had spread out their bedding mats and were taking a nap. Needless to say, the short and fat thirty-something-year-old driver was their informal leader. He had stripped down to his underwear and was sleeping next to everyone else, looking as though he wasn't at all concerned that the villagers weren't passing him any money.

It appeared that the wholers had organized everything very thoroughly. Along the wide cement path leading down the mountain, under the white sunlight, it was as if there was a layer of smoke and dust, and everything was bright and pristine, without a soul in sight. The tourists who had come up the mountain the previous day had all gone back home, and now the weather was so hot that no one seemed to have any interest in visiting. Or perhaps the people who had come up the day before had all been gathered and tricked into returning home, while the people who now wanted to come up were being blocked at the base of the mountain. Whatever the reason, the mountain ridge was extraordinarily quiet, and apart from those seven or eight wholers, there was no one around.

Through the window, One-Legged Monkey could see the pines and cypresses that surrounded the memorial hall on all sides, while the chestnut and locust trees next to the gorge were all green and budding in the heat. From this greenery, the cicadas also quietly emerged, and they sat on tree branches and leaves crying a torrent. In the blink of an eye, the wild grass and brambles on the mountain slope had become densely overgrown, and within that greenery there were countless grasshoppers and other insects flying about. All of the vegetation on the mountain was green and blooming.

As the weather grew warmer, the villagers locked in the memorial hall felt even more suffocated and oppressed, as though they were indeed locked inside a bamboo steamer. One-Legged Monkey gazed out of this window for a while, and then moved the box and chairs over to a different window and peered out, confirming that they were indeed locked inside the memorial hall as though it were a steamer. This figurative steamer, furthermore, was suspended in midair, such that if you were to try to leave through the window you still wouldn't be able to get down. The windows in back and on either side of the building all faced out over a cliff, and were positioned several dozen feet above the ground. The window in front was slightly lower, but even it was as high as a typical second-story window. In front of the kowtow steps, on the other hand, the window above the door was low enough that you could push it open with your shoulder and crawl in or out. But there were two young sentries watching the door, each with a three-foot-long club he was prepared to use if the need arose.

It was impossible to escape through the windows. Not even a wholer would dare jump from them, much less one of Liven's disabled villagers. And, furthermore, how could they go down the mountain while in plain sight of the people outside?

When One-Legged Monkey climbed down from the window, everyone gazed up at him expectantly. His face was covered in dust, as though he had just walked into a wall.

They asked, "Is there any hope?"

He said, "Not a trace."

They immediately lost their last remaining hopes of escape. Instead, they opened several windows to air out the memorial hall. The breeze brought in the smell of the mountain vegetation, and they could peacefully sit or lie down in their respective rooms. Time inched forward like a horse or an ox trudging through tall grass, and when the sun finally passed its zenith, there was a shout from outside the memorial hall door:

"Hey, are you hungry in there? . . . Are you thirsty in there?

". . . If you are hungry and thirsty, just pass us the money under the door, and we'll send you in some soup and food through the window."

This shout entered the memorial hall, where it reverberated loudly. But the villagers didn't respond, and instead merely let the sound fade on its own. Once the hall was silent again, the villagers' hunger and thirst became even more acute, as though they had been awakened from a deep sleep. They felt as though there were herds of animals galloping through their stomachs. In this way the day passed, and eventually dusk was about to fall.

At that point, however, there was a thump on the memorial hall window. People emerged from their side rooms to take a look, and then returned and reported that all of the windows had been nailed shut. They reported this as though they had known all along that something like this would happen. It was as if they felt that, since they were all disabled and couldn't climb out even if the windows had been within reach, they might as well have the windows nailed shut. Therefore, no one paid attention to the villager who was speaking, and instead they all focused on the sound of hammering on the windows. They kept sitting or lying silently where they had been, trying to use silence to suppress their hunger and thirst. It was as if they were trying to use a mosquito to control a fire that kept burning ever hotter.

The hammering sound at the windows echoed like thunder inside everyone's heart. With each thud, the villagers' hearts would pound, and as the sun traversed the hundreds of li of sky from late afternoon to evening, they continued to endure this incessant pounding.

As the sun set, everyone's hunger and thirst once again erupted with a vengeance. Some people had been sleeping, and at this point they woke up in a daze. The sunlight streaming in through the window had shifted from blazing white to bright yellow, and then again to blood red. The sun had moved from the window in the front of the memorial hall to the window over Lenin's portrait and crystal coffin, and then on to the window in the back of the memorial hall. It appeared as though there were a sheet of red silk over each pane of glass. From inside the room, you could see the cover that had been nailed over the windows, like a little cap. The people outside were all tall wholers, and despite the steep cliffs and gullies below the windows, they had still been able to easily nail the covers over them.

Grandma Mao Zhi hadn't lain down this entire time, and merely sat there staring stupidly at the door. Through it she could see the crystal coffin in the center of the main hall, together with the white cloth draped across the coffin, on which ten or twenty people had left their fingerprints affirming their support of withdrawing from society. No one had any idea what Grandma Mao Zhi was thinking as she sat there. When the sun went down, she finally turned away from the coffin and gazed instead at her four granddaughters: Tonghua, Huaihua, Yuhua, and Mothlet. Then, she looked at Paraplegic Woman, who was lying across from her. Speaking half to them and half to herself, she asked,

"Are you hungry?"

They all looked at her.

"If you have money, then go buy something," she said. "It won't do for everyone to starve to death."

"It's almost nighttime," Paraplegic Woman said. "Maybe tomorrow they will open the doors for us."

Grandma Mao Zhi went into another room. She looked at the villagers who were sitting or lying there, and said,

"If you are hungry, then buy something. It won't do for everyone to starve to death."

No one spoke. They just gazed out the window at the setting sun.

She proceeded to another room, and said,

"I've decided that if you need to buy something, you should. It won't do for everyone to starve to death."

She went to yet another room, and repeated,

"If you need to buy something, you should. It won't do for people to starve to death."

She went to each of the individual side rooms, telling everyone the same thing. In the end, however, no one went to buy a bun or a bowl of water. One person said, "I don't have a single cent on me!" Another said, "All my money was fucking stolen!" They all claimed that they didn't have any money and that if they were about to die of hunger and thirst, there was nothing they could do about it.

Day changed to dusk, and dusk to night. Around dinnertime, the people outside the door repeatedly called to the villagers inside the memorial hall, saying, "If you are thirsty and hungry, just pass the money under the door." Apart from one villager who couldn't endure it any longer and passed fifty yuan under the door in exchange for half a bowl of water, no one else paid them any heed. No one could bring himself to spend two hundred yuan for a bowl of noodles, or five hundred yuan for a bun.

In this way, the night passed.

A new day arrived.

By the third day, the villagers were so hungry that their eyeballs looked as though they were about to fall out of their sockets, and when they walked they had to support themselves by leaning against the wall. But the sun was still as piercingly hot as on the preceding days, and when it shone in through the glass window, it was as if countless red-hot iron rods had been extended through the window. Everyone's lips were so dry that they bled, and in order to stanch their thirst, the villagers didn't stay in the side rooms but rather all went into the main hall or to the latrine. The air there had a little more moisture, but because the pump was no longer working, there was also crap and urine everywhere.

The people outside had hardened hearts and resolved to wait things out. They knew that when the villagers had endured all the hunger and thirst they could stand, they would eventually hand over their money. Therefore, except for calling out at mealtimes to see if the villagers were hungry and thirsty, the people outside didn't bother them, and instead merely used time itself to torment them.

And, in the end, the villagers were indeed worn down.

At noon of the third day, the people outside called to the villagers in the memorial as if they were peddling goods, saying,

"Hey, do you want some water! One hundred yuan for a bowl . . ."

"Hey, do you want soup? Two hundred yuan for a bowl of egg noodle soup, so full that the bowl is overflowing. . . ."

"Hey, do you want a steamed bun? Our white buns are as big as a child's head or your wife's breasts, and our burned yellow baked scallion buns are as yellow as gold, and as tasty as a fried dough cake. Do you want one? Five hundred yuan for a white steamed bun, six hundred for a yellow baked bun."

They kept hollering outside the door, and periodically would climb the ladder and peer inside. They would shout the same thing through the window over and over, like a loudspeaker repeating an announcement ten or more times, and then would extend a bowl of water through the window, asking, "Does anyone want this? Do you want it? If you don't, we'll just pour it out." Then, they did in fact pour the bowl of water into the memorial hall. The water was like a sheet of silvery white beads, shimmering briefly in midair before splattering onto the cement floor. The ground was immediately covered in a layer of water.

They also extended a bun through the window and asked, "Does anyone want this? Do you want it?" They crumbled the bun into tiny crumbs and scattered them outside the window, as if they were feeding birds, leaving the memorial hall with only the savory aroma of the bun, like the fragrance of wheat wafting over during that earlier period of famine.

By crumbling up the bun and pouring water all over the ground, they attracted the villagers into the main hall of the memorial hall, where they all stood or sat, watching as one bowl of water after another was poured out and bun crumbs rained down like sand onto the ground outside the window.

The noon sun was so hot it couldn't possibly get any hotter. It hadn't been this hot for several hundred years. Inside the memorial hall there wasn't a trace of a breeze. The air felt as though it had already been breathed. Everyone seemed as if they needed to sweat, but their bodies didn't have any moisture to release. If the heat continued, everyone would soon start sweating blood. Because there was no water to flush away the urine and feces that people had deposited in the memorial hall's latrine, by this point the stench filled the room and enveloped everyone.

The wholer who had been pouring water and crumbling buns through the window left to take a nap, and inside the hall everything became as silent and stuffy as a tomb. The villagers were all so hungry and thirsty that they were about to pass out, and everyone sat on the ground as though paralyzed.

Their lips were as white and shriveled as cracked sandstone.

Apart from the sound of those wholers talking, there was absolute silence outside the memorial hall. That is to say, over those three days, no one else had come up the mountain, and therefore no one knew about the unprecedented event that had taken place. No one knew that the residents of Liven were locked up in the Lenin Memorial Hall and for three days hadn't had a taste of food or water.

No one knew that little Polio Boy was running a fever, or that each time the villagers wanted to get him half a bowl of water they had to pass fifty or a hundred yuan under the door.

The boy's uncle had already passed out next to one of the memorial hall's marble pillars.

Deafman Ma had been lying motionless at the base of the wall for an entire day and night. It was as if not even his eyes wanted to move.

The paralyzed woman who had been traveling with the troupe to help cook for them had become so hungry she couldn't endure it any longer. She used a bowl to capture her own urine and then drank it, but immediately proceeded to vomit it up again.

Eventually, in the heat of the afternoon of the third day, Grandma Mao Zhi emerged from the side room where she was sleeping. She was holding her crutch and leaning against the wall. Her face was ashen as a result of her having endured three days and three nights of misery. Her hair was gray and disheveled. Her blue shirt used to fit her just right, but now it looked like it was draped loosely over a clothes hanger. When she walked out of her room, the villagers paid her no attention, figuring she had nothing to report, since, like everyone else, she had spent the preceding three days sitting or lying down. But now, she opened her mouth and spoke, such that everyone had no choice but to listen, hanging carefully on her every word. She had not been in the main hall when the people outside splashed water and crumbled buns through the window, but she knew very well what they were doing. She stood there, holding her crutch in one hand and leaning against the wall with the other. She asked,

"They're not splashing water or crumbling buns anymore?"

Everyone just stared at her.

She said,

"I know most of you still have money on you, and I also know exactly where you keep it. If you don't believe me, then let's have everyone take off their clothes and let someone look through them, or lift up the bricks beneath their bedroll and let someone look under them."

She said,

"It won't do for people to die of hunger and thirst. One hundred yuan for a bowl of water, two hundred for a bowl of noodles, and five hundred for a steamed bun—if you buy them, you'll live, but if you don't, you'll die. So, will you buy them or not?"

She concluded,

"You don't need to hide your cash. Every family can drink the water and eat the steamed buns they buy with their own funds. Trust me, those who don't have any money will die of hunger or thirst before they use a cent of any one else's."

The entire hall fell into a deep silence. Then there was the sound of people looking around. Soon, they were all looking toward the corners of the room where they had hidden their money. It was as though they were all afraid that Grandma Mao Zhi had found their secret stashes of cash, as if she had revealed their secret weakness. Some of them hated her for this, some simply felt embarrassed, while others were grateful that she had finally torn down the artificial facade that had been erected inside the hall. However, they all remained where they had been sitting or lying, looking silently at one another. It was as if they each felt Grandma Mao Zhi was talking about someone else. It was as if they all felt as though if others took out their money to buy some water, they couldn't possibly avoid sharing it with them, and that conversely, if they themselves took out their money to buy a bun, they would have no choice but to give some to the others. What made them particularly anxious and fearful was the thought that if they were the first to take out their money, everyone might jump on them and beat them, saying, *Fuck your mother, you had all this money on you, and yet you made us endure three days of thirst and hunger*, and then would proceed to steal their money and use it to buy water, noodles, and steamed buns for themselves.

So instead, they all remained where they were without moving or saying a word, as if the hall were completely empty.

The air became increasingly noxious.

It was fouled further by the stench from the latrine.

The main hall was so quiet that it seemed as though a leaf or feather would create an enormous pit if it fell to the ground, and would carve an enormous gash in one of the marble pillars if it happened to brush against one of them. It was as though the leaf or feather might shatter Lenin's crystal coffin into countless shards of glass. Indeed, the hall was so quiet that you wouldn't find a quieter place anywhere in the world. It was also so stuffy that you wouldn't find a stuffier place anywhere in the world. As everyone gazed up at Grandma Mao Zhi, they gradually began to feel somewhat ill at ease, and they remained focused on some indeterminate spot in front of them.

In this way, the confused time inched past, as though it were counting individual strands of hair; perhaps it covered a hundred-long li, or perhaps it was the equivalent of several strands of hair. Eventually, Grandma Mao Zhi shifted her gaze to Polio Boy.

The boy was sitting in the corner closest to the hall's main door. He was leaning against the door frame, and the water that had been thrown in through the window had reached his feet and splashed his face. Whenever the people outside threw water in, he wanted to go try to catch it with his mouth, but was afraid that afterward he might find himself stuck there and unable to move. Needless to say, his face had a deathly pallor from hunger and thirst and had become as swollen and shiny as a rotten apple or peach, while his lips were covered with dry, bloody ridges and were extraordinarily engorged. Grandma Mao Zhi looked at him, and he looked back at her. It was as if he were seeing someone who resembled his mother. He seemed to want to call out to her, but was afraid that he had misrecognized her. Therefore, he just stared at her silently, as though waiting for her to recognize him.

Grandma Mao Zhi watched him for a while, and then said, "Boy!"

He grunted in response.

She asked, "Do you want to eat?"

He nodded, and said, "I'm very thirsty."

Grandma Mao Zhi said, "Give me the money you have stitched inside your pants pocket, and I'll go buy you something."

The boy took off his pants in front of everyone, revealing his floral underwear. On the underwear there was a bulging white pocket with the opening stitched shut. The boy leaned down and ripped the pocket with his teeth, as Grandma Mao Zhi came over and took his money. After counting out six bills, she handed the rest back to him, and then went over to the memorial hall door and knocked a few times, saying, "I want a bowl of water, and a steamed bun!" Then she stuffed the money under the door.

In the blink of an eye, a bowl of water and a steamed bun were passed in through the window over the door. The boy stood behind the door to receive them, and began drinking and eating in front of everyone. He was just a boy, and initially no one paid him any mind, even as the sound of his drinking reverberated throughout the hall like a river, while that of his eating was like food frying during the village's livening festival.

He ravenously devoured the steamed bun, heedless of everyone around him.

The aroma swept through the memorial hall like a tornado, followed by the sound of the boy chewing. His right leg was as shriveled as a stick and he was as skinny as a stalk of grain, and normally when he opened his mouth he couldn't even stuff an egg inside. But now this small and skinny boy brought his mouth up to the edge of the bowl and, in two or three swallows, managed to gulp down two-thirds of the steamed bun, which was as big as a rabbit's head.

Everyone's eyes remained fixated on his steamed bun, and on the boy delightedly enjoying his food.

No one said a word. Everyone was consuming the sight of him swallowing the water and the sound of him eating the steamed bun. One-Legged Monkey was standing to the side licking his cracked lips. Deafman Ma for some reason was covering his mouth with his hand. Tonghua, Huaihua, Yuhua, and Mothlet were not watching the boy, and instead were just staring at their grandmother as if she, who was standing right next to them, might suddenly pull out a wad of cash and buy each of them a steamed bun and a bowl of water.

By this point it was already afternoon and it seemed as though the air in the room, and even time itself, was being chewed up by the boy.

Suddenly, Deafman Ma unbuttoned his pants, and muttered, "If we're all about to die, then what the hell do I need money for?" He pulled twelve hundred yuan from his underwear, and shouted at the door,

"Give me two steamed buns, and two bowls of water!"

He passed the money through the crack under the door.

The smiling face of a thirty-something-year-old appeared at the window, and handed down buns and water.

The Mute wailed several times, stomped his feet, then suddenly went back to the side room where he slept. He started counting the bricks along the wall behind his bed, and when he reached the fifth one, he lifted up the corresponding bricks beneath his bedroll and removed several wads of cash. He removed a pile of bills, and as he walked forward he stuck out three fingers and wailed. Grandma Mao Zhi took his money and explained to the smiling face in the window, "He wants three steamed buns, and three bowls of water. Here is eighteen hundred yuan. Count it yourself." She then passed the wad of bills through the window into the person's hand.

The smiling face accepted the money. Without even counting it, the man immediately shouted out to the people below him, "Quick, bring us three steamed buns and three bowls of water."

In this way, the situation slowly began to shift. The villagers no longer needed to avoid one another. As Grandma Mao Zhi had claimed, their money had been stolen three days earlier, but they still had some cash stashed away on their persons. The women opened their shirts in front of everyone, and most of them had money hidden away in little pockets that they had sewn inside. There was one woman who didn't have this sort of pocket, but she retreated to the latrine and, in the blink of an eye, reemerged holding several hundred yuan.

The boy's uncle sat there without moving. Eventually, he ripped open his pants leg, revealing several hundred—or perhaps even several thousand—yuan.

The old man who had gone on stage playing the role of a hundred-and-twenty-one-year-old didn't rummage around in his clothes for money, and neither did he retreat to the side room to retrieve it. Instead, he went over to Lenin's crystal coffin and, lying down, starting feeling around on the ground underneath the coffin, eventually withdrawing the sort of wallet that usually only city folks use. The wallet was full of crisp, new hundred-yuan bills. He pulled out who knows how many bills, muttering, "Fuck her grandmother. If everyone is going to die, what use will our money be to us?" He didn't buy a steamed bun, though, nor a bowl of water. Instead, he purchased three baked buns and three bowls of noodles. The buns were baked to a succulent shade of brown, and the noodles were similarly cooked to perfection.

After the old man accepted the three baked buns and three bowls of noodles, he placed two of the bowls at his feet and held the third in his left hand while cradling the three baked buns in his right. He then took the buns and bowl over to Lenin's crystal coffin before going back to collect the remaining two bowls of noodles. The coffin was light and bright, and when he placed his noodles and buns on top, it was as if he were placing them on an imperial jade table. In this way, it wasn't as though he were eating simply because he was hungry, but rather as though he were saying, *Eat and drink, because the important thing is simply to survive. What use is your money? What's special about it? Food is the most valuable thing in the world.*

He savored his bun as happily as a cow chewing its cud, and drank his noodles as if he were guzzling water in the middle of a desert. He focused only on his eating and drinking, completely ignoring everyone else. It was as though he were on stage performing the role of a starving man.

Several people stood there watching him, while others retrieved money from various places and, like him, bought armfuls of buns and noodles. As they did so, they said, "Grandmother! If people can't even survive, they should at least eat and drink well."

One-Legged Monkey had been hiding motionless behind the crowd of villagers, but after watching everyone eat and drink, he suddenly took out some money from somewhere. Then he saw Cripple: the "hundred-and-twenty-one-year-old man." He was eating and drinking on top of the crystal coffin, while peering beneath the coffin at the brick from which he had just removed his money. From this, One-Legged Monkey began to develop a suspicion, whereupon he cursed, "Fuck your mothers!" It was unclear whether he was cursing the old cripple or himself. He took off the special hard-soled shoes that he wore while performing his Leaping-Over-a-Mountain-of-Knives-and-Crossing-a-Sea-of-Fire routine and removed several hundred-yuan bills, then used them to buy some buns and noodles.

As One-Legged Monkey ate and drank, he looked around, and his gaze would periodically come to rest on that area below the crystal coffin, where Cripple kept glancing.

Meanwhile, the main hall erupted into tumult, with everyone calling out for buns and water. The villagers all hobbled over to the door of the memorial hall, where, like the old cripple, they would say, "That's right. Fuck your mother! If people are starving to death, what the hell do they need money for!"

They said, "Eat, drink. It won't do if everyone dies of hunger or thirst."

They said, "It doesn't matter if a bowl of water costs one hundred yuan. Even if it cost a thousand yuan, I wouldn't accept this sort of death sentence."

Soon, the entire hall was filled with the sound of people eating and drinking.

One person gulped down a bowl of water, then extended a hundred-yuan bill toward the window and shouted, "Sell me some more water! I need some more water!" Another person devoured a bun in a few bites, then shouted, "Sell me another bun, sell me another. I want that oil-baked bun!"

At this point, however, the four small windows above the memorial hall door were pushed open, and in them appeared the faces of four wholers. In the middle window appeared the face of the driver, but he wasn't smiling contentedly like the wholer beside him. Instead, he stuck his head in and looked around, cleared his throat, and said,

"If you had done this earlier, you wouldn't have had to go hungry for so long!"

He added,

"I apologize. . . . The price of the buns has gone up. . . . They now cost eight hundred yuan each. The price of water has also gone up, to two hundred yuan a bowl."

All of the villagers immediately fell silent, as though the driver had suddenly thrown water onto a burning fire. Some of the people holding up their money to buy buns and water promptly pulled their arms back down, but one woman remained frozen there with her arms suspended in the air, the money still in her hands. One of the wholers in the window quickly grabbed her money, and the woman shouted,

"You stole my money. . . . You stole my money. . . ."

The person who had taken her money leaned into the hall and said with a laugh, "If we had wanted to steal your money, why on earth would we have waited here for three days and three nights to do so?"

Her scream faded into silence, as she quickly backed away from the door, grasping the pocket sewn into her shirt. From a distance, One-Legged Monkey saw the old man with the crutch instinctively glance over at that area beneath the crystal coffin. He saw that all of the people in the hall had been left speechless, and were watching Grandma Mao Zhi.

The entire time this was going on, Grandma Mao Zhi simply stood in the middle of the hall next to a column. Huaihua, however, had already retreated to one side, holding in one hand half a bun and in the other half a bowl of water, which she was enjoying happily but silently. No one knew when she had gotten the money to buy them, but now, as she hid in a corner eating, she repeatedly looked back, with large, vivid eyes, at her grandmother, her blind older sister, and her other nin sisters. The sun was shining in through the window as brightly as before, and depite the earlier stench, the air now also had the fragrance of buns and of moisture. Huaihua was standing there chewing her bun and drinking her water, but now she was quieter than before, as though afraid someone might hear her, as though a swarm of rats or sparrows were about to steal from her.

The villagers who hadn't managed to buy water or a bun miserably watched Grandma Mao Zhi, as though simply by watching her they could get something to eat and drink. They all had expressions of bitter regret, that they had missed an opportunity to survive and were about to die of hunger and thirst. All of them were lying limply at the base of the wall, gazing at Grandma Mao Zhi and at the wholers in the window, and then bowing their heads.

At that point, the situation quickly changed, as the wholers started smiling deviously. The sunlight behind them was blindingly bright as it shone in the villagers' eyes. The sun was hovering above the wholers' heads, and their faces were bathed in sweat. They had all taken off their shirts and gowns, and their shoulders were as red as if they were covered in black and red oil. The driver was still standing on a ladder, telling the people inside loudly but deliberately,

"I know that many of you have a lot of money hidden away on your persons. For each performance, each of you received one or two seats, so who knows how much you've earned over the course of the past six months. The others only stole about one- or two-thirds of what you must have had. I am now telling you the truth when I say that if you give me eighty or a hundred thousand yuan, I won't ask you for anything else, I'll simply sit here selling buns and water. The price of water just went up again, to three hundred yuan a bowl. The price of buns has increased as well, to a thousand yuan a bun. If you want, I also have packets of pickled vegetables. These are comparatively cheap, and you can buy some for only two hundred yuan each."

He added,

"Do you want them or not? If you do, this is the price. If you don't, then you are welcome to wait until tomorrow, but the price may well go up again."

He looked at Grandma Mao Zhi, and said, "I am the leader of the wholers outside, and you are the leader of the disabled people inside. I know you've endured a lot, and that the bridges you've crossed are far longer than the roads I myself have traveled. But you mustn't get confused and do things you will regret, like not passing me the money."

Staring intently at Grandma Mao Zhi's face, he said,

"This is the price. Do you want water and buns?"

He continued looking at her. "Do you want any or not? I'm sorry, Grandma Mao Zhi, if you don't want this bun, the price will rise again. A steamed bun will soon cost twelve hundred yuan. The price of water will also increase, to five hundred yuan a bowl. A packet of pickled vegetables will cost three hundred yuan. That is the going price, and if you want to starve to death, you are welcome to not buy anything. Think about it. I'm going to step down for a rest period.[3] After you have decided, give me a shout."

After the driver finished his explanation about the price increases, he smiled again at the villagers from the window, then told all of his people to come down from the window, saying, "Hey, Grandma Mao Zhi, you should urge the other villagers to hurry up and purchase what they want, because if they don't, I might get angry and raise the prices again."

Then, he disappeared from the window.

The hall returned to its earlier silence. Those who hadn't yet finished their water and buns quickly stuffed them into their mouths and placed the empty bowls at their feet. Others who hadn't finished their steamed or baked buns either quickly ate them or hid them somewhere. In any case, the villagers all quieted down again, and the window also reverted to its former state.

The hall became as silent as a grave. One after another, the villagers retreated from the main hall to the side rooms where they slept. There, they sat or lay down, as if waiting either to die or for the wholers outside to open the door and permit them to walk out with their money.

One-Legged Monkey, however, did not return to the side room. He noticed that before the old man with the crutch left the crystal coffin, he had leaned over and felt around beneath the coffin—but it was unclear whether he was looking for something or placing something there. One-Legged Monkey therefore decided that he, too, would go feel around beneath the coffin. First, he went to the latrine and stood there for a while, as though taking a piss. By the time he emerged, the main hall was empty, as everyone had retired to the side rooms. Even Grandma Mao Zhi, grasping Tonghua with one hand and Mothlet with the other, sat with her daughters on her bedroll, their eyes closed and their heads leaning against the wall.

Everything was quiet. Deathly quiet. So quiet that it was possible to hear the sound of dust flying around the room.

At this point, One-Legged Monkey emerged from the latrine and discreetly went over to feel around underneath the crystal coffin. The coffin was positioned on a marble table, and was supported by two stone bars. Apart from a layer of dust, there was nothing beneath the coffin. Needless to say, though, the old man with crutches had previously kept his money here but must have just removed it, leaving behind only a layer of dust. One-Legged Monkey was somewhat disappointed, and hated himself for having watched for so long that the old man with crutches had noticed him.

One-Legged Monkey pulled his hand out from beneath the coffin and wiped off the dust. He was petrified with fear, but refused to give up. He glanced over at the side room doors, then proceeded to lie down and peer under the coffin. He saw not only three marks in the dust next to the support rods, where Cripple had kept his money, but also a black hole half as big as a book in the center of the table. It was as if when the workers were building the table, they had forgotten to add a slab of marble.

One-Legged Monkey reached into that dark hole. He accidentally pressed something, and suddenly the two slabs of marble on which he was standing began to sink into the ground. Before he knew what was happening, they had sunk down several inches and receded to the side.

A deep, black pit appeared beneath his feet.

He was so startled that he sat down on the floor.

He peered into this two-foot-long and one-foot-wide pit in front of the coffin, suddenly realizing that when he had reached into the hole beneath the coffin, he must have accidentally tripped a mechanism of some sort. By this point, the main hall was completely empty, and there was no one in the doorways of any of the side rooms, either. The windows to the main hall were also empty. One-Legged Monkey's palms were sweaty and his face was pale. Using the light from the crystal coffin, he peered into the pit that had opened beneath his feet, and noticed with surprise that beneath the coffin there was another pit. It was somewhat smaller than the marble table, and was about five feet wide, eight or nine feet long, and three feet deep. The sides of the pit were also lined with milky white marble slabs, as though lined with a sheet of white silk. Inside this milky white pit, there was another crystal coffin that was identical to Lenin's coffin above it. Perhaps this second coffin was slightly smaller than the first, but otherwise the two were virtually identical.

One-Legged Monkey was so startled by the sight of this second coffin that he broke into a cold sweat. His legs, which were dangling into the pit, began to tremble. He wanted to pull his feet out, but something seemed to be holding them there, making it a struggle just to move them. He peered into the pit, whereupon he heard the sound of the sunlight shining in through the memorial hall window onto Lenin's crystal coffin, turning the coffin red, as though it were made of pink agate. That gentle light also shone down onto the second crystal coffin inside the pit, which turned the color of black jade. The second coffin began to glimmer, but its glimmer was deep and murky, like a piece of black jade immersed in water.

At this moment, One-Legged Monkey saw clearly that there was a row of Chinese characters on the lid of the second crystal coffin. The characters were bright yellow, and while they didn't shine they nevertheless were very bright. Every character was as big as a bowl, and they began from the head of the coffin, with a space as wide as several fingers between characters. These characters were written in an ancient chancery script, and were each as thick as a piece of tree bark.

The characters were inscribed directly on the lid of the coffin, and there were nine of them in all. One-Legged Monkey read them carefully from beginning to end:

May Comrade Liu Yingque Be Eternally Remembered by Posterity

One-Legged Monkey felt somewhat at a loss. He immediately realized that Chief Liu had prepared this second crystal coffin for himself, but what he couldn't understand was why Chief Liu would want to prepare his own coffin while he was still alive, why it had to be a crystal coffin, or why it had to be positioned in Lenin's Memorial Hall, next to Lenin's coffin. One-Legged Monkey stared into the pit at those nine characters inscribed on the lid of the coffin, but waited until later to ponder their significance. The golden color of those nine embossed *li* script characters attracted him. They didn't produce light in themelves, but rather emitted a yellow glow into this underground pit—like a row of nine suns hidden behind the clouds. He stared intently at the nine characters, focusing in particular on their color and wondering what they were made of. Of course, if the characters had been made of brass, they would have oxidized quickly in the humid pit. Instead, however, they remained bright yellow. What, then, could they possibly be made of?

One-Legged Monkey thought of gold.

When it occurred to him that the characters might be made of gold, the chill in his legs immediately disappeared, and he felt instead a surge of warm blood rush from his feet up to his head. Without wasting a second, he slid monkeylike into the pit, leaned over, and stroked the characters. Then, as if crazed, he grabbed at the characters on the lid of the coffin. But it appeared as though every single stroke was firmly nailed down; and this, combined with the fact that his hands were sweaty, meant that he wasn't able to pry off a single one.

The sounds in the main hall resonated loudly down inside the pit, as though there were an underground river close by. One-Legged Monkey stood up, bumping his head against the bottom of Lenin's crystal coffin. There was a thud, which startled him so much he became covered in sweat. He had a sudden urge to pee, just like six months earlier when he'd first performed on the Shuanghuai stage.

He managed to control himself, however, and didn't permit the urine to leave his body. Instead, he began tugging at the gold characters, eventually managing to break off a single stroke from one of them. This piece was the size of a fingernail and the shape of the tip of his index finger, and was as thick as a piece of tree bark. He held this tiny piece in his hand, and tried to estimate how much it weighed. It felt as though this little piece pressing down on the palm of his hand was as heavy as an iron hammer.

It turned out that those characters were indeed made of gold.

The nine gold characters on the lid of Chief Liu's crystal coffin read:

May Comrade Liu Yingque Be Eternally Remembered by Posterity

Upon realizing that the embossed characters were made of actual gold, One-Legged Monkey sat there stupefied, then tried to pry off another piece. After he failed to loosen even half a stroke, he could no longer think about anything other than urinating and proceeded to climb out of the pit. He immediately went over to the two marble slabs and began pressing down on the opening between them. He didn't know what button he pressed, but it pricked his hand like the end of a tree branch. He pressed against this branchlike stub, moving it back and forth until eventually the open pit was covered up again.

At that point, One-Legged Monkey realized he really had peed in his pants, and the damp area was rubbing against his thighs like a clump of wet sand.

Seeing the deathly quiet memorial hall, he quickly hobbled over to the bathroom, but succeeded in secreting only a few more drops.

Given that over the previous three days he had drunk only half a bowl of water, he'd had the urge to urinate without actually having had anything in his bladder. Moreover, he had already pissed out all of the excess liquid inside him when he'd wet his pants down in the pit.

After peeing out those few drops, One-Legged Monkey felt as carefree and livened as though he had finally relieved himself of the urine that he had been holding back for the past three days. He stood erect in the latrine, without tying up his pants, his shoulders thrust back and his arms in the air. At this point, he heard someone at the window above the main door of the memorial hall shout inside:

"Hey, come on out. People of Liven, come out. My elder bro here wants to organize a meeting for you—there's something he wants to tell you."

After some of the villagers emerged, the person at the window repeated,

"Someone get Grandma Mao Zhi. My bro wants to organize a meeting for you, and after you've listened to what he has to say, he'll let you go."

One-Legged Monkey heard the sound of many footsteps. He emerged from the bathroom and saw that the villagers were coming out of the side rooms, walking behind Grandma Mao Zhi. They proceeded to the center of the hall, where they stood in a group. Not a single one of them, not even Old Crutches, glanced over at the crystal coffin. At the window the faces of those four wholers reappeared. One of them still had the condescending smile that he'd had earlier, while another had turned pale. The truck driver, whom the others called "Elder Bro," looked utterly calm. He was standing at the center window, gazing into the hall, and let his gaze come to rest of Grandma Mao Zhi. He said,

"Hey, people of Liven, Grandma Mao Zhi, listen to me. I'm going to level with you. We've grown impatient waiting for you. It's hot and we all want to go home, and I'm sure you're even more eager to return home than we are—to return to your carefree days of livening. We all want to return home, so let's be honest with each other. You are all disabled, so you don't *really* need any money to enjoy a carefree life. Even if you were to cook and eat like crazy, you couldn't possibly spend very much money every month. On top of it, I can't bear to see you locked up in this hall with nothing to eat or drink. Some of you are missing an arm or a leg, or are unable to see, hear, or speak—life for you must not be easy."

He said, "We wholers have been thinking about you. We've been watching you, and we know where each of you has hidden your money. We've calculated that, for every performance, each of you has earned half a seat, on average. We don't know precisely how much you have earned over the past six months, but the thieves could not have stolen more than a third or half of it. The remainder must still be hidden on your persons. You need to hand over that money, every cent of it."

He said, "After you have done so, we will issue each of you three thousand yuan. You've been traveling and performing for the past six months, so it's only fair that we give you three thousand yuan, which amounts to your having earned five hundred yuan a month. Five hundred yuan a month—that would be a good salary even for someone in the city. Three-quarters of the residents of Shuanghuai are workers who don't earn a salary at all, but I propose to give each of you five hundred yuan for each month you have worked, over and above what we've have already given you in food, clothing, and housing, none of which you've had to pay for. If you add everything up, it amounts to our having given you the equivalent of between nine hundred and a thousand yuan a month."

At this point, the driver paused. The setting sun shone down on the right side of his face, revealing that it was covered in sweat. He wiped his forehead and looked into the hall, where he saw that the villagers appeared more lively. They exchanged glances, suggesting that they were considering this proposition. He saw that, in the end, the villagers all turned to Grandma Mao Zhi, as though waiting for her decision, waiting for her to say something to them and to the wholers.

Grandma Mao Zhi, however, didn't utter a single word. Instead, she remained in the front of the hall, half standing and half leaning against one of the marble pillars. She simply stared at the faces of those wholers in the window, and at the mouth of the driver. She appeared pale, as though someone had just slapped her several hundred—or even several thousand—times, and as if those slaps were still continuing.

"Hey, people of Liven and Grandma Mao Zhi, did you hear me?" The driver wiped the sweat again, then cleared his throat. "Let's settle our accounts. You hand over all your money, and then each of you can return to your village with three thousand yuan, to enjoy a carefree, livening existence. Or do you prefer to remain locked in this memorial hall, paying five hundred yuan for a bowl of water, twelve hundred yuan for a steamed bun, and three hundred yuan for a packet of pickled vegetables?"

He said,

"If you can't bear to part with your money and refuse to buy anything, then you will slowly die of hunger and thirst. Or maybe you think it's not so bad to die of hunger and thirst here. After all, you do have Lenin's crystal coffin, so whoever dies can use it."

Then he asked,

"Hey, think about it. Do you prefer to die and be placed in that crystal coffin, or would you like to hand over your money, take your three thousand yuan in salary for the past six months, and then return to Liven and live happily ever after?"

After that, he didn't say anything else. It was as if he had concluded the meeting and said everything he wanted to say, and was now waiting for everyone to vote.

The villagers silently watched Grandma Mao Zhi. The atmosphere in the main hall had become extremely oppressive, as though they all had thousands of pounds of pressure weighing down on their heads. At that point, Grandma Mao Zhi moved away from the column she had been leaning against, and shifted her gaze away from the windows above the door. She slowly turned and looked at the villagers. After regarding them for a while, she appeared to reach a decision. She looked back at the window and asked,

"If you don't open the door, how will you collect the money?"

The driver didn't even need to think about this. Instead, just as he'd typically needed only a quick glance to park the truck carrying the villagers' performance props, he waved at the window and said, "Have you decided? If you have, then listen closely. I want you to all line up at the southern end of the hall. Then, you should lay a sheet on the ground and place all of your money on it. After everyone has done so, you can each proceed to the northern side of the sheet." When he finished, he looked at Grandma Mao Zhi, as though he was trying to discern something from her expression.

But he wasn't able to make anything out. Grandma Mao Zhi didn't go to the side room to fetch a bedsheet, but rather removed her light blue shirt and laid it on the ground in the center of the hall, then led Tonghua and Mothlet over to the southern end of the hall.

With this, the situation abruptly changed. Either because the villagers had just eaten some buns and drunk some water, and no longer felt as famished as before, or because they had already become limp from hunger—after looking first at Grandma Mao Zhi, and then up at the face of the wholer in the window, they all promptly followed Mao Zhi to the southern end of the hall.

One-Legged Monkey and Huaihua also followed Grandma Mao Zhi.

The stuffy atmosphere began to congeal.

The expressions of the wholers in the window glazed over, as though they had become frozen.

No one uttered a single word. Grandma Mao Zhi, Deafman Ma, and Blind Tonghua and her little nin sisters, Yuhua and Mothlet, were standing or sitting in the first row, while Old Crutches, Polio Boy, and his uncle were all standing in a group slightly behind them. In the final row, Huaihua and One-Legged Monkey were standing shoulder to shoulder. One-Legged Monkey nudged Huaihua, then laughed softly and said, "Hey, after we return to Liven, I want to marry you." Huaihua squinted at him, and merely snorted in response. He smiled and said, "You see yourself now as a beautiful wholer, but I can still use my money to marry you."

She looked at him coldly, and stepped away from him.

He stepped closer to her, then smiled once more and said softly, "If you don't marry me, I guarantee you'll regret it for the rest of your life." He didn't look at her again, and she didn't look at him. The hall was deathly quiet and no one spoke, or even moved. After a long silence, Grandma Mao Zhi emerged from the crowd, went to the northern side of the hall, and said to her granddaughter,

"Tonghua, your entire life you've never been able to see what color money is. What do you want money for? Why don't you take out the money you've sewn into that pocket, and then we can go home."

When Tonghua heard her grandmother address her, she began to tremble. Following the sound of her voice, she turned toward her grandmother, and it seemed as though she could see her grandmother's calm and inscrutable face. She stood there silently, looking as though she wanted to take out the money she had hidden but couldn't bear to part with it. She hesitated, locked in a stalemate with her grandmother. At this point, One-Legged Monkey abruptly left Huaihua's side and jostled his way to the front of the crowd. To everyone's astonishment, he hobbled over to the blue shirt lying on the ground, took off his left shoe, and removed several thousand yuan in brand-new bills from beneath the insole, together with another wad of several thousand yuan from the waist of his pants. Then, he bent down and placed all of the cash on the shirt.

"I've put all of mine here. After all, what is money worth? Returning to the village to enjoy a life of livening is more important than anything." Having said this to the villagers, he looked at the driver in the window and added, "The important thing is for you to open that door and let us leave. I don't even care if you give us those three thousand yuan or not. The critical thing is that we be permitted to return home."

Having said this, he obediently moved from the southern side of the hall to the northern side, where he stood next to Grandma Mao Zhi.

The driver in the window nodded in satisfaction.

At this point, the situation was abruptly transformed. It was as if One-Legged Monkey had opened a door, and after he passed through it everyone else could then follow. Blind Tonghua silently took off her floral shirt, ripped it open, and removed one wad of cash after another, then felt around on the ground for her grandmother's shirt. When she finished, she too confidently went over to the north side of the hall.

Grandma Mao Zhi said, "Mothlet, do as your grandmother says."

Mothlet proceeded to untie her finger-thick red velvet hair ribbon, and from inside removed several wads of cash. She placed them on the shirt, then moved over to the northern side.

Little Polio Boy removed his money from a pocket and placed it on the shirt.

Deafman Ma walked up from the back of the crowd, removed the money from his pants legs, and placed it on the shirt.

Some of the other villagers hesitated. The fifty-year-old One-Arm, who with only a single arm could cut radish and cucumber into paper-thin slices faster with his one hand than a wholer chef could with two, had earned a considerable amount of money with this skill, but no one knew where he'd hidden it. Most of the villagers had already gone to the northern side of the hall, and only a handful remained on the southern side. One-Arm looked at the four faces in the window, then back at the villagers standing across from him, and then went to the side room to fetch a winter hat and removed the money he had hidden inside it. He placed several wads of cash on the shirt, then proceeded to the northern side of the hall. At this point, the driver in the window said coldly, "Place the hat itself on the shirt as well."

One-Arm gripped his hat tightly and didn't move.

The driver cursed, "Do you fucking not want to live? Remember that you only have one arm!" With this, One-Arm deposited his hat on the shirt. The hat's earflaps were so stiff it looked as though they had wooden boards inside them. Needless to say, they were stuffed full of cash.

By this point, all of the villagers had moved to the northern side of the room. Those who had money had taken it out, while those who didn't had claimed they really didn't have any, since it had all been stolen, and then they too moved to the northern side of the room. There was a small mountain of cash on Grandma Mao Zhi's light blue shirt, like a pile of vegetables or broken roof tiles. The sun was shining directly on the money, illuminating the colorful designs on the bills. Half of the bills in the pile were brand-new—so new that the scent of their ink filled the room like the smell of fresh paint. Those who had placed money on the pile had each deposited thousands or even tens of thousands of yuan, so that once all the cash was gathered together, the pile was amazingly large, so large that the villagers felt they were seeing a tower of gold or a mountain of cash. They didn't look at the people in the window, but rather kept their eyes fixed on this pile of money, as if they were gazing at the face of their own children and wanted to go hug them close. Everyone standing, together with the two paralyzed women lying on the ground, crowded together on the northern side of the hall.

At this point, the driver said coldly, "Grandma Mao Zhi, come over here, and nobody else move. Now, bundle the money together, every single bill, and pass it to me with your crutch."

Everyone stood there in a dead silence, staring intently at Grandma Mao Zhi, as though hoping she wouldn't walk over. She hesitated for a moment, then proceeded to do as she had been instructed. She tied together a corner of the shirt and its collar, then did the same with the two sleeves. After the bundle was all tied up, she patted it with her hand, as if to make sure it was secure. Then, as she was lifting it with her crutch, she looked calmly at the driver and said, "Son, I'm already seventy-one years old, and it was I who led the people of Liven out to perform. If I give you the money, you must open the door and let me lead them home again."

She said this very softly, as though she were an invalid asking the doctor to give her a prescription, and when the doctor—which is to say, the driver—replied he became very gentle, his face flushed. He looked down at her, then at the bundle of money, and said softly,

"Once I receive the money, I'll certainly open the door." As he said this, he took a bundle of keys out of his pocket and showed them to Grandma Mao Zhi. He shook them back and forth, making the keys clink and clank, and said, "Hand me the money; I'm good for my word."

With great effort, Grandma Mao lifted the bundle of money to the window.

The driver unhurriedly accepted it.

The entire transaction was completed in less time than it takes to swallow a bite of steamed bun or a gulp of water. It took no longer than the length of a needle, and then the money was in the driver's hands. He unhurriedly took a loose corner of the bundle and retied it, then handed it down to the person standing on the ladder below him, saying, "Hold this." Then he looked through the window at Grandma Mao Zhi, and asked softly,

"Is all the money here?"

"It's all there."

"Are you sure no one has any more on their person?"

"Weren't you watching as they all took out their money?"

The driver didn't say anything else. He stuck out his tongue, then used his lips to push it back in. He repeated this gesture several times until his lips were wet and the color of blood, then he pursed his lips and thought for a while, and finally asked gently,

"Are Huaihua and her three nin sisters your granddaughters?"

Grandma Mao Zhi looked over at Huaihua, Tonghua, Yuhua, and Mothlet. She didn't know why the driver was asking her this, but nodded.

"How old are they?"

"They are seventeen."

"How about this?" he said. "I know there are several wholers among you, and they are now energized after having just eaten some buns and drunk some water. In order to guarantee that they don't make trouble when we open the door, you should let your granddaughters crawl out through the window first." He said, "Once we have your granddaughters in hand, we will open the door and each go our separate ways."

With this, the situation took an abrupt change of course. The driver's flushed expression immediately changed hue, like the sun disappearing behind the clouds. After briefly considering what he had said, the villagers decided it sounded reasonable. The villagers behind Grandma Mao Zhi started moving forward, into the center of the hall. The sun had already passed over the memorial hall, and the sun rays that had been shining in through the front window had at some point shifted to the back window. The main hall was covered in a gentle red light, and the midday heat had started to dissipate.

A cool breeze began to blow through the hall, and with this breeze everyone gradually came to their senses. Some of the older villagers walked up and stood next to Grandma Mao Zhi, and said to the driver in the window, "Son, look at us down here. We are blind, crippled, deaf, mute, and paralyzed. Some of us are missing an arm or a leg. While it is true that there are a few wholers among us, they are all over sixty. How could we possibly make any trouble? If you let us come out and return to Liven, we will bow down to you in eternal gratitude."

"Don't waste my time with this." The driver looked up at the sky and said, "Will you let the four girls out or not?"

No one responded, and instead everyone looked at Huaihua and her three nin sisters, and then at Grandma Mao Zhi. Grandma Mao Zhi was as pale as a sheet, and the corners of her mouth were trembling. The wrinkles on her face were twitching, like a spiderweb that had been blown apart by the wind. She wasn't sure whether or not she should let her granddaughters go out first, and wasn't even sure whether or not they themselves would be willing. The main hall again became completely silent. The sound of the setting sun shining in through the window was as loud as the cicadas crying under the sunset, reverberating in everyone's ears. In this deathly silence, Huaihua suddenly announced in a loud voice,

"I'll go. I'd prefer to go out and die rather than live in this stifling place."

Having said this, she pushed the table to the window, then placed the three-legged chair on top, leaning the side without legs against the door frame. She climbed up onto the table, and then onto the chair. From there, she extended her arm and the wholer outside grabbed her hand and pulled her through the window.

Yuhua also climbed up and was pulled out.

Mothlet also climbed up and was pulled out.

Now only Blind Tonghua remained standing next to her grandmother. Grandma Mao Zhi looked to the driver and said, "She is blind." He replied, "The blind one has to come as well, because that way I know you'll worry about her." Tonghua turned to her grandmother and said, "Grandma, I can't see a thing, and don't have anything to fear." She began walking over to the door, and Grandma Mao Zhi led her to the table, then helped guide her onto the chair on the table, so that the people outside could pluck her out through the window as though she were a chicken.

With this, the villagers had done everything they were supposed to, handed over everything they were supposed to, and said everything they were supposed to. They waited for the people outside to open the door. At this point, however, the driver peered in at them with a faint smile. That smile was as sallow as a field of turnip mustard blossoms in the summer, both accommodating and unyielding. He abruptly shouted, "Fuck this. Are you trying to fuck around with us? Did you think we wouldn't know? Did you think I really believed that you passed over all your money? I saw that many of you still have money hidden on your persons. You have money hidden under the bricks beneath your bedrolls, in the cracks in the wall of the latrine, and under the crystal coffin. You've hidden your earnings from the performances everywhere. I'm telling you . . ." He suddenly started roaring, opening his mouth as wide as a city gate, "I'm telling you, if you don't pass *all* of your money beneath the door, tonight I'll let my people enjoy Huaihua's beauty, and before nightfall I'll let them ravage the bodies of her three nin sisters."

Having said this, he immediately climbed back down the ladder, like someone sinking below the waves. Soon, there was no trace of him.

The setting sun continued shining in through the windows in the back of the hall, shining onto the villagers' bodies and faces.

Further Reading:

1) **Well water.** *Refers to cold water that has just been drawn from a well.*

3) **Rest period.** *Refers to a midday nap.*

Chapter 7: The door is open.... The door is open....

The sky was almost completely dark.

All of the money had been passed beneath the door. None of them had a single cent left hidden on their persons or in their rooms. First, Paraplegic Woman passed over the money she had earned for the last few performances and sewn into her sleeve, next Deafman Ma passed over the cash he had hidden in the crease of his two-layered metal billfold, and then Mute passed over the bills he had hidden under the bricks beneath his bedroll. Eventually, everyone's money had been sent outside. By now the sun had set, and not a trace of red remained in the back window. As the villagers were waiting for the door to be opened, the man collecting the money shouted to the people inside,

"Hey! The sun has gone down. You can come out tomorrow. Just spend another night inside with Lenin's crystal coffin, and tomorrow when you leave we'll issue each of you your salary for the past six months."

After he finished speaking, everything became silent again.

Night fell, and a humid atmosphere pervaded every side room in the memorial hall. The person had said that it was dark, and that tomorrow they would discuss leaving, but by this point the villagers were all too exhausted to say anything, or even think about anything.

It was as if the question of whether or not the door would be opened, and even whether or not they would be allowed to leave, had become completely immaterial.

The villagers returned to their respective rooms, where they lay down and stared at the ceiling. The moonlight poured in through the windows like water. The snow-white ceiling appeared pale green in the evening light. No one said anything, or asked anything. It was as if they were all extraordinarily tired, and just wanted to lie down and rest and wait silently for whatever was to follow.

They assumed that the rest of the night would pass like this, but shortly after dinnertime the villagers began hearing Tonghua's, Yuhua's, and Mothlet's sharp screams coming from far away, like bloodcurdling wails emanating from the mountain or the gorge. The sound was bitingly cold, and seemed as if it was coming from the dead. It stopped and started, like a chunk of ice flowing down a river on a bitterly cold winter day. Periodically, they could also hear the wholers' maniacal laughter as they shouted, "Come do them. They are small, so their holes are small, tight and livening. . . . Whoever doesn't do them will regret it the rest of their lives!" These shouts were followed immediately by the nins' screams and cries. As the villagers heard these sounds, there were so startled, they all sat up in their beds.

Eventually, they all went to Grandma Mao Zhi's room, and saw that the light in her room was shining bright, as she sat in the corner listening to the cries. Over and over again she slapped her face, as if she were slapping someone else's face or a wind-dried board. She cursed hoarsely,

"Go die. . . .

"Go die. . . .

"Go die. . . .

"Go die right now. . . .

"Go die right now. . . ."

Grandma Mao Zhi's slaps and curses drowned out the wails and struggles of the nins outside, just as the sound of a storm outside might drown out the sound of someone knocking at the door. Grandma Mao Zhi was in her seventies, and the villagers found it nearly unbearable to see someone so elderly beat and curse herself in this way. They rushed over and restrained her.

Paraplegic Woman, who shared a room with Grandma Mao Zhi, came over and grasped her hand, saying repeatedly,

"Auntie, no one is blaming you. . . . Auntie, really, no one has uttered a word blaming you."

The villagers all hurried over and restrained Grandma Mao Zhi until she calmed down. By the time she recovered, the nins' cries had ceased. The entire world became deathly quiet, and there was only the sound of the moon rays and starlight shining in through the window.

In this way, the night passed.

The villagers remained in their respective rooms, unable to sleep. Without saying a word or moving a muscle, they were waiting for the next day to hurry up and arrive. Only One-Legged Monkey sat restlessly in bed. Eventually, he exclaimed, "Fuck this!" and proceeded to drink the unboiled water the wholers had passed through the window, after which he had diarrhea and spent the entire night running back and forth to the latrine. While doing so, he systematically pried off all of the embossed gold characters from the lid of Chief Liu's crystal coffin in the pit below Lenin's. From this point on, he became Liven's most extraordinary resident.

But as everyone was waiting for daybreak, little Polio Boy got up to do something, and as he passed in front of the memorial hall door, he suddenly cried out,

"It's open! The door's open!

"The door's open! The door's open!"

Everyone hurriedly got out of bed. The paraplegics, cripples, blind people, and deaf people all rushed toward the door of the memorial hall. A cripple fell to the ground; a woman was pushed into a door frame and started bleeding. Deafman Ma didn't hear the shouting, but when he saw everyone rushing toward the door, he also ran out of his room, naked. It was true—the two red doors were now wide open. The early morning breeze was blowing in as though it were blowing over directly from the city wall. The sky was still cloudy. There was a glistening layer of water on the limestone kowtow steps in front of the memorial hall, and the pines and cypresses on either side of the hall were like a row of shadows in the darkness. The villagers rushed out like people emerging from prison or a cave, and stood in front of the memorial hall doors rubbing their eyes. Some stretched their arms, as though trying to grasp the sky and hold it tight. Then someone remembered Huaihua and her nin sisters, and said, "Quick, let's go look for Tonghua, Huaihua, Yuhua, and Mothlet."

They all started running down the stone kowtow steps.

They quickly found Tonghua, Huaihua, Yuhua, and Mothlet in the empty rooms that were used to sell odds and ends at the base of the kowtow steps. The rooms were full of empty bowls, chopsticks, and clothing that the wholers had left behind when they departed, and there was also a noxious odor of uneaten food. The girls had been left completely naked, each of them tied up in a different small room. Tonghua and Huaihua were each tied to a bed, while Yuhua and Mothlet were tied to a couple of chairs. Tonghua, Yuhua, and Mothlet had not only been beaten by the wholers, but because they were all tiny nins, their genitalia had been ripped open, and the area between their legs was covered in blood. In order to prevent them from crying out, their shirts and pants had been stuffed into their mouths. Mothlet's mouth had been stuffed with her underwear. By the time the villagers found them, it was already light outside, the white fog having been replaced by clear light, and the villagers could clearly see that the girls' tender bodies were all bruised, and that beneath the bruises the girls were as pale as death.

It occurred to everyone that Grandma Mao Zhi had not yet emerged from the memorial hall, so they all hurried back to the side room and saw that she had put on the burial outfit that she normally wore only while performing. The black silk shimmered and sparkled in the dark room. Grandma Mao Zhi was just sitting there, expressionless, as though she already knew what had happened outside the memorial hall.

The villagers said, "Auntie, the door is open."

Grandma Mao Zhi replied, "I just want to die. Tell everyone to go back down the mountain and return home."

The villagers said, "Last night the wholers ran away. Auntie, lead us back to Liven. You must lead us back."

She said, "You should all quickly return home."

The villagers said, "Huaihua and her nin sisters have all been violated."

Grandma Mao Zhi stared in shock, then pondered for a moment and said, "That's fine. This way, in the future, everyone in the village will know that wholers are to be feared. This way, it won't occur to anyone to want to go out and perform again, and they'll appreciate the advantages of remaining in Liven."

When the sun came up, the mountain ridge became as hot as summer. Grandma Mao Zhi was wearing her burial clothes as she led the villagers, who were pulling, pushing, carrying, and dragging the luggage and bedrolls they had taken with them when they originally left the village of Liven. Together, they descended Spirit Mountain and headed back to Liven. In the end, it was in fact still winter, and the land outside the Balou mountains was covered in snow and ice. It was only in the mountains that the seasons had skipped over springtime and proceeded directly to summer. The trees were beginning to bud and put out new leaves, and even the grass on the pockmarked slope had turned green, transforming the entire slope into a verdant expanse.

The group of villagers headed down the mountain together. They saw many things along the way, including sighted wholers standing in the fields with black blindfolds over their eyes and tapping various objects, practicing the Acute-Listening technique, and people with their ears stuffed full of cotton or cornstalks, a board or piece of cardboard hanging next to their face, practicing the Firecracker-on-the-Ear technique. There were also women and girls sitting in a sunny area in front of a village, embroidering images on tree leaves or pieces of paper, together with some people in their forties or fifties wearing black burial clothes as they hoed the fields, carried manure, and spread fertilizer. As the villagers slowly walked through the mountain ridge, they saw many wholers wearing burial clothes. In one village, tens or even hundreds of villagers were gathered on a hillside hoeing wheat sprouts, all of them wearing black silk and satin burial clothes with

427

large golden *longevity, sacrifice,* and *libation* characters embroidered on the back. They were laughing as they raised and lowered their hoes, and the entire mountainside was filled with the rustling of their silk clothes and the shimmering of their burial outfits in the sunlight.

After the residents of Liven passed this village, it was no longer merely people in their forties and fifties who wore burial clothes, but boys and girls, wearing them to school. Even nursing babies had golden *longevity, sacrifice,* and *libation* characters on their backs.

Throughout the land, these *longevity, sacrifice,* and *libation* characters could be found everywhere.

The entire land had become a world of longevity, sacrifice, and libation.

Book 13: Fruit

CHAPTER 1: JUST BEFORE DUSK, CHIEF LIU RETURNS TO SHUANGHUAI

Just before dusk, Chief Liu returned to Shuanghuai.

Chief Liu and the delegation that had been assigned to travel to Russia to purchase Lenin's corpse initially arrived at the county seat around noon, and from there Chief Liu instructed the delegation to get out of the car and return home for the moment. As for himself, he drove to Spirit Mountain to examine the Lenin Memorial Hall.

By the time Chief Liu arrived back at the county seat's eastern gate, it was already almost dusk. He did not immediately proceed into the city, however, but rather told his driver to go home while he himself waited just outside the city. He stood by the side of the road, as if afraid of running into anyone. He wandered back and forth, hovering like a specter at the city gate.

He wanted to wait until the sky was completely dark before returning home.

This was a day at the beginning of the *jimao* Year of the Hare, 1999. Although it was the middle of winter, it was not very cold. There were a few blocks of ice on the sides of the river, but the water in the center was still flowing freely, producing a white belt that stretched in both directions. In the depths of the Balou mountains, meanwhile, it

431

was as sweltering as in the middle of summer. The trees were all green, the plants were budding, and the Lenin Mausoleum was surrounded on all sides by lush, green vegetation.

But in the end, this was merely a peculiarity of the Balou mountain region, and in the outside world, circumstances and the climate both remained unchanged. Winter was still winter. The trees were all bare, and the mountainside was dark and ashen. In the fields, the dull and pale green wheat sprouts were still dormant, but seemed to have an oppressive air. The villages were all so quiet that they resembled ghost towns. There was a slight breeze from the north, and it blew like a knife under the eaves of the houses and through the streets and back alleys.

There was no sun.

The sky was gray, and some fog began to develop in the evening, though it would probably be more accurate to say that a thick layer of winter air spread out over the ground, over the face of the mountain, and throughout the deep gorge. In the depths of the region, people seemed lazy, as if they had not slept enough but still needed to get up and go about their day. When they looked up, they saw that the sun was hidden behind the clouds, like a corn pancake hidden inside a skillet.

Ordinarily, it would have been snowing at this time of year, but it had been a dry winter and therefore had merely been bitterly cold. Everyone throughout the land had a fever, and the sound of sneezing and coughing could be heard all night long. Cold medicine sold like grain during a famine.

The livestock, however, were in no danger of getting sick. The pigs hid in the pigsties, sleeping all day and waking up only to eat, and after eating they would sneeze brightly and go back to sleep. The sheep, meanwhile, grazed on the mountain slope during the day and at dusk returned to their pen to pass the frigid winter night. As for the chickens, when the sun was out they would scratch for food where it was sunny and swallow some sand to aid their digestion. When there was no sun, they would hide at the base of the mountain wall or in a corner of the village alleys.

It was in the middle of this sort of winter that Chief Liu abruptly returned to Shuanghuai, together with the delegation he had sent to Russia. He came in a car with six people, all of whom had frosty expressions. The situation surprised everyone, as if they had set out for Beijing but arrived at Nanjing instead.

Half a month earlier, Chief Liu had visited Spirit Mountain with red silk for the memorial hall's ribbon-cutting ceremony. A flower had already been placed in the middle of the silk strip, and the red-handled scissors had already been prepared. Chief Liu had taken the scissors and tried them out on a book, finding them to be so sharp that they immediately sliced off a corner of the cover. He also watched the residents of Liven perform their special-skills routines at different scenic spots throughout the area, but these routines were already somewhat stale after six months of continual performances, and he decided that for the ribbon-cutting ceremony they would need to develop a completely new routine, which would cause the tens of thousands of spectators to cheer in astonishment.

Chief Liu had decided that he definitely couldn't cut the ribbon before the memorial hall's inaugural performance, but rather would do so immediately following the conclusion of the performance, whereupon he would announce the official opening of the memorial hall. He would announce that the delegation he had sent to purchase Lenin's corpse had arrived in the capital, where they were filling out the paperwork needed to go to Russia. In two or three days, once the paperwork was complete, they would depart for Russia. Then, in ten days or two weeks—or, at most, twenty days—they would ship Lenin's corpse back from Russia and install it in the memorial hall's crystal coffin.

Chief Liu would use his sonorous voice to announce to the tens of thousands of people in the audience that the following year Shuanghuai's revenue would increase from nothing to fifty million yuan, then double to a hundred million the following year and double again to two hundred million the year after that. Within four years, the county would be able to issue each of its residents a Western-style house with a gable and a pointed roof. Beginning on the day that Lenin's corpse was installed in the memorial hall, none of the Shuanghuai peasants would ever need to pay any more grain tax, and instead the local treasuries would send all of the requisite funds to the national coffers in a series of monthly installments. Beginning in the first month after the installation of Lenin's corpse in the memorial hall, every family of peasants in the county would drink calcium-fortified milk for breakfast every morning. Those who didn't drink the milk would not receive the refrigerator and color televisions distributed by the county, and if they had already received them they would have to return them. Whichever family didn't eat ribs and eggs for lunch wouldn't receive nutritional supplements like ginseng and black-boned chicken at the end of the month.

In short, during the six months after the installation of Lenin's corpse, the lives of the people of Shuanghuai would improve immeasurably. Peasants working in the fields would be issued salaries, which would be determined not by how much grain they harvested but rather by the number and size of the flowers they planted in the fields along the road. Those who planted more than half a *mu* of flowers would receive several thousand yuan a month in salary, and at the end of the year they would receive a bonus of more than ten thousand yuan. Because Lenin would be resting on Spirit Mountain in the depths of the Balou mountains, the Shuanghuai county seat would become a bustling metropolis. Water would flow nonstop through the streets, and there wouldn't be a single speck of dust to be found anywhere. The sidewalks on either side of the road would be paved not with brick, but rather with granite or marble, and at key locations like major intersections and in front of the county committee and county government buildings, the sidewalk would be paved, not with granite or even marble, but rather with Nanyang jade from Funiu Mountain.

As Chief Liu was speaking, someone objected that having a lot of money was not necessarily a good thing, since money can change people. Chief Liu, however, had already anticipated this objection, and took this opportunity to warn Shuanghuai's seven hundred and thirty thousand peasants and its eighty thousand city-dwellers that, by that point, all the people—from the county seat to the depths of the Balou mountains—would have so much money they would either have more than enough to pay for their house and food and a car, or become suicidal, treating money as though it weren't worth anything at all. He warned them that, after the county's hundred thousand or so households all became rich, they shouldn't permit their children *not* to study and read newspapers, and they shouldn't just ride around all day, enjoying fancy meals, going through money like dirt, and reveling in the fruits of other people's labor. They shouldn't hire people from other counties to come to their homes to work as nannies and order them about as though they weren't even human. Even distant rural areas could develop problems with gambling and drugs, and when they reached that stage, Shuanghuai would need to pass some new laws, among them:

1) *Any peasants who fail to plant at least two* mu *of flowers in front and back of their house, along the road, and in front of their field will have their year-end bonus cut in half (but not to less than fifty thousand yuan).*

2) *All households whose children do not graduate from college will have three years of their salaries and bonuses cut, and all households with a child who has gone to college will receive double salary and bonus (and not less than two hundred yuan).*

3) *All families who donate their extra money to charitable causes—such as changing the card tables in their village's geriatric residence and paving the paths to the village's gardens with bricks and covering them with limestone—will be reimbursed for twice as much as they have donated; however, if they spend their extra money on gambling and drugs, the county will send them to the poorest area in a neighboring county to work the land, thereby returning them to their former poor life; their family's entire salary of several tens of thousands of yuan will be transferred to a poor school or village in a neighboring*

county; and they themselves won't be allowed to return to
Shuanghuai until they have been successfully reeducated.

In order to prevent the residents of the county from going crazy as
soon as they became rich, Chief Liu had jotted down a dozen or so
new laws and regulations in his notebook. He recognized that the real
climax of the memorial hall's opening ceremony would lie not in the
villagers' special-skills performance, but rather in his own emotional
and moving speech. He knew that as soon as he finished speaking,
everyone on stage would immediately begin jumping around like crazy,
and he was afraid that they might start cheering him the way people
had cried out, "Long Live Chairman Mao" at the height of the Cultural
Revolution, and that each household might hang his portrait in the
center of the wall of the main room of their house, and that they might
kowtow to his portrait the way they would to Lenin in the memorial
hall. Actually, from the day that the delegation charged with purchasing
Lenin's remains left Shuanghuai and headed to Beijing, Chief Liu had
hardly been able to sleep. His blood was coursing through his veins,
and by the time the residents of Liven began arriving at Spirit Mountain for the performance, he couldn't sleep at all. He hadn't closed his
eyes in more than seventy-two hours, but he nevertheless remained as
wide awake as if he had just had a long bath and a good night's rest.

For Chief Liu, waiting for the day when he would finally be able
to announce the opening of the Lenin Memorial Hall was like a lake
waiting for a man dying of thirst. Regardless of how thirsty the man
is, it will still take several days for him to arrive at the lake. Chief Liu
became increasingly impatient, but he was after all the county chief,
and therefore the more impatient he became the more important it
was that he remain calm.

After escorting the delegation to their car, and then returning to
the district and provincial seat to attend some meetings, Chief Liu led
Secretary Shi back to the countryside, to the rural side of the county
beyond the Balou mountains. In order to calm his sense of agitation,
he went to a mountain region at the southern end of the county, where
they didn't even have telephone coverage. He didn't go there to conduct

any research or to visit the poor, but rather simply to hang out next to a reservoir and to liven for a few days. Not until the day before the ribbon-cutting ceremony, when Liven's performance troupe returned to Shuanghuai and went up to Spirit Mountain, did he return to Spirit Mountain and begin feeling fully livened again. However, it was at this point—when Chief Liu and the villagers had just climbed the mountain, he had just seen the new acts that the special-skills troupers had added to their repertoire, and he had just sat down in the Lenin Memorial Hall—it was at this point that an urgent matter came up.

This was an extremely urgent matter.

It was as if an earth-shattering thunderclap suddenly appeared in the middle of a cloudless sky, after which clouds immediately moved in from all sides and rain began pouring down, without a trace of sun or moonlight.

"District Secretary Niu wants you to come back to the district as soon as possible."

"What's the matter?"

"You must return today. Right now. At this very instant."

"Tomorrow the memorial hall will have its ribbon-cutting ceremony."

"Secretary Niu says you must return immediately."

"Do I definitely need to leave today? Couldn't I go tomorrow after the ceremony?"

"He says you have to be at his home tonight."

"What can possibly be this urgent? Am I the only person he wants to see?"

"Chief Liu, do you think there is anyone else whom Secretary Niu would personally invite to his home?"

The person speaking to him was one of the county's deputy secretaries. After taking the phone call from the district seat, the deputy secretary had tried desperately to contact Chief Liu, and when he couldn't find Liu he proceeded to get a car and drive up to Spirit Mountain himself. As he was speaking with Chief Liu, he hadn't even had a chance to wash the dust from his face, and sweat was still dripping from his forehead like drops of mud.

Chief Liu said, "Fuck, not only does he not show up for the inauguration ceremony, but he has to pick this precise moment to interrupt."

The deputy secretary said quickly, "Chief Liu, if you leave now, then you can probably be back tomorrow in time for the ceremony."

So, Chief Liu went. He didn't take anyone with him, and instead drove urgently down the mountain and toward the district seat. On the way, when he was able to get a phone connection he called up Secretary Niu, who said, "What do you mean a momentous matter? This is a thousand times—no, ten thousand times—bigger than a momentous matter. You'll see once you arrive!" With this, Secretary Niu hung up the phone as if snapping a branch in half. Then, Chief Liu told his driver to drive like crazy, and by nightfall they managed to cover the five hundred *li* to Jiudu, where they proceeded right up to Secretary Niu's front door.

The moon was cold and bright, and it seemed as though there was a thin layer of ice on the ground, but Secretary Niu lived in a large courtyard, and inside it was as warm as the abnormal summer weather atop Spirit Mountain. In the past, whenever Chief Liu came to visit, he would plop down on the sofa in the central building, as though he were in his own home. This time, however, when he entered and saw Secretary Niu's frosty expression, he just stood in the doorway. Secretary Niu hung up the phone and tossed Chief Liu the newspaper he was holding, as though tossing a rag onto a table.

Chief Liu said, as he was accustomed to doing in the past, "I'm starving."

Secretary Niu said, "Then starve. Something extremely urgent has come up."

Chief Liu said, "No matter how urgent it is, I still need to eat."

Secretary Niu squinted at him, and said, "I myself haven't been able to eat all day, and yet you want to eat now?"

Chief Liu still had no idea what had happened, so he merely stood there and stared at Secretary Niu. He asked,

"Could I at least have a glass of water?"

Secretary Niu stood up from the sofa, and said,

"There isn't even time for you to drink a glass of water. The provincial governor wants to see you immediately. He wants you to come in tomorrow and go to his office."

Chief Liu's gaze followed Secretary Niu, and he asked,

"What has happened?"

Secretary Niu poured him a glass of water, and said,

"The group that was sent to buy Lenin's corpse from Russia was detained in Beijing."

Chief Liu didn't take the glass of water, and instead his face turned deathly pale.

"What happened? Their paperwork was all in order, and they even had several blank letters of introduction that they could fill out when necessary."

Still holding the glass of water, Secretry Niu said,

"What happened? You'll know when you see the governor tomorrow."

Chief Liu said,

"But I've never met the governor before."

Secretary Niu leaned against the old, dark red sandalwood table, and said,

"This time, the governor wants to meet with you alone."

Chief Liu took the glass of water from Secretary Niu, and quickly downed it. Then he wiped his mouth and said,

"If he wants to see me, then I'll go see him. After all, it's not like he's Chairman Mao."

Secretary Niu looked at Chief Liu, then paused and said,

"If you leave now, you can make it to the provincial capital by nightfall. It is quite possible, however, that after this meeting you will no longer be the county chief, and I will no longer be the Party secretary."

Chief Liu paused, then raised his voice and said,

"Secretary Niu, don't be afraid. I'll take responsibility for whatever happens."

Secretary Niu slowly broke into a smile, and said:

"What should I be afraid of? I was already planning to retire at the end of the year."

Chief Liu went to pour himself another half glass of water. The water was still a little hot, and as he waved it back and forth he said,

"I'll have another sip of water and then will leave for the provincial capital. You can rest assured, Secretary Niu, that there is no river that cannot be forded, and no bridge that cannot be crossed. When I see the governor, I'll emphasize to him how important it is to Shuanghuai that we bring Lenin's corpse back, and will also stress that it will be enormously beneficial for the district, and even the entire province."

Secretary Niu continued smiling, his bright yellow face resembling a baked bun enveloped in a cloud of steam. Without saying a word, he took the glass from Chief Liu and refilled it. After Chief Liu drank the water, Secretary Niu urged him to quickly proceed to the provincial capital, saying that the road from Jiudu to the capital was under repair and traffic would probably be backed up, and therefore he needed to set off as quickly as possible.

Chief Liu proceeded to make his way back to the provincial capital in the dark. On the way there, his driver said that the foot he was using for the accelerator was tired and swollen, and that the car's tires were crowding the moonlight on the side of the road and frightening away the sparrows perched in the roadside trees. Finally, at dawn, they reached the provincial capital, where buildings were as abundant as trees in a forest.

When he had set out for the county seat the previous evening, the only thing Chief Liu had been able think about was that he should kowtow to himself, burn some incense, and perhaps shed a few tears. After all, for better or for worse, he was the county chief, and there were eight hundred and ten thousand people who, when they saw him, would want to kneel down. After arriving at the provincial capital that morning, he hadn't dared to even eat a bowl of jellied tofu, so afraid was he that he would lose time. Instead, he rushed to the government building on an empty stomach. After explaining why he was there and signing in, he entered that brown marble courtyard. When he arrived at the ten-plus-story building, he took out his county chief ID card and had the gatekeeper get in touch with the governor's secretary. The governor said he should wait downstairs "for a while."

This "while," however, became a virtual eternity, to the point that he ended up spending more than ten times as long waiting than it had taken him to get there from Shuanghuai in the first place. Finally, when it was almost noon, a message came from upstairs instructing him to proceed to the sixth floor. To his surprise, the governor spoke to him only for the length of time that it takes a drop of water to fall from the roof of a building.

The governor said, "Have a seat."

He said, "I don't have anything to say. I summoned you here just to see what kind of person you are. I couldn't believe that there was an official below me who would dare to raise money to go to Russia to purchase Lenin's corpse."

He said, "You won't sit down? If you won't have a seat, then you may go now. I already know how great you are. Go out and find a place better than the Kremlin to stay at. I've already sent someone to Beijing to retrieve the delegation you assigned to go to Russia, and when they arrive here in two or three days I want to see them as well. No matter how busy I may be, I will definitely want to have a chance to meet Shuanghuai's glorious leaders."

He said, "After I have met Shuanghuai's leaders, you can escort them back to the county seat, and prepare to hand over the county's work to your next-in-commmand."

After having traveled through the night to reach the capital, Chief Liu discovered that this was all the governor wanted to say to him. The governor did not speak very loudly, sounding instead like a breeze passing under a door that has been closed tightly to keep out the winter chill. But when Chief Liu heard him, he felt his mind go blank, and all that was left was some black mist and white clouds. He had already missed three meals in a row, not having consumed anything at all since the two glasses of water that he had had at Secretary Niu's house. Now, he suddenly felt so hungry that he was about to collapse on the governor's desk, his legs as weak as a willow branch in the spring, or as the noodles that the people of Shuanghuai rolled just for him.

Needless to say, he couldn't very well collapse in the governor's office. He was after all a county chief, and was responsible for looking after eight hundred and ten thousand people, all of whom would kowtow when they saw him, and therefore he naturally couldn't just collapse in the governor's office. Outside, the sun was shining brightly on the roof of the building, and its rays were beaming in through the governor's window. As his eyesight started to blur and he began to feel faint, Chief Liu gazed at the governor—the same way that, two years earlier when he visited the Shuanghuai county jail, those criminals had stared at him. Chief Liu wanted to sit down. There was a sofa behind him, but given that he hadn't sat down when the governor originally invited him to, he naturally couldn't very well do so now that the governor had already asked him to leave. He was also dying of thirst, and was desperate to find some water to wet his parched throat. Behind the governor there was some mineral water that someone had brought from the mountains. Chief Liu looked at the jug of water, and although the governor saw him staring, not only did he not offer Chief Liu any water to quench his burning throat, but he even took a black leather attaché case from the desk and tucked it under his arm.

The governor gestured for him to leave, the way one might brush away a fly.

Chief Liu had no choice but to depart.

Before departing, Chief Liu took one final glance at the governor's office. This was the first time he had ever stepped foot inside and it would probably be the last. He told himself he must make an effort to examine it carefully. The office was not as big as he had imagined, nor as stately. All told, there were three rooms, with a desk, a leather chair, and a row of bookcases, together with more than a dozen flowerpots and the sofa behind him. In addition, there were three or four telephones on the desk.

Later, Chief Liu was not entirely certain what else had been there. Of course, he saw and remembered the governor's expression and appearance, just as he remembered the precise size of the crystal coffin in Lenin's Memorial Hall. The governor's face had a layer of deep red beneath its surface swarthiness, as shiny as if it had been soaking in ginseng soup for many years. The governor had a round face, narrow forehead, and white hair. His face resembled a well-aged apple, which had developed many wrinkles over time but which, because it was originally of high quality, still retained a delicious apple fragrance. The governor was wearing a light yellow sweater, under a well-made gray jacket and a tan wool coat. He was wearing a pair of black round-toe leather shoes, and his pants were made from a dark blue fabric. Actually, there was nothing particularly extraordinary about his outfit, it being no different from that of any older man of a certain class whom you might encounter in the street.

The only difference was his tone of voice, which was very calm and measured, but carried a trace of icy coldness. He was the governor, and could discuss a cataclysm the way other people would discuss a light breeze and drizzle. Things that would leave other people petrified, he could discuss as though they were icy hot—when, in fact, those embers contained a piece of ice that would never melt.

The governor mentioned this cataclysmic event as though it were a willow catkin floating to the ground, or a sesame seed that had gotten wedged in an ox's hoofs. At this point, Chief Liu did not realize that the governor's speech was deeper than the sea, and instead he was merely thinking that he had traveled all night and then waited all day only to find that the governor merely intended to say a few words to him. Chief Liu desperately wanted to offer a remark, even if this remark was as short as a bean sprout or as fleeting as a flame, but the governor took his leather attaché case and prepared to walk out, leaving Chief Liu with no choice but to depart as well.

With those few words—which lasted no longer than the length of a chopstick, or the amount of time it takes a drop of water to fall from the roof of a house—and before Chief Liu even had a chance to come to his senses, he was ushered, weak-kneed, out of the governor's office. It was only then that he suddenly awoke to the fact that the governor had actually seen him—and he had seen the governor—and that the governor had said everything he wanted to say, and in the process had thrown away everything Chief Liu had worked for his entire life. Chief Liu felt as though he had been hurled from a hot summer into a bitterly cold winter, that his life's work had been tossed to the wind. In the blink of an eye, everything was blown away to who knows where. However, even though Chief Liu and the governor had just seen each other, as Chief Liu was leaving the office it occurred to him that he had not had a chance to utter even a single word.

While staying at a guest house in the provincial capital, Chief Liu got sick. He caught a cold and started running a fever. If he had been in Shuanghuai, his secretary and the county hospital would have sent him the very best medicine, but here in the provincial capital he had no choice but to spend the next two or three days in a delirium, popping one fistful of pills after another, as though they were fried peas. He was afraid that his fever wouldn't break, and that he would keep coughing until his cold developed into pneumonia. By the time the delegation had been summoned back from Beijing by cadres from the provincial Party committee, and the governor had spent a drop of time seeing them, Chief Liu found that his cold was somewhat improved and that his fever had begun to subside. It was as if he had come down with the cold and the fever solely in order to have an excuse to sleep while waiting for the delegation to return from Beijing—waiting for them to return so that he could speak to them.

"What did the governor say?"

"The governor didn't say anything. He just wanted to see us, to see what was wrong with us. He said that if we needed, he could have the provincial psychiatric hospital set up a clinic in Shuanghuai."

"Set up what kind of clinic?"

"He said it would be a political psychology clinic. He said he was concerned that we were all suffering from a form of political insanity."

"Fuck his grandmother. What else did he say?"

"He told us to return to Shuanghuai, where we will report to our post for the final time, because in a few days he was going to send someone to relieve us of our responsibilities."

"Fuck his grandmother. Fuck his great-grandmother. Fuck his grandmother's grandmother."

After cursing for a while, Chief Liu had no choice but to lead the delegation from the provincial capital back to the county seat. They felt like people who, after studying diligently for an exam for more than a decade, discovered just as they were about to enter the examination room that they had been denied entry by the site's managers, and as a result their ten years of diligent study had disappeared in the blink of an eye and the dreams they had nurtured their entire life had collapsed behind them.

The delegation set out when the sky was still dark, and first took a train to the district, then proceeded back to Shuanghuai in a car sent by the county. For the duration of the trip, there was commotion everywhere, but neither the country chief nor his companions uttered a word. Chief Liu resembled someone on his deathbed, and it was truly heartrending. During this entire journey of several hundred *li*, he sat in the front row without saying a single word, and therefore no one dared to say anything to him either.

The delegation had left for Beijing after having filled out a mountain of paperwork to go to Russia. They had even bought the tickets to fly from Beijing to Russia. But it was at this point that—because they were traveling to Russia for the express purpose of purchasing Lenin's corpse, which was interred beneath Moscow's Red Square— they discovered that they needed to get one of China's departments to stamp the forms they had brought with them from the county seat. This was a round, red stamp, containing only a dozen or so characters. But when they went to that department to get the stamp, someone asked them to sit down and wait for a moment, inviting them to have a drink of water and not to worry. The person brought them each a glass of water, and then left.

Soon someone else arrived to lead them away. He asked them many questions, such as whether they had prepared enough money to buy Lenin's corpse, where the memorial hall housing Lenin's corpse was located, how big it was, and whether they had worked out the technology needed to maintain the corpse. He also asked about the Spirit Mountain Forest Park where the corpse would be installed, including how much admission tickets would cost, and how they planned to use the money after the county became rich. Eventually, after he had asked everything that could conceivably be asked, and they'd answered everything that could be answered, he told them not to worry, saying that the person in charge of issuing the stamps had just left that morning with some other cadres to visit the Great Wall at Badaling. He said they had already notified him and told him to return immediately, and therefore asked the Shuanghuai delegation to wait patiently. He said, "When it is time to eat, we'll have someone bring you some food, and that way you can wait for the provincial cadres to return. If necessary, we'll send someone to lead them back."

In the blink of an eye, everything had ended, and it suddenly felt like a theater after a performance has concluded and everything has been put away. No one knew what Chief Liu was thinking during the ride home. No one knew what he had seen as he was climbing Spirit Mountain to visit the memorial hall. In any case, it was nightfall by the time he arrived at the eastern gate of the county seat. Chief Liu's face looked like a dead man's, and his hair had gone completely gray. It wasn't clear whether his hair had turned gray following his meeting with the governor or upon his return to the memorial hall. At any rate, it was now as gray as a nestful of white sparrows.

He had aged overnight.

He had become completely and utterly old.

Like an elderly man, Chief Liu trudged back to the county seat. His legs were weak, and it seemed as though he would topple over if he wasn't careful.

From the time Chief Liu left the debut performance at Spirit Mountain led by Grandma Mao Zhi, pace by pace,[1] only a few days had passed. Yet, he felt as if he had been away from Shuanghuai for several years, several decades, even half a lifetime. Now it seemed the people of Shuanghuai didn't even recognize him. In the past he would always ride in a car, with the scenery passing by outside the car window like wind blowing by his eyes. What was past was past, however, and now nothing was left.

Occasionally back then, he would get out of the car for some reason, and all of the people in the streets would recognize him and

erupt into a tumult. In the commotion, they would call out affection-
ately, "Chief Liu, Chief Liu," and would immediately surround him. If
they weren't trying to drag him home for dinner, they were bringing
a stool over for him to sit on, inviting him to rest in their doorway.
Some people would stuff a newborn baby into his arms, asking him
to hold it and begging him to grant the infant some good fortune and
to give it a name. Others would ask him to use his rather mediocre
handwriting to write out a couplet that they would then paste beside
their front door. Students would bring him a textbook or homework,
and ask him to sign it. When he walked through the city, he felt like
an emperor strolling down the street, and his mere presence would
make people deliriously happy, such that he wouldn't even pay attention to the scenery.

But today, it was dusk and fairly chilly, and there were very few
people out in the street. The doors to the shops and stores were all
closed, and even the little alleys had barely anyone in them. The main
street was as quiet as an empty room, and the only people still outside
were the streetwalkers.

It was because he was afraid of being seen that Chief Liu had
gotten out of the car before reaching the city gate, in order to cross
the old city streets on foot. However, the street was completely empty
and there was no one to be seen. No one was there to recognize him,
as people would have done in the past. Chief Liu craved that sort of
recognition. This was *his* county seat, and Shuanghuai was *his* county.
In Shuanghuai, there wasn't anyone who didn't know who he was.
When he walked down the street, everyone should have reacted in
surprise. Today, the street was nearly completely still. Occasionally he
would see someone, but he or she would quickly scurry away, hurrying
home without even glancing back. At one point he saw a woman, but
when she opened her door to call her children to come home and eat
dinner, she gazed at Chief Liu for quite some time, acting as though
she didn't really recognize him, and proceeded to call out, then closed
her door and went back inside.

The old city could not compare with the new one. The street was
full of houses with broken bricks and cracked tiles, though occasionally

there might be one or two houses with new tiles. Those houses were square-shaped with redbrick walls, and on this winter day they were like red pine coffins that had just been completed and had not even been painted yet.

Chief Liu walked alone, feeling that he had entered a graveyard, as if he had died and been brought back to life. Therefore, when people saw him, they didn't dare look him in the eye.

At one point, two people walked by him bearing shoulder poles full of fruit, heading to the market to sell their produce. Needless to say, they were both from Shuanghuai, and probably were from families that had been living there for many generations. Chief Liu told himself that as long as they recognized him as the county chief, and stopped and greeted him by name, the next day he would make sure to appoint one of them to be deputy director of the business bureau and the other to be deputy director of the foreign trade bureau. He was still Shuanghuai's county chief and Party secretary, and if he wanted to appoint someone to a certain position, there was nothing to stop him. Not only could he appoint them to serve as deputy directors, he could even appoint them to serve as bureau directors. All he wanted was for these two fruit-sellers to recognize him, put down the produce they were carrying, bow to him, and address him as Chief Liu, just as people used to do when they encountered him in the street.

Chief Liu stood there without moving, waiting for the men to recognize and address him.

The men only glanced at him before walking past. The rattling of their carrying poles gradually died off as they moved away, until eventually it could no longer be heard.

Chief Liu stood there in shock, watching the two figures as they disappeared into the darkness. They hadn't recognized him as the county chief! This made him feel as though there were snakes and bees in his heart. However, he continued smiling. It occurred to him that these two men would feel utterly wronged[3] at having missed out on their chance to be named deputy director.

Chief Liu walked all alone from the old city to the new one. Whenever he encountered someone, he would stop and wait for them to recognize him. If they did, he was prepared to promote them to the position of bureau chief or something. In the end, not a single person recognized him. Unlike the past, not one person, when they saw him, rushed over to stand by the side of the road, wearing a broad smile, nodding or bowing to him, and intoning softly, "County Chief Liu." By this point the sky was already dark, and he had moved from the city streets to a series of rural alleys. Not until he reached his family's courtyard did the street lamps behind him finally come on.

Chief Liu had never before been so anxious to have someone recognize him and call out to him by name. He had originally decided to return to the city under the cover of darkness because he had been afraid of running into anyone, but when no one ran into him—or if people saw him, they didn't recognize him—his heart felt as empty as a warehouse that had been robbed clean, to the point that only the empty building remained. At the very least, he told himself, the door-keeper of his family's courtyard would recognize him and would hurry out to greet him, but when he arrived at the entrance, the gatekeeper didn't come out to meet him as he normally did. From a distance, Chief Liu had seen a light on inside the house, but when he arrived the entranceway was as quiet as a tomb.

He had no idea where the old gatekeeper had gone. The gate was open, but no one was there.

After dusting his feet in the entranceway, Chief Liu walked into the courtyard.

He had to return home.

He couldn't remember how long it had been since he was last there. It seemed like a long, long time ago. His wife had told him that, if he could, he should stay away for three months, and he had replied, "Just watch me! I'll stay away for half a year."

It seemed that he had in fact been away from home for half a year. It was early spring when he left, and now it was the dead of winter.

Between visiting the countryside, attending meetings, and staying at the construction site of the Lenin Memorial Hall, it seemed that it had already been more than half a year. In fact, it was almost as if he had been away for several years. Sometimes he would be in the county seat, but he would prefer even to stay in his office rather than return home. And now, as he walked into his family's courtyard, he suddenly felt he couldn't remember what exactly his wife looked like. He couldn't remember whether she was thin or fat, light- or dark-skinned, or even what kind of clothes she liked to wear.

By this point the sky was already dark but the moon and stars were not visible, as clouds covered the sky like black fog. As Chief Liu stood in the dark entranceway, he concentrated for a while until he finally remembered that his wife was in her mid-thirties, was short, and had a white face with jet black hair that she would often wear down to her shoulders. He remembered that she had a mole on her face, or what people called a beauty mark, and that it was black and brown, but for the life of him he couldn't recall whether it was on the left or right side of her face.

The first thing he wanted to do as soon as he walked in was to check and see which side of her face the mole was on. He glanced up at his house, where he saw his wife's sparrowlike shadow flit past the kitchen window. It passed in an instant, and his heart felt as if it had been gently stroked by something. He immediately strode forward.

He wanted to return home.

After walking only a few steps, he turned left, thinking that he should stop first at his Hall of Devotion to pay his respects. It had been half a year, or perhaps even several years, since he was last home, and who knew what condition the hall was in.

He therefore went first to his Hall of Devotion. He opened the door, closed it behind him, then turned on the lights. When the lights came on, he gazed at the portraits on the wall, but no longer felt the sense of livening that he used to feel when he looked at them. The portraits of Marx, Engels, Stalin, Chairman Mao, Hoxha, Tito, Ho Chi Minh, Kim Il Sung, and Carlos Mariátegui were still hanging on the wall, just as before, and those of China's ten great military leaders were still hanging below them. The only difference was that Chief Liu's portrait was no longer on the second row where Lin Biao's had been, but rather was now on the first row behind those of Marx, Engels, Lenin, Stalin, and Mao.

Chief Liu stood in the center of the Hall of Devotion for what seemed like an eternity, letting the time in the room slowly flow past. In the end, he removed his portrait from its position behind Mao's, and instead placed it in front of Marx's, hanging it at the very front of the first row. Then, he filled in all of the empty rows on the sheet below his portrait, underlining them in red, and in the final space he wrote two rows of characters:

> *The greatest peasant leader in the world*
> *And the most prominent proletarian revolutionary in*
> *the third world.*

He drew nine red lines beneath each of those two rows of text. Those nine lines were like the thick red dragon he had described, dazzling and eye-catching. He stared at those two rows of text and the red dragon for a while, then knelt down and kowtowed to them, and to his own portrait. Next, he turned around and gazed at the portrait of his adoptive father, and lit him three sticks of incense. Finally he left the Hall of Devotion.

In the quiet night outside, he could hear the sound of a car in the distance. That low rumble sounded somewhat familiar, almost like the sound of his own car. Maybe Secretary Shi had received the news that he had returned and was coming to see him. Needless to say, at least his secretary, when he saw him, would address him as "County Chief Liu."

Chief Liu emerged from his Hall of Devotion and turned off the light. His black sedan was in fact parked in front of his house, and it was in fact Secretary Shi who had come to see him. From the time he was appointed as county chief and had designated Secretary Shi to be his secretary, the secretary had always addressed him as "County Chief Liu," and surely he would again now.

And, in fact, Secretary Shi had not stopped calling him "County Chief."

Further Reading:

1) **Pace by pace.** DIAL. *This refers to the act of stretching time out, and means to calculate everything to the fullest; it has nothing to do with taking actual steps.*

3) **Utterly wronged.** DIAL. *This refers to the act of completely missing out on an opportunity, and thus feeling wronged.*

Chapter 3: Chief Liu, Chief Liu, may I bow to you?

"I'm sorry, Chief Liu. I've wronged you, Chief Liu."

"Fuck your grandmother! I'll cut off your head! I'll shoot you! But even beheading or shooting you wouldn't be enough to relieve my fury."

"Chief Liu, Chief Liu, I've really wronged you, Chief Liu."

"Bow down, everyone bow down to me!"

"Don't blame him, don't blame Secretary Shi. Blame me for everything!"

"Get out! You lewd woman, you sow, you bitch, you weasel!"

"Chief Liu, don't beat her. Beat me instead. Look, her face is covered in blood. If you keep beating her, you'll kill her. Everything is my fault, it's all Secretary Shi's fault."

"Are you telling me not to beat her, and to beat you instead? Did you really think I was going to let you go?"

"Ah, ah, ahya. . . ."

"I've already fired you. After you've done your time in prison, I'll arrange for you to return home to work the fields."

"Beat me, Chief Liu! You are welcome to kick me to death, stomp me flat, or tread me to a pulp."

"I'll fuck eight generations of your ancestors, that's what I'll do. But for now I'll have the Public Security Bureau send you to prison. With one word, I can exterminate your entire family. I can drag your name through the mud, reducing you to the status of a rat in the street. I can make it difficult for you to even walk in Shuanghuai. I can make it such that there won't even be anywhere in Shuanghuai where you can go beg for food."

"I'm begging you, please don't beat him. Look, he's already lost consciousness. Old Liu, Chief Liu, I'm begging you to beat me instead."

"Fuck your grandmother. Tell me the truth: When you leave the house, everyone recognizes you as the county chief's wife, and addresses you as the first lady. Do you know that?"

"I know that. But I don't want to be a first lady. I just want to be someone's ordinary wife. When I get off work, I want to cook dinner and mop the floors, and while my husband sits on the couch reading the paper, I want to be working in the kitchen. When I bring the food to the table, he'll put down his paper and we will eat together. After we have eaten, I'll sit on the couch reading the paper while he goes to the kitchen to wash the dishes. After he has finished, the two of us will sit on the couch watching TV and chatting, and eventually we will go to bed together."

"Chief Liu, you must complete us. If you don't forgive us, we'll keep kneeling here before you all night long."

"Water? Water? Fuck your mother! Doesn't this house even have a drop of water?"

"We don't have any drinking water ready.... I'll go boil you some now."

"Fuck your grandmother! I never expected, when I appointed you to be my secretary, that you would turn around and stab me in the heart. Even my failure to purchase Lenin's corpse did not hurt me as much as you have."

"I've wronged you, Chief Liu. I've really wronged you."

"Okay, okay. Even if you kowtow to me until your forehead bleeds, I still won't forgive you."

"I'm not asking you to forgive me. One should pay for one's crimes."

"Please have some water.... It's still hot, though, so let it cool off first."

"Do we have any tea?"

"Do you want green tea or red tea?"

"I don't fucking care."

"Okay, I'll fix you some green tea. I have some right here."

"Stand up. Tell me what you're going to do about this."

"Chief Liu, if you don't offer your forgiveness, then I won't stand up even if my life depends on it."

"Then just kneel there, and tell me what you are going to do."

"I beg Chief Liu to complete us. . . ."

"Complete us, because if you don't we'll die right here kneeling in front of you."

"Tell me how you want me to complete you."

"Let us get married. I've caused you to lose face in Shuanghuai, so afterward you are welcome to have us transferred somewhere else."

"Chief Liu, we won't forget your benevolence and generosity. I've been your secretary for many years, so no one knows better than I what you want. If you complete us, I'll have everyone in the entire county bow down to you. I know that you weren't successful in purchasing Lenin's corpse. Even so, I'll have the entire county bow down to you. I'll have everyone in the entire county bow down to you whenever they see you. If you don't believe me, give it a try. Starting tomorrow, I'll have everyone on the street bow down to you whenever they see you. I'll have everyone in the new and old city hang your portrait in the main hall of their house. Is that okay?"

"Huh? . . . Do you think that you are a celestial being? I'm telling you, even God himself doesn't have the ability to do that."

"Chief Liu, I can do what I propose."

"Get out! Both of you, get out! Get out of my sight!"

......

"You didn't return for half a year, so I thought . . . that I would stay overnight to speak with you."

"Needless to say, you can have whatever you want in this house."

"I don't want anything. The only thing I'll take is my father's portrait."

"You can take it. You can take anything you want."

"Okay, then. We'll be leaving now."

"Go. Hurry up and leave. I don't want to see either of you again."

"Thank you, Chief Liu. . . . I know that benevolence must be requited. I'll remember your generosity and benevolence. Tomorrow, I'll have all of the people of the county kowtow to you and treat you like a deity."

Chapter 5: The entire world bows down

Chief Liu's tears of livening finally fell to the ground.

To his surprise, when he came out of the house the next day, everyone was in fact bowing down to him.

When he woke up, the sun had already passed the highest point in the sky and it was almost time for lunch. What Chief Liu never expected was that after the earth-shattering events of the preceding few days, he would be able to sleep soundly that night. Even Secretary Niu's telephone calls couldn't wake him.

Chief Liu was exhausted, and needed a good night's rest. Therefore, he slept soundly for a while.

"If you were home, then why didn't you answer the phone?"

"I'm sorry, Secretary Niu, I was too tired."

"The governor called, and all he said was that he wanted the district to send a new Party secretary and a new county chief to Shuanghuai within three days."

Chief Liu's mind was in a fog. Secretary Niu asked, "Didn't you send the documentation for purchasing Lenin's corpse over to Russia?" Chief Liu replied, "How could we not have sent it? For such a major business transaction, how could we not have sent the paperwork? We even sent two copies of the intent-to-purchase statement, together with duplicates of all of the accompanying documentation."

He added, "After all, Russia is far away, and consequently we are not able to discuss everything face-to-face, but rather had to first send an intent-to-purchase statement."

Secretary Niu roared, "That's just great. . . . You send someone to the capital with an intent-to-purchase statement together with a separate refusal-to-purchase statement, whereupon the provincial leaders explode with fury, becoming so angry that their intestines leak out."

Chief Liu knew that he was Shuanghuai's county chief as well as its Party secretary, but at this point he felt as though he had come up to the edge of a cliff and had nowhere to turn. He added, "Then, what do I do now?" Secretary Niu said, "I'll find you somewhere to go." He added, "The district just established a new imperial tomb museum, and they moved the tombs of all of the emperors, imperial family, and ministers who were buried in Jiudu, so that people could observe and appreciate them. The museum is a first-tier work unit, and you could be the museum's director." After Secretary Niu finished, Chief Liu felt as if he still wanted to say something, but Secretary Niu hung up the phone.

Chief Liu was thereby relieved of his position, and as for what kind of appointment he would be given next, Secretary Niu told him to wait to see what plans the provincial authorities might have. If he was going to be demoted, so be it; as far as punishments went, this was not such a big deal. The important thing, however, was that he still wanted to say something, but Secretary Niu avoided him like the plague and hung up the phone without even waiting to hear what he had to say. The sound of the phone hanging up echoed coldly, like a knife chopping through ice. Chief Liu sat dumbfounded on the edge of his bed, and a long time passed before he realized that he was still undressed. He threw the telephone receiver onto the table as if it were a small whisk broom, and then put on his down jacket. Apart from words associated with the ancient tomb museum, such as "corpse" and "coffin," Chief Liu's mind was a complete blank.

As he sat on the edge of his bed staring blankly into space, he didn't feel the slightest sense of sorrow or unhappiness, and instead merely felt as though everything was unreal, as though he had not yet woken up and these new developments were all just a dream. He wanted to pinch himself to prove that everything was real, and even raised his hand to do so, but at the same time he was afraid that the pinch would confirm that everything was in fact as it appeared to be. Therefore, he lowered his hand again and continued sitting woodenly on the edge of the bed. He gradually sensed something moving in his head, like a breeze blowing away the fog inside. He tried to grasp at the shadows fluttering through his brain, and stared at the wall across from him and thought intently. It occurred to him that although he had agreed to permit Liven to withdraw from society, he had not yet convened a county-level meeting to this effect. Upon remembering the business about Liven withdrawing from society, Chief Liu suddenly stared in shock as a crack opened up in the fog in his brain. This crack developed into an opening, and a bright ray of light shone through it as though a door had just been opened.

Chief Liu emerged from the room.

He wanted to convene a meeting of the county's standing committee. Given that the new county chief and Party secretary were already on their way to replace him, this would be his final standing committee meeting.

But as soon as Chief Liu walked out of the building, he found that everyone in the city, and even the whole world, was bowing and kowtowing to him. First, the old man who picked up the trash and swept his courtyard every day walked over, smiling. The man was over fifty, and had been cleaning and sweeping the courtyard for more than a decade. He was smiling silently, as though he had just discovered some gold or silver in the trash. He went up to Chief Liu without speaking, then bowed deeply. Only after he had straightened his stick-thin waist did he open his gap-toothed mouth and say, "Thank you, Chief Liu. I hear that after the end of the year, I'll start receiving several thousand yuan a month for sweeping the courtyard."

Chief Liu picked up his trash and headed toward a box of garbage. For a moment, he couldn't understand what had happened. When Chief Liu arrived at the gate of his family's courtyard, the old gatekeeper was busy washing his dishes, but when he turned and saw Chief Liu, he immediately dropped the dishes and, shaking the water from his hands, ran out and bowed, saying, "Chief Liu, I should kowtow to you, but I'm too old and am no longer able." He said, "I really never expected that, despite not having any children, I would one day be able to retire and relax. But now you have constructed a nursing home for the county and announced that everyone over sixty is guaranteed a room there and will receive retirement benefits equal to twice their original salary." When he finished, the water on his stove began boiling, and he rushed back in.

Chief Liu then went out to the street. To his surprise, upon seeing him, the peddlers who had spent the entire winter selling melon seeds, sugarcane, and winter apples, regardless of whether they were men or women, young or old, broke into broad smiles, and thanked him profusely: "Chief Liu, we are grateful to you. Thanks to you, Shuanghuai now has good fortune, and from now on we will no longer need to stand here in the middle of winter selling melon seeds." Or, they said, "Thank you, Chief Liu, I never expected that after selling apples for most of my life, I would be able to rest at home when I got old and still have enough to eat and drink."

A thirty-something-year-old woman crossed the street. She had come to the city from the countryside to sell the tiger-headed children's shoes she had made, and was huddled against a wall to find shelter from the sun and wind. She timidly came over and, once she was standing in front of Chief Liu, began kowtowing, her face covered in tears. She said,

"Chief Liu, people say that after the end of the year we will no longer need to work the land, and instead every month we will be issued free grain, vegetables, and meat. They say that tourists who come to Shuanghuai will pay several dozen yuan for the tiger-headed shoes I make, so that they can take them home and hang them on their wall."

Chief Liu realized that the county seat must have undergone an enormous transformation overnight; not only was everyone bowing and kowtowing to him, but furthermore people were walking around with oracular smiles, as though the bodhisattva had come to this city the previous night and said something to everyone. And whereas the previous day the entire land had been enveloped in mist, now the skies were completely clear. The sun was shining down brightly, and the sky was an expanse of blue, so pristine that it looked as though it had been scrubbed by hand. If occasionally there was a trace of clouds, they would appear as white silk. It was warm, as warm as springtime. If this sort of weather could last another three to five days, the willows and poplars would soon begin budding and the wildflowers would begin blooming, just as they had begun on Spirit Mountain a couple of weeks earlier.

Perhaps this warm weather was some sort of omen.

Chief Liu permitted everyone to crowd around and thank him, and as he proceeded from his courtyard to the county's government building, the crowd kept growing. Those bowing to him kept increasing in number, as did the elderly people kowtowing to him. In the blink of an eye there were suddenly so many people surrounding him in the less-than-one-*li* stretch of road that he could no longer continue forward, as if he were a virtual deity who had suddenly emerged out of nowhere.

It turned out that earlier in the morning they had heard that the previous reports that the attempts to purchase Lenin's corpse had failed were merely rumors, and that the reality was that both the district and the provincial seats had wanted to install the corpse in their respective cities for a few days, and had deliberately created problems for both Shuanghuai and Chief Liu. Now, however, the problems had been resolved, and Beijing was supporting Shuanghuai and Chief Liu. In all likelihood, the plan would be back on schedule within three to five days, and Shuanghuai would be permitted to purchase Lenin's corpse from Russia and ship it back to Spirit Mountain. Chief Liu, furthermore, had already sent someone to Germany to arrange for the purchase of Marx's and Engels's personal effects, and the representative had sent back word that not only had their German counterparts agreed to sell Shuanghuai a pair of Marx's knitted sleepwear, but in recognition of the villagers' extreme devotion to Marx, they had also offered to give the villagers Marx's desk, chair, and fountain pen. They said that Engels's descendants were willing to give Chief Liu all of the swallowtail dinner jackets their ancestor had ever worn. They said that when Lenin's cenotaph in Shuanghuai was completed, his descendants would all attend the opening ceremony, and wouldn't even ask Shuanghuai to pay for their airfare tickets. They said that the descendants of Vietnam's Ho Chi Minh said that they were willing to grant Shuanghuai half of their ancestor's personal effects. They said that Albania's and Yugoslavia's current leaders had readily agreed to give Shuanghuai everything that Hoxha and Tito had ever used, and furthermore weren't asking for a cent in return; they were even willing to send their former leaders' cremated ashes. They said Cuba's leaders had agreed even more quickly, saying that they wanted to keep Castro's corpse, but the people of Shuanghuai could take anything else they wanted. The only remains they could not obtain easily were the personal effects of North Korea's Kim Il Sung. They said that Kim Il Sung's son Kim Jong Il was currently the nation's leader, and was asking for anywhere from a hundred and ten thousand to a hundred and fifty thousand yuan for every pen his father had ever used and every button that had ever fallen from his clothes. They said that if Chief Liu wanted to buy Kim Il Sung's old revolver, they would have to pay at least nine million yuan for it.

Even at nine million yuan, Chief Liu still agreed to purchase the revolver.

This way, not only could the Lenin Memorial Hall open immediately for business, but by the following year they could set up a display room featuring the ashes, clothing, and personal effects of the other world leaders. This way, Spirit Mountain's ten peaks would each have a memorial hall of one the world's ten great leaders, and every day they would attract at least three to five times as many tourists as the Lenin Memorial Hall alone. This would include visitors from neighboring counties, from the district, from the province, from throughout the nation, and even from other countries around the world. Just as foreigners who come to China cannot fail to visit Beijing, if they visited Beijing they would have no choice but to also visit Shuanghuai. In fact, some people might even come to China for the express purpose of visiting Shuanghuai, without even having any interest in visiting Beijing. It was mind-boggling to think how much income that would bring in!

The people said that Chief Liu had already arranged to have Shuanghuai build new roads, and even an airport. They said that in order for Shuanghuai to be able to sell tickets for a hundred yuan each, the county would need to build three to five large printing factories, for the express purpose of printing these tickets around the clock. They said that all of China's banks were preparing to establish their largest satellite branches in Shuanghuai, so that the county's residents could deposit all the money they wouldn't be able to spend. They said that in order to compete for the enormous amounts of money every resident would have in a few years, and in order to encourage everyone to deposit money with them, the banks were jockeying to be the first to give the county a loan to build a highway leading up to Spirit Mountain, both sides of which would be lined with guest houses.

Indeed, the lives of the residents of Shuanghuai had been turned upside down overnight. Their heavenly days were almost here. So, why *wouldn't* they all express their gratitude to Chief Liu? Who in Shuanghuai didn't know how hard Chief Liu worked to purchase Lenin's corpse? Who didn't know how hard he struggled to establish the Liven performance troupes?

Who knew, however, that even as he was working to purchase Lenin's remains, Chief Liu was already making plans to obtain the personal effects of all of these other world leaders? No one had expected that all of these seemingly impossible tasks would be accomplished virtually overnight, that everything would be purchased and would immediately be ready to be shipped to Shuanghuai.

Chief Liu laughed and asked, "Who did you hear all this from?"

The person replied, "From your secretary. If your own secretary said it, how could it not be true?"

Chief Liu's heart skipped a beat, but at that moment his astonishment was drowned out by the people surrounding him, as they kowtowed to him and crowded around just to say something to him, shake his hand, or have him caress their child's head. They crowded him to the point that he could barely keep his balance. Indeed, with some people jostling in and others pushing back, in an instant the people surrounding Chief Liu had clogged up the entire roadway. The street peddlers started shouting,

"You've knocked over my apple stand! . . . You've knocked over my apple stand!"

"You're trampling on my bags of melon seeds! . . . You're trampling on my bags of melon seeds!"

The crowds knocked over the door plank that a peddler had set up as his stand, and the red paper and firecrackers he sold at New Year's, together with his red couplets, gate couplets, and kitchen god portraits, were strewn all over the ground. The peddler stood to one side and beat his chest as he cried,

"Aren't you afraid that the firecrackers will go off? . . . Aren't you afraid that the firecrackers will go off?"

All of this was merely so that people could bow and kowtow to Chief Liu, to express their gratitude. People who were out shopping immediately put their things down and walked out of the store. People who were out eating or drinking immediately put down their cups and chopsticks and emerged from the restaurants. They bowed and kowtowed, murmuring words of gratitude. Naturally, they didn't forget to ask him, "Chief Liu, I hear that next year the street in front of our house will be paved in marble?" They also didn't forget to ask, "Is it true that everyone will be guaranteed a monthly salary of five thousand yuan?"

Someone also asked, "I hear that whenever we want to eat something, the county will issue it to us?"

"Is it true that every family will be given a new house?"

Someone asked worriedly, "But then won't people become lazier and lazier?"

"Perhaps our children won't even want to study?"

This was all real, Chief Liu realized, as everyone swarmed in front of him. Under the sun, there was the rancid odor of people's sweat, the smell of sweltering dust, and an oily stench of the hats the peasants had been wearing for many years without ever washing them, together with the scent of cotton from the city-dwellers' new coats and scarves. Standing in the middle of this crowd, Chief Liu was jostled back and forth. He shook one person's hand, and answered another person's questions.

This true livening was as real as the warmth you feel when you put on clothes, or the pain you feel when you bleed. One group of people after another kept surging toward Chief Liu to bow and kowtow to him, and to express their gratitude. As soon as one group receded, another would take its place.

The sun was directly overhead, with warm air blowing through the streets. People's heads were as densely arrayed as a field of melons. Some of the men were wearing padded hats, while others were wearing single-layer ones, or even going bareheaded all winter. The result was a colorful assortment of black, blue, and gray heads. Most of the women, on the other hand, were wearing scarves. The city women were wearing long red, yellow, green, or blue wool scarves, and they would each pick their favorite color depending on their age and fondness.[1] When it was cold they would wrap their scarves around their heads, and when it was warmer they would pull them down to their necks, or would drape them over their shoulders, using them merely as an accessory. Some of the young rural women pursued this urban fashion, wearing long knitted scarves, but most of them remained fond of the traditional square scarves people had always worn in the country side, particularly cheap ones they had bought on sale. Although this was discounted merchandise, the colors were still bright red and green, filling the entire street with color. Regardless of whether people were bowing or kowtowing, the entire world became filled with dancing colors.

The entire world was greeting Chief Liu.

The entire world was crowding forward.

Chief Liu experienced an intense feeling of happiness. He'd thought that this sort of scene would be possible only after the Lenin Mausoleum had been established and Lenin's corpse had been brought back and installed, or once the county became so rich that it would seem as though money were growing on trees, and the residents of every town and village would no longer need to work the land to be able to have whatever they wanted, and would instead be able to simply go to the public center to get it.

But now, here was this scene suddenly appearing before him. He saw that there were many peasants carrying the red paper, firecrackers, and stove god portraits they had prepared for New Year's. He saw that there were oil paintings wrapped around many of the stove god portraits, and he instantly recognized that those outer paintings were in fact two-by-three-foot portraits of himself that people had purchased on the street, and that it seemed as though there was a red halo surrounding them. Having already noticed the portrait's red frame and determining that this was his portrait, Chief Liu attempted to ask one person whether red paper and firecrackers were expensive this year. The person replied that the prices were not too bad, and added that the places selling Chairman Liu's portrait also sold red paper and firecrackers for half as much as other places.

Chief Liu said, "It's not a good idea to buy my portrait to hang on your wall, and you would be better off buying pictures of the elderly or of the demon chaser Zhong Kui."

The person replied, "We've been hanging pictures of the elderly and Zhong Kui at home for several generations, but they never granted us a good life. Only you, Chief Liu, have made it such that our good life is just around the corner."

Hearing this, Chief Liu felt a warm, livening glow surge from the center of his being. He was grateful for Secretary Shi's preparations and felt that, after so many heartbreaking calamities, to have these thousands of people bowing and kowtowing to him was enough. He knew he should be content. And it was worth it. A red blush covered his face as he slowly walked out of the crowd and toward the front of the street. When he was almost at the county government and committee building, he suddenly felt that this stretch of road was actually very short. He regretted having walked so quickly, and that he hadn't extended this road to make it eight to ten *li* long, like Beijing's Chang'an Avenue.

Fortunately, however, in front of the county government and committee building there wasn't a square but rather a wide street. People were already standing there in a dense crowd, all reverentially holding portraits of Chief Liu rolled up and tied with red string—as though

466

they were bundles of incense sticks. It was as if they were gathered there awaiting his arrival. They were standing on their tiptoes, their heads craned and their gazes fixed intently on him, as though they had been waiting for him for a hundred, or even a thousand, years. Now that he was finally there, they all looked grateful and livened, happy and blissful. They waited for him to approach, and when he arrived at the gate to the county committee and government building, several dozen fifty-something-year-old people from the city and the countryside suddenly bowed down to him in the middle of the street, kowtowing to him in unison, and shouting the same phrases:

"Thank you, Chief Liu! Thank you for granting us this heavenly fortune. . . ."

"May Chief Liu enjoy long life, may he live for a hundred, or even a thousand, years. . . ."

"Chief Liu, the people of Shuanghuai all kowtow to you in gratitude. . . ."

The people shouted these greetings loudly and in unison. Suddenly, the thousands of people assembled there all kowtowed together, as if on command. All of the heads, be they black or colorful, bent down like grain blown by the wind. Everyone lifted their heads, and then bowed them again. The entire world became silent during this process, so much so that the sound of people breathing was louder than the wind. Much louder, and as solemn as when, in the past, the emperor would visit Shuanghuai and stand in front of the county's tens of thousands of residents. The sky was clear, the sun was blazing, and people could even hear the sound of clouds moving across the sky.

At this point, Chief Liu heard the sound of someone's forehead striking the asphalt, like a wooden mallet striking the surface of a drum, and tears immediately began streaming from his eyes. He wanted to go over and lift up several of the old people in the front of the crowd, but at the same time he wanted them to finish their three resounding kowtows, to let them finish expressing their gratitude. He knew that whenever people kowtowed, they did so three times, and that only then could they be said to have successfully completed the ritual.

As he was hesitating, and as the thousands of residents were all kowtowing to him, Chief Liu glimpsed over the bowed heads of the populace the county cadres standing in the doorway of the government building. There was also the deputy county chief, who had been responsible for going to purchase Lenin's corpse but had returned empty-handed, together with Secretary Shi, who had worked with Chief Liu for many years but who the previous night had accompanied Chief Liu's wife back to her and Chief Liu's house.

All of the cadres had baffled expressions, and only Secretary Shi had a knowing grin. Chief Liu wiped away his tears and walked over to them.

"Let's convene a meeting," he said softly to Secretary Shi. Then he added by way of explanation to the confused-looking deputy county chief's secretary, "Have the standing committee members come to the meeting room. We are going to convene a standing committee meeting."

Having said this, he looked back at the thousands of people in the street. He saw that these Shuanghuai residents, after having kowtowed three times, were all still kneeling there and had not yet gotten to their feet. It was like when, in the past, they did not dare stand up until the emperor had spoken.

Chief Liu took a step toward the door. He stood in the meter-high flower bed at the entrance, but because it was winter the basin didn't have any flowers, and the soil inside had been trampled flat by children who climbed it to play. Standing on the edge of that flower bed, Chief Liu gazed ahead along the rows of heads in front of him, and saw that behind the crowd there were thousands of peasants who had come in from all the villages and towns surrounding the county seat. They were all carrying rolled-up portraits of Chief Liu, like so many bundles of incense sticks. Because there were too many people, they could not come closer to Chief Liu, and instead they started kneeling down there in the street, one after another. It was as if they were lined up to the end of the earth.

Chief Liu knew that the reason everyone was kneeling before him was that they were afraid of blocking the view of the people behind them, which is why they knelt for so long, so as to allow the people who had arrived late to catch a glimpse of Chief Liu. After the latter had seen him, they too would kneel down and kowtow three times.

As these crowds of people surged into the county from the surrounding countryside, and to the street in front of the government building, they stood a *li* or half a *li* away, gazing up at Chief Liu. Then, they too knelt down and began kowtowing.

By midday, as the sun began moving west, there was already a sea of people gathered in front of the building, appearing to fill the entire city—and even the entire world—with their kneeling bodies. At this point, Chief Liu smiled silently, as tears of livening streamed down his face and onto the ground.

Further Reading:

1) **Fondness.** *DIAL. Preference, or excessive love.*

CHAPTER 7: EVERYONE WHO DOES NOT AGREE TO LET LIVEN WITHDRAW FROM SOCIETY, PLEASE RAISE YOUR RIGHT HAND

The people gathered outside the main courtyard were still kneeling when Chief Liu proceeded to the office of the county committee to convene his final standing committee meeting as county chief.

He said, "Regardless of what you may say, I've already decided to move to Liven. From this point on, I will be a resident of Liven. Of course, there is a condition for settling down in Liven, which is that you can't be an able-bodied wholer. If you are a wholer, you can't become a resident of Liven."

Chief Liu said, "Now, please agree to permit Liven to withdraw from society—so that from this point forward the village will no longer fall under the jurisdiction of either Shuanghuai county or Boshuzi township. Everyone who agrees, please raise your hand."

There was a long silence in the room. Apart from Chief Liu, no one raised a hand.

Seeing that no one other than himself was raising a hand, Chief Liu put his own hand down and then said, "How about this—how about everyone who *doesn't* agree to let Liven withdraw from society please raise your hand in my presence."

There was another long silence, and still no one raised a hand.

"If no one raises their hand, this means that all the votes go to permitting the village of Liven to withdraw from society." Chief Liu said to the recording secretary sitting beside him. "The vote is unanimous. After you have recorded this decision, please go implement it." Then he added, "Have the driver immediately bring the car over."

Finally, Chief Liu turned back to the members of the standing committee, and asked, "None of you want to relocate to Liven?" He added, "If not, then the meeting is adjourned." After announcing the meeting's adjournment, Chief Liu was the first person to step out of the conference room. Everyone thought he was going to greet the thousands of people kneeling outside the courtyard of the government building, so who could have expected that as soon as he walked out of the building, there would be a bloody scream,

"Come quickly, there's been a horrible accident. The county chief has been run over by a car. . . ."

"Come quick, the county chief's own car has shattered both of his legs. . . ."

Those shouts rained down from the sky like blood, splattering the government building courtyard, and the entire world.

Book 15: Seeds

CHAPTER 1: AS FOR WHAT COMES LATER, IT WILL COME LATER

Grandma Mao Zhi departed.[1]

By that point the new lunar year had arrived, and the weather had gotten somewhat warmer. The willows, poplars, and wild grass were all green and budding. Spring had indeed come early, in the first lunar month, and in the Balou mountain range, there was the fragrantly foul smell of grass everywhere. In this transition from winter to spring, someone showed up from Boshuzi township. He was on his way to a relative's house deep in the Balou mountains, and when he passed Liven, he stood in front of the village and began shouting,

"Hey . . . people of Liven . . . people of Liven . . .

"Do you hear me? . . . This is a letter for your village. . . . It is a document. . . ."

Although it was warm on this day, the winter chill had not yet fully gone away. The villagers were all sunning themselves around the old honey locust tree in the center of the village. Grandma Mao Zhi had aged so much she didn't have a single black hair left, and instead her entire head had turned as gray and brittle as a patch of dried grass. When she returned from Spirit Mountain after having led the villagers on their performance tour, she didn't remove her burial clothes. In fact, she wore them all day to cook, eat, and even sunbathe, and at night she wore them to bed.

She rarely spoke anymore, her lips being so tightly sealed that it seemed as though she were already dead. But when she did open her mouth, she always repeated the same thing:

"I'm about to depart for a cause. If I'm going to die, so be it. When you die, your body becomes stiff. When I was alive I wasn't able to help the villagers withdraw from society, and I let down the entire village. When it comes time to dress me in my burial clothes after I die, they will take the opportunity to tear me apart limb by limb."

She added, "That is why I won't remove my burial clothes, and neither will I give the villagers an opportunity to tear me apart limb by limb."

Therefore, she wore her burial clothes all day long—and regardless of whether she was resting at home or walking through the village, she always had those sixteen or seventeen blind, crippled, or half-paralyzed dogs following her around.

The side of Deafman Ma's face was completely disfigured as a result of the six months he spent performing his firecracker routine. He actually didn't have any problems while he was still performing every day, but as soon as he stopped, that half of his face became covered with pus, and while he was idle that winter he frequently went to the center of the village to sun himself, orienting the injured side of his face toward the light. It is said that the sun can cure many illnesses, and after Deafman Ma sunned himself the entire winter his face did in fact gradually heal. Paraplegic Woman no longer embroidered anything on paper or leaves, but rather spent her time sunning herself and mending shoes. While she worked, she kept muttering about her children, saying that they must have grown teeth on their feet, because otherwise how could their shoes fall apart so quickly?

When One-Legged Monkey returned to Liven, he didn't have a cent to his name, but he did have a large pouch of gold strips that would last him his entire life. Even though he couldn't eat or drink the strips, he often said that he wanted to build a two-room house at the top of the ridge and open a store and a restaurant. He said that he wanted to be the boss, and before turning thirty he hoped to transform the gold deposit into a substantial investment. At this point, he borrowed all his tools from the carpenter, and worked at home every day building shelves for his store, until the entire village and the hillside were full of the sound of his hammering.

Huaihua was pregnant, and even though her belly was growing larger by the day, she still always wore her red wool shirt. Given her slender figure, as her belly grew she came to resemble a carrying pole with a round willow basket tied to it. Because she was pregnant, and particularly because she was pregnant with a bastard child as a result of what happened on Spirit Mountain, her mother Jumei felt humiliated and didn't want to see anyone, and stayed at home day after day. Just as everyone who saw Huaihua's belly knew what had happened to her, they also knew that Blind Tonghua and her nin sisters Yuhua and Mothlet had also been violated by that group of wholers and, consequently, had dropped out of sight.

The fearless Huaihua, however, began walking through the village every day, since she had been told that it was good to keep active while pregnant. She would stroll around like a ball rolling back and forth, with a bright smile on her face and always eating a snack of some sort. As she strolled back and forth, she looked proud of the baby in her belly.

People would ask her, "Huaihua, how many months along are you?"

She ate her melon seeds and replied, "Not very long."

They would ask again, "When are you due?"

She replied, "It's still early."

They asked, "Is it a boy or a girl?"

She said, "I don't know, but at least I know it will be a wholer."

Little Polio Boy wanted to learn to become a carpenter, and he spent every day at One-Legged Monkey's house, running errands for him and helping out with other tasks.

No one knew what One-Eye was doing all winter, and when the other villagers were hanging out in the streets he was nowhere to be found. When the villagers were not around, however, he could be seen strolling aimlessly about. He would occasionally ask someone, "Where is everyone? Where did everyone go? Did they all sneak out to perform?"

In this way, everything went back to the way it had been. But though it appeared as though nothing had changed, in reality everything was different from the way it had been before.

On that day, as Grandma Mao Zhi was sunning herself under the honey locust tree in her burial clothes, surrounded by those sixteen or seventeen dogs that she treated like her own grandchildren. Paraplegic Woman was sitting on a wooden stool on the western edge of the village, mending shoes, and Deafman Ma had set up a door plank in a location where he could get direct sunlight while being shaded from the wind on the pus-covered side of his face. Some people were off to the side playing poker and chess to while away the winter boredom, when a loud shout was heard from the mountain ridge,

". . . Residents of Liven . . . did you hear me? I have an official document from the township for you. . . ."

Little Polio Boy had gone to the mountain ridge to cut down a dead locust tree that he planned to have One-Legged Monkey make into a cabinet leg, and he brought the letter down with him. He hobbled along with the trunk of the locust tree resting on his shoulder and the rest dragging on the ground, leaving a cloud of dust in his wake and a long trail. When he arrived at the center of the village, he stood in front of Grandma Mao Zhi, who was still sitting beneath the honey locust tree, and said,

"Granny, this letter is for you."

Grandma Mao Zhi seemed surprised.

The boy said, "The person said that this is an official document from the county seat."

Grandma Mao Zhi's surprise became open astonishment.

As she was reaching out to accept the leather envelope, the movement of her arm made her satin burial clothes rustle loudly. Once she had taken the letter from Polio Boy, her hand was trembling so hard she had a difficult time opening it, but finally she ripped open the envelope and was able to remove the thick, folded letter inside. When she unfolded it, she saw the black characters and the two round seals from the county committee and the county government at the bottom of the page. Grandma Mao Zhi suddenly began to cry. She abruptly stood up and began sobbing, as her gray tears rolled down her sallow face like pearls.

The sun was warm. It was almost noon, and the stillness of the village was shining everywhere like sunlight. At this point, Grandma Mao Zhi suddenly cried out, as though she were an old person who had already died and surprised everyone by suddenly coming back to life. An "*Ah, ah!*" sound erupted from her throat, like burning kindling inside a woodstove. The disabled dogs lying beside her all suddenly opened their eyes and looked up, gazing at her in confusion.

Little Polio Boy took a step back.

Paraplegic Woman stabbed her shoe needle into her own palm.

Deafman Man sat on the door threshold, the pus released by the heat of the sun flowing down his neck.

The villagers who were playing cards held their cards in midair, as though their hands had died.

The pregnant Huaihua walked over from the other side of the village. From a distance she heard her grandmother cry out, and she rushed over, holding her belly. Before she reached the honey locust tree, her shouts rolled over:

"Grandma! Grandma! . . . What's wrong?"

"Grandma, Grandma, what's wrong?"

Paraplegic Woman, Deafman Ma, and the idle people playing cards all cried out together,

"What's wrong? . . . What's wrong?"

Grandma Mao Zhi instantly stopped crying. Her tears, however, continued streaming down her face. Despite the tears, her face was gradually covered in a flush of excitement. She looked at the surprised villagers, and then bent over and carried her bamboo chair to the bell hanging from the honey locust tree. As she was walking, she muttered hoarsely to herself,

"Withdraw from society; we're going to withdraw from society.

"This time we're really going to withdraw from society. The documents were sent down more than a month ago. They must have arrived at the township at the end of last year, but didn't reach the village until now."

Grandma Mao Zhi continued muttering as she walked, not looking at anyone as she moved forward. It was as though no one was around. Still muttering to herself, she arrived at the bell. She placed her chair beneath it, then picked up a round stone. She climbed onto the chair and began striking the oxcart wheel bell, making a crisp *dang, dang, dang, dang* sound. Under the midday sun of this day at the end of the first month of the *jimao* year, the village and the hillside were filled with the bright tolling of the bell, the entire Balou region was fllled with the pink ringing of the bell, and even the entire world seemed to be filled with this *dang, dang, dang* sound.

The residents of Liven all emerged from their homes. Men and women, young and old, the blind, crippled, deaf, and mute, together with those missing arms or legs, were all summoned by the tolling of the bell. One-Legged Monkey emerged with the canvas apron still tied around his waist and a wood plane in his hand. Jumei was inside cooking, her hands covered in flour. Tonghua, Yuhua, and Mothlet were busy doing something or other, but they all came over and joined the other villagers. The entire village stood like a dark mass beneath the honey locust tree.

"What is she doing?"

"I don't know."

"Why is she ringing the bell now?"

"You're only supposed to ring it in the event of an emergency."

In the hubbub, Grandma Mao Zhi gazed at One-Legged Monkey, who was standing in front of the crowd. She handed him the letter she was holding, saying, "Read this to the other villagers—in a loud voice!" One-Legged Monkey asked what exactly it was he'd be reading, and Grandma Mao Zhi replied that once he read it he would know. One-Legged Monkey took the letter, unfolded it, and then gasped in astonishment. He stared in shock for a moment, then, like Grandma Mao Zhi's, his face erupted in delight. He hobbled over to the stone riser beneath the tree, jumped up onto it, cleared his throat, waved his arms, and then cried out as though he were an important personage, "Quiet please, quiet please. Fuck your grandmother, the documentation for Liven's withdrawal from society has arrived. Now I am going to read this motherfucking document aloud to everyone! . . . This will be a presentation!"

Under the honey locust tree, everything became absolutely silent—so silent that it seemed as though no one was even there.

Standing on the stone riser, One-Legged Monkey read aloud in a shrill voice this document that had been sent down by Shuanghuai's county committee and county government:

> *To the Party committees from every department, office, and township:*
>
> > *In accordance with Liven's repeated requests that it be permitted to "withdraw from society"—which is to say, to voluntarily leave the administrative jurisdiction of Shuanghuai county and Boshuzi township—the county committee and county government have carefully studied this matter and reached the following conclusion:*
>
> 1) *As of today, the village of Liven, located in the depths of the Balou mountains, will no longer fall under the administrative jurisdiction of Shuanghuai county and Boshuzi township. Shuanghuai and Boshuzi will no longer have any authority over Liven, and conversely Liven will no longer have any obligations toward Shuanghuai and Boshuzi;*
>
> 2) *Within a month of the day when this document is issued, Boshuzi township must collect and destroy all of the residency permits and identity cards that had previously been issued to the residents of Liven, and if it is discovered that anyone in Liven is still using the township's residency permit and identity cards, they will be treated as illegal counterfeits;*
>
> 3) *From now on, all of the administrative maps printed by Shuanghuai must have their borders revised such*

that they no longer contain the section of the Balou mountains where Liven is located, and the county's administrative maps must never again include the village of Liven;

4) *Beginning today, Liven's freedoms and rights—including the right to citizenship, the right to property, the right to housing, the right to disaster relief, the right to medical treatment, and so forth—will no longer have any relation to Shuanghuai or Boshuzi. On the other hand, Shuanghuai and Boshuzi must not interfere with Liven's informal contacts with the county, township, or any of their associated regions.*

At the end of the document, there were just the signature and the stamps of Shuanghuai's county committee and county government, together with the date on which the document was issued.

When One-Legged Monkey finished reading, he folded up the document and placed it back in the envelope. At this point, the sun was directly above the tree, and its heat flowed over the village like boiling water. Several turtledoves and flocks of sparrows alighted on the branches of the honey locust tree, and their chirps poured from the sky like rain, pounding down on everyone's head and body. Even after the villagers had heard and understood the announcement, they kept standing and sitting there, staring intently at Monkey's hands, as though he had not finished reading, as though he had not read the most understandable part and consequently there were still many parts that were not yet clear. Everyone looked calm, as though Liven's withdrawal from society had been expected and was nothing to get excited about. It was also as if this earth-shattering news of Liven's withdrawal from society could not be announced just like that, with a sheet of paper and two stamps. The withdrawal seemed somewhat unreal, and the people almost didn't allow themselves to believe it. Each of them just stared in a daze, like someone who has only half woken up from a deep sleep.

At this point, One-Legged Monkey hopped down from the stone riser. Then, something occurred to him, and he asked loudly, "But now, if we want to establish our own performance troupe, to whom will we go for a letter of introduction?" He added, "If we don't have a formal letter of introduction, will we still be able to earn as much money from our performances as before?"

This question was directed to Grandma Mao Zhi, but just as One-Legged Monkey was asking it he turned around and saw that she was leaning against the tree on her bamboo stool, completely motionless, as though she were fast asleep. Her burial clothes sparkled as though they were still brand-new, with the sunlight shining on them just as the spotlight had done when she was performing. She just sat there on her stool, leaning against the honey locust tree, her head cocked to the side. Her glowing face had a calm smile and a livened appearance, like a child in the middle of a pleasant dream. One-Legged Monkey repeated his question, and again he didn't receive a response, and he was about to ask a third time when the question got caught in his throat.

He exclaimed with alarm, "Granny Mao Zhi, Granny Mao Zhi. . . ."

Jumei added her own cries, "Grandma . . . Grandma . . ."

Huaihua and her three nin sisters jostled their way into the crowd and cried out together, "Grandma, Grandma, what's wrong? Why can't you say anything?"

The crowd then erupted, as the entire hillside began crying and shouting at Grandma Mao Zhi.

Despite all the shouts and shaking, Grandma Mao Zhi didn't respond.

She had departed.

She passed away peacefully, with a smile on her lips. When she died, that look of satisfied livening on her face was as warm and bountiful as the sun.

She was seventy-one years old, and hers should have been a joyful funeral. It was inevitable that there would be cries of mourning, but privately people remarked that she had earned her death and that the peaceful look on her face when she died was something very few people could hope for.

They buried her three days later. There was no need to hurriedly prepare her burial clothes, and she had even prepared her own coffin. As a result, everything proceeded calmly. On the day that they picked up her coffin and walked toward the graveyard, located several *li* from the depths of the Balou mountains, something happened that the villagers would never have expected. Huaihua was pregnant, and therefore couldn't escort her grandmother to her grave. This was an age-old rule. Jumei and her daughters Tonghua, Yuhua, and Mothlet, meanwhile, were women and girls, and since Mao Zhi had no male descendants, the women had to recruit some men and boys before the funeral procession set out. The villagers—be they young or old, blind or crippled—were all younger than Mao Zhi, and they all felt a certain sense of filial obligation toward her, and felt that it was correct and sensible to escort her to her grave.

On the day they were about to set off with the coffin, they saw that pack of sixteen disabled dogs abjectly following it. The dogs were not weeping and crying like the humans as they escorted Grandma Mao Zhi's corpse, but each one of them had two streaks of dirty, dusty tears below its eyes. As they followed behind the coffin and the procession of filial mourners, just as they used to follow Grandma Mao Zhi around when she was alive, their tears continued to fall. By the time the coffin had been carried half a *li* out of the village, the original pack of sixteen dogs had grown to include more than twenty animals, and then more than thirty. Perhaps they had come from neighboring villages, or perhaps they had come from beyond the Balou mountains. They included black, white, and gray dogs, together with a handful of thin and dirty disabled cats, and as the funeral procession advanced, that pack of thirty dogs gradually grew to over a hundred, eventually outnumbering even the human residents of Liven.

By the time the procession reached the graveyard, the entire mountainside was full of domestic dogs, wild dogs, feral cats, and what have you, the vast majority of which were either blind, crippled, missing an ear or tail, or suffering from some other disability. Not a single one of them moved or made a sound. Instead, they all just lay there peacefully, watching as Grandma Mao Zhi was put to rest.

As the mourners were leaving, someone remarked, "That's an awful lot of dogs. I've never seen so many dogs before in my entire life."

Someone else said, "Yes, and they're all disabled."

Then, everyone suddenly heard a wailing sound coming from the area around the grave. The sound was coming from that enormous pack of disabled dogs and cats. Unlike people, who complain about things while they are weeping, these animals instead just opened their mouths and wailed, like a winter wind blowing through the village's back alleys. Grandma Mao Zhi's relatives and fellow villagers on the mountain ridge all turned around to look at the grave area, where they saw that the dogs and cats that had been scattered across the mountainside had waited for the people to leave and had then proceeded to gather in front of Grandma Mao Zhi's grave. The mountainside field where the grave was located was blossoming, the bean sprouts were already green and craning their necks, and the red earth from the new grave was eye-catching. The dogs lay down in that green field, their heads facing Grandma Mao Zhi's grave. As they gazed at the site where she had been buried, the dogs resembled a pile of multicolored stones lying in a pool of water. And then, as they lay there wailing, dozens upon dozens of disabled dogs started digging at the new grave, scattering earth everywhere, as though they were trying to dig Grandma Mao Zhi right out of the ground.

The villagers on the mountain ridge all shouted,

"What do you think you're doing? If someone is already dead, what good is it trying to dig them back out?"

They shouted, "Come back. . . . . Grandma Mao Zhi is already gone, but Liven is still your home."

Gradually, the huge pack of dogs stopped digging at the grave, and instead proceeded to wail even louder, as though the entire world were filled with a winter wind blowing through the village's back alleys.

The blind and crippled villagers said many things to the dogs and cats, and then slowly made their way back to Liven, mutually supporting one another. When they reached the mountain ridge where the village was located, they suddenly saw wave upon wave of people streaming toward the village from outside the Balou mountains. Like the villagers themselves, these people were almost all disabled—either blind, crippled, paralyzed, deaf, mute, missing a limb, or having an extra digit. Very few of them were wholers. They were supporting one another, one family after another, pulling carts and toting carrying poles full of bedding, food, or other things. Clothing, pots, chopsticks and utensils, sand and tiles, jars, tables, chests, chairs, bed frames, electrical cords, and ropes, as well as chickens, ducks, cats, piglets, and sheep—all this and more was piled high on those carts and carrying poles. Dogs were running behind the crowds of people, their tongues hanging out. Oxen were being slowly led forward, together with stout mountain goats.

One group after another poured into the valley. The blind were pulling carts with paraplegics riding on top, directing them where to go. Deaf and mute people were toting carrying poles, shouting and signing. Cripples were leading oxen and goats, and when the animals stopped walking the cripples would beat them with a stick to urge them on. There were wholers pulling carts, on which there were no possessions, only children and the elderly. Some of the children were blind or mute, and the blind ones would ask a question while the mute ones would sign something in response, but since the former couldn't see what the latter were signing they would inevitably start fighting. In this way, the procession gradually moved toward the mountain ridge where Liven was located.

As the villagers returned from escorting the coffin, they stood on the side of the road staring in surprise. They asked, "Where are you moving to?"

The people in the procession asked in return, "Are you from Liven?" They said, "We have come from far away, where the government built a dam and forced everyone in the way to move. They gave every family a sum of money, and said that we could either relocate together or each take the money and relocate separately." They said, "We have already found a new location, which is even better than this village in the depths of the Balou mountains." They said that Liven was located at the junction of Shuanghuai, Gaoliu, and Dayu counties, while the place where they were going was located at the junction of six different counties, including Baishizi, Qingshui, Mianma, and Wanbozi, where there was a small gorge that didn't appear on any administrative map and didn't fall under anyone's control or jurisdiction, and in which there was fertile soil and abundant water. Therefore, these hundreds of disabled people had all agreed to relocate to that gorge in order to pitch a camp and establish a village, to farm the land and liven.

They said, "Don't worry. We will enjoy a better life than you have here in Liven."

The villagers asked, "And where exactly is this place you are talking about?"

They replied, "It is over on the far end of the Balou mountains, on the other side of Spirit Mountain."

While this conversation was still going on, the migrants began pulling their carts and hoisting their carrying poles. Then they bade farewell to Liven and the villagers and proceeded into the depths of the Balou mountains. The residents of Liven stood on the mountain ridge path and gazed at that slowly disappearing crowd of hundreds of blind, crippled, deaf, and mute disabled people from the land of wholers.

The villagers waited until their shadows had faded into the distance, then continued toward Liven, looking as though they had just lost something. When they passed Sister Hua Slope,[3] they looked at the mountainside full of fertile soil, which was not planted with crops but instead was full of carriage-wheel chrysanthemums, moon grass, and green summer flowers. The villagers said,

"We've already withdrawn from society. Why are we still sowing loose earth?"[5]

Others said, "Of course we're sowing loose earth. Having loose days,[7] how could we not sow loose earth?"

Someone asked, "What is this about having a Dragon Day,[9] Phoenix Day,[11] or Old People's Day[13] on these loose days?"

Someone replied, "Don't ask me. Now that Grandma Mao Zhi is gone, you should ask whoever is the eldest."

Someone asked, "Then how do you sing the livening song?"[15]

"Now that Grandma Mao Zhi has departed, I'm afraid there is probably no one who remembers the words."

Someone else asked, "Now that Grandma Mao Zhi is gone, who will manage the village's affairs?"

Someone else replied, "Given that no one here manages anyone else, why do we need anyone to handle things?"

At that point, a paraplegic, a cripple, and a blind man reached Liven. When they arrived in the village, a pregnant Huaihua was waiting for them at the entrance to the village, an astonished look on her face. When she saw the villagers returning from the funeral, she called out to them from a distance,

"Chief Liu has had a car accident. . . . Both of his legs are broken, and furthermore he is no longer the county chief. . . . He has come to live in Liven. At the moment he is in the temple guest house. He said that he will stay there from now on."

The villagers at the entrance to the village all stared in astonishment. Tonghua, Yuhua, and Mothlet stood in the crowd like chicks that had just fallen from the nest. Their mother, Jumei, was right behind them, pale from shock, as though someone had just hit her or kissed her.

The villagers all stared at one another, not knowing what to do. Only One-Legged Monkey looked pleased.

In this way, Chief Liu settled down to live in Liven, becoming one of the village's disabled residents.

As for Huaihua, she gave birth six months later. She gave birth to a thin and frail daughter.

Although it was a daughter, at least she belonged to the next generation. As for what the future held, only the future would tell.

CHAPTER 3: FURTHER READING— SISTER HUA SLOPE, HOLIDAY, AND LIVENING SONG

1) **Departed.** *The term means "to die," but also connotes a degree of respect for the deceased. This is the way in which people in Balou pay their respects when someone highly esteemed passes away.*

3) **Sister Hua Slope.** *"Sister Hua Slope" is the name of a place in the village of Liven, and "Sister Hua" is the name of a person. Everyone in Liven knows the story of Sister Hua and of Sister Hua Slope.*

It's said that the story began four jiazi cycles ago, in the gengzi Year of the Rat, when Sister Hua was seventeen years old. One of her parents was deaf and the other was mute, and while Sister Hua herself had sharp hearing and a sweet voice, her legs didn't work very well. She nevertheless had a graceful beauty, with skin as white as pristine clouds in the sky, beneath which there was a shade of light pink like that of a water orchid.

Sister Hua lived with her parents on a mountain slope not far from Liven, in a house consisting of several thatched rooms and a well. The family had oxen and goats, chickens and ducks, and the soil on the slope was so fertile that if you stuck a chopstick in it, it would immediately start budding.

One day followed the next, and by the time Sister Hua turned seventeen she was already one of the most beautiful women anyone had ever seen.

It was in that year, at the height of the Qing dynasty, as the entire realm was enjoying peace and prosperity, that a young man coming from Xi'an attempted to cross over Funiu Mountain to reach the Shuanghuai county seat, where he had been assigned an official post. But because the young man felt the route was too long, he decided to cut across the Balou mountains. By the time he arrived in Liven he was parched, and he proceeded to Sister Hua's house to request a bowl of water. It was there that he encountered Sister Hua herself.

As he stood in front of her house holding a water bowl, he noticed that the crops Sister Hua's parents had planted were growing exceptionally well. The wheat stalks on the mountain slope were full of grain, and a single year's harvest would give them enough grain to last them another three years. Closer by, there was row upon row of bundled corn hanging under the house eaves from previous years, and even if the village were to have poor harvests for the next decade the family would still have more corn than it could eat. All of the vegetables, flowers, and sunflowers planted in front and back of the house were in full bloom, bright red in the springtime and green in the summer, with carriage-wheel chysanthemums, white mountain orchids, and moon grass combining with cloudy shade and red sunlight. There were also wild purple wisteria and chaste tree shrubs, geckos climbing the walls, and red flowers and green willows, vegetation and plant fragrance everywhere.

Having encountered this idyllic setting, the young man, who had just been appointed to a seventh-grade prefect position, decided not to continue on to Shuanghuai to become the county magistrate and to instead stay in Liven, marry Sister Hua, settle down with her, and set up a business.

Of course, Sister Hua's family adamantly rejected this proposal to permit her to marry a man who would then move in with them as their son-in-law, rather than having her marry out. They asked her, We are just villagers, so how could we presume to have you marry a county official?

The prefect proceeded to take out his imperial letter and stamps, together with the paperwork he had brought with him in his quest for fame and glory, and tossed them all into the ravine.

Sister Hua's father said, Everyone in our family is disabled. How can we accept a healthy wholer as our son-in-law?

The prefect went into the family's kitchen. Everyone thought he was going to put away his water bowl, never expecting that he would instead grab a cleaver and proceed to chop off his left hand at the wrist, thereby leaving himself permanently disabled.

Sister Hua therefore had no choice but to marry him.

From that point on, the prefect ceased being a prefect, and instead became Sister Hua's husband and moved in with her. Sister Hua's father began teaching this young man, who had been studying ever since he was young, how to farm and use a hoe. Her father taught him to use one hand to hold a sickle and thresh the grain, while Sister Hua herself taught him how to plant vegetables and flowers. From that point on, they enjoyed their heavenly days.

By the time Sister Hua's parents passed away, the prefect could already use one hand to plant millet and sow beans, pick sorghum and harvest wheat, and transplant seedlings. As a result, in summer the hillside was always covered in wheat, and in autumn it was covered in corn that grew as large as a wooden club. When the cotton turned white, it was as though clouds had descended from the sky, and when the rape plants bloomed in spring, it looked as though the sun had been swallowed up by the water. All year round, there were fresh flowers and vegetables, and the ducks and chickens were able to feed from dawn to dusk.

Because Sister Hua not only was incomparably beautiful, but from the time she was young had loved to plant flowers behind the house, she would transplant magnolias, wild crysanthemums, and moon grass to the mountainside, so that in spring the slope would be full of the fragrance of magnolias; in summer it would have the red and green aroma of sunlit flowers and moon grass; in autumn there would be the scent of wild crysanthemums, melons on vines, and beans laid out to dry; and in winter she would plant a kind of wild bramble that grew over the eaves of the house and mountain plums to grow along the cliff. She would let the moon grass grow in the warm sunlight at the head of her bed, where it would produce little red flowers like those of carriage-wheel chrysanthemums, and in winter she would plant fragrant purple Chinese roses and Chinese peonies, which always wilted in the sunlight but bloomed when it was overcast. In this way, it was like spring throughout the year, and she could always enjoy the smell of fresh flowers. All year round, you could smell this spring fragrance from far, far away.

This was an excellent place, a heavenly place.

During the day, while the prefect was working in the fields, Sister Hua would be either sewing or mending shoes. With one of them working in the fields and the other in the doorway of their home, they would always be carrying on a conversation,

She asked, How could you have decided to simply chop off your hand?

He said, If I hadn't been disabled, would you have agreed to marry me?

She said, No, I wouldn't have.

He said, Well, there you have it.

Sometimes, when he was working in the fields and happened to stray too far from the house, such that the two of them could no longer hear each other, she would move her spinning wheel over to where he was working, and would spin cotton or mend shoes while he worked.

He said, This soil is very rich; it's full of oil.

She said, Actually, you should have accepted the position of magistrate —that is a man's true honor.

He said, To tell the truth, when I was seven I had a dream that if I wanted to enjoy a heavenly existence, I should study hard. If I studied hard and became an official, heavenly days would await me. So, I studied diligently for thirteen years, passed the jinshi exam, and was appointed county magistrate. When I passed in front of your house, that dream from thirteen years earlier suddenly reappeared in my mind's eye, with you and the fields of crops appearing just as they had in my dream. I remembered that in my dream there were nine chickens, and your house also turned out to have nine chickens. In my dream there were six or seven ducks, and your house also turned out to have six or seven ducks. In my dream the girl was three years younger than I, and when I met you it turned out that you were seventeen while I was twenty. In my dream there was a pile of grain as big as a mountain, and the mountain slope was covered in fresh flowers, and it turned out that your house also had a pile of grain as big as a mountain and a mountain slope covered in fresh flowers.

He asked, Why wouldn't I have stayed behind?

Needless to say, each night they would hug each other tight. He told her countless stories he had learned from books, and she would tell him endless stories about life in the mountains. Time flowed like water, grass, or wheat fragrance, as one day followed another, year after year. Eventually she said, Someday, I want to give you a child.

He said, I worry that the child might turn out to be a wholer.

She said, Actually, I hope we have a wholer.

He said, If it is a wholer, then when he grows up he won't understand people's lives here, and might miss out on this heavenly life and instead leave and wander aimlessly. He would endure immense hardship and sorrow.

She reflected for a moment, but didn't respond. She ended up getting pregnant anyway, and while she was pregnant provincial officials discovered that as the new magistrate was on his way to assume his new post in the Shuanghuai county seat, he had happened to encounter days of livening and had decided not to take his assigned post after all. The provincial officials reported this matter to the emperor, who thought, Are you not using the livening days of the disabled to mock the prosperity of the able-bodied? He therefore replied angrily, Having only one hand, he can't very well fight, but he can certainly cook, so send someone to make him join the army, to cook for the troops.

At that time, there were many uprisings in the area around Yunnan, so the prefect was told to go there to serve as an army cook. When he left, Sister Hua gabbed him by the leg and sobbed. He said, I should have chopped off both of my hands, because if I had, today's events would never have come to pass. He added, These past few years of livening have been worth it. I'm just worried that after our child is born, you won't be able to bring yourself to render him disabled. He added, Mark my words. First, wait for me to return, and second, after our child is born, you must at the very least make him lame in one leg, so that he can't walk properly and would be counted as disabled.

Having said this, the magistrate was taken away by the troops.

Sister Hua gave birth to their child on Sister Hua Slope. The child was a perfectly healthy wholer. Afraid that Sister Hua might have a difficult delivery, the women of Liven all came to watch over her bedside, and *they were delighted when she gave birth to a wholer. Given that she was the child's own mother, how could she possibly bear to maim him? Even the prospect of shaving off a layer of skin from the back of his hand was enough to make her burst into tears. She and the child therefore waited at Sister Hua Slope for her husband to return from Yunnan. They waited and waited, and when her son turned seventeen he announced that he wanted to leave the Balou mountains and go look for his father. One day, the son did in fact leave Liven and set out in search of his father, wandering through distant lands.*

Like his father, the son never returned.

In order to encourage her husband and son to come home, Sister Hua stopped planting crops on the hillside, and instead covered the hill with flowers and grass. She planted carriage-wheel chrysanthemums, rizhao plums, magnolias, and white orchids. They were fragrant in autumn and bloomed red in winter, and all year round there was a floral fragrance that could be smelled for more than ten li in every direction.

Sister Hua hoped her husband and son would smell her flowers and return to Balou. Every year when the flowers were in season, she would sit on the hillside gazing out at the world with tear-filled eyes. The year when the flowers and grass were most verdant, and their fragrance spread to permeate the entire region, she was sixty and blind in both eyes, having lost her sight staring out from that flowery hillside.

In the end, Sister Hua's husband and son never returned. The people of Liven and of Balou never again planted crops in the rich soil of that hillside, and instead just let it continue growing flowers and grass. The hill came to be known as Sister Hua Slope.

5) **Loose earth.** The term refers not only to the land that each family has planted for itself, but also to a form of farming and a style of life that Liven has practiced for a long time, and that are directly antithetical to those associated with the land and labor collectivization movements. More specifically, the term refers to an existence in which one eats what one grows, does not pay grain taxes, and has no relationship whatsoever with the government.

7) **Loose days**. This term refers to a kind of free and unfettered life, a form of existence that, from time immemorial, has been made possible by loose earth.

9) **Dragon Day, 11) Phoenix Day, 13) Old People's Day**. These are unique holidays honoring men, women, and the advanced age and accumulated wisdom of the elderly, which Liven used to celebrate but which disappeared many decades ago. Dragon Day honored men, and was held every year on the sixth day of the sixth month; Phoenix Day honored women, and was held every year on the seventh day of the seventh month; and Old People's Day honored the elderly, and was held every year on the ninth day of the ninth month.

The origins of these holidays can be traced back to the Ming dynasty. After the Great Migration, Liven was founded in the Balou mountains, but because the vast majority of its residents were blind, deaf, paraplegic, crippled, or mute, most of the men were not able to plow the fields or harvest the crops. They enjoyed a solitary existence, but many people were not content with Liven's style of life and mode of existence. One day, an elderly person arrived in the village and reported that if people headed southeast, the blind could regain their sight, the deaf could have their hearing restored, paraplegics would be able to walk as energetically as if they were flying, and mutes would be able to speak and sing. Even unattractive wholers, as long as they were willing to head southeast, could become handsome and powerful. Therefore the men, behind their wives' backs, all agreed to leave, and secretly departed in the middle of the night, heading southeast.

If they got hungry along the way, they would help people work the fields, do odd jobs, or even beg for food, and if they were thirsty they would get water from a river or pond. They endured immense hardship and were exhausted, but one day, after walking for a year and a half, they encountered a gray-haired man lying by the side of the road. The old man was extremely hungry and thirsty, and asked them for something to eat and drink. In handing him food and water, the men noticed that he was blind, crippled, and deaf. After the man had had his fill, they said, Although we are all disabled, *we are nevertheless young, and each of us has only a single disability. You, however, are already over eighty and furthermore have multiple disabilities, including being blind, crippled, and deaf, and missing a leg. Why didn't you just remain at home?*

The old man replied, I've already been on the road for sixty-one years, for more than a full jiazi cycle. He said, When I was nineteen I tried to take my life several times, on account of being disabled. But later God sent me a dream, telling me to head northwest, where there is a Balou mountain and a village called Liven. In Liven, there is an enormous old honey locust tree, beneath which there is buried a secret that can enable the blind to regain their sight, the deaf to regain their hearing, the mute to regain their voice, and cripples to run again. The old man said, It was in order to find that secret that I left my home in the Southeast and have been walking for sixty-one years. I set out when I was nineteen, and now I'm already eighty-one. He added, I know that if I continue for another year and a half I will reach Liven, but unfortunately I'm already over eighty, and am afraid I won't survive long enough to see it.

As he was saying this, the old man started sobbing.

The people from Liven immediately turned around and headed back to the Balou mountains, carrying this severely disabled man with them. However, despite the fact that they were diligently attending to him, the old man passed away three days later, in the middle of the night. Before dying, he said, I've lived for eighty-one years, and have been traveling for more than a full sixty-year jiazi cycle. But it was all worth it, just to have enjoyed these past three days. Then he went to sleep, and the next morning he didn't wake up.

After selecting a grave site for the old man, the villagers spent another six months on the road, until they finally made it back to Liven. Once there, they quickly took out their pickaxes and shovels and started digging beneath that old honey locust tree. They dug out a large porcelain jar, inside which there was a small redwood box. The mouth of the jar was so narrow they had to shatter it to get the box out. When they finally succeeded in opening the box and peered inside, they discovered that it was actually empty, without even a scrap of paper or a speck of soil.

The villagers threw the box away, cursing the old man, then they each headed home to rest. Because they had spent a full year and a half traveling southeast, and another year and a half traveling back to the Balou mountains, they had spent a total of three years on the road. They were all exhausted, and no one brought up again the possibility of leaving Liven and their wives. Instead, they focused on working their fields and being with their families.

However, during this season of harvesting the wheat and planting sorghum, the one-armed men discovered that, after having spent three arduous years on the road, they could one-handedly reap the wheat and dig the fields, even doing the work of two-armed wholers. The cripples discovered that after having been away from home for three years, they were now so used to walking that they were even faster and more vigorous than able-bodied people. The blind discovered that, because they had walked so far, they could now use their canes even more effectively than sighted people used their eyes. The deaf similarly discovered that after having spent three years on the road and spoken with so many different people, they had learned to guess what anyone was saying just from watching their lips. The mutes discovered that as a result of having needed to sign to people while on the road, they had gradually developed their own sign language.

All those who'd been on the road found they could farm and live as well as wholers. When they remembered the benevolence of that eighty-one-year-old man, they decided to designate the ninth day of the ninth month Old People's Day. In order to congratulate the men not only for having returned, but for having learned special skills to compensate for those that they lacked, the women designated the sixth day of the sixth month—which is the day the men returned—to be Men's Day, and called it Dragon Day. In order to thank their wives for having remained so busy and raised their children during the three years they were out traveling, the men decided to designate the seventh day of the seventh month to be Women's Day, also known as Phoenix Day. On Old People's Day, all members of the younger generation would kowtow to their elders, and not only would give the elderly good things to eat and drink, but would take out the unlined and lined garments that they had prepared for the elderly to wear all year round and would compete to see whose was the most attractive, and afterward they would donate the garments to the elderly.

The sixth day of the sixth month is generally a busy time of year, but after this day was designated Dragon Day, the men would not do any work on that day, and instead the women would be responsible for preparing food and drink and working the fields, while the men would stay home all day and rest. After spending the day resting, however, the men would then have to go into the fields and work overtime to compensate. On the seventh day of the seventh month, meanwhile, the busy season had already passed, and by this point the women would also be tired, so it would be their turn to rest for a day. On this day, the men would not only cook the meals, but also prepare their wives' favorite foods.

Of course, it was also necessary to invite people to sing Balou tunes on Dragon Day, Phoenix Day, and Old People's Day, and the village would spend an enormous sum of money hiring a group of wholer lion dance performers from several dozen li away. Naturally, the children would want to light firecrackers and wear new clothes, just as they would on New Year's.

15) **Livening Song.** The Livening Song was the earliest prototype of the Balou tune. Its melody was mostly that of a call-and-response song, and less frequently would take the form of a solo. However, the performance of the Livening Song could take many different forms: Some people sang the tunes while alone on the mountain ridge when they felt lonely and tired; others would sing them back and forth from one mountainside to another; and there was even a group of people who might loiter at the entrance to the village singing the songs together. The melodies had set patterns, but the lyrics varied depending on the setting and the season.

The lyrics that were most popular among the older generation of disabled villagers were:

Hey, hey hey hey . . .
You deaf man on the hillside, listen up.
In the sky there is a celestial fairy who is singing.
If you can hear her clearly, she will marry you,

But if you can't, you will need to spend the rest of
    your life alone.

Hey, hey hey hey . . .
You blind man on the other hillside, watch this.
There is a golden rabbit sleeping at your feet.
If you can catch it, you will enjoy good fortune for the
    rest of your life,
But if you can't, you will need to eat plain bread for
    the rest of your life.

Hey, hey hey hey . . .
You cripple down in the gorge, listen up.
You must run up the hill in a single breath.
If you can make it up, you'll become a wholer,
But if you can't, you'll limp for the rest of your life.

Hey, hey hey hey . . .
You paraplegic on the mountain ridge, listen up.
The celestial maiden in the sky is lonely.
If you can stand up, she will give you her hand,
And if you lead her home she will become your wife.

Usually, the person singing this would be someone farming on the mountain ridge, who would start singing to relieve his loneliness. The melody would be similar to the duet's, only more carefree and lyrical. In order to write this novel, I lived in Liven for several years, but the only lyrics that I was able to collect were the following.

The lyrics of the first song:

The soil is rich, oh yeah, it is flowing oil.
The wheat grains are as large as stones.
I pick up a wheat grain on the side of the road,
And when I toss it aside, I accidentally break open
    your head. . . .

And the lyrics of the second song:

I am a blind man, and your leg is lame.
You sit on the cart while I pull it.
My feet stand in for yours,
While I borrow your eyes from you....